THE GRAND PACT

JC HAWKE

IVY ROSE PUBLISHING LTD

Editing: Ellie McLove – My Brothers Editor

Proofing: Rosa Sharon – My brothers Editor

Cover: Murphy Rae

Photographer: Michelle Lancaster

For the ones who need a little holding up

The over-thinker

The planner

The comfort seeker

Coño - Jason Derulo

Ain't No Mountain High Enough - Marvin Gaye (For the girls)

If You're Meant To Come Back - Justin Jesso

On Your Way Home - Patrick Droney

Location - Khalid

Ghost Town - Benson Boone

No Right To Love You - Rhys Lewis

Breathe Me - Sia

Walked Through Hell - Anson Seabra

A Little Bit Yours - JP Saxe

All For You - Cian Ducrot

Slide - James Bay

Follow me - Sam Feldt & Rita Ora

Dancing In The Moonlight - Jubël feat. Neimy (For the whole gang)

Never Say Never - The Fray

Rainbow - Kesha (Lucy's catchy beat)

PROLOGUE

Elliot

Lowerwick Estate, London: Antlis Memorial Ball

"Going once, twice, sold." My jaw tics as the hammer comes down on the wooden stand, echoing through the speakers with a resounding thud.

"Well," Charlie utters, nestling his hands deeper into his tux pockets. I twist my head to look at him fully, my face stoic. I find him watching me from my right, his lip twitching with a knowing smile. "Wasn't how I saw that going at all."

My back is to the stage, and as I lift my hand to catch a bartender's attention, I feel multiple sets of eyes settle on me.

Lance Sullivan, my head of finances, slides his drink across the bar and into my hand, grinning at me just as wide as my best friend. "Nah, can't say I'm shocked, to be honest."

They're referring to the ten thousand pound bid I've just placed—and won—on our friend Lucy.

The prize?

A date with her.

Fucked-up thing is, no one would bat an eyelid if it were Charlie or Lance bidding.

Bunch of nosy fuckers, the lot of them.

When the girls announced there would be an auction, I knew it wouldn't end well. Both Lucy and Nina auctioned off dates with themselves, and while I watch on as Nina's date ends up with a business rival of mine and Mason's (Mason, who just so happens to be Nina's ex and also the guy now putting her over his shoulder and leaving the marquee), I'm glad I didn't let Lucy go cheap.

She wasn't going to be a laughingstock.

Charlie slips a hand across his face, thumbing the side of his mouth as his fingers pinch at his cheek. A laugh slips past his distorted lips, and I roll my eyes. "Tonight has been wild."

"Fuck off. Pricks."

My eyes are trained on the amber liquid that lies unmoving at the bottom of my glass—still and calm.

I can still feel lingering eyes on me. Do I care? No. They can make their assumptions—including my friends. "I wasn't going to have her made a fucking joke of." I lift my eyes, giving them both a look loaded with warning. I don't need to explain this to them. "You think I was going to leave it go to Vinny. Really? He's nearing retirement."

Vinny is Mason's head of security and driver, and who fucking knows what else. The man practically brought us all up and is like a dad to Mason these days.

"Hey! I think Vin is well fit!" Megan grins wide as she slips her arms around my waist and smiles up at me. I peer down at her over my shoulder. "Mr Montgomery, we'll need a signature. Scar!" she yells, looking around for her friend. I reach out and take the clipboard from her hand, signing my name and adding to my original bid.

It wasn't my intention to bid on Luce, but it made complete sense to *me* that I did. She deserves more than the lousy numbers thrown around the room in jest, and with Megan and Scarlet in charge of the money and bidding, I knew anything could have happened.

I knew the moment I tipped my head that they would make it out to be more than what it is.

My gaze finally seeks her out, and fuck, I shouldn't be mad at her, but I can't help the frustration that comes from her choice to stay with a man like Miller. Like now, she doesn't come to us like she usually would. Instead, she steps down from the stage and makes her way through the crowd and over to her drip of a boyfriend.

I watch as he turns to face her, a smile slipping into place and masking the annoyance he has with my ostentatious bid. He hates me and what I've just done, but he wouldn't tell her that.

Her head twists as if sensing my stare, and as our gazes lock, her icy-blue eyes widen a little before she catches herself.

"Excuse me," I tell my friends, slipping from Megan's hold and stepping through the crowd.

I can see the panic flittering over her face, and I watch as she leans in to say something to Miller, brushing a blonde curl behind her ear to keep her hands busy.

"A word, Luce," I say as I near, tipping my chin at her as I slide my hand around her waist and into the back of her dress. I smooth my hand over her silky skin, smirking slightly when it grows pebbled beneath my fingertips.

"Uh, sure," she mutters, blushing. More from embarrassment than my touch if I know her like I think I do. "Miller, you don't mind, right?" she asks, looking sheepishly over at him.

What do you get when you take two overly polite people and put them into a relationship?

"No, of course not. I will go… over there." I follow his finger to the few chairs that line the wall of the marquee.

A fucking train wreck.

Lucy watches him as he slips away and over to the seats.

I watch her.

Her dress is gold with sequins covering every inch of it. It's high at her neck but low at the back, leaving me with an in.

"Walk with me." I propel her forward with my hand on her back.

"I'm pissed at you, you know."

"I know." I smile. "But I'm pissed at you, too."

"At me?" she retorts, turning to look up at me as she shuffles through the crowd. "How could you be mad at me?"

"You've barely spoken to me all night," I counter. "You didn't even come to say hello." I pop a brow accusingly, although I'm really not mad at all. She seems to slash away at my annoyance without even trying to. "Also, why are you with him?"

"No. No, no, no, no." She stops walking and turns on

me. "You don't get to do that. You won the bid and get to take me on a date—I don't find anything you do weird anymore; you'll have a reason for it, I'm sure."

"I do—"

"Which is fine by me. But you're my friend, Ell. You should be here for me when I need it, not coming at me and telling me I shouldn't be with Miller."

Her eyes start to well, and she dips her head, hiding from me.

I realise she's upset.

"Luce–"

"Just go enjoy your night. I'm good, okay."

She turns and walks towards the bar, and I contemplate following her, but I know she needs the space.

I also know she isn't okay.

"Luce."

"Elliot!" she drags it out as if she's annoyed, but how could she be?

It's me.

"I said, walk with me. I wanna know what's up."

"Let me grab a drink real quick." She sighs, relenting easily before she peers over at Miller and then brings her gaze back to me. A lazy smile dances across her face, and I can't help the grin I flash her.

"You don't need it."

I take her wrist without breaking eye contact, then lead her from the tent. I wrap her arm through mine and stand up straight. "Elliot Montgomery at your service, Miss Morgan. Now how can I be of assistance?"

Her snort could wake the dead. "Shut up, you dork."

I smile at my feet as she pushes me away, but I quickly

draw her back to me by the neck. Her hand slips around my waist, and we fall into a comfortable walk.

"Talk to me."

She inhales heavily through her nose, drawing in the fresh country air. Lowerwick Estate belongs to the Lowells—well, what's left of them. Scarlet and Mason are brother and sister and as good as family to me. We grew up out here on our family's estates, but when Mason and I took over our fathers' real estate company, we had to move into the city.

"What the hell am I doing, Ell?"

"You actually want me to answer that?"

She gives me a pointed look, and I shift my gaze out to the countryside, not being able to stick the look on her face. She will be a ballbuster of a wife for some fortunate prick one day.

"I don't know what I want—"

"With Miller?"

She shrugs, defeated. "With life." Rolling her lips, she pulls her arm from mine and steps away from me, using her hands to articulate her words. "I'm thirty. I'm in a relationship that's…."

"Fucking dead."

Her head drops to her shoulder. "That's not true or fair."

"Isn't it?" I ask. "Luce, I bid on you tonight, and he didn't do shit. He let it go for me to take you on a date."

"Miller can't afford that kind of money."

"It's dead," I reiterate. She knows it too. "If it were my girlfriend on that stage, I'd bullshit my way to a date with her, money or no money. And what's that crap before with him just strolling off when you tell him to?" I scrub my face, trying to dispel my frustration. "Come on, Luce, you deserve better."

"I don't think I have time. It's not like I can just leave him and then find someone and settle down. What if I don't meet someone else now? It takes time. I've put the work in with Miller."

"It's been a couple months. And there isn't a cutoff point here. You go on and on about it like you're old."

"I am. Or I'm getting older. I want kids, Elliot."

I sigh and come to a stop, sliding my hands into my trouser pockets. I've heard this a million times over the two years I've known her. "I know you do."

"You don't understand because you don't have the same life goals as I do, and that's okay; I get it. But it doesn't mean you'll be able to convince me to throw away a relationship because it's lacking a little spark."

"A little spark?"

"Yes! It's not like me and Miller don't have anything going on. We are just fine."

"Is fine going to be enough for you though, princess? When you're curled up in your bed late at night, and you're still dreaming of the life that could've been, you going to be fine then?"

"What do you want from me? To leave him?" Her eyes search mine, hungry for an answer I don't fully understand.

"I want you to be happy. To be confident in your life choices. Make them for you; the girl stood in front of me now, not the girl you might be in five- or ten-years' time."

"That's easy for you to say!" She shakes her head. "You don't get it. You don't want kids, so you don't have the goals or the guy you'll be in five years' time pushing you to make choices. I want to work towards something in life."

"I have goals."

"Yeah?" She frowns, and I know she didn't mean to sound so surprised.

"Yes. But I choose to live in the moment." I step up to her, lifting her chin. "Tell me this. You want to wait it out, see if you can make it work with Miller, but you're not truly happy. I know you're not, so don't bullshit me. But what if something happens? What if you're chasing your five-year goal, fighting to make the *dead* relationship work, and you die at year three? Huh? What then?"

"That's ridiculous and morbid." She chuckles, lifting a hand to cover her mouth as if she can't control it.

I smile along with her because it is morbid, and she's fucking beautiful. "But I'm right. What if you're wasting time right now? What would five-year Luce think about that?"

"She'd think it's dumb."

"She really is a silly bitch sometimes," I agree.

She breaks out into another laugh, and I sober my features. Deciding in this moment that the girl in front of me deserves more, I make a rash decision that I know I won't regret.

"Luce, I wanna see you live your life."

"I am."

"Leave him."

"No."

"Keep looking."

"Elliot!"

"And if in two years you haven't found him—No. Fuck

him, actually. If in two years you haven't found *her*, if you're not settled and well on your way to 'five-year Luce,' I'll give you the kids."

"You'll what?"

"Kids. It's what you want the most, right? It's not a big thing for me and not something in my future. I can be as supportive as you need me to be." I shrug, feeling pretty sure of myself. "I'll give you kids."

I say it as if it's the last bite of my sandwich and not my offspring.

She stands frozen, utterly shell-shocked. "Like… in a tube?"

My lip curls at that, and I lick at my bottom lip, watching as her eyes follow the movement. "You can have them whatever way you want them, princess." I step forward, swiping her hair from her shoulders and pulling her to me. My hand grasps the back of her neck, and I angle her face up to mine. "Go live. Without restraint. I bet you won't even need me come the end."

"Ell," she murmurs, lifting her dainty hand to smooth it across my cheek. "You're the sweetest man sometimes, you know that?"

1

Lucy

Nineteen Months Later

And they lived happily ever after.

That's the dream. A bar I set high at the tender age of six, completely out of reach of every man I'd ever encounter.

It's not that I date the wrong men, although my girls would say different, but I seem to cling to the mediocre, the safe, simple men of the world who don't ever make it past the first year.

I'm a firm believer that once you get the ick, you're done. There's no coming back from the ick. But my problem—and it's a real kicker—Cinderella didn't quit when Prince Charming didn't recognise her at first glance. Aurora wasn't mad that Phillip took one hundred years to wake her up. And the most bittersweet of them all, Beauty loved Beast, even after he locked her father away, held her captive, and showed her his true self. She loved him at his worst.

So, now I live in hope, too afraid to give up on the wrong man in case he is my Prince Charming.

How messed up is that?

"Princess, are you crying again?"

"Leave me alone." My hands lift to cover my face, shielding my tears.

"Luce." I can hear the smile in his voice as he pries my hands away. I find him on his knees beside me at the sofa. "Come on, you've seen this movie a thousand times." His boyish grin pokes at the five-year-old in me, threatening to pop her sad little bubble.

Elliot Montgomery was thrust into my world a little over three years ago when my best friend Nina met Mason Lowell, Elliot's best friend and business partner. He's my friend, someone I spend almost all my spare time with these days, and one of the first people I call with any important news and cry to when I'm sad. And then sometimes, when it's late, and the warmth from his body hits different, well then sometimes, on those nights, I curl in closer, and he stays till dawn.

We have an understanding—a friendship which comes with an invisible line that we've toed along for the past two years.

Somehow London's most notorious playboy managed to worm his way into my fairy tale.

"I thought you were leaving after you finished your muffin?" I ask, letting him pull me up from the sofa.

"You wouldn't have let me leave. You'd have fluttered those pretty lashes and made me stay."

I grin up at him as I find my feet on the hardwood. "It's late. I need to get some sleep. We both have work tomorrow." I bend to collect our wineglasses, then slide past him and into the kitchen.

"Is that a hint for me to tuck you in?"

"No." I roll my eyes as my lip curls into a full smile. "We have Nina's showcase tomorrow evening. Are you still okay to pick me and Meg up? I think we're going for food first."

"Yep, Lowell booked the Landarlin. Probably got his balls strung up for being so over the top."

Elliot isn't wrong, but I don't tell him that. As much as Nina has changed for the better over the years, she will always have her quirks.

I place the glasses into the sink then turn to face him. "I don't know; Mase loves it when she gets fiery with him. It's like their kinky foreplay or something."

"True," Elliot agrees, watching me for a second before sharpening his eyes on me. "You sure you're okay? I know you liked the fucker."

The *fucker* he's referring to is my boyfriend, Miller. Well… I guess you'd call him my ex-boyfriend after he dumped me this morning. I probably should be sad, and I am. Miller and I were together on and off for a little over two years—a record for me. It was okay. Not bad. Not… special. And then last Christmas, when he tried to propose, and I hesitated for a second too long, he checked out. It was like he gave up, and I don't blame him. The poor guy's been trying to take things further for months. It's what I've always wanted. More. The marriage proposal, house, kids. The *happily ever after.*

So why wasn't Miller enough?

The clock's ticking, and all I can think about is how I won't be where I want to be when it strikes out.

I think back to this morning and how things ended so bitter.

"Miller, just give me a second to articulate what I want to say!"

He rounds on me before I fully get my words out, stopping me in my tracks. "What? What could you possibly have to say after last night?" His eyes transfix on me as if he's crazed, yet they hold nothing. Or if they do, I don't see it.

Miller shakes his head at me before looking away to continue packing the last of his things. There isn't a lot to take with him, and in this moment, I wonder if I should've pushed us to live together sooner. Maybe it would've sparked something.

"Is this to do with Beth?"

He twists to face me again. "Beth?" The arch in his dark eyebrows as they reach for his hairline makes my throat ache. I shouldn't be passing the blame when I know this is on me. "Fucking Beth!"

I swallow around my clunky words and pray they come out better. "I'm sorry. I shouldn't have asked that."

With his hands resting on his hips, he takes a deep breath and lifts his eyes to mine. This is probably the first time I've seen any real reaction from him in the two years we've been dating, and it sends a twinge of pain through my chest to think we might have nearly been there. Or he might have been.

"Lucy, you don't want me."

My eyes fill with tears, and I take a half step toward him. "I do."

"No, you don't."

He's right. I roll my lips as emotion builds, blurring my sight. I want to want him. Why isn't that fact enough? And why for once, just this one time, can't I fall for the good guy? "I'm so sorry, Miller. It's not you, it's—"

"You." He nods, sniggering as he lifts his duffel bag from my bed and pulls the strap to lie against his firm chest. He doesn't mean for his words to hurt me—he hasn't got it in him to hurt someone intentionally—but they do. "I hope you find what you're looking for in life, Luce." He stares at me through a mask of indifference, not moving. And I know I could keep him. I could beg this man to stay in a relationship with me, and he would.

It's the sort of man Miller is.

And it's why I don't say a word.

But I do cry. I don't feel what two years of dating should bring me at its end, but I do shed a tear. For me? Miller? The fucked world we live in? I don't know, but I have an overwhelming sense of loss as I stand alone in my apartment, clinging to a dream that has just been squashed once again.

A dream I've never felt further away from.

"I'm fine, Ell." I swallow past the lump in my throat as I push a wayward strand of blonde hair from my face. Licking my lips, I look up at him, and like every other time our eyes connect, he sees. "Ell…"

"Bed." He tips his head towards my room. "Come on, Megs is gonna be a while yet, and I don't want your mascara staining my shirt with those tears I can see brewing."

The warmth of his palm encases mine, and he pulls me through to my bedroom.

"Ell, you should leave."

That's what I should say. I should tell him to leave. I shouldn't want him to stretch out his six-foot-four body on my bed or pull my head down to his sculpted chest or hold me while I sleep.

Elliot has become something he shouldn't have over the years, and I'm not afraid to admit it. My family see it. My friends see it. Fuck, even Miller saw it. They know me and how my mind works.

Elliot Montgomery isn't just my friend.

He's so much more.

"Sleep, Luce. Leave your worries in today and sleep into tomorrow with me. You'll be alright."

He's my safety blanket.

2

Lucy

"Seriously?"

It's Friday night, and I'm standing alone at my kitchen counter holding what my friends consider the perfect "get over Miller gift."

"Seriously!"

A small laugh bubbles up my throat and slips past my lips as I examine my new toys. I look around my tiny apartment that I share with my best friend Megan, checking that she didn't slip in here whilst I was in the shower—because someone clearly did—then I slide open the card.

Girl, go fuck yourself!
You deserve it!
xoxo
kisses and orgasms

Ever the ladies are my girls.

Reaching in, I pull the little silver balls from the plastic casing. They roll in the divot of my hand, the shiny metal cool against my heated palm. My brows lift slightly when I discover how weighty they are. "Surely they aren't staying inside of me," I say to myself.

Shaking my head, I go deeper into the parcel, freezing when I grasp something thick. I don't bother fighting my smile because why should I? I need some fun. It's been too long since I've allowed myself to let go. Miller definitely didn't get me to the point of—

"Oh, it's a vibrator!"

I'm not a toys kind of girl, and the girls know this. It will be precisely why they gifted them to me. Fortunately—or unfortunately (I suppose it depends on the type of person you are), we are extremely open with one another. Always have been.

It's a Friday, the night of my lifetime best friend's dance showcase, and I know I should start it with a bang. She wanted this for me. I should have some fun.

"Are there batteries in this thing?" I hold up the impressive fake penis and examine it. It's been a *long* time since I've had anything this large.

If ever.

I trace the lifelike veins wrapping around the silicone-like vines with a frown firmly in place. "Why did they go so big?"

With a fear of being broken by my new pal BOB, I collect the smaller silver balls and make a calculated guess that they are the safer option. I have around an hour before Megan will be back from the hairdressers, and then Elliot should be here not long after to pick us up. I have some time, and it might be nice to wear the balls whilst I get ready.

Nerves flit through me as I rush to collect up the parcel and disappear into my room. I chuck the boxes onto the bed and then go to the bathroom to wash my new friends. Not thirty minutes later, I'm standing in front of my mirror, hair and makeup done with an excited smile on my face. I wasn't sure at first, and it took me a couple of minutes to figure out the best way to get the little suckers in, but I did.

I smooth my hands down my robe and move my hips from side to side, letting the balls follow the movement and brush my walls. My cheeks flush.

Oh, yes!

I bite my lip and walk to my dresser for no real reason other than the pleasure it gives me.

Is this what I'm supposed to do? Do I just walk around the house, letting them jiggle around inside of me?

I start to do a little dance in the middle of the room, shaking my butt and laughing when my stomach tightens with arousal.

"Oh, shit."

Stalking to the bed with an amused grin on my face, I drop down on the sheets and grab the box. I flip it over and read the back.

"Remote control?" I start to search the box for one and come up short. Then I read the box again. "There isn't a damn remote control!"

And I'm miffed. The idea of what it might feel like with an added buzz makes my core ache.

Damn it!

"Princess?!"

I freeze on the spot at the sound of the distant voice. The box still clutched tight in my hands.

No! Why is Elliot here already?

"Just a second!" I yell, completely ruffled.

Shit!

I grab the packaging and BOB up from my bed and launch them into my open wardrobe.

Bob doesn't want to be silenced, though, and ricochets off the back panel, landing proudly at my feet. In a mad panic, I swipe the giant penis with my foot and send it flying under my bed.

Deep breath.

The second I stop still, the balls settle, and my stomach quivers. Goddammit. I can't take them out. Can I?

"You decent?" Elliot calls from the other side of the door.

"NO!"

Calm down.

Calm down.

"I missed that." I can hear the playfulness in his voice as he pushes open my bedroom door.

"Elliot!" I scream, utterly mortified. I'm wearing my robe, and I'm fully covered, so my dramatics are going to seem a little much to him.

"There she is." He flashes me the most swoonworthy smile, and it sends my face three thousand shades deeper red.

"Get out! Now!" I point at the door.

"Why aren't you dressed yet?" he asks, resting his shoulder against the doorframe.

My eyes drop down his grey pinstripe suit.

He looks edible.

The balls get a cuddle.

"I have another half an hour, thank you very much!"

"Why are you yelling?" He frowns. "Are you okay?" He steps forward, genuine concern on his face as he places a hand on my forehead. "You look a little hot. Your cheeks are all pink." I see his cheek tic, a slight smirk playing on his mouth. "What is it, Luce?"

"What's what?" I swallow past the thick lump of mortification that's lodged itself in my throat.

He darts his tongue out and wets his bottom lip as panic rises like fire in my gut.

"I'm ready to go," I announce, not processing my words.

"You are?" his gravelly voice questions me while his eyes drop down my robe.

I quickly unhook my two-piece from the hanger and shimmy the skirt over my hips. "Yes!" *And I also have two deliciously torturous balls lodged inside of my happy canal, which I should remove, but for some reason, I insist on rushing us out of the door instead.*

This couldn't have gone any worse.

I'm going to kill those girls.

Once I have my skirt in place, I grab my white cropped top and give Elliot the evil eye. He turns around and waits.

"Why are you early anyway?" I ask, still frustrated and trying to keep my mind off my *situation.*

Maybe I could make us a drink and then "go for a wee" before we leave.... That could work.

"I had a meeting with the new developers and finished

early. Mase called, asked if I could go over sooner tonight and give him a hand."

"He did?" I frown as I smooth out the band on my top that hugs my ribs, making sure my breasts are in the right place. That puts plan *A* out the window.

"Uh-huh." I look up and find Elliot facing me and his gaze glued to my chest before he brings it up to my face. "Megan will go to Charlie's and get a lift with him and the others instead."

I roll my eyes and reach for my clutch bag. *Thanks for the heads-up, Megs!* I will have to sneak away at the meal and remove the balls. It's a completely shit and unsanitary plan, but it's all I have right now. "So, we have to go now? I haven't even had a drink yet."

I take a deep breath and blow it out through my mouth, my stomach churning with nerves.

I'm with "my people" tonight, so I shouldn't be so nervous.

It's the balls. They have me all wound up.

"Not unless there are things you need to do first?" He gives me a cheeky smile.

I narrow my gaze on him and wonder what his problem is. "Why are you acting weird?"

"*I'm* acting weird?" he utters, lifting his brows.

What's that look? Have I given myself away? If I go to the bathroom, would I look suspicious?

Good God, this is stupid.

"I was a little emotional before," I lie, knowing he'll believe it. I'm the biggest crybaby. "With everything that happened with Miller this week."

"Ah, of course." He tips his chin in understanding. "Shall we hit the road then?"

I nod, rolling my lips as I follow him out of my apartment.

Why am I like this? Too embarrassed to say something when in reality, I'm close enough with Elliot to tell him the truth. But no, I stand here and swallow my words, knowing I'm going to have to sit in the car for the next thirty minutes, or however long it will take for us to get to the restaurant, with these damn balls lodged inside of me.

"You know it's looking like it's going to rain out." Elliot looks at me over his shoulder, his face awash with something playful as he tells me, "You might get a little wet."

I flinch and instantly pray he doesn't catch it. "I am."

"You are?"

What? "No." I shake my head. "I mean, yes. I am going to get wet." Oh my god, could I be any more twatish? "If it rains," I snap, walking past him and pulling open the car door of his Aston Martin in a fluster.

I slide in, not looking across at the idiot climbing in beside me as I click my seat belt into place. I fiddle with my clutch bag and make sure I have everything before we leave, using it to distract myself. Something tells me I should've found a different mode of transport tonight. As much as I appreciate Elliot, he didn't understand Miller or our relationship. I'm not in the right frame of mind for his shit tonight, and it shows when he gets in the car and starts to sing "Coño" by Jason Derulo.

"Elliot," I groan.

He fiddles with his phone and hits a button on the dash, and the song starts to blare.

"Someone's clearly feeling himself this evening." I take a deep breath as the beat of the music sets my body thrumming in the seat. Glancing across at the stupidly loveable human to my right, I roll my eyes and crack a smile because it's impossible not to when he's around. "Just drive, Montgomery."

"You're looking good tonight, Luce." He nods his head to the beat. "Straight up, you look hot."

My insides warm at his compliment. He knows I will be fretting over how I look this evening.

I've not always been such a worrier, but as I've got older, I've stupidly allowed things to hold me back. I tend to lean on the people around me to guide me in life instead of making the big decisions for myself. In a way, I think it comes from being fortunate. I have so many people around me who care enough to have an opinion.

I even picked a university-based on where my best friend would be. Then I got a job as an assistant to a fashion designer because it seemed like a more *me* choice.

I've never been alone or independent.

From a young age, I had Nina, who practically lived with us. My parents are super close and would do anything for me. And my cousins and extended family are the type to meet up almost every weekend as kids. I guess this is why I feel so selfish about Miller and the news I broke to him the other night.

It's so far out of my comfort zone to even be thinking about such a life-changing decision.

"You'll hurt yourself thinking that hard."

I let my head roll to find Elliot's gaze flicking between me and the road. His blond hair is styled perfectly tonight—

gentlemanly, almost. Although that's a ruse I don't think he intends to give off.

Elliot Montgomery isn't a gentleman. He would tell you that himself. He's a self-proclaimed playboy and proud of it.

He's also a beautiful human being. I know that. I see it. It's in the way he cares for everyone he loves.

There are times in life when you meet a person, and they give off an aura so strong you're immediately drawn to them. Their mood is uplifting and wholesome—it's addicting, and in a moment of bizarre need, you become almost desperate to gain them as a friend. You want to know them and for them to notice you, to love you, for them to pull you into their lives and never let you leave, because when they do, you know you'll benefit from having that person in your life.

That's Elliot Montgomery.

An enigma, a beautiful friend, and a top-shelf playboy women trip over themselves to know.

"You're wonderful, you know that, don't you?" I tell him, still staring at the side of his head. I'm not the only one who feels this way. I see it time and time again with everyone he meets.

Men included.

"I do." He gives me that panty-melting grin. "But what's got you mushing up? You still upset over fuckface?"

With a deep sigh, I gaze back out through the windscreen. "No."

I just don't know what to do.

"You're overthinking. You need to get drunk and go dancing. Or maybe you need to come." He winces as if he knows it's inappropriate, then grasps my bare knee, sending goose bumps fluttering under his large palm. "We're nearly at the restaurant, hang in there, baby. The girls will know what to do."

"Stop!" I chuckle, brushing his hand off. He has no idea what his words and touch do to me. I need to keep it that way. "I have so much in my head."

"Then spill it." He tightens his hands on the steering wheel, and my stomach clenches, making the balls knock and my eyes roll.

Mustn't forget about them.

"I don't know. It's like I don't even know myself. It's lots of things."

"You don't know what you're thinking?"

"No, I do." *I just don't want to tell you.* "I'm letting heavy thoughts settle, and it's hard."

"Because of Miller?"

"Because of life." I dip my head, knowing he must be tired of this conversation by now. "I guess I'm scared I have to start all over again now."

"No, Miller had to go, even if it took you over twelve months to realise it. This will be the best year of your life. Just you wait." His hand glides across my chin, the soft tips of his fingers tipping up my face. I lift my head and look at him, catching his eyes before he darts them back to the road. "You know I meant what I said. Our pact."

I dip my head to the side with a shake of the head. "You can't promise me that, Elliot."

"I can," he snaps, making a smile fight its way onto my face. "It's my life. I'll do what I want with it." He looks at me pointedly. "Because *it's my life*, Luce, and I make the rules, for me, when I want to without worrying about what it might mean later."

"You're crazy, though."

"Suppose it doesn't count then, huh." He taps his finger on the steering wheel, and I wait, knowing he has more. "What would fuckface do?"

"What?"

"Miller. What would he do?"

"You mean, would Miller offer up his… his…"

"I think spunk is pretty fitting."

"God. I'm not having this conversation with you." I shake my head and look out the window.

It's like dealing with a child.

"Hey, I'm serious, talk to me. What would he do?"

I throw my hands up and let them flop to my lap in defeat. "Well, of course, he wouldn't do that. He's too… proper."

"Exactly that. He is too proper—boring."

"You're mean."

"But not wrong." He pops a brow.

"He had his moments of fun."

"Did he make you come?"

"Elliot!" I scold, tightening my lips to hold back the laugh that begs to join his free one. "You're such an asshole!"

His smile doesn't leave his lips as he says, "I'm just playing."

"Well, it's none of your business." I peer out the window, shielding my heated face from him.

The car speeds up, and I'm forced back into the seat, my

torturous body screaming out for more as my fingertips grasp the smooth leather under my thighs.

I sit straight, squirming a little when the balls roll. Chancing a look up at him, I find his blue eyes laughing with unspeakable promise.

"I know he didn't."

3

Lucy

Mason Lowell doesn't know how to do things by halves. We arrived at Landarlin before anyone else and quickly helped him decorate the area he had booked. You'd think the restaurant was fancy enough as it was with the floor-to-ceiling windows and panoramic views looking over the city. Still, Mase insisted we add a canopy of flowers over the area and then placed candles around the tabletop himself. It's beautiful, over the top, and Nina will love it. Once upon a time, she would've questioned his motives. Or just outright told him it wasn't what she wanted. She couldn't help it. Yet I know, without a doubt, that she has worked her butt off for tonight. This dance showcase has been years in the making and something she's put off time and time again. I know Mase feels pressure to make it perfect for her.

Once everything is done, Elliot slips off to the bar to get us some drinks. I clock Mason standing with his phone clutched in his hand, and with the balls still sitting tight inside me, I consider it the perfect time to slip away.

"We're here!" Megan sings, entering the restaurant with Charlie and Scarlet following close behind.

"For fuck's sake." I just need five minutes.

Mason's head lifts from his phone, a frown marring his brow. "You alright, Lucc?"

I plaster a smile on my face. "Grand."

"You sure?" he questions, running a hand through his dark waves. The man looks delicious tonight, and I mentally high-five my best friend for her choice of husband.

"What time is Nina getting here?" I ask.

"Vin's bringing her." He tips his chin towards the door. "Any minute now."

"Perfect." I clasp my hands together and try to act unaffected by my stupidity. Why did I leave the house with these things inside me?

"Hey, babe!" Megan grins as she walks toward me. She looks stunning. Her hair is freshly dyed dark, poker straight, and silky smooth. Her lips are painted her signature red, and her dress matches. "Sorry I didn't make it back home. You okay?"

"I'm wonderful." I reach forward and grasp Scarlet's wrist, pulling her from her conversation with her brother and Charlie and over to us. My eyes drop down her lacy grey wrap dress, and it gives me pause. "Scar, you look hot!"

"Thanks!" she chuckles, seemingly a little tipsy.

I look at Megan, worried. Scarlet has been through a lot. Not just last week, last month, or last year, but a lifetime of pain that she carries with her every day. Still, she smiles through it all.

I check no one is looking or listening, then bring my voice to a hushed whisper. "Sex toys! Really?"

For a split second, they don't react, but then a knowing look crosses both their faces.

I knew it was them.

"You are so welcome." Megan winks.

"Let me know how you get on with them, please. I need to add to my collection." Scarlet chuckles.

I tighten my gaze on her. "You used to be so sweet, Lowell."

"Hey, that's my brother's name, not mine!"

"He's a filthy animal, too."

"Whatever," she muses.

I check around for listening ears. "They're inside of me."

Megan snaps her wondering gaze back to me, giving me all her focus. "I'm sorry. What?"

"They are inside of me." I nod, rolling my lips as I let my panic show. "The balls. I put them in to try them, and then Elliot flipping showed up and needed to come here to help get set up, and I don't know, I panicked, he was all question, question, question, and I felt like he knew I was being shady. The box was on the bed, and I had to chuck it in my wardrobe. I was worried he would see."

"Wow." Megan's jaw hangs wide open.

"You said the balls?" Scarlet asks to clarify.

"Well, duh. I'm not walking around with a fucking monster cock lodged up in there, am I?"

Megan throws her head back, laughing, drawing eyes our way. "This is gold."

"How do they feel?" Scarlet asks with intense fascination.

"Stop it, now!" I snap at them both, pulling them closer and lowering my voice. "I need to go to the loo and take them out."

"Now? Eww, no! Screams UTI to me." Megan grimaces.

"What choice do I have?"

"Just leave them be. They aren't hurting, right?" Scarlet tilts her head with a frown. "Do they hurt? How heavy are they?"

"Scar, will you not!" I take a deep breath and try to calm down.

"Will do wonders for your pelvic floors. I'm always working on mine."

I watch my friend for a moment in pure astonishment. She has, without a doubt, been fully corrupted by the lot of us. There was a time when she would be weirded out over this conversation.

"Okay, don't get worked up." Megan flattens her hand and gets to the point. She knows I'm stressing over this. "If they aren't causing discomfort, I would leave them be for now. No one knows they're there. I promise. And I mean what I say about taking them out here. You don't know what the state of the toilets is."

I look around at the immaculate dining room and then back at her.

"It's a bit of fun, Luce." She shrugs.

I puff out my cheeks and take the drink Elliot slips into my hand. He's slid up beside me, but I already know he didn't hear our conversation.

"Fine," I tell Megan. "Thank you, Ell," I add.

"How are we, ladies? Megan and Scar, looking beautiful tonight."

"Thanks!" They both lean in to kiss his cheek, then Charlie and Mason join, stepping up behind the girls.

"Where's Nina?" I ask impatiently as if it's all I can think to say.

"She just texted; she's on the way. Made Vin stop off at George and Liam's place to say good night to the kids."

I smile at that.

Nina is a wonderful mum.

George is Mason and Elliot's floor manager. He's worked for them for years now and has become a massive part of all our lives. George and his boyfriend Liam have a little boy of their own called Oliver and tend to offer up babysitting duty for the Lowells when they have no one else. It doesn't happen often, but when nights like tonight roll around and we're all together, it's peace of mind for us to know they are safe with George.

I spot my parents walking into the restaurant and smile. "Mum and Dad are here." I step around everyone and move towards the door. "Hey! You guys made it!"

"Wouldn't miss tonight for the world!" my dad murmurs into the top of my head. I wrap my arms around his waist and hug him close. I knew they wouldn't miss it, but I did worry when Dad was caught up at work this afternoon. Growing up, my family was Nina's. My parents practically raised her.

"Hello, darling." My mum gives me a warm smile and pulls me into an embrace. "You look just perfect!" she says, holding me at arm's length.

I slide a strand of blonde hair back behind my ear. "Thank you, Mum."

"We beat Nina here, I hope?" my dad asks, looking over my head and waving to the others.

"Only just, old man!"

He whips around at the sound of Nina's voice. She's standing in the doorway looking phenomenal in a white pantsuit.

I don't know why I do, but I turn to look at Mason, melting a little when his face transforms into the most wholesome smile. I couldn't ask for a man to love her better than he does.

My eyes flick past him to Elliot, whose eyes are stuck on me. I give him a little wink to break his trance, then smile when his face softens.

Mason comes to Nina, and says hello to Mum and Dad, then we all get seated at the table.

It's rounded, and Megan sits on my left, Scarlet on my right and Nina next to her. Mum and Dad are next to Mason, and then Elliot and Charlie sit opposite us alongside Vinny, who is next to Megan, forming the full circle.

The minute we're sitting down and the girls feel it's loud enough, they fill Nina in on the situation between my legs.

"You're wearing them now?!" she hisses.

"Yes." I nod, taking a swig of my drink.

"You! This isn't very you, Luce!" Nina flashes her teeth at me as her smile stretches her face. I watch as Mason catches her glee, and his hand instinctively settles on her thigh. "I'm… proud, maybe. I don't know." She laughs.

"I'm glad we're finding it funny, that's for sure." I huff, and Megan waves me off.

"Oh, chill, will you? It's not like you have razor blades shoved up there. I'm sure it's *satisfying needs*."

"Umm, no, actually it isn't. The remote control wasn't in the box."

Megan frowns, tipping her head to the side. "Huh? No, couldn't be. I put the batteries in it for you. Left it in the package."

"Well, it wasn't there. I looked."

"You'll have to find it when you get home." Scar waggles her brows at me suggestively.

"I plan to!" I lift my bum from the seat, and my stomach coils tight. My wince has the girls snickering. "I'll be using the monster cock at this rate."

"I said it was huge!" Nina blurts.

"Excuse me?" Mason questions, leaning over her shoulder.

"Nothing, bossman."

"Doesn't sound like nothing."

"Luce has a giant spot on her ass. She didn't believe me when we went dress shopping the other day."

The frown that pulls at Mason's brow is as deep as mine, although mine is real. "I don't believe that for a second, and you know it, Pix."

"I'll tell you later," she promises, slapping a kiss on his cheek.

"No, you will not," I hiss.

Mason regards me for a moment and senses my distress. He retreats back to his spot next to Nina, and I give her an evil stare.

"That's it. I'm going to go take them out."

"Don't be so dramatic," she groans.

"I'm not being dramatic. This is like… fucking wonderful fucked-up torture. It's like almost great. Almost."

"We need to find that remote when we get home. I'll play with you if you want."

"Megs, I will take this knife and play with you, if you want." I stab the air with the knife.

The girls all chuckle, and I can't help but laugh with them.

"Seriously though, Luce, are you okay? I've been so busy with the showcase I feel like I've been a shitty friend," Nina asks.

"I'm okay," I tell her quickly, not wanting to make the night about me even for a second. If there's one thing I hate, it's attention. Or all eyes on me. I haven't told any of the girls the real reason why Miller and I broke up. They knew I had been struggling for a while, but that's about all I've let on. "It needed to happen. I'm ready for what's next."

But what is next?

"Either way, it's gonna be a buzz." Scarlet winks.

Megan lifts her glass in a toast. "You've outdone yourself with this one, Luce. Fucking queen!"

"Agreed." Scarlet joins, lifting her glass.

"We are not toasting this. How about to Nina, on an incredible night to come?"

"Nope. We're toasting you and your balls." Nina chuckles quietly, diverting the attention from herself and toasting with the girls.

"Whatever." I lift my glass and let it clink. "I think I should toast to Miller and his tiny HOLY… Wowww." I finish on a whisper as I catch myself, but my hand hitting the table seemed to gain the attention of everyone in our party. I close my eyes and try to ignore the buzzing at my core.

I think on my feet. "These cocktails. Woooo. Just… yum!" I try to hide my blush behind the lock of hair that hangs loosely against my cheek.

"The fuck is wrong with you?" Megan mutters into my ear.

I look across to my parents, and my dad gives me a concerned grimace. I close my eyes as if blocking out the world would also miraculously make me disappear.

The balls are vibrating.

The balls are fucking alive and riveting relentlessly against my walls.

I might come, right here, surrounded by my family.

I might go to hell.

I definitely can't move.

"I don't know about anyone else." My eyes peel open and land on Elliot Montgomery. "But I am *buzzing* for this showcase."

My stare is dead set on him.

"I'm like a big *ball* of excitement." His shoulders widen as he leans back in the chair, cocksure and not a care in the world. "My body is practically *vibrating* and making me giddy."

"Giddy?" Charlie mocks into his glass, none the wiser.

You bastard.

"That's what I said, my friend." He bites his lip, smirking at me. "Fucking gidddddy."

My hand clenches as the buzz intensifies.

He turned it up.

I'll kill him.

"Anyone want a drink?" he asks, looking around the table with a smug look on his face.

4

Elliot

Standing from the table, I eye the few empty glasses and mentally note what's needed.

I can feel Lucy's gaze glued to me, but I don't look her way. She'll follow after me any minute now anyway. I laugh inwardly as I replay the look on her face when I turned on the device.

I'm a bastard.

"I'll give you a hand." John, Lucy's father, stands, rounding the table and heading off towards the bar.

My eyes land on Lucy's mortified ones, and she shakes her head.

I drop to level zero before cranking it up four clicks.

Her face blushes a deep pink hue, and her shoulders tense.

I'm going to have so much fun with this.

"How are you, John?" I ask as I take up position next to him at the bar. It should probably be awkward standing here chatting to him whilst I control his daughter's arousal, but it's not.

Not for me anyway.

I turn and watch over my shoulder. Lucy makes a sign for me to cut it out.

"I'm good now that I'm here." He huffs as he raises a hand at the barman for another beer. John's your typical geezer. As laid back as it comes, happy when he's at the football or with a pint in his hand. "Maggie's been worried about Lucy. It's all I've heard this week."

"Luce is alright," I tell him with complete certainty. John knew I disliked Miller. We shared the same opinions many times over the few years I'd known the Morgans.

"I think it's the move. Mags doesn't want the distance between them. And she worries. We want her to go, but I have to agree. I don't know if she has it in her."

My brows knit as I dip my head to the side in confusion. Righting my shoulders, I turn to face the bar and process his words before I reply.

"Maggie's worried about the move." I nod, not letting on that I'm clueless to what he is talking about.

"It's bloody New York, Elliot. Can you really see it?"

I swallow, trying to loosen the lump that's moulded to the back of my throat. "New York." It slips past my lips before I can stop my tongue from forming them. I turn my head to look at her.

"It got rid of Miller. That's one plus."

"I didn't know," I mutter, still watching her.

John whips his head around to face me. "You didn't know?" He blanches. "About Miller?"

"I didn't know about New York."

"She didn't tell you?"

I glare at her, and her face falls the slightest bit, her facade slipping. I don't want her to feel uncomfortable, but I can't help the annoyance building inside me.

I up her another level and look back at her dad.

"No. If I'm honest, I don't think she's told anyone." Disappointment runs deep, seeping through my skin and plastering to me like armour.

"She would've told the girls," he tells me, his eyes fixed and wide on my face as realisation sets in that he's just told me something he shouldn't have.

I frown. "You said it got rid of Miller. Is that why he left? Because she's going to New York."

"She told him she got the fashion designer role and was considering it. He wasn't happy, and after the shit show at Christmas. It's been a long time coming."

He's referring to Miller proposing to Lucy.

She said no.

Thank fuck.

We all knew he wasn't right for her. Not a bad man—by any means—but she should be busting at the seams with life and laughter, not walking around glazed eyed and worrying about things that might never happen. If she could see herself through my eyes—her family's, she wouldn't be questioning an internship at all. If she could see herself through my eyes, she would have gone the first time she got the offer. Again, she turned it down because she didn't think she had it in her. She didn't think she was the "type of person who ups and leaves her life for a new one."

I'm not having it.

"Can you get this round for the guys?" I ask John,

waving over another staff member. "Can you get the next order delivered to the table and have it added to my tab, please?"

"Of course," the girl replies.

"Excuse me, John."

Slipping my hand in my pocket, I step away and hit the button on the remote to turn it off. Then I pull out my phone and shoot off a text.

Elliot: Move that ass. NOW. Restroom

She sits and stares at her phone for a solid thirty seconds before she considers getting up, her face paling as she chews at her bottom lip. It irritates me.

She irritates me.

Elliot: Get out of your head!

She looks down and starts to type. I watch three dots appear and bounce along the bottom of the screen as if she is writing an essay.

Luce: Not tonight

I look up and watch as her eyes try to escape my heavy stare.

My feet set off towards her, stalking through the restaurant. Bending at the waist, I lean down and speak low so only she can hear.

"Up. Now. Or I will have you screaming out my name at this table for the whole restaurant to hear."

She rises like I knew she would. Her fear of causing a scene far greater than her mission to avoid my questioning. My hand forms to her back, and I guide her from the room, not giving a single fuck about the eyes that follow us.

It's always been this way.

Friends with no benefits and a whole ton of shit in between.

"Why did you do that!" She blushes as she turns on me.

I ignore her until we're further down the hallway and away from prying eyes.

I do a quick sweep and check that the women's bathroom is empty, then flick my head for her to come. "In," I tell her, holding open the door.

She brushes past me and crosses her arms in front of her chest, waiting.

I lock the door and stare down at the stainless steel knob.

"Give me the remote."

When I don't answer, she repeats it. This time with more grit mixed into her words. "Elliot, give me the control."

"You want control? How ironic." I snap, shaking my head as I finally turn.

I instantly lose the anger from my words as I take her in. I adjust my stance and scrub my hands over my face, not knowing where to start or even if I want to. It's been this way since I met her, and although I know she's more than her fears, she doesn't. She doesn't see or believe it, and *that's* fucking draining.

Still, my feet carry me to her spot at the hand dryers. Grasping her slim neck in my heated palm, I pull her into me, knowing she needs it.

"The fuck you doing, Luce?"

"What do you mean?" she asks, sliding her hands up my back as if it's the most natural thing in the world to do so.

I pull back and look down at her. I don't hide the disappointment from my face. As much as I don't want to add to her load, she needs to know bottling everything up isn't just detrimental to her. It affects us all.

"Does Nina know?"

Her spine stiffens under my hold.

"She doesn't, does she?" I snigger. "Who *did* you tell?"

"Who did I tell what?" she questions, and I have to hand it to her, she voices it with pure confidence.

"New York. The internship—with Almendo, I presume?"

She steps back, covering her delicate lips with her fingers. Her other hand flattens on my chest. "I was going to tell you all after the showcase. A couple of days."

"Bullshit," I spit.

"I'm not going, Elliot." Annoyance flares in the backs of her eyes, and I root for it. Crave it. "There was nothing to tell. I already made a decision, and I know it's the best choice for me."

"Best choice for *you* or for the box you reside in?"

Hurt flashes in her eyes, and I ache. From top to toe, my body roars at me to rein it in.

"You have to go, Luce," I stress.

She shakes her head, her shoulders dropping. "I can't."

"But you want to?"

"No."

I crowd her again, and she welcomes me into her warmth. "Please don't lie to me."

"Elliot."

"You'll regret it. If you don't go, you'll regret it. This is an opportunity of a lifetime. And you've had it twice!"

"I know."

My face draws tight with agony but not with my own pain. I know how much she wants this. “You’re going.”

“I can’t.”

“You. Can.”

I watch her throat bob, her gaze shining.

“Luce, your life won’t wait for you to be brave. You’re destined for more. You just have to take it. Before it’s too late.”

“I’m scared,” she admits on a whisper. “I rely on too many people around me.” Her wide eyes pierce through me, a desperation to make me understand. “I can’t do it on my own. New York is fucking huge. It’s never going to happen, Ell.”

I don’t say a word. We stand together, my body aligned with hers with an unnecessary closeness, one I never intended to create.

I don’t know if even I can convince her.

I don’t know if I want to convince her at all.

“It was always my dream, but I’m thirty-two soon; I can work my way up at the shop. Jean…”

I tune her out, not wanting to hear her excuses. Because that’s exactly what they are. I slip my hand into my pocket and turn on the remote. Her hand comes up and clenches my bicep, her nails digging into the skin beneath and most probably leaving a mark.

“Elliot,” she moans, and it goes straight to my dick.

“Don’t say my name like that, princess.”

“You have to stop.”

I wonder if she can feel me, the hardness taking shape in my suit pants.

“You should go to New York,” I tell her softly. “Take the

internship, have some fun, be a little reckless." I click it twice, my watchful gaze transfixed on the contours of her face. The way her lips part, her eyelids pinched and fighting to stay open. "How does it feel?"

She wets her full bottom lip with her tongue, and I follow the motion like a shrinking tide, desperate to get lost in her. "Good. It feels too good."

"Sometimes, I wonder just how sweet you really are, Luce."

She watches me with hooded eyes.

"I want to know what it feels like."

"What, what feels like?" she asks, her breathing laboured as she shifts her hips.

"You."

She drops her face to my chest. "Oh, God."

"He isn't going to help you."

She raises her head as an amused smile tips up her lips.

I should have more control, but I don't. I smooth my hands over her shoulders and push her away to stand on her own.

Backing away, I lean against the wall at the opposite end of the room, my gaze just as lust filled as hers.

"We don't… do this," she remarks as her eyes roll.

"We aren't doing anything."

She gives me a droll stare as if what I just said is untrue. "You told me in the car that it wasn't my business. Well, tonight it is. It's very"—click—"much"—click—"my"—click—"business."

"Elliot." Her hand reaches out to hold the vanity, her eyes lifting to look at me. She laughs nervously, lightness filling her eyes and replacing the heaviness in the room.

"That," I rasp. "That is exactly what I'm talking about. Look at what happens when you let go. Let go, Luce."

"You need to leave." She starts to panic, but I stay rooted in place.

"Can you not come with me in the room?"

"I can. But I don't want to."

"Let. It. go."

She bites down on her lip, her hips rolling. A loud moan falls from her mouth, and I grow stiff to the spot and in my pants.

"Touch yourself," I tell her, the air in the room shifting and becoming something else entirely. We've never gone this far. In all the times we've fucked about, we've never been this riled. This close to crossing the line completely.

"Elliot. Leave."

"You want me to leave? 'Cause I'll go." I groan as she arches her back, searching for friction that's not there. "But is that what you want? 'Cause I don't want to go, Luce. Not even a little bit."

"Why are you so bad?" She huffs, her gleeful look full of arousal and hot as fuck.

"You make me bad." I grin. "Touch yourself."

Her hand drops without the trepidation I was expecting from her, and it shocks the shit out of me. A hiss passes my lips, and I clench my jaw to silence it.

"Talk to me." I swallow the saliva that pools in the base of my throat.

She slips her fingers up under her skirt. "Friends don't do this."

"Friends don't help one another when they need a little push?"

"I split up with my boyfriend less than twenty-four hours ago," she reminds me.

"I've easily slept with three women in that time frame before."

She stills her hand. "Eww! Gross, Ell!"

"Look at me."

Her gaze meets mine, and I smile despite the sting in my ribs because she believes I'd do it. I mean, I have.

"I'm kidding," I lie, pacifying her. "Are you wet?"

"Stop it!" she snaps, her tone playful yet dripping with desire.

"Do I need to come over there—"

"I'm wet," she interrupts, her eyes fixed on my left hand.

I follow her line of sight to the remote control, and my brows pop before a hungry glint rips my top lip. "You want more?" I chuckle.

I set it to the max, pocketing it and grasping my erection through my pants. Lucy doesn't even notice; her eyes are closed, and her body rocks against her hand.

I just need a squeeze.

"So, so… good!" she rasps.

I don't know what's happening right now. Am I getting off on my friends' arousal? Or are we merely finding pleasure in joined company? Are those two things any different?

Fuck knows, but I can't stop, and I don't want to.

There's never been a right time with Lucy. She's been with Miller for the majority of the time I've known her, and when she wasn't, we've fucked around a little. Nothing more than a look that would linger for a couple of seconds too long or a cheeky spoon in bed after a night out in the city. She's the woman you marry and far beyond the likes of me.

She deserves more than anything I could ever give her.

We have a level. An understanding, if you will. Lucy's looking for her happily ever after, the man that will tick all the boxes. And I'm the guy looking for the next hot fuck to warm his bed.

Notorious.

What a word that is. It followed me throughout college, university, and my adult life. Mostly because Mason Lowell tag-teamed me through every party we ever went to and then some. We fucked, drank, dominated in our business field and did it all with a ruthlessness nobody should be proud of.

Women know what they get with me, and Lucy knows what I have to offer—which isn't a lot and nothing she looks for in a man.

She deserves the world, and I'm nothing more than a player to her, who makes money while he sleeps and fucks women before breakfast.

I am funny.

That's one thing I have going for me.

I love my life, and I wouldn't change it. But if I could do my family proud, not have my mum's gaze on me at parties because she's worried I'll "hook up with a floozy." She tells me she's proud of me all the time and how much she loves me, but that's just words. Her eyes speak the truths she's had to learn to accept. I'll give her what she wants one day, but right now, I have no idea how I'll get there.

I decided a long time ago that I wouldn't put an expiry date on my life, and I won't. I choose to live each day as it comes. I have great friends, family, a fucking multimillion-pound company that grows annually. I don't need to chase a damn thing.

The thing is, when you're labelled throughout your whole life—fairly or not—you end up becoming a product of that.

Intentionally or not.

5

Lucy

THE SMELL OF OUR ABANDON SEEMS TO WRAP ITSELF AROUND me like a scorched blanket as I slide my fingers from my clit, and into my sex. My arousal drips down the inside of my thighs, and I know I should stop. I shouldn't be doing this. But I cannot and will not voice the words that would cease this ecstasy.

I've never had a problem with bringing myself to the point of orgasm but never, in my entire thirty-one years, have I got myself off in front of another man. The fact I'm stood here now, with my fingers dancing across slick flesh, all while Elliot Montgomery watches me—I'm questioning my sanity, but it's all but shattered, tethering on the edge of oblivion along with my impending orgasm.

"What are you thinking? Tell me."

My eyes split open. A gasp falls from my lips when I find Elliot palming himself through his trousers.

"Your eyes were closed." He frowns as he utters the words, maybe not meaning to say them at all.

With his vulnerability threatening to unravel at our feet, I give him an inch.

"I'm thinking about how I've never done this."

"You've never given yourself an orgasm?"

I shake my head no. "I've never." I look down at where my hand curves beneath my skirt. "Not whilst being watched."

Paper-thin wrinkles crease the corners of his eyes as he observes me, his mind ticking overtime. For a man who claims to live life on the edge, he sure knows how to get deep into that handsome head of his.

"Get out of your head." I bite my lip and try for a sexy smile, throwing his words right back at him.

His chin tips up. "Did he make you come?"

My pussy throbs. It's as if his words are connected by a thread, teasing the intimate parts of my body expertly.

My heart jerks as realisation sinks in. "You've done this before," I state, not needing an answer.

Of course, he has.

"How many times have you had to finish yourself off after he came inside you?"

"Ell," I moan, my cheeks flushing red hot. "I'm so close."

Raising my hand, I palm my breast, gritting my teeth when my nipple hardens under my gentle touch. There's no doubt in my mind whether Elliot can see them through my top, and the filthy bitch inside of me wants him to see. It's as if every late night in bed when I'd push into his embrace a little too provocatively is now coming to a head. We're going into a territory that's always been forbidden.

"We should stop."

Please, God, don't stop him.

"Not until I get what I want." His words are husky and laced with need, and I wonder how close he is. As close as me?

"And what's that?" I breathe out, my chest visibly moving.

He takes a couple of steps toward me, and I gasp, fear gripping at my veins and making my blood pump a fraction slower through my body.

"I want you to go to New York—"

"Elliot—"

His hand comes up to grip my jaw in a firm hold, his fingers splaying across the smooth skin at my neck. "Shut that pretty fucking mouth up for a second and listen to me."

My eyes drop to his lips as his tongue flicks out and traces them.

"Go. Try it. If you hate it, you can come home. But don't sit around here waiting for Prince Charming to ride on in and give you everything you ever wanted. I may not be the man to take dating advice from, but what I do know is that he isn't real. What is real is your career, and it's waiting for you. The rest will come, and when it's time, it will all happen like you want it to." His hand shifts between us, and I tense as I wait, apprehension swirling in my lower body over what he's about to do.

There's no way he is about to touch me.

He wouldn't.

We don't.

"Tell me you'll go."

"I can't—"

Something firm pushes against my aching clit, and I drop my head to see the little black control poised in his strong hand, white knuckled and steady as he toys with me.

"Elliot." I drop my head back to the wall, and he chuckles, a deep grumble in his chest that travels all the way to the pits of my stomach.

His hand slides from my neck and plants beside my head. "I made a mistake."

"You did?" My brows knit in confusion.

This is too good.

Too dangerous.

He eases up on the pressure and begins swirling the smooth plastic around my pulsing bud. "You're adorable, you know that?" He smirks, flashing me his sexy smile. "I don't want you to tell me you'll go." His eyes darken, his face getting impossibly closer. "You sat on this news for what? A month? More? You want to go, I know you do, and you will."

I swallow the lump in my throat, hating that he can see so clearly through me. It's thrilling and devastating all in one.

"I want to go," I admit.

Because I do. It's been a dream to work with a company like Almendo, and the only thing holding me back is me. I hate myself for it. I preach to my friends to love themselves, to be positive, brave, empowered. Yet I fail to do that for myself.

It's stupid small things that make up a lifetime of disappointing choices.

I'm afraid life won't go how I want it to, and it's debilitating.

"I'm scared, Elliot."

"I know, princess." He glides the control over my clit. "And I'll be here for you: night or day. I can be in New York in what? Five hours—maybe quicker. It's going to be scary; you'll be in new situations with new people and an unfamiliar city."

My stomach tenses. That's everything I've spent the past eight weeks thinking about. Walking the subway, sleeping in a tiny apartment in a high-rise, my neighbours, my colleges—where I will eat, shop, bank—everything.

"But Luce, you're going to be living your dream. You'll find a new normal, a new routine with new people. And you will thrive. I *know* you will."

My eyes roll as he glides quicker in an up and down motion. Relentlessly. He knows I'm close.

"I might not be the best man to take advice from, and I know you'll probably take what I say with little regard." My fingers grasp his wrist, anchoring his hand harder against me as I work my hips shamelessly. "But you know I'm right. I want this for you, and as much as it will suck not having you around for a little while, I'm not selfish enough to keep you."

Elliot

"OH MY GOD."

"Let them see what we all see."

"Elliot," she whispers. Her legs tremble as her body

rocks desperately into mine, causing my thumb to slide over the remote control and lightly graze her slickened folds.

We both hiss.

"Please," she begs, fisting my shirt.

My eyes clench tight, knees bending as I try to refrain myself from grinding against her. My cock is rock solid, desperate for the warmth of a tight little pussy to sink into.

"You'll go to New York."

"Yes," she moans.

"Good girl." I place a kiss on her forehead. "Now, come on my hand so we can go back out there and celebrate your news with our friends."

"We…" She shudders, and I quickly flatten my thumb, fucking off the controller completely along with all rational thought. A couple of inches, and I could slide my finger into her.

I'd be lying if I said I hadn't fantasised about touching Lucy before. She's a fucking hell-raiser for any man with a dick. I've lost count of the number of times she's slept over after a night out, and I've woken up with my cock nestled in the line of her ass.

"We shouldn't… Elliot."

"You want me to stop, then *you* need to stop moaning my name," I growl, using the tips of three fingers to motion over her clit in slow circles.

"We're crossing a line. What if we fuck up this friendship?"

I tsk, and she whimpers as my palm connects with her pussy, a loud slap echoing around the restroom and momentarily reminding me where we are. "We fucked up our friendship the day we met, princess. It's insulting to me that you think we are friends."

Desperation takes over, and she begins to work herself on my fingers. Large ocean-like pools lift to fix on my own eyes, and I see the silent plea shining through—or maybe it's a question, because the way her hips lift, higher and higher, bringing me dangerously close to slipping low enough to her entrance.

"Luce." My jaw clenches and her face sparks with uncertainty, making me feel like a dick for building her up, then questioning her when she pushed.

On the next roll of her hips, I give her what she wants, and the bravo I showed moments before gets lost along with each finger she takes.

Should we be doing this?

Does this change anything?

Fuck, I don't want to mess this up with her.

"Oh my god!"

"Shh." I chuckle, feeling my shoulders loosen. "I really would love for the whole restaurant to hear you come for me, but I don't think it's what *you* want, is it?"

"God… no. Don't stop. Please, Ell, just this one time, don't stop."

"Wouldn't dream of it."

The tips of my fingers brush over the vibrating balls, and I focus my stare on her face, watching to see what she needs—what she likes.

"Does that feel good?"

Her head drops back, and I fight the urge to ravish her throat. "Yes! So good!"

"How about." I push one of the balls against her pulsing

wall, directly where her G-spot should be. "Here."

"Oh my god, stop. No! It's too much… I'm going to…."

I use my thumb to work her clit, swirling it around and around, then down and flat.

It drives her wild.

Her hips buck, her body growing heavier in my arms as her core erupts around me, clamping around my fingers like a vise.

"You might wanna cover your ears." Her sated eyes capture mine, her jaw slack as her body comes down, rolling over my touch and trembling uncontrollably. "What I would give for you to be coming on my cock. You're tight, Luce. Real fucking tight. Any man's wet dream, yet it's your cum that's leaking down *my* wrist, the inside of your legs—they're covered. You'd make the hottest fuck, princess."

She rides it out, her back arched as soft whimpers escape delicately past her parted lips. I watch the moment she comes down and the panic and shame that creeps up her neck in a scarlet flush.

"Outta your head." My forehead meets hers. Our eyes lock. "I just wanted to show you what happens when you break the mould, stepping outside your normal and throwing yourself into the unknown. Tell me, how did it feel to be so reckless? Coming in the middle of a restaurant because of your 'friend's' touch."

"We're in a bathroom," she mutters, sultry and sarcastic and still fucking sexy as hell.

I expose my teeth in an uncontrollable smile as our breaths mingle.

"Don't overthink this." I sober, gesturing between us as if what we just did didn't mean shit, and it's completely fucked up, but once I've said it, I realise it's probably what she needs to hear. An out. She doesn't need to try and make sense of this.

I slip the balls from her pussy, and she sucks in a sharp inhale as they pop out with a loud slurping sound.

I grin like a pubescent teen seeing porn for the first time.

"If we could do that again, I'd like to record it and set it as my morning alarm sound."

"Stop!" She chuckles, pushing on my chest and covering her face.

Pocketing the balls, I step out of her space and watch as she slips past me and into a stall.

"Everyone's going to know."

I roll my eyes at her already racing thoughts. "No, they won't. And if they do, what does it matter?"

Her head pops around the door, her brows pulled together in dramatic outrage. "It matters."

She finishes up and moves to the vanity, fixing her already perfect hair and placing her hands over her pink cheeks to cool them down.

"My legs are like flipping jelly," she complains, and it has my shoulders pulling back. "It normally wears off by now, but I feel like I can barely walk."

I keep my mouth closed.

I don't tell her what goes through my dirty fucking mind.

"What if someone questions us, we need to get our story straight."

"Save the stories for the grandkids."

"Can you be serious for five seconds!" She shakes her head, but her face tells me she's amused.

"That doesn't seem like any fun." I smile down at her

and flick the lock open.

Pulling open the door, I nod my head for her to go. "Let me do the talking, okay?"

I try to convey my seriousness, but I doubt she sees it. She thinks I'm fucking around.

"Trust me." I place my hand on her back and guide her from the restroom.

We stroll down the corridor, and her body shrinks in on itself with every step. "Don't make it obvious," I whisper close to her ear, running a finger up her spine and forcing her shoulders back. My eyes drop to her tightly drawn lips. "And smile, for fuck's sake."

"Don't tell them!" she hisses as she looks up at me with wide eyes.

I frown down at her. "What?"

"It's Nina's night—"

"Here they are!" Maggie calls. "What took you so long? Everything okay, Luce?"

"Please, Ell. I'll tell them Monday morning once I accept the offer, but don't mention it tonight." She slips out of my light hold and rounds the table with a terribly fake smile on her face.

"Everything is fine." Lucy nods at her mum, and I see the silent exchange between them. Her mum knows about New York. She probably thinks that's what's wrong.

John gives me a grim look, and I advert my eyes fast as I take my seat. I don't need Daddy John giving me any looks across the table. It's bad enough with the rest of our friends right now.

They aren't stupid, but they also don't know a damn thing.

At least nothing that I've ever told them. And what's even to tell?

"Where have you two been?" Scarlet asks, twirling a lilac strand of hair around her finger.

"Just for a cheeky finger."

"Elliot!" Maggie scolds.

"Sorry, Mags." I chuckle lightly as the whole table eats up my ruse in amusement—all but John. I don't even look in his direction.

No one at this table expects anything to happen between Lucy and me. We've known each other for over three years without so much as a kiss—we still haven't kissed—but our unique relationship over the years has desensitised them right now, and sneaking off for a "cheeky finger" means something entirely different for them. They think I'm fucking around.

It's glorious, really.

"Let's eat," Mason announces, pulling my focus to him.

Okay, maybe Mase doesn't think I'm fucking around, and perhaps I should be prepared for the look on his face to be transformed into a string of words at some point in the night.

He can't be mad. Lucy and I are just a bit of fun.

It's all we'll ever be.

In fact, that's one thing I'm certain of. I'm Elliot Montgomery, the notorious playboy who doesn't have a plan in life. And she's Lucy Morgan, the hopeless romantic with a blueprint to her life tattooed across her heart.

Our eyes meet, and she swallows thickly, not returning my smile.

She knows it's a bit of fun, right?

6

Lucy

I MADE IT TO WEDNESDAY BEFORE I MADE MY FIRST MOVE. After fending off a killer hangover all day Sunday, feeling like I might die of mortification over what happened between Elliot and me most of Monday, and then coming to the realisation that I definitely shouldn't be going to New York, only to break down in my shower—because I know I should go—I decided the best place to start when it came to moving forward was to speak to my boss, a dear middle-aged lady named Jean. I've worked as a designer for her since I left university, and the thought of leaving Venty's terrifies me. Jean has looked after me over the years, and she was one of the main reasons I declined the internship the first time it was offered.

Will she be mad?

Can I come back once I'm done?

I couldn't ask for a better boss than Jean. She's bent rules on numerous occasions, saved my ass over huge mistakes, picked me up on bad days, and made me laugh harder on good days.

"Lucy, my love?"

I place my hands flat on the corded carpet and let my fingers tips flex against the beige threads. I turn my head to hear her. "Yeah?"

"Did you want to have that chat now?"

My palms heat with her words. When she called my name, I knew exactly what she was going to say. I asked her if we could chat this morning, and she was all for it. I needed a minute to gather my thoughts, so I asked if we could do it later in the day. She was busy at the time and agreed.

"I'll be right down," I call back.

"Shall we have a cuppa?"

Is this a tea occasion? She obviously wants one if she is asking. "Yeah, sure!"

All the words I've been practising in my mind swirl over my tongue silently as I place the last few garment bags on the rails. I'll finish displaying them later. I practice how I can word everything I have to say. The reasoning, the dates I can work to if I leave, the thank-yous for all she's done for me. Everything.

Then I go downstairs.

"I presume this is about New York?" She catches me off guard. Completely. It throws me, and I'm left standing mute on the spot as I try to figure out how she'd know.

I open and close my mouth a couple of times, but nothing seems to filter through.

"They called me." She bends to grab the milk from the fridge in our tiny kitchen. You can barely swing a cat in here, but we also don't spend much time in here either. "Weeks ago, actually. I was beginning to think you weren't going to tell me." She gives me a pointed look, and I know I need to say something.

"I wasn't going to go before," I rush out the words awkwardly, then realise what I've said and cringe. God, I basically just told her I'm leaving. "I changed my mind, literally this weekend—maybe."

Her smile is instant and genuine, and it makes the grip I had on the bannister loosen.

"You did?"

"I think so," I mutter, still knotted up at the idea of leaving. I can't visualise it, not fully. It's so out of my comfort zone I find it impossible to think it's real. "It's what I *should* do."

"Absolutely it is!" Jean sings. She hands me a mug of tea and nods to the stairs to sit.

She wears the same smile as my mum did when I told her I received the offer. She's happy for me. They all are.

I sit beside her and wait, choosing to let her say what she wants to.

"I was surprised when you didn't snap up the offer the first time. This is wonderful news, Lucy."

"You didn't say anything?" I say, instead of agreeing.

She gives me a pensive look as I sip my tea. "I knew you'd make the right decision for you. You always do."

"No, I don't." I laugh.

"Yes." She nods. "Yes, you do."

I frown as I watch her.

"So, you lack a little self-assurance." She waves it off, and her infectious grin pulls at my lips. "I know who you really are and the designer you'll become. I have every bit of faith in you. You just need a little time to see it."

"What will you do?" I ask, my tone full of concern.

"I'll find someone else," she quips. "How long do I have?"

"They want me now. I told them it will depend on how soon we can fix everything here."

"Lucy, with all the love and respect—and yes, I'm likely to crash and burn without you around." She nudges my shoulder playfully. "But there isn't anything to 'fix' here. You need to go, then you go. Don't wait around for me to sort myself out. We both know how long that'll take."

"You think I should go now?"

"Do you want to go now?"

I lick at my lips, then quickly pause.

I don't even know if I want to go at all.

Nerves clench my stomach tight, and I think about the excitement my mum had when she found out I had the offer again, the way Elliot was so adamant it was what I needed. I go with that. "Yeah. Yeah, I think I do."

"You've said, *I think*, three times now. That indecisiveness won't take you anywhere far."

"I want to go," I tell her, nodding my head. I feel better now that she knows. Something sparks in my stomach, a flare of something warm.

Dare I say I'm excited.

Indecisiveness won't take you anywhere far.

"Thank you so much, Jean. I wouldn't even be in this position if you didn't take a chance on me all those years ago." Tears well in my eyes, and she quickly throws her arm around my shoulder, pulling me into her.

"Come on, love. None of that." Her hand rubs at my arm in a brisk but comforting motion. "And thank *you.* You've kept me going, you know. You're a special human being who deserves everything coming your way. I'm excited for you."

Why am I leaving?

I should stay.

I could have an easy life here.

But would I be happy?

I'm not sure I would be.

It's just after one when I leave the shop. We don't work long days on Wednesdays because it's never busy enough to warrant staying open late six days a week. We split it, so every other is a late, and we stay until five thirty—or at least one of us stays.

Before I head over to my mum and dad's house to tell them my news, I go and tell the person I worry about the most. And not because she can't manage without me, but because she will miss me—and I will miss her.

Over two decades of friendship, and we've never been apart.

My throat burns, tightening as I push through the doors at L&M fitness. It's a multilevel building that houses a gym and leisure facilities and my best friend's dance company. It's gorgeous—the whole place. The gym is top of the line with a boutique feel in the decor, which just works, and the dance studio, which sits on the top floor, was designed by Mason himself. It's so Nina; it's scary. He knew what she'd want, and he made it happen.

I wave at the receptionist Gemma and skip up the stairs, a slight spring in my step. It feels good to be positive when I feel like it's been forever since I've allowed myself to believe in this dream.

Nina is still with students when I get to her level, so I move to sit on the piano in the corner of the room while I wait. I watch as she instructs them, picking up on things I can't even see wrong. She's a perfectionist and an insanely talented dancer. To see her finally living her dream after all life has thrown at her gives me hope. Hope not only for myself but for anyone with a heartbeat, trying to withstand perfectly in a world filled with so many hurdles.

I still haven't spoken to Elliot about Saturday night, and I know I need to. It seems off to leave what happened hanging in the air without having a conversation about it, but also, what is there to say? What if what we do say messes with me going to New York? Am I being naive to think it meant something? You don't do that with someone if you don't at least hold some sort of feelings for them, right?

"Hey!"

Nina bounces over and interrupts my deep thoughts, and I plaster on a smile as she shimmies up onto the piano. "Good day?" I ask, watching as the group leaves the studio.

"Wonderful. Yours?"

I sigh heavily, and she twists her head to look at me. "I have news." Her eyes drop to my bottom lip that's being torn to pieces between my teeth. Her defined brows pinch in. "I quit at the shop."

"You what?" she snaps, sitting up straight. "Luce?"

I swallow around the lump in my throat. "You remember in Bora Bora that time I told you about the internship in New York—"

A gasp falls from her lips. "Shut the front door!"

"I got offered the same position."

"Oh my god. Luce!" Her eyes instantly fill with tears, wild but happy. "And you're going? How? That was what? Three years ago."

"They reached out. I didn't even apply."

"They want you," she whispers in amazement.

I nod, not managing the smile I know I should give.

"You're going; you're really doing it," she says, her face awash with pride. "This is everything."

"It's why Miller left. I told him I might go, and he left."

Nina's arms slip around me, clinging on tight. "Oh, babe."

"What if I hate it, Nina?"

"Then I'll come get you. In a heartbeat."

"You think I should go?"

Her brows knit, and she recoils as she shakes her head in disbelief. "Absolutely!"

I swallow and nod. A tear slips down my cheek, the weight of my decision hitting me like a ton of bricks as I offload on my best friend.

"Hey! Don't cry!" She starts to laugh, and I fall into her chest. "You're making me cry, bitch. Come on, what is it?"

"I don't know if I want to go." I sniff. "I feel like everyone else wants me to go, but I don't know if it's what *I* want."

"Well, I know that your family and friends—and Jean, they all want what's best for you. Simple."

“What if I say no, and then regret it? What if it’s just me stopping me like before?”

“I thought you said you already quit at the shop? You sound so unsure.”

“I did. I have.” And not even three hours later, I’m doubting myself. “I’m going to go.” I look down at my hands as the sadness washes from me.

“Do you think it’s because of today? Having to tell us? Because we’ll be okay. We can call, come out and see you literally whenever. Maybe you’re feeling down because you feel like you’re saying goodbye.”

“Probably.” I nod.

“But, that being said… Luce, if you don’t want to go, you don’t go. You’re not letting anyone down, and you can still accomplish your dreams and more right here in London.”

“What if I don’t know?”

She grimaces. She isn’t used to not knowing. She’s so strong minded she wouldn’t allow the doubt in if it were her. “What does your gut tell you to do?” she asks.

I look at her and shrug.

Her face falls, and the disappointment bleeding through the creases of the loving mask she tries to front seals it. “I’m going to go,” I ramble on. “It’s just nerves, and no wonder, it’s New York. I have to give it a shot.”

“Maybe you should think on this—”

“I’ve thought on it for the last eight weeks, night and day.” Maybe that tells me more than I care to admit. Perhaps that means something. “I should go, and I want to.”

She frowns at me, openly watching me for a sign of something. “You’ve told me you’ve felt lost for years, that you want to be more independent, step outside of your comfort zone. I think this could be it. I'd hate to see you make the wrong decision, but if you need some kind of reassurance, I think this could be that step."

"Like a sign." I swallow, my tears slipping slowly down my cheeks.

"They came back for a second time." She reaches out and palms my cheek, then wipes it across her tights. "You're special. Fucking insanely talented in your field, and they want you. New York wants you, Luce! Fucking New York!"

She shakes me in disbelief as she says it, and I chuckle in her hold.

"Will you… with Ellis… I don't want you to—"

"Luce." I look up at her, my face wet and probably a mess. "We're going to be just fine. It's your turn now. Go get 'em, okay."

I nod and then hide my face back in her chest. "I wish I had your balls." I huff.

"I wish I had your soul," she whispers.

"Would it be very me of me to say you already have it?" I grin, feeling soppy but happy.

"Yes. Stop it before you melt me completely." Jumping down from the piano and wiping her face, she turns and faces me. "We're dancing. Tonight," she decides. "Fuck, Luce, you're leaving. I'm so proud and sad, and… god, I'm so proud of you."

"Shit, stop." I laugh, my chin wobbling.

She walks over to her phone in the corner of the room and then turns around and starts to sing along to "Ain't No Mountain High Enough" terribly.

I throw my head back and laugh as she shimmies toward

me with her hands outstretched. I come in strong on the female vocals, and she fist pumps the air.

Jumping down from the piano, I meet her in the middle of the dance studio and grasp her hand. "This is cheesy as shit!" I shout over the speakers while bouncing on the balls of my feet.

"I don't give a fuck!" she hoots.

I try to stop the tears, but they still come, and so do hers. This girl has been a constant in my life for over two decades. She became my best friend before we even knew what it meant. My mum took her in when she needed love the most, yet she taught me more about love than anyone ever could. I saw the fire in her eyes as she got back up after every knock back, and it's inspired me every day since. From drunken nights to scathing secrets we'll never tell and shitty boyfriends we live to forget. There's nothing she doesn't know, and I'll be completely fucking lost without her.

I grab her in a hold and hug her tight. "You'll come visit, promise?"

"Promise." She grins. "Who else knows?"

"Elliot. Jean." I sniff and dry my face on my sleeve, cringing at the foundation that stains it in my carelessness. "Mum and Dad know, but they don't think I'll go. I'm going to tell them after this."

"You have nothing to be worried about, I promise. They will be so proud of you."

I nod, not managing words.

"You okay?" she questions.

I shrug randomly with an awkward pull of my shoulders. I want to tell her how I feel about Elliot, and I will, but saying anything aloud makes it real, or at least it will mean I have to face the truth of what's in my head.

I don't even know what I feel.

"You're scared. I can see it radiating from you, and it's gutting. You're going to be amazing."

I take a short step back, looking down at the polished floor before sitting and lying flat. It's easier to let Nina think that, and it's true. "I am scared," I admit, looking up at Nina. "But I think I'm also excited. Like, I might love it."

Nina grins and moves to mirror my body.

"The fact you want to give it a shot is what's important. Scared or not, you're going for it. You'd regret it if you didn't."

I turn my head to look at her. "I would."

"When are you—" The sound of her phone blaring through the speakers has the tiny hairs at the base of my neck standing on end. I flinch. "Crap!"

Jumping up, Nina rushes over and answers the call.

"Hey!" she sings.

I close my eyes and think about everything I need to figure out between now and leaving. From Elliot to my bank account, my car—which will have to be sold. Or I could just leave it at Mum and Dad's, but if it isn't being driven, it will die on me.

"Is she okay?" Nina asks, drawing my attention to her with the concern that laces her voice. "No, it's okay. I will come and get her. Bless her. Scar said she was quiet this morning."

I frown and sit up.

"Yeah, I just finished anyway. I'll come and get her, then grab Ellis… Okay, bye."

"What is it?" I ask when she hangs up.

"Waverley's sick. She was sent home from the nannies."

"Wasn't Scar supposed to pick them up today? It's your working day."

"No, she's doing overtime at the hospital, and Bethany called Mase before me. I'm going to go grab her from Mason's office now."

"I'll come with, I want to see the kids anyway, and you won't have to drag Ave out of the car at school then."

It will be a good time to speak to Elliot, too.

We need to talk.

Mason and Elliot's office is located three buildings away from L&M fitness in the prestigious Montwell building. Previously owned by their fathers, the two of them spent the majority of the past decade building it up to be one of the most renowned property-developing companies in the country, Ellis and Frey—named after their mothers.

Where Mason was thrown into the hot seat under the watchful eye of his father straight out of university, Elliot was much more relaxed about taking on his father's role. His dad didn't retire for three years after Anthony Lowell had, and from what I've heard, it took Elliot a while to take the position seriously.

I haven't seen Elliot since Saturday, and we haven't spoken about what happened either. It makes me nervous to see him now, and I don't want to ever feel that way with him. I don't know what there is to say, but I do know it needs to be aired. We're good friends, and we can't lose that.

He can probably brush it under the carpet and carry on as normal, but I can't. When I told the girls about what went down, they weren't even surprised. They were just over the top excited that *something* had actually happened.

Elliot is a good guy. My friends adore him. I adore him. But he isn't the man I should be crossing that line with. Don't get me wrong, it was fun—so much fun, but now I'm left feeling off with a need to figure out if he feels an ounce of the confusion I do.

The way he touched me lit a fire in my gut that didn't fully fade when he let me go.

"Stop bouncing your knee." Nina eyes me in the elevator mirror, her face assessing and full of questions. "What is it? It's not just New York. Something's up with you."

I don't snap back at her like I want to. I should say something witty and shut her up before I blabber my mouth and tell her everything I'm standing here thinking about. My silence has her going deeper.

"Is it what happened with Elliot?"

There it is. She always knows. It's the bittersweet side of having someone so paralleled to your life that they know your shit before you do. She doesn't know what I'm thinking, but she knows who I am and how I will be feeling.

"I need to talk to him." I pull my lip between my teeth and look across at her. "Clear the air before I leave."

Nina nods, her eyes dropping before covering her concern that momentarily flashes on her face. "You guys have been playing this game for years. He probably shouldn't have done what he did, but you didn't stop him either." She shrugs unapologetically.

"That's not at all helpful."

She makes a face and gives me an innocent shrug as the elevator doors slide open. The reception area is empty when we arrive, and we quickly make our way to Mason's office.

I look down the hall before we slip in through the door and wonder if Elliot is in.

"Look who's here!" I turn at Mason's enthusiastic voice.

Waverly sits on the sofa, nestled in his suit-clad lap as she watches the TV. It's mounted on the only solid wall. The rest is glass and looks out across the city.

"Hey, Ave," Nina coos, walking around the office and crouching down in front of them. "You feeling poorly?"

Waverly frowns and turns into Mason's jacket, holding on tight with her tiny fist. "This is going to be fun." I chuckle. "Ave, do you want to come with us and get Ellis? I'm coming too!"

She gives me a death stare, and Nina sighs.

Waverly has a favourite, and that's Mase.

"I'm going to pop down and see Ell quick. I'll let you tackle little miss." I give her a wink and back out of the room.

Elliot's office is at the other end of the floor. It's out of the way of everyone else and is an exact mirror of Mason's—although it's much less clinical. I spent a lot of time coming and going with Ellis when he was a baby, so I usually feel comfortable being in the space. Only today, as I stroll down the corridor, I feel different because now I have a heavy ache in my stomach from the weekend's antics. I wish I'd called him over the weekend or at least sent him a text. He's so calm and cool he'd have come over and spent the day and probably put me at ease about the whole thing.

But I wasn't in the right frame of mind on Sunday, and

he would've been in my head about New York, which leaves three whole days between Saturday and now.

My palms are sweaty, and my steps are clunky and harsh. I feel like a ball of energy that can't calm.

Calm down, Luce.

It's Elliot. He's my friend. He'll say something stupid, I'll laugh, and we can go back to being *normal* again.

I puff out a breath and knock once, then walk in.

I find him sitting at his desk. He looks perfect as always.

And so does the brunette who's half-dressed and sliding back into her tights at his side.

7

Elliot

THERE ARE MOMENTS IN MY LIFE WHERE MY CHOICES—NOT many—have gutted me. I pride myself on owning everything I do. No excuses.

"Luce, it's not what you think."

My heart sank when I heard her knock. I knew it was Lucy before she opened the door, doe eyed and looking lost. She catches herself fast, and then I watch in anticipation as her shoulders draw back, and she looks me dead in the eye.

I swallow, my jaw clenching as her judgement paints everything her eyes cast over.

"Sorry. I should've waited outside when I knocked." She turns to leave, and I quickly stand, panic kicking me in my gut and setting me in motion.

She knows me. Knows what I'm like. "It's fine," I tell her. "Harriet's leaving now."

Lucy flicks her eyes to Harriet, who is slipping on her

shoes. She gives Lucy a once-over, then twists her lips up as if she knows something she doesn't.

"How convenient." Harriet laughs.

"Hurry up," I mutter impatiently. She knows how unprofessional this looks.

She sighs as she grabs her bag and coat, then gives me a seductive wink as she shoulders past Lucy. I catch the look on Lucy's face, and it makes my heart drop to my ass.

"Sometimes, I think I know who you are." My jaw stiffens. "Like… you go from this incredible…." She shakes her head and laughs. "Jesus Christ, Ell."

I roll my lips and rub my hands together, not understanding her at all. "What?"

"Nothing. I'm going to go."

"Luce." I grasp her wrist, and she turns towards me.

"What?"

"I'm—"

"Don't apologise." She frowns accusingly. "Why would you apologise?"

"Well, with what happened on Saturday night, it's shitty of me, and I'm sorry you walked in on this."

"Saturday was just a bit of fun, right? You said it didn't matter."

"I don't think I said—"

"It's fine. Seriously." She watches me as if I'm wasting her time. "We're friends, you helped me, and I came to tell you I accepted the offer."

My heart seems to do something wild in my chest. "You did."

"Yeah, I did." She pulls her shoulders even squarer. "I quit at the shop."

"You did?" I repeat.

"Yep." Her eyes glisten as we stare at one another, and I swear I can see hurt in them. I dip my head and scuff my shoe along the floor as I step back to lean against the desk. "When do you leave?"

"Tomorrow." Her lip trembles, and I tighten my gaze on her.

"Tomorrow?" I question with a frown. "Why so soon?"

"I should have left three years ago."

"No. You shouldn't have. What are you doing, Luce?"

"Stop asking me that!"

"Why?"

"I know what I'm doing. Why I'm doing it, and I want to do it. I want to go to New York, Elliot."

I nod, my arms crossing against my chest.

I should let her go without questioning it, but something feels off.

I didn't give Harriet a second thought in the moment, but standing here now looking at Lucy as she tells me she's leaving—something I told her to do—why do I feel like utter shit?

"How are you getting to the airport?"

She frowns as if she hasn't thought about it. "I'm not sure. Mum and Dad will be working, but I'll probably be able to get a lift with one of the girls." Her eyes flutter as she thinks about it. Realisation seems to flash on her face, and then she nods. "Or I can get a taxi or something."

"I will take you."

"You don't need to."

"I want to. What time is your flight?" I round the table

and open up my diary, my knee bouncing. When she doesn't answer me, I lift my head. "Luce, what times your flight?"

"I… I, umm… I haven't booked it yet. I plan to do it when I get home."

The fuck is this woman up to?

"Come here."

She watches me but doesn't move.

I go to her and pick her up. Nothing sexual, just a defiant child getting carried to where they're supposed to be. I sit in my chair and pull her into my lap. I wrap my arms around her shoulders like I have many times before, and she slips her arms around my back, slotting against me.

Neither of us says a thing for a good minute.

She breaks the silence first. "Do you think Nina will be okay?"

I think about that before I answer because it's not an easy one. "We will make sure she is."

I feel her nod against my chest. "I know."

"You can't worry about everyone else."

"I know."

I smooth my hand over her back, wishing she didn't walk in here like she did. "Ell,"

"Hmm?"

"Tell me something no one else knows—a secret or fear. Something I can think about when I need something to fixate on that will make me feel less alone. I want something important to take with me."

I frown down at her, my face as hard as stone. "I don't have any fears. You know I live every day as it comes."

"You're lying," she hums, and it smothers across my

chest, making me feel like Sundays, blankets, and warm apple pie. "Everyone's afraid of something."

"What are you afraid of?" I counter.

She lifts her head from my chest, looking up and cutting me in two. "You already know. I mean, there's a list." She laughs, but I don't flinch. "I'm afraid I won't get to have children, that I'll be too old, and it won't happen for me."

I smile and take her chin, bringing her face closer than I probably should. "We have a backup plan for that." She pouts and then snuggles back into me. "And your secret? Something unknown."

She sighs, and I know she has her eyes closed. "Okay… I hate that I can't stand lying in your arms knowing someone else was in them ten minutes ago."

I try not to move. Try to calm my blood as it rushes through my body and towards my heart like a wildfire. If I don't, she'll hear it—feel it beat out of rhythm.

"And I don't want you to apologise. If anything, I'm sorry."

I shake my head, still catching up. "What are you sorry for?"

"For telling you that." She chuckles. "And for being so irrational."

She's jealous?

"You don't have to tell me your fears," she whispers. "I know you're strong and live on an ever-changing track, but if you need someone, like those nights you sneak over and spoon me because you *feel like it.*" She says it so frankly I worry I might've let my guard fall a little too low and let her see too much. "You can call me. FaceTime. I'm still going to be here for you. It's probably going to be a much healthier friendship."

She wiggles her hips, and I chuckle.

"My biggest fear?" I think about it, although I already know. I just don't know if I want to tell her. "I'm afraid I will die suddenly, and you'll say something sappy at my funeral and embarrass me."

"Ohhh, that's a good one." She grins as she sits up and stares at me with an amused look on her face. It's warm and wholesome and should be on a wall someplace. "It will ground me for sure."

"I don't know what you want me to tell you," I sober.

"It's fine." She waves me off, letting me avoid her question with my shit banter. "I should go home. I really do need to book a flight. And pack!"

I pull her back to me as she goes to stand. "Why tomorrow?"

"If I don't go then, then I won't go at all."

"You don't want a party? A night with the girls? Where are you going to live?"

"I'll find somewhere. I have savings for now, and I can stay in a hotel until then. And I'd love a night with the girls, but it will make me sad. I just need to leave."

I nod and give her a tight smile. "Good. This is good." I swallow the lump in my throat.

She smiles. "Sorry I turned up here unannounced."

"You don't ever have to apologise. And, Luce, I *am* sorry about Harriet. You didn't need to see that."

"Don't be!" She rolls her lips as if she has more to say, but she isn't sure. She's never been closed off with me, so I'd hate for her to be now.

"And I agree that we should forget about Saturday. I'm not even a little bit sorry." I bite my lip at the same time I break a smile. "But it wasn't a good time, so I am sorry if it was confusing for you."

"You don't need to apologise." She stands and smiles down at me. I'm glad we talked, especially with her leaving so soon. "Who was that woman anyway?"

"No one important."

"No one important." She rolls her eyes.

"Don't do that."

"What?!" She smirks, being all playful.

"Your jealousy is hot as fuck, you know."

"I'm not jealous!" She's still smirking.

"If you say so."

"It's fun to mess with you," she informs me. "You're single, Ell. You can bone whoever you want."

"I know I can."

"Harry-art seems like a dream too, so I totally get it."

"Harriet," I correct, steepling my fingers and bringing them to my lips.

"Same thing. Why are they always so posh? I'm genuinely curious."

"What, you decided to go to New York, and it automatically brings out sassy ass Luce?"

"I'm no longer in crisis, so yes, I feel much better. *And* if I were wrong, you'd defend your poor penis."

"You are dismissed."

"Okay. Bye. See you on the other side, mother—"

I'm on my feet before she can pull open the door. My hand wraps around her waist from behind, and I pull her up and off her feet. She squeals, and I quickly dip my head to her neck, swathed by her hair.

"Can I take you to the airport? Please?" I ask, squeezing her.

"Okay. If you must!"

I let her free and drop her to her feet, pulling open the door and slapping her ass as I send her on her way.

Lucy

Not only did Mum and Dad take the day off work to come to the airport with me, but Megan, Nina, Scarlet, the kids, Mason, Charlie and of course, Elliot are all here to see me off. It's not what I wanted, and I would have preferred to have left quietly, but I am glad they came.

The only issue is, I'm now a snivelling, snotty mess as I walk towards the escalators and my gate.

I know this is a big deal, and I understand why my parents and friends wanted to be here. But I was doing great. I was pretending it was nothing and that it wasn't a big deal. As I packed, called the bank, even when I called and told Almendo I was coming out as soon as today. I was on autopilot and doing it with ease—not an easy feat for me.

Megan invited Nina and Scarlet over last night, and we had takeout and wine. One final girls' night for a little while. To be honest, we've been slack over the past twelve months, everything with Scar and getting her back to work, Nina and her studio, the kids. Megan is the only one who seems to live a relatively uneventful life, and she seems the most grounded out of the lot of us. Our time together as a foursome seems to be getting stretched thinner and thinner, and it's to be expected with how our lives are changing.

This is just another change, and it won't be forever.

"How are you feeling?" Megan asks, bumping my shoulder.

Nina looks up at me as we walk together in a line, Scar on the other side of Nina. "Shitting it," I tell them all.

"Remember what we said last night," Nina reassures me. "You only have to give it a shot, and if you hate it, you can come home. Did you take the tablets?"

"No, I was worried about being too out of it boarding the plane. I will take them when I get to my seat."

"It's hardly anything strong, Luce." Nina shakes her head, eyes soft and encouraging. "You'll be fine."

She's talking about the medicine but also everything else: the flight, hotel, my first day, first night. I'm crapping it and barely slept a wink last night.

I got up early when I was sure sleep wasn't coming and cleaned the apartment. Megan will be taking over the rent and said she would tell me if it became too much. She has a good job and can cover it, but I still feel bad. We've lived together since university, and I'm almost certain she will love living alone. It's always been me who hasn't wanted to change our setup.

"Luce, they're calling your gate again." I turn and look at my mum. She's standing with my dad watching me. Everyone is. It's hard to read the uncertainty on their faces right now.

Is it because they don't believe I can do this? Is it all in my head? Maybe they're just as sad as me. This is a good-bye, after all.

"Okay. I better go then." I shrug and stop at the bottom of the escalators.

My blurred gaze drifts around the group, and I don't try to hide it. I don't focus on anyone for too long, but when I see my parents take a step forwards, I step into their arms. My face nestles between them, and I use it to shield my emotions.

I knew I'd cry.

"You'll call me when you land, yes?"

I nod and lift my head, smiling at my mum. I take in her dark hair peppered with little greys that are nearly ready to be covered again. Her small nose and perfect brows, I always loved the way Mum did her brows. The technician lady always told me she couldn't do mine the same because they weren't as naturally thick. I memorise everything as if I don't have access to photos and I won't see her again. Silly.

"I'll miss you guys so much!" I sniff, hiding my face again.

"We are so proud of you, Darling. You know that, don't you?" my mum tells me, my dad nodding in agreement.

"Thank you, guys."

I step away and turn to Charlie. He pulls me into a hug then gives me a wink. "Good luck."

"Luce, babe, you need to go!" The panic in Nina's voice makes my heart squeeze and my stomach knot.

I'm not ready.

I don't want to leave them all.

"Lucy." I turn and find Mason. Ellis is clutched up in his

arms, and I grab up his hand. "Come on, girl. You can do this."

I step closer. "Mase—"

"She. Will. Be. Fine," he tells me, knowing what I was going to say. "If not, expect her first class and encased in bubble wrap."

I chuckle and hug him quickly. "You be good for Mummy and Daddy, Ellis."

He blows me a kiss, and I pretend to catch it.

My flight gets announced again, and I swallow the lump in my throat, but it doesn't stop the tears. It just makes it burn worse.

"Come here, Morgan." Elliot heaves me up, and my legs instinctively wrap around him.

"Elliot, put me down!" I hiss, feeling mortified and hiding my face in his neck.

"If I only get thirty seconds to say goodbye, I'm doing it properly." He strolls towards the escalator and takes my bag from Nina. She has tears streaming down her cheeks, and it makes my smile drop along with my heart.

"Elliot, put me down." I panic.

"If I put you down, you'll miss your flight."

He's right, which I hate. I watch over Elliot's shoulder as Nina gets wrapped up in my dad's arms.

"I don't think I can do this," I whisper.

Elliot turns his head. The escalator is carrying me further and further away, and I hate it. I was brought up in a big family, with people around me constantly. How am I supposed to go to New York?

Once we reach the top of the floor, Elliot walks to the

gate and lets me down. His forehead meets mine, and a tear slips free and down my face.

"Outta your head."

I smile and take a deep breath to control my emotions.

"You should be excited."

"I am." I nod and force a smile. "I do want this. It's just hard to say goodbye. I've never had to."

"It's not forever."

"I know."

"Twelve months."

"I know."

"Here." He slips me an envelope, and I frown down at it. "Don't open it now. It's for when you need something to fixate on or whatever you said."

A secret or fear.

"Ell—"

He pulls me into him tight, his heart beating strong and making everything seem okay momentarily.

"Come back to me, yeah?"

My mouth drops open a little, and I nod, not knowing what else I should do. Come back to him?

"Go! You're going to miss your flight."

I turn and grab my case, my lips rolling as I look between Elliot and the gate. "Bye." I wave awkwardly, and he gives me a killer smile.

It sets me on my way, and I move to stand in line with my suitcase. I'm late, and there are only two people before me.

"Wait!" I spin as Nina's voice calls from the top of the escalators. She runs for me and all but takes me to the ground as she bashes into the dividers that form the queue. "I thought it was best to not say goodbye because of hormones and shit, but then I couldn't not, and I had to come say it."

I laugh through another bout of tears and hug her tight to me.

"Luce, I want you to promise that you'll go to New York and be you," she says in a rush and out of breath, knowing the lady at the desk is looking at us. "Don't feel like you need to leave to find yourself or to become anything more than you are right now because you don't. Who you are is exactly who you should be, and the world will learn to love you regardless."

"Excuse me, miss, we need to get you on board."

"Okay," I tell the lady. "Sorry."

I look back at Nina, and she smiles. It's what I needed to see before, and it gives me the strength I need right now. "Okay," I tell her with a nod, pulling her into one last hug. "I love you!"

"I love you, too!"

I hand my boarding pass to the lady and give her an apologetic smile. She gives me a semblance of a smile back, but it doesn't reach her eyes and feels forced. Like she's being paid to provide me with this sympathetic look.

Taking my ticket, I walk to the tunnel and look back over my shoulder. Nina and Elliot are standing together, Elliot's arm thrown over her shoulder and her arm around his waist.

I give them a wave and walk around the corner.

Once on the plane, I reach into my carry-on and find a tissue, wiping my face and taking a few calming breaths. I find my seat and put my bag in the overhead.

Elliot put me in business class—he wanted me to go first, but I refused. He told me it was a going away treat and that he would be offended if I said no. And right now, while I'm sitting here feeling like my throat is about to close in on me, I'm glad I'm in business and wish I had gone for first. At least I wouldn't have as many eyes on me. It feels like everyone is looking at me, but I'm not spiralling enough to forget that they aren't. It's just me being me and worrying about things that aren't real.

The seat to my left is empty, and I wonder how a plane that's at full capacity has an empty seat.

"Can I get you a drink, miss?"

My nerves seem to settle, and I ask for a glass of fizz, hoping it will calm my nerves. I remember that Nina gave me the tablets, but I feel rooted in my seat and don't want to get up and risk causing a scene. It makes my stomach ache. I should have taken them before. Crap. I breathe in through my nose and try to pull air into my lungs, but it seems impossible. I'm having visions of me having a panic attack and someone calling the cabin crew over and then my family having to come and get me. Being escorted back through the plane because I can't breathe.

I bend the corners of my boarding pass, and the edges cut into my sweat-covered palms.

I don't think I can breathe.

I look at the white envelope underneath my pass and frown.

Elliot's fear.

Don't open it now. It's for when you need something to fixate on.

I inhale and manage to gather half a breath. I peel back the corner of the envelope.

"Are you okay?"

"Me?" I rush out, looking up at the man in the next row.

He nods, then drops his gaze to my hands. "You seem nervous."

I swallow. "I am."

"Here." He riffles around in his laptop bag and pulls out a box of medication. "It's Xanax." He hands me the box and nods as if to say, "check it."

I do, and I find it's similar to what Nina had given me. My eyes lift again to the kind man, a feeling of gratitude washes over me that he noticed my panic and reached out to me. "Thank you. Thank you so much; that's really kind of you."

He nods, his eyes lingering for a second before he looks away again. He's a good-looking guy with a buzz cut, a five o'clock shadow covering his jaw, and from what I can see, an athletic physique. I'm still caught off guard that he noticed my distress and tried to ease that.

I'm always looking for signs in life, something to tell me I'm on track and where I should be. Why does him being here with a similar medication as Nina's and knowing I need it feel like one?

"You're American?" I ask although it's evident by his accent.

"I am. You're British." He grins, and I can't help smiling back.

"I am. Have you been here on holiday?"

"Business." He nods to his laptop open in front of him. "You?"

"I live in England." I smile, laughing internally at my

one-eighty. I feel comfortable with him. "I'm moving to New York for work."

"Wow, that's pretty cool. What is it you do?"

"I'm a fashion designer. You?"

"I'm in tech. Security and servers and all the fun stuff. I was a Navy SEAL for eight years, left last year."

"Cool." I grimace at my use of the word cool.

His face transforms into a smirk, and he tries to hide it, tries to go along with this terrible conversation.

"So… you don't like to fly?"

I drop my eyes and decide I want to be honest with him. "I don't like anything outside of routine, if I'm being truthful. I once had a panic attack on a plane to Paris. I was with my boss at the time."

"Ahh, I can understand that. Not many people enjoy flying. In fact, before you boarded the plane, a young girl barfed back in economy."

"Oh, no." I cringe, taking a hasty sip of the sweet champagne the flight attendant places in front of me.

"Can I get you anything else?"

"Yes, we will have two more of those." He nods to my glass and closes his laptop, and then he looks back at me. "Tell me, where is it you're going to be working?"

I smile on the inside, knowing he will have heard of the brand. I've waited my whole life for this moment. "Almendo. I'm going to be in their Soho headquarters."

He grins wide. "I work on Prince Street." He leans over the arm of his seat, getting closer as he whispers, "Are you stalking me?"

"Is that close by?"

"It's in Soho."

"What? You're kidding me." My smile is instant, and I can't help my blush from his closeness. "And, no! I am not stalking you." I laugh.

"It's nice to meet you…" He looks at me, waiting for a name.

"Lucy! Although my friends call me Luce."

"Luce." He slips his hand in mine and gives it a soft squeeze. "Maxwell."

I feel the knot in my stomach ease a little. "It's great to meet you, Maxwell."

I place my boarding pass, Xanax and the envelope on the empty seat. I might have just made a friend, one that will be a stone's throw away in New York, but I'm not silly enough to take tablets from a complete stranger.

"I'd be more than happy to be your tour guide when we land." He gives me a wink, and I take another sip of champagne.

"Yeah? I tried using Google Earth to find everything I'll need, but I'm undoubtedly going to get lost."

"Well, then it's a good job you met me."

I smile into my champagne flute and settle in for the flight, feeling ten times better than when I boarded.

I can do this.

8

Lucy

We touch down in New York in the late evening, and I'm completely drained by the time my feet hit the tarmac. It's like every worry I ever had about being here was wiped from the depths of me, and I'm running on some kind of wild adrenaline rush. I know I should make the most of it because it won't last.

I pull up Maps on my phone and find the information I saved this morning. My taxi should be waiting for me outside the airport, and then it's taking me directly to my hotel, but still, I want to have my Maps on so I know they are driving me to the hotel and not down some back road where they will kill me.

Maybe I'm still a little wired in.

"You know, I'm going right by your hotel." I turn and find Maxwell standing behind me on the curb. His coat is thrown over his arm, and his shirt looks fresh and crisp. He must have changed. He cocks his head back towards what I presume is a car park. "I can give you a lift."

"Oh, that's okay. I have a taxi booked."

I look up at the row of waiting cars and try to figure out which are taxis and which could be mine.

"People aren't so bothered here." He smiles, and it makes me feel warm. "We blow off our taxis all the time."

I frown at that. "People do that at home too, but I'd call that type of person an asshole. I couldn't and wouldn't let them down. That's someone's wages. Someone's child who won't eat tonight because I couldn't follow through with a simple plan." I shake my head as I get caught up.

He stands on the spot smiling at me. "Does that make me an asshole?"

Shit. I shrug, my eyes widening and looking anywhere but at him.

"You want a lift or not, lady? Last chance."

I dip my chin slightly and smile. "No, I'm going to get the taxi. But thank you." I swallow and meet his stare. He seems like a really nice guy, and he kept me talking the entire flight. I like him. "I would love it if you could show me New York, though? Maybe we could grab a coffee?"

He starts to back away from me with a cheeky smile on his face. Is he going to just walk away?

"I'll call you," he tells me.

"Call me?" I utter, but he doesn't hear. "Okay!" I shout, looking around at the quietening area and wishing he'd waited for me to find my taxi. Or I could have got a lift. Why didn't I just say yes and be on my way already?

Silly bitch.

I make my way down the row of cars and start checking each one by knocking on the window.

Fifteen minutes later, and freezing my tits off, I find my guy.

Twenty minutes later, I arrive at the hotel.

One hour later, I realise Maxwell never took my number.

"It's good, Mum! I'm starting on Monday, so I've got a couple of days to get settled. And I plan to start looking for an apartment as soon as possible."

"Oh, that's wonderful, darling. I was so worried you'd waste money at the hotel."

I drop back onto the bed with my trainers in hand. Slipping the phone between my ear and shoulder, I put them on. "I'm pretty sure Scarlet knew someone or did something because it's definitely not as expensive as I expected it to be. I should be okay here for a couple of weeks, if not longer. I'm so excited, Mum. I actually feel really good."

I listen to her inhale then let out a heavy breath. "Perfect. Just perfect."

"You okay?" I ask.

"I am now. I barely slept last night."

"Oh, Mum. I'm so sorry." My shoulders sag, and I lift the phone to my ear as I pause tying my laces.

"No, no, no! It's not your fault. It's just me being irrational. It's so good to hear you're happy this morning. The way you left at the airport worried me, that's all."

"I think it was this buildup of months and months of

what-ifs—I didn't tell anyone for so long, and I didn't know how it was going to be. This is only day one." I chuckle, my stomach clenching. "But it's a good day today, and I'm going to make the most of it whilst it lasts. You know what I'm like. Honestly, Mum, it was a little of everything. Now I'm here, I feel a whole lot better."

A traitorous wave of tears mist my eyes, and I shake my head as I try to blink them away.

"Okay, I believe you," she tells me. "You'll call me if you need me?"

"Yes, Mum."

"I love you, darling. Your dad said he does too."

"I love you both, too."

"Bye, Luce."

"Bye. Love you," I add again.

Sitting in the middle of my bed, I drop my phone down and then let my mum's words settle for a couple of seconds too long. She was worried about me at the airport, and it takes me right back. The way Nina broke down in my dad's arms.

Am I selfish?

No.

"No!"

I jump up from the bed and grab my headphones.

I can bloody do this.

Walking to the door, I slip my key card into my pocket and leave the room, ready to start this new venture with a spring in my step.

Elliot

I WAS INVITED TO THE LOWELLS' for dinner this evening. It's not out of the ordinary for us all to meet up, but it's very obvious that Nina is trying to pull us all together after Lucy's sudden departure.

Slipping my phone from my pocket, I check my messages for the tenth time in a matter of hours. I'm not sure what I was expecting, but apparently, it was more than nothing at all. I know she landed safe and checked in at the hotel because when the girls booked it, I made sure Scarlet sent me all the details so I could track the flight. I'm certain Luce would've spoken to her mum or Nina by now, and that's one of the reasons I had no issue with driving all the way out to the estate for dinner tonight.

Pulling into Lowerwick, I manoeuvre my car alongside the neatly parked vehicles on the circular drive and climb out. Everyone is already in the dining room when I walk in, and I apologise to Nina for being late as I take a seat between Charlie and Scarlet at the table.

"You alright?" Charlie asks, not casting a full glance my way and keeping his voice hushed.

Charlie has been one of my best friends since university. He studied law and only became acquainted with Mason and me because of his first-year antics around campus. Charles Aldridge was a fucker in his day. Now, not *so* much. He mellowed when he got his degree, became reserved and less about women and more about his work—and some family shit he had to deal with for a while. He's the good guy and a fucking impeccable friend.

"I'm good," I tell him with a nod.

Looking around at the people surrounding me, I can't help but feel off. Lucy is absent, Lance too. It's hard to imagine the fact we likely won't see him at this table for at least another five years.

It's missing energy in the room, and it sucks.

"Ell, do you want a drink?" Scarlet asks from my right, giving me a nudge.

I turn towards her as she pulls me from my thoughts, noticing the table quiet and eyes on me. "The fuck are we all looking at?" I question.

Small smiles pull at their lips, and I shake my head as I rise from my chair. "I'll grab it." I spin the red and white bottles of wine in the centre of the table and then go to the wine cellar to grab a couple more bottles. I'm not gone for more than a couple of minutes when Mason joins me.

"Did your wife send you?" I ask, popping a brow as I throw a look over my shoulder. I continue my search for the wine. "She was giving me a look at the table. Fuckers all were," I mutter.

"You know how she is. She's probably feeling like Luce is gone forever. It took hours before she stopped crying last night."

I take that reminder and chuckle. "True." Lucy might not be gone forever, but she isn't here right now. And it doesn't feel right.

"Is it weird for you? With half the gang?" I ask him.

He dwells on it, his hands stuffed in his pockets as he walks over and eyes a row of wine I was nowhere near. He slips one from the rack and hands it to me. Once upon a time—not all that long ago—he wouldn't have had a clue where to find this wine. "I guess." He shrugs.

I nod, running a hand through my hair.

"You seem off, Montgomery. In the office today, too. It's why Nina's looking at you like that. She's worried."

"Worried about what?"

He gives me a look that says, "who fucking knows" and throws his hands up. "You, I guess."

"You told her I was off."

"I tell her everything," he defends.

I roll my eyes and sit back on a stacked barrel. "Luce hasn't called or texted. Has Nina heard from her?"

"Yeah, she landed and crashed pretty hard, I think."

Mason knows I give a shit, and I know he gives a shit too. Lucy quickly inserted herself in all our lives when our worlds meshed together, and I've never met a single soul who can sit in a room with her and not be drawn to her.

"She needs this."

I glance at my best friend. "I know."

"I'm just saying. You've been playing a dangerous game for a long time. I reckon this will make or break the two of you."

"What?" I spit, screwing my face up.

"You know what I mean."

"Nothing is going to happen between me and Luce."

"Alright." He tips his head. "You do you, Montgomery; I don't know what I'm talking about."

"You sound like fucking Charlie."

He looks at me, offended. "My wife would have my balls if she knew what I thought you should really do."

I tip my chin. "Which is?"

"What you do best. Get fucked and fuck. It will at least take the edge off."

"Pretty sound advice."

He shakes his head and laughs with me, but I know he doesn't truly mean it. He hates to see me still chasing tail when he's at a completely different stage in life. He pushes the kids on me all the time like it will make me want what he has. Truth is, I don't know what I want, and I'm good with that.

I've always been good with that.

"You're all way off. I'm good. Just with Lance in fucking prison and now Luce gone. It's a different vibe to what it once was."

"It is," he agrees, face hard and lips drawn into a tight line.

"Well, this is entirely too deep for us," I tell him. "Come on, asswipe."

I stand up straight and leave the cellar with him.

We go back to the dining room, and I watch as Mason sits down and Megan leans in to whisper something in his ear. His eyes meet mine, and then he shakes his head at Nina, who's sat on the other side of him.

Interfering pricks.

Why do they think I'm not okay?

Sliding out my phone, I sneak a look and see I have no new messages. I check socials for updates but get nothing more than a story from six hours ago of downtown New York.

Annoyance slaps me in the face as I go to check my messages again.

I'm fucking obsessed.

Needing a distraction, I pull up Harriet's number,

wondering if she would want to finish what we started yesterday.

"Wine, Elliot?" Scarlet asks as she fills her glass.

"No, thank you." I catch Mason's gaze and then continue. "I have someplace else to be later."

Mason shakes his head with a knowing smirk.

Why change a habit of a lifetime?

I'M HOME for no more than fifteen minutes when Harriet knocks at my door. She's dressed in a peachy-coloured silk dress that hugs her slender body. She's hot as fuck and way too overdressed.

"Harriet," I greet her, leaning forward and kissing her cheek.

I'm not a complete asshole.

"Can I get you a drink?"

"Yes, please. Slimline tonic and whatever gin you have."

I stroll to the kitchen and make her drink, pouring a rum for myself while I'm at it. I down one glass before pouring another, rolling my shoulders as it burns my chest.

"Here." I hand Harriet her drink and take a sip of my own as I lean back against my sofa.

"Cheers." She smiles and clinks my glass before bringing herself even closer, sliding herself between my legs.

My hand glides around her waist, and I smooth it over the material until I have her ass in my palm.

"I was surprised you called after yesterday. Who was that girl?"

She says *girl* like it's a jab, but Lucy isn't here, and she's only offending *me*. "That would seem to be none of your business."

"Of course." She starts to finger the knot in my tie to remove it. "But I should know if you're sleeping with other women."

"Why the issue now?"

"No issue." She licks at her lips, palming my cock through my pants. "Just curious."

"You know what they say about curiosity."

She frowns. "It killed the cat?"

"It definitely won't get your pussy any attention."

"But you are sleeping with her?"

I drop my hands from her and sigh. "No, Harriet. I'm not."

Her lips turn down, and she pouts in surprise. "Didn't think she seemed like your type."

I can't help but bite at her assumption. "You don't know a thing about my type. Why so many questions tonight?"

"I'm done, sorry." She grins and reaches her hand out to place her drink on the sideboard. "Want me to suck you off?"

My lip tips up, and I watch her slide to her knees on the cool tile. "Attagirl."

She giggles, and it goes straight to my dick. She's halfway through unbuttoning my slacks when my phone chimes, five times back to back.

There's only one person I know, so unbothered by her sleekness, to send messages so bashfully, and I curse her internally for choosing this point to message.

Fucking typical.

Harriet takes me in her icy hand and sucks on the tip of

my cock. I swallow and try to focus on her, but my phone burns a hole in my thigh. Still, I ignore it.

It pings again.

"Need to get that?" Harriet asks, tipping her head back to look at me whilst my precum leaks onto her bottom lip.

Fuck.

I pull her to me, gliding myself to the back of her throat. She takes me with ease, and I slide my hand into her hair to keep her head drawn low and my cock deep.

I pull out my phone quickly and glance at the screen.

Two images and four texts.

Not being able to help myself, I slide across the screen and open the messages.

Princess: I did it!!

Princess: Look at me go!!

The first picture comes next, and it's similar to the one on her story, only this time it's got her face in the shot, and she has her face screwed up from the sun. Her petite nose is bunched and cute as fuck.

Princess: It's so different to what I expected. Busier, smellier and such a buzz.

Princess: I miss you Ell!!!

I open the next image, and it's of her in bed. The covers are pulled up to her chin, and her eyes look glassy. She's makeup-free which I don't get to see enough, and her cheeks are slightly flushed.

Princess: You're at Nina's tonight right? You probably won't get these till later so catch up tomorrow? Good night! xo

I scroll back to the image of her in bed and sigh as Harriet swallows around me.

Lord, give me strength.

Elliot: You still up?

Three dots bounce moments later, and I grow harder—closer.

Princess: Sure am batman. I thought you were ignoring me.

Elliot: You messaged me five minutes ago

Princess: I thought I was #1

I tilt my head back to the heavens and try to hold off. I should pocket my phone and concentrate on Harriet.

Fuck, I'm a first-class prick.

My phone chimes with another text, and a picture of Lucy's feet pops up on the screen. Her toes are painted a light girly pink shade, and I wince at the blisters that strain across the planes of her skin.

Princess: Think I fucked my feet

Elliot: I don't want to see your grubby feet Luce. Make sure you wrap them up before bed.

Another message comes in, and I open it to find a video—or a boomerang. She's rolling her eyes at me, and as it rounds off, she smiles and licks at her lip innocently. I can tell she's laughing to herself.

My cock *innocently* jerks.

I watch it again.

Again.

Again.

"Harder," I rasp out as I thrust my hips forward.

Elliot: I wish you were here Luce

My head drops back, and I see stars as I squeeze my eyes tight, and I come down Harriet's throat.

Princess: Wanna FaceTime?

I pull out of her mouth. "You need to leave."

"What?"

I shake my head, finding my balance on the back of the sofa again. "Sorry. I need to handle something. Work." I lift my phone, and Harriet's brows lift.

"Are you kidding me?"

"I wish I was." I drag a hand down my face and zip up my slacks. I take Harriet's hand and pull her to her feet. "I'm sorry, Harriet. I shouldn't have called tonight."

"Oh god, just lie to me." She waves me off and steps away, picking up her coat and bag. "Bless you." She strolls out of my home without looking back and clearly without an ounce of her pride knocked.

My phone starts to ring, and I look down at it in disgust.

What am I playing at?

"Luce," I answer, not turning on the camera.

"Hey!"

I run my hand through my hair and let her voice settle over me. Fuck, it's good to hear her voice.

"You okay?" I ask.

"I'm fine, actually. It's weird being here, but it's also been nice. It feels like I'm on holiday at the minute, but I'm sure once I start at work on Monday, it'll seem more real."

"Yeah." I squeeze my eyes tight as I think about her boomerang and how it was all I could see while I blew my load into someone else. I don't know what happened between the restroom incident and now, but it's clearly fucking with my head. "Can I call you back, Luce? Tomorrow."

"Of course. Is everything okay?"

"Yeah, I just have some things to tie up before the end of the week. I was in the middle of it when you called."

I shake my head and pinch between my brow. I'm snowballing the fuck out of this.

"The girls said you left dinner early. Don't go working too hard! I'm not there to pull you out of the office anymore."

"No. No, you're not." Could I feel any shittier?

"Cheer up, Montgomery. You're like day one without me. It can't be that bad." She chuckles, and it makes me smile.

"You sound happy. I worried you'd be too worked up to enjoy it."

"I'm still running on adrenaline, I think."

"You need to wrap your feet. Don't let the blisters burst, or you'll be like you were on New Year's all over again."

"Yes, Sir."

"Don't be a little shit."

She chuckles. "I'll let you get back to work. I need to sleep anyway, I'm not used to the time difference yet, and I'm whacked. It's still light out now."

"Yeah, it'll probably take some time."

"Promise you'll quit it before it gets too late? It must be past midnight there."

"I promise. I'll call tomorrow, okay?"

"I'll hold you to it. Good night, Montgomery."

"Night, Morgan."

9

Lucy

It's just after six the next evening when I call Elliot. I've spoken to my mum and dad and all the girls in a group call, and now it's time to soak in the bath while I try to figure out what's up with Elliot Montgomery. He's always so easygoing, happy in his world of fuckery and never lets a thing get to him.

He sounded stressed last night on the phone, and when I spoke to the girls, they said he was abnormally quiet at dinner. I didn't believe them. It's Elliot. He's the loudest man in the room with something filthy or smart to say at all times.

When I messaged him this afternoon and told him I'd call tonight, and he agreed, I was relieved. For a minute, I worried what happened between us at the restaurant might have been playing on his mind. We both agreed to brush it under the carpet, and it's what I want. I can't deny that I have some kind of feelings for Elliot. We've always had that attraction. But then he touched me, and it made me feel like maybe he felt something more for me—and insanely good.

Walking in on Harriet in his office seemed to squash that thought pretty quickly, which leaves me wondering why my friends would label him as a "a little lost puppy" at dinner.

"Hey, pretty girl."

I grin into the phone as the call connects, and Elliot fills the screen.

He's in bed.

"Hey!"

"You okay?" he asks, sitting up and positioning himself so I can see him better.

"I'm good. Tired today and haven't done too much. Someone from Almendo emailed me some documents to help me prepare for Monday. Learning the schedule and planning for the week kinda thing. It's made my day fly by."

"Do you feel ready for Monday?"

"No. I'm crapping it, to be honest. Bear with me; my bath is ready."

I place the phone face down on the cabinet so he can't see me, then I pull off my robe and slide into the warmth of the claw-foot tub.

"Lucy Mae Morgan, are you stripping on our first FaceDate."

"Shut it." I chuckle, grabbing up my phone. "You can't see a thing."

"My eyes can't, no. But my mind…."

"Did you say FaceDate just now?" I question, smiling.

"I did." He matches my smile with an even wider one. "I'm already excited for the next one. I'm hoping to get to second base."

"Second! What was first?" I laugh out loud, and the water sloshes.

He watches me with a warm look in his eyes. "That smile," he says as his teeth flash.

I don't know what I was so worried about before.

It's Elliot.

My eyes follow my hand as it dances through the water, collecting up the bubbles. "Nina said you were quiet last night. Is everything okay?"

He runs his hand through his hair and looks back at me with a hardened stare.

"What?" I question.

"Don't let them fill your head with their bullshit, Luce. Lowell tried it with me last night."

"They only care, Elliot," I defend. "So you're okay?"

"It was weird having dinner with you and Lance missing, that's all."

"It's been odd without Lance for the past couple years. I can't imagine being there without one of the girls too."

"Exactly," he agrees, swallowing and darting his eyes around the screen.

I watch him, sensing he has something on his mind. "Did you go out today? I know Dad was watching the game."

"I caught some of it. Was at the gym with Lowell and Charles this morning." He licks his bottom lip and stares at me, and I know he wants to tell me something.

He can't keep secrets for shit.

"What is it?" I snap. "Whatever's on your mind, out with it."

"I don't want to upset you, but I don't want to lie to you."

My heart sinks. "Right…"

He runs his hand through his hair as my mind races with the possibilities. Is something wrong with Ellis, Ave, one of the girls? Surely Mum or Nina would have said. He wouldn't lie about something like that, though. Is it about what happened in the restaurant? It has to be. Shit.

He's caught me completely off guard.

"Last night when you called, I had someone here. Or she'd just left, actually, but I felt shitty for it. I lied on the spot for no reason and then couldn't sleep a wink knowing what I did."

"Oh." An ache forms in my throat, and I try to swallow it down. "I didn't catch on, sorry. You should have said. I would've called back."

"I didn't want you to go. I wanted to talk to you."

"Elliot—"

"I thought of you."

I snap my mouth closed.

What did he just say?

"I thought of you while she sucked me off, Luce. I think you've fucked me, and I don't know…." He runs his hand through his hair again, and I watch silently as his bicep bulges. "I guess I hadn't shaken off what happened in the restaurant fully."

Oh, fuck.

Fuck.

Fuck.

Fuck.

"Say something." He settles again, the muscles around

his shoulders relaxing. It's as if all that was plaguing him is wiped from him with his admission.

"What if I have no idea how to respond?"

A smirk pulls at the corner of his mouth. "Have I embarrassed you? Are you turned on?"

His efforts to lighten the mood are welcomed, and I fan my face as I try to process. "You shouldn't have lied to me. But I get it. It's you."

His face drops, and my heart instantly pangs with guilt.

"I didn't mean it like that," I rush out. "I just meant—"

"You're not wrong." He shrugs, agreeing. "Can we start this FaceDate from scratch?"

I nod, my insides feeling a little rotten from what I insinuated. He was with someone last night; that's not out of the ordinary. He definitely doesn't need to feel like shit over it.

"You're not what you think you are, Elliot."

He turns his head to the side as if to say, "really?"

"You have your ways, but it doesn't give people a right to label you. I shouldn't have said that. It was wrong, and I'm sorry. You're single, youngish—"

"Watch it," he warns.

"You can do what you want, and you don't have to tell me or explain yourself to anyone else."

"I know, but it didn't feel right lying to you."

My brows pinch together as I process the entire conversation.

What is happening here?

This wasn't what I was expecting tonight. I don't know how I feel, but I don't feel mad. Maybe sad. Knowing that Elliot was thinking about me whilst with another woman rocks me a little.

It's unexpected.

"It's because you're a good man. But it's okay, and I'm glad you told me. About the restaurant thing—"

"I shouldn't have brought that up. I meant what I said. We should forget about it."

Forget about it.

No matter how confusing this man is, he's right. I'm two days away from starting my new job at Almendo, and I can't be distracted.

There's a reason nothing has happened between us before now, and I need to remember that.

We aren't for each other.

We're better as friends.

We want completely different things in life.

"I agree," I say, not putting as much grit behind it as I should.

He watches me for a minute, and I soften. "What?"

"Nothing." He grins, and I smile back.

It's always this way. I can't name a time he's been off with me for more than five minutes. "Wanna get in bed and watch a movie with me?" I ask, knowing we need something to pull us back a little.

He tips his chin, tightening his eyes on me in curiosity. "What movie?"

"I'm thinking *Cinderella*, the 2015 version. I shouldn't prefer it, but I do."

"Absolutely not," he sniggers.

"Ell!"

"We've watched it already. What about something else? The new SAS episode is up."

I huff and roll my eyes playfully. "Fine. But only because

I got to pick last time. Let me have five more in here, and I'll call you back."

"Alright."

I sneak fifteen more minutes in the steamy water before I relent and climb out, wrapping myself in a fluffy towel. I slip into my comfy pyjamas and then slide into bed.

I call Elliot back.

"Ready?" he asks, distracted and not looking at me fully. The room is now dark, and the TV lights up his face. I always appreciate these rare moments with him. It's as if all the bullshit he fronts to the world slides off with his Oxfords and Armani suit, and what's left is this unknown man who sits for hours watching Disney movies with me. He's soft, caring and nothing like what everyone thinks he is.

I wish people could see it, but I also don't want anyone else to get the Elliot I do.

"Yep, still devastated I have to watch your rubbish, though," I tease, giving him a heavy dose of eye contact when he glances at the phone.

"Don't do that."

My bottom lip protrudes.

"Luce."

"It's fine." I sigh, tilting my head as I fight a smile.

"Dammit! Fucking every time."

My shoulders shake as I laugh silently. I search for *Cinderella* and sit back in triumph.

He flaps about with the TV, trying to act pissed off, but I know he loves it, really.

"Ell."

"What?" He types in the movie, not looking at me.

"When will you admit you prefer my movies over yours?"

He swings his eyes back to the phone and tightens his gaze on me. "You opened the envelope already?"

My face falls, but it's quickly overcome with surprise. "What! That's the secret?" I smile. "I thought you said it was a fear!"

He's laughing at me. "You didn't open it."

"No! I forgot. I was about to on the plane when I met Maxwell, and he calmed me down. I put it in my bag and thought I'd save it."

"Save it." He nods.

"Does it say you love my movies?" I grin.

He carries on searching for the film. "You'll find out one day."

"I want to open it now."

"You'll ruin it if you do. What happens when you need it and you've wasted it?"

"I don't know. I'll ring you and take another."

"Savage, Luce."

"Tell me! Or I'm going to go get it."

"No. Press play and shut your mouth."

"Not what you said last night," I mutter, pulling the duvet up to my chin, amused.

He stops and gives me a calculated look through the screen, and I don't know what he's thinking, but his frown wipes the smile from my mouth and makes my cheeks heat instantly.

"Who the fuck is Maxwell?"

They say New York is the city that never sleeps, but as I peel back the covers and tiptoe to my hotel window, I stare out at the overcast sky and wonder how the night can turn everything so dreary and cold. I'm still trying to adjust to the time change, and it's bound to take time, but I also know that the worry running rampant through my head is the reason behind my four a.m. wake-up call.

I have one day before I start at Almendo, and I plan to get out and explore a little today. Anything to make myself feel less of a tourist on Monday.

It was easy to stay in the hotel yesterday and work on the emails Monica had sent, but it also ended up being an excuse not to get out and sightsee.

Now it's four a.m., I'm wide awake, and I have nothing to do.

I consider calling Nina, knowing she and the girls will be up and likely getting the children breakfast. Well, Megan won't be up. But I don't want to ring them. Although I promised to call them if I needed them, I don't want to be constantly calling home.

I want to do this on my own.

Breathe, Luce.

With a shaky hand, I grasp the window handle and push it open. The city assaults me in all its energetic glory, making the dull sky come to life in an instant. A police siren wails, sounding close before it fades and becomes distant—but not completely silenced. One thing I've noticed in the two days I've been here is New Yorkers don't let a lot of things bother them. Back home, an ambulance roars down the street, and you stop for a second and watch as it goes by. Here, people are in another world. It's thrilling. They sidestep anything in their way.

I watch as a group of teenagers emerge from a side street, falling around and shrieking as they laugh in their intoxication. They don't look old enough to be out this late. It reminds me of my uni days when I'd burn the candle at both ends, then crawl in from a party at five and be in class by nine.

I miss being so carefree. I want to yell down at them to enjoy this moment, that it will be gone, and life will catch up soon.

God, that's pathetic.

I sound old.

I need to snap out of this mood and be my own vibe.

Grabbing my phone from the bed, I sit back in the plush tub chair and lie my legs along the windowsill. The full moon lights up the sky and illuminates my skin, making my legs look milky and super smooth. I snap a quick picture and upload it to Instagram.

I caption it *4 a.m. thoughts.*

Not even one minute later, my phone rings.

"Princess, you should be sleeping."

I tip my head back and rest it against the chair. "I tried."

"What's in your head?" Elliot asks as if it's a normal question.

I sigh, not dwelling on my reluctance to tell him. "How I miss old times. The easiness of being young and carefree."

"Fair. But why at four o'clock in the morning?"

"I don't know. I think my body clock is off."

"Give it a couple days, and you'll start work; you'll find a routine, and your body will follow."

He's right. "Why are you up already? It's a Sunday." I frown.

"I was up early to work out. Couldn't sleep."

"You couldn't? You sleep like the dead."

"I had a fucked-up dream."

I smile up at the ceiling. "What was it about?"

"If you laugh," he says accusingly.

"I won't. I swear." I cross my heart even though he can't see.

"I was in this castle and couldn't get out. These weird Viking people were yelling shit about coming outside, and then I was in The Montwell, and Mase was smashing up his office, telling me the ball was going to drop, and he'd missed it. I was bollock naked the whole time."

"What?!" I howl. "Hold on, hold on. Back up to the Vikings." I laugh.

"I don't even know. It's hazy as fuck now but felt real in the moment. You were there," he tells me as if he's just remembering. "Megan too. You thought we were going to die and wanted us to jump out the window."

I hold my stomach to stop the ache. "Stop!"

"I said it was fucked up. It's all the Disney shit you've had me watching."

"Well, we won't be watching *Rapunzel* for a little while." I chuckle.

"Fuck no," he grumbles, and I imagine him running his hand through his hair. "Nina was talking at dinner about coming out on New Year's to see you and watch the ball drop."

"In your dream?"

"No, for real."

"Really?" I sit up a little as excitement sparks.

"I don't know if Charles and Megs can get away yet, but everyone was game."

"I'd love that. I've been thinking about when I'd come home and what I can afford travel-wise."

"I own my own plane, Morgan."

"Wow. Congratulations. Are you going to tell me your dick size too?"

His light chuckle rasps down the phone as he says, "Eight solid inches and thick enough to fuck you for any other man."

"Elliot!" I proclaim. "You're a filthy bastard sometimes."

"Did it get you out of your head?"

"It did; how lucky am I?" I say sarcastically.

"Seriously though, you want to come home, then we'll have you on the next flight out. It's important to me that you use us for that."

He says it so matter of fact, I sink down in the chair. I don't get authoritative Elliot very often, and it always sets me squirming. And it's not the tone or demand. It's the reasoning.

He cares.

"I know you want to keep your pride but not with this. We want to see you as much as you want to come home."

"Okay. I promise to tell you if I want to come home."

"Right then," he says, final. "Are you going back to sleep?" he asks, his voice growing smoother.

"Maybe." I yawn and pull the blanket from the end of the bed off and over to me. "Tell me what you're doing today."

"I plan to go out and see Mum and Dad. Mum's cooking Sunday lunch."

Elliot's parents own Rosestone Estate. It sits next to Lowerwick and is equally as breathtaking. It's peaceful and picturesque and a place I know Elliot holds dear to him. I imagine him in the orangery drinking tea with his mother from their finest china.

"What's the weather like?" I ask, wanting to see everything he can. To feel home through his fingertips.

He huffs out a laugh and says, "Rain. It's raining, Luce."

"I'm shocked," I say, full of sarcasm. "Are you going to pop in to see the kids?" A pang of jealousy etches across my chest. Not seeing Ellis and Waverly will be the most challenging part of this whole new chapter of my life.

I make a mental note to call them later.

"Of course, I am. Ellis wants to get out on the lake."

Between the two estates lies a massive lake that spans miles. The Montgomerys and Lowells are the only people who have access, and it's become a spot for the families to create a lifetime of memories together.

"I wish I could see him out there. He was so fearless last time. Make sure he wears his vest."

"Luce."

"I know. I just can't stand the thought of him out there and falling in."

"You know I wouldn't let anything happen to him."

"I know." I yawn and close my eyes. "Ell?"

"Yes, Luce."

"Thank you for calling me."

"Get some sleep." He pauses for a minute, and I think he's hung up, but then he rasps out. "One day, you'll look back and wish you were in New York again, up at four a.m., watching on while the world slept because you were buzzing with the anticipation of chasing your dreams. Don't wish this away, princess. You dreamed of it once."

A soft smile pulls at my mouth as I drift off to someplace else.

10

Lucy

I WAKE THE NEXT MORNING WITH A SORE NECK AND STIFF legs. The wind whips through my hotel room and has me pulling my blanket tight as I lean up and pull the window closed.

I slept for hours.

Picking up my phone, I realise it's died and go and plug it in. Not wanting to stop for a second to let any thoughts in, I take a shower and get ready for my day.

I'm walking through the main reception a little over an hour later when the receptionist halts me. My stomach knots as she waves me over. "Hi, is everything okay?" I ask.

"Yes, we have a note for you." She reaches under the desk and then holds it up. "Here you go!"

I take it from her and say thank you.

Stepping outside of the hotel, I stand off to the side so that I'm not in the way and open it.

Have lunch with me today. Max. 212-555-0199

Maxwell?

I hold the piece of card to my chest as excitement buzzes inside of me. He told me he would show me around. This could be perfect. I have no idea where I'm going or what I'm even supposed to do in the city. What better way to see New York than with a New Yorker?

I dial the number, and he answers on the fourth ring.

"Hello?"

"Maxwell, it's me, Lucy!" I try to control my voice, but it raises and draws the attention of the other pedestrians.

"You got my note."

"I did. Thank you so much for taking the time to stop by. That was so kind of you."

"I thought you might like to meet today?"

I smile. "You did?"

"I figured you probably haven't made many friends in the city yet, and it would be rude of me to know that fact and not take you out for lunch."

"I've not made a single friend," I inform him with a light laugh. "And lunch would be great." I look around the street and wonder which way I should go. It's just after ten, so that leaves me at least a couple of hours before lunchtime.

"Maxwell, how do I get to the empire state building from my hotel?" I ask.

He chuckles, and I hear him rustling on the other end of the line. "Where are you now?"

"Outside of my hotel." I glance around. "With no idea where I'm going."

"Walk to the end of the street and turn left. Wait by the little coffeehouse. I'll be twenty minutes tops." He hangs up before saying goodbye, and I make my way to the end of the street.

Fifteen minutes later, Maxwell arrives looking fresh from a shower and wearing a black T-shirt with black jeans. He's an attractive man, and I have to take a second to appreciate that as he pulls me in for a quick hug.

"How are you? Settling in?"

"Yeah, I think I'm doing okay."

He tuts. "That indecisiveness will get you killed."

His comment jars me, and I can't help the frown that forms on my brow.

"Shit, sorry. Ignore me. I'm still civilising."

"Oh, no. It wasn't what you said." I shake my head. "Well, actually, it was. It's something my boss once said to me. Just last week."

Indecisiveness won't get you anywhere far.

"You looked ready to bolt," he teases.

I grasp his strong forearm. "No, no, I need you!" I chuckle. "I have no idea where I'm going."

"Alright, lady. Have you eaten today?"

I look at him sheepishly, my stomach growling at his words. "Not yet."

"Well then, let's have brunch. Then I'll get you out into the wild."

My feet are going to fall off, I'm sure of it. There can't be a square inch of the big apple my trainers haven't touched, yet Maxwell's convinced we only covered a tiny percentage of it.

"You looked at him as if he stole your puppy or chucked your ice cream cone on the ground."

"He just walked straight up to the counter, right in front of all of us and spoke to them like complete crap. He didn't have a care in the world."

"I'm pretty sure he worked there."

We laugh in unison as we round the corner of the street. My shoulders relax when I spot the sign for my hotel.

Finally.

"I cannot thank you enough for today, Max. You've been the best tour guide I could ask for."

"It's been my pleasure, and you can repay me with dinner. One night this week?" Maxwell's top lip twitches as he twists his head, gauging my reaction.

I want to say yes. I should say yes. I need friends here, someone I know in New York, looking out for me. My family would want that. But I also don't want to fall into my usual clingy ways. I want to do things for myself here. Find my independence. That's literally the whole point of me being here.

And as much as it's been amazing having Maxwell show me around, a part of me wishes I could go out and do it all alone.

I can't say no, though, and I don't want to. I just need to give myself some time to find my feet.

"How about Friday? I can imagine work will be hectic this week."

"Friday works for me."

"Perfect. You have my number now." I smile. "I should

probably go soak these blisters for the rest of the night." I cringe at the grim information I didn't need to share. "You've kept me from stressing about tomorrow all day, so thank you for that."

"You don't need to thank me." He steps back, and I can tell he's turning to leave.

I've noticed Maxwell never says goodbye properly. He pays you attention while you're engaged in conversation but checks out almost instantly when he's done. I've seen him do it all day with everyone he meets. It seems rude, although I don't think he means to come across that way. "If you get stuck and don't know where you're going tomorrow or in the week, just give me a text."

"Thank you, Max."

He gives me a smile and nods, turning on his heel. I watch as he walks down the street.

Inside the hotel, I change into my comfiest pyjamas. Then, I drop back to the bed, exhausted, and open the folder I filed all my work documents in yesterday. Maxwell walked me to my new office today. It's a fifteen-minute walk from the hotel and in a really lovely area in Soho. Scarlet was obsessed with finding me the most practical place to stay, and she's nailed it.

I just have to find an apartment or room to rent that's a little more permanent now.

Once I've finished reading over the schedule for the morning, I iron my favourite black Gucci dress and hang it in the wardrobe. With everything checked off my list, I give Nina a call.

"Hey, babe."

"Hey!" I smile as the call connects.

"Luce," I hear Mason's deep voice echo through the phone. I can imagine them curled up in front of the fire together at the estate.

"Hey, Mase!"

"You sound happy," Nina observes.

"I do?"

"Uh-huh." I can tell she's smiling. "Talk to me, tell me about New York. Is it wonderful?"

"It's honestly incredible. Everything and nothing like I expected."

"How do you feel about tomorrow? I'm buzzing for you."

"I'm terrified." I chuckle. "But excited too. It feels like everything I've worked for has been leading up to this moment."

"Which is why we're so proud of you. I still can't believe you've gone. I went to see Meg earlier, and it was just off. I guess it will take some time to get used to you not being around. Have you been exploring?"

"I have. I met a guy called Maxwell, and he offered to show me around the city."

I hear shuffling in the background. "Maxwell," Nina repeats.

"He's a Navy SEAL. Or used to be. He's in tech now."

"Well, I'm glad you're making friends." It goes quiet, but I can hear Nina mumbling something as if she's covering the speaker. "What's his last name, Luce?"

"I don't know." I frown. "Why?"

"Hold on." I hear more shuffling, then the sound of wind rippling before a door closes. "Sorry, Mase is being an ass."

"What's he doing?"

"He's just worrying over nothing."

"He asked for Maxwell's last name, didn't he?"

Nina sighs. "You know what he's like. I won't tell him anything more about it. You can talk to me and know that he won't interfere."

"I don't mind that he asked. He's a good friend, and I'd want the same if it were you. And I get it, but Maxwell seems like a pretty sound guy." I smile. "I get a good vibe so far."

I contemplate telling her I met Max on the plane, but I don't want her to know I had a mini-meltdown and that he offered me medication to calm down.

Instead, I tell Nina all about my day, from breakfast to the moment I called her. She sits and listens to me ramble on until I catch her yawn through the phone. I look at my watch and see that it's just gone six p.m.

"Nina, it's past eleven there. You need to sleep."

"I do," she agrees, sounding shattered. "Scar's working crazy shifts this weekend. It's killing me a little trying to work around her and the kids."

Nina lives with Mason's sister at the estate. They get along, and the house is huge, so it's no issue. If anything, I think it works better for everyone. Scarlet was able to help with childcare when Nina went back to work, and when things set Scarlet's world spinning, she relied just as heavy on them. I can't imagine her on her own after what she's dealt with. "Scar never stops. I don't think either of you knows how."

"True," Nina hums.

"I'm going to find a movie to cry over that will keep me

awake past nine. Or maybe Henry Cavill or a Hemsworth is what I need. Get some sleep, okay? Don't let that handsome husband of yours corrupt your ass."

"Corrupt my ass… are you okay?"

"I didn't mean your actual ass." I laugh out loud. "That's already at full corruption levels. Breached and fucking sore." I snort. "You're safe, though; it's a Sunday."

"I'll have you know we did it on a Friday the other week. Asshole," she sounds so proud, and it has me doubling over.

Nina once revealed that she lost her anal cherry on a random Tuesday night, and we've *never* let her live it down.

"Right, I'm hanging up." She huffs.

"I love you!" I tell her, my cheeks still stretched wide.

"I love you, too." I don't hang up because I know she isn't done. "Luce, just be careful, yeah?"

"Nina." I sober, letting her know I hear her. "I'm not silly. I'll be as careful and smart as your butt on a Tuesday."

"I'm never going to live it down, am I?"

"We wouldn't be your best friends if we let you. Can you imagine being boring and not ribbing each other over the stupid shit we do?"

"I think about that life often. My true dream. It's punless and glorious."

"Now you're making up words. Go to sleep!"

"Good night," she sings before hanging up.

My head hits the pillow, and I smile up at my phone, feeling good after such a long day.

I get the urge to call Elliot, and I don't know why. It's not like we spent every day together at home. It's late anyway, and I don't want to wake him.

Maybe we should leave it a day or two.

Let things cool off a little.

I find a movie and cosy up on the sofa.

Elliot

"What can I get for you, gents?"

I lean into the bar and reel off my order to the petite brunette on the opposite side. She busies herself making our drinks, and I turn my eyes on the club.

"Let It Go" by Armonize pumps through the speakers as men continue to fill the downstairs bar. The Nightingale is a gentleman's club and the only place in the city Charlie will come to pick up women, and I have to hand it to him. It's a sound setup.

A safe one for the likes of him.

"Busy tonight," I remark, losing my train of thought when a woman strolls past us in a slinky piece of nothing. I twist my head and pop a brow at Charlie.

He grins back at me. "Honestly, I'm surprised you were up for it."

"When am I not up for it?" I throw back in confusion.

He doesn't answer me right away, choosing to take the drink from the bartender and take a leisurely sip.

I wait.

"Have you heard from Lucy yet?"

My gaze tightens on him accusingly. When his lip curls and he smirks into his glass, I know he's fucking with me. "Fuck off, Aldridge."

"I like the way you think." Charlie clinks his glass with mine and starts to stroll off towards the second floor.

He looks over his shoulder at me as the security guard opens the gate. "You going up tonight?" he asks, tipping his chin towards the most private area in the club. It's where the women will be *entertaining* before they go downstairs later tonight.

I push past him. "Luce and I are friends. Nothing more and nothing less."

He shakes his head as he levels with me, walking up the steps beside me. "I only asked if you'd heard from her, mate. You were pretty worked up at dinner on Friday."

I look around the second floor, feeling eyes settle on us as we cross the room and ease into one of the empty booths. My leg bounces under the table as I down my drink.

"I had Harriet at mine after the meal."

Charlie meets my eyes but doesn't say anything. Mentally, I know he's already dissecting everything I've already said. No doubt he knew I had something on my mind. "Lucy ended up messaging me late evening, and I let Harriet suck me off while texting her back."

He watches me, nodding after a solid beat of silence. "And she's settling in okay?"

I snicker and look at my drink, spinning the glass on the table between my fingers. "I fucked around with her before that. At the meal on the evening of Nina's showcase. We've never..." I shake my head as if it will tell him the rest.

"I get it." He sits forward, bracing his forearms on his knees. "You and Luce have always been a paradox; doing too much just by doing nothing."

"That's just it, though. We both want it this way. We've got it right, and I don't want that to change."

"But it doesn't feel like something you can control?"

I turn my head to look at him fully.

"No," I disagree, shaking my head as realisation kicks in. "It doesn't feel like something I *want* to control."

He nods. "And instead of telling Luce this, you come here with me, pick up some random woman, and fuck her until that control's a little quieter?"

"You're turning into your fucking therapist," I tell him, deadpan.

He laughs at that and tips his head back. "As long as someone's getting my money's worth—"

"Charlie!"

We both turn towards the woman approaching us.

"Amber," Charlie drawls out, eyeing me as she positions herself between the two of us.

"You've not been in for weeks," she complains, sounding genuinely concerned.

"I've been busy." I watch as Charlie's eyes appreciate the pretty blonde, and then her hand as it slips into his. She leans forward to whisper in his ear, and I look away, signalling to the waitress for another drink.

In my peripheral, I see Amber get up and walk away.

I twist around, pinning Charlie with a frown, but he just nods his head in the direction Amber slipped off in. My eyes seek her out, and I spot her speaking to a group of girls.

When she returns, she isn't alone.

"Hello, Mr Montgomery." Olivia, one of the women I'm well acquainted with at the club, steps forward, smoothing a hand over her long blonde ponytail as her lips drag up and out at the sides.

"Miss Vessen." I tip my chin at her in greeting, and she takes a step forward. Closer. "You wear that coy smile of yours convincingly well." I lean in and whisper in her ear, "But you and me both know how dirty those lips can really get."

Her head tips to the side. "I don't know what you're talking about."

I snigger and glance at my friend. He's sat with Amber, a challenging glint in his eye. He knows exactly what he's doing. Maybe more so than the little vixen stood at my feet.

Charlie doesn't think I'll hook up?

"Do you want a drink, Liv?" I ask, slyly cocking my head towards the private rooms at the back of the club.

The waitress appears at Olivia's back, and she turns slightly to catch her wrist. "Could you take it to room four, please, Bec?"

"Of course."

I stand and button my jacket with a heavy stare on Olivia. Then, I reach out, dancing my fingertips from her shoulder, across her collarbone, up her slim neck and over the seams of her swollen lips.

"Shall we?" I ask, pulling down on the pouty flesh and exposing her near-perfect teeth.

She watches me as her throat bobs, then her head follows, nodding in agreement.

I smile as I take her hand and walk to what I know is room four. They aren't numbered, but anyone who's a member at The Nightingale knows how the club works.

I wait at the door as Oliva slips her hand past my waist

and unlocks it with her key. I quickly throw a glance over my shoulder to see Charlie watching after us.

Jackass.

As we slip inside, I shut the door and question my own damn sanity over what I'm about to do.

"Look, Liv, you're fucking beautiful. One of the smartest girls on Louis's payroll, and I've purposely led you on here like an absolute prick. But I'm just trying to throw off a scent, so to speak. Charles thinks—"

My words drop off the tip of my gaping jaw as I turn and face her.

"You're taking your top off," I say, not stunned enough to keep my mouth shut.

"Charles thinks what?"

"You didn't wear a bra tonight." I swallow, shaking my head. "You didn't need one," I add, dazed and fucking rattled as I take in her perfect tits.

I clench my teeth hard.

Stick to the fucking plan, mate. She's not that hot.

Olivia hums, her eyes sultry and full of something my cock begs for. "I even wore matching panties."

"Yeah?"

"Do you want to see?"

"No." I nod my head yes.

She takes my hand and laughs, pulling me over to the makeshift bed. It's more like a giant fuck chair, but you can sleep on it.

As I sit down, I grasp both sides of her shirt in my fists and pull them together, covering her nipples from my hungry gaze.

Still, I clench my eyes tight and reevaluate the last week in my mind.

Olivia lowers onto my lap, squashing my hands between us and effectively smothering her breasts in my palms.

"Mr Montgomery, open your eyes," she whispers.

"Just a sec."

I should definitely fuck her. Right?

"You're not what you think you are, Elliot. You can do what you want, and you don't have to tell me or explain yourself to anyone else."

Did Luce really mean that?

"About the restaurant thing—"

"I shouldn't have brought that up. I meant what I said. We should forget about it."

"I agree."

Fuck.

"Who the fuck is Maxwell?"

"I met him on the plane, and he said he would show me around the city. He's a friend, Elliot."

He's a friend. *Why'd she tell me that?* And why did I care?

Olivia's hips gyrate slowly over my lap, and I groan, releasing her shirt to grip the tops of her thighs.

I should stop her. If I let this happen, it's going to be on Lucy's terms. She's taken over my mind this week, living in my head rent-fucking-free.

But if I don't do this… It will still be on Lucy's terms.

Conclusion: I'm fucked either way, but a whole lot less if I walk out that door.

When I open my eyes, I find Olivia's mouth dangerously close to my own. Darting my tongue out, I wet my lips, then encourage her to move back. She rolls over my erection, just like I wanted her to.

As I lift my knees, she falls forward, and I bring my mouth to her exposed neck.

Fuck it.

She works herself over my trouser-covered dick, searching for her release while my tongue dances across her salty skin.

From her smooth neck to her taut throat, down her chest to the swell of her full breasts, and then across to her—

"Yes!" Her head falls back, and she lets out a moan that doesn't belong to Luce.

Fucks with me a little.

She rights herself, smirking at me as she comes closer.

I frown.

"God… No. Don't stop. Please, Ell, just this one time, don't stop."

I squeeze my eyes tight, trying to forget that voice.

That night.

The way Lucy rolled her hips higher and higher until my fingers slipped inside. The way she was dripping for me, begging me to not stop.

Olivia's mouth brushes mine, and I reach up, forcing my hand between us and flattening my finger against her parted lips as I push her back.

"Sorry. They don't belong to you."

They don't belong to anyone.

I sigh as I stand, letting Oliva fall to her feet. "Wait here," I tell her.

As I emerge from the room, I find the second floor quieter than it was five minutes ago, but Charlie's still in the same spot I left him.

No Amber in sight.

He smiles smugly as I approach him.

"Fuck you, asshole," I snap, not needing his shit.

He holds his hands up. "I've got you, Montgomery. You get home to that phone and hand of yours."

I shake my head as I stroll past him, my shoulders drawn back as I try and shake off his words.

I shove my hands in my pockets as my knees bounce with every step I take down the stairs.

I look up at the bouncer, who gives me a slightly puzzled look.

Yeah, me fucking too.

I make my way through the crowded club and back out into the city.

11

Lucy

I'M HALF-AWAKE, LYING ON MY BED AND DOING ANYTHING I can to stay awake a little longer.

I watched a film, scrolled on my phone for half an hour, and now I'm going over my schedule for the millionth time in two days.

The worst thing I could do is fall asleep too early and then be up hours before I need to be in the morning.

It's going to be my first day at Almendo.

I drop the file on the bed and grin wide, my excitement too much.

God, if I could tell ten-year-old me that this was where she'd be at thirty.

I might not have the man, house, or kids, but I have a killer job. Something I've worked my ass off for and I can be proud of, and something that could potentially allow me to have all the other things on the list one day. If I can work my way up at the company, which was discussed during the interview, then I could probably buy my own home. I could support a family.

You can't buy a man, but there's always BOB and the balls.

I glance down at my phone as it lights up with an incoming call.

Elliot.

"You must be tracking my thoughts, Mr Montgomery?"

"No… should I be?"

I sit up and shrug as I smile, even though he can't see. "No. It would be totally inappropriate."

He tsks, and it reminds me of the balls, the restroom, and… shit. "So we're going straight in with the dirty talk tonight? Good to know."

"I've not said anything dirty!" I laugh.

"You implied inappropriate thoughts and me in the same sentence. I'm hard, princess."

I stick my tongue in my cheek and smile. "Sounds like a you problem. I wasn't thinking about you."

"No?"

"Nope."

"What then?"

How do we keep falling into this so easily?

I swallow and tell the truth. "I was thinking about the balls."

"Oh." He chuckles, and it's deep, orgasmic, and full of something sinful. If hot, dirty sex had vocal cords, it would scream in the tune of Elliot Montgomery, I'm sure of it. "I've been thinking about those balls, actually."

My brows knit, and I gulp around the lump in my throat. "You have?"

"I found them in my tux pocket. Forgot I slipped them in there at the meal. I'd be lying if I said it wasn't a pleasant surprise finding them when I went to the dry cleaners. I'll take good care of them until you get back." His voice grows raspier with every forbidden word he utters, and I wonder if he's intentionally messing with me. "Unless you want me to ship them out to you, do you need them, princess? How inappropriate are we talking?"

"Do not ship them! Can you imagine customs getting hold of that parcel?" I start to panic. "I'd be mortified collecting them from main reception too. Send them, and I'll have *your* balls!"

"And what do you suggest I do with them exactly?"

"I don't know… bin them."

"Think again. They're too much fun for the bin."

Every sensible word inside of my head scatters, turning me to mush. "I—"

"Luce, I'm messing with you." He chuckles down the phone, and I sink back further into the mattress. "Tell me about your day."

I palm my scarlet cheek and close my eyes, letting go of the heated thoughts thrashing around in my mind. "I've been out in the city. I timed my walk to work and checked out the building—"

"How was that?"

"Good, I love the area, and from what I can see, the office is amazing."

"Have you had any luck finding an apartment?"

"Not yet." Truthfully, I'm happy here at the hotel, and it's only been two days. The idea of having to move to a different area makes me anxious. "I need to focus on settling in at work this week, and then I'll start looking for a place to live. One thing at a time."

"Will you be okay when you do find somewhere? We could fly out and help move your things."

"You guys have already done enough. But, thank you. You know I appreciate it."

"I wish we could be there to help you."

"Hmm, If I remember correctly, you hate moving." I smile, thinking back. "In fact, you were utterly useless when we moved Nina and Mase out to Lowerwick."

"I was on Ellis duty."

"You're always on Ellis duty. When there are dishes, or when there's a queue you don't want to wait in. We all see it."

"You're just jealous that he prefers Uncle Elliot."

I laugh because it's true. "Because you buy him everything he wants."

"Would you not if you could?"

"No." I roll my eyes, knowing he doesn't get it. "He'll end up spoilt. He's lucky that Nina's so grounded, although Mase is getting better at saying no to him. He knows how to work you, that's for sure."

"Good, I'm glad he does."

"I know." I smile, pulling out my wash bag and moving to the bathroom. "Can we FaceTime? I need to do my face."

"You're going out?" he questions.

"No, I mean take it off. I'm knackered and have work in the morning. It's only nine here, and I need to try and stay up. If I lie down any longer, I'll be flat out in ten minutes."

He starts to FaceTime me, and I answer, smiling down

at him as I place the phone on the vanity. "Did you sleep last night?" he asks.

"A little. I was up early, but I definitely got a couple of hours." I lean down and look at him, taking in his handsome face. He's in a crisp white shirt, and his hair is styled back in mussed waves. "You're still up?" I ask, making out his lounge behind him.

"Hmm, I was out with Aldridge but came back early. Wasn't feeling it."

I watch him intently, and his lip twitches.

"What?"

"Nothing!" I reply.

He tips his chin. "No, what's that look for?"

I relent. "When does Elliot Montgomery not feel it?"

"Wasn't a lot on." He shrugs. "Charles was out, but he has his head caught up in a case, and Mase no longer has his balls."

"That's bullshit." I point down at him as I pump my cleanser into my hand. "Mase chooses to stay in."

Elliot chuckles. "Fair. I would, too, if I had a Nina at home waiting for me."

"Right." I'd want to be at home if I had what they had.

"What's that you're putting on your face?"

"Face wash." I hold up my hand to show him before smoothing it over my face.

"Can't you just use a wet wipe?"

"Of course, I could, but I'd get spotty." Some girls get away with that life, but I'm not that fortunate. "This gets all the dirt off my face. It's awful living in the cities; probably be worse here than home."

His face is scrunched up, and I smile to myself as he

starts flicking through the channels on the TV. It's how we'd be at home, only he wouldn't know what I was up to in the bathroom, and I'd be teasy about him changing the channel while I was gone.

It's keeping me busy and my mind off of the morning.

"What we watching?" I ask with a smirk, spritzing my cotton pads and swiping them around my eyes and nose.

"What's that now?"

I hold up the bottle and shake it. "Toner?"

"What does that do?"

My heart flips in my chest. He has no idea how adorable he is. "It basically balances my pH levels."

"Right." He frowns as if it's silly.

"What are you watching?"

"I started season two of *Peaky Blinders* last week."

"I thought we were going to watch it together? Meg will kick your ass," I tell him, grabbing up my moisturiser and massaging it in.

"I'm only on episode two. You haven't missed a lot."

"You're the worst. It's like me watching the new *Bridgerton* without you."

"It's not," he assures me. "In fact, I *encourage* that."

"You'd be gutted, don't lie."

"I mean, I'd need to know what happens—"

"See!" I laugh.

I brush my teeth, then pick up my phone and move to the bed. I pull back the covers and slide in. "Oh, God. I'm so tired; this is dangerous."

"You're not going to fall asleep on me, are you, Morgan?"

"I might. My body is ruined from today, but my mind is on overdrive because of tomorrow."

"You can call me in the morning if you want. I'll keep my phone on loud just in case."

"I'll be fine. I've set my alarm for an hour before I need to be there. I don't want too much time to think about it."

He nods his head, not looking convinced.

"What?"

"Nothing."

I smile at how stupid we are. "You obviously think that's as bullshit as your *wasn't a lot on* line."

"I just know you'll be up before your alarm."

"Well, I won't be calling you if that's the case. It's stupidly late home there, Ell. You should go to bed. You have work in the morning."

"I will soon."

My eyes drift over him, from his dirty-blond hair to his tired blue eyes. He looks boyish and lazy, and something about him screams home.

It's hard to think he doesn't see himself as I see him. He thinks he's so out of reach, being a *notorious playboy*—his own words. But what he doesn't get is that I see him away from all the women, parties, and the ruthless business world he revolves in. It's only in moments like these that I truly see it.

Deep down, he's the softest man, with an even softer heart.

"Outta your head," he tells me, his eyes flicking between me and the TV. "You'll do great."

"I'm not thinking about work," I say softly, already melting into the fresh sheets.

"What are you thinking about?"

"You."

His smile is dirty. Pure filth. "Course you are. Tell me more."

"No."

"You sound guilty."

"Guilty of what?"

"I don't know. Do I need to go grab those balls?"

I laugh. "What are you going to do with them from all the way over there?"

"I'm sure we can get inventive."

"Ell," I warn.

"Don't *Ell* me. You're the one with your head in the gutter."

"That's crap! I wasn't even thinking dirty things about you. Just you in general."

"But now you are, aren't you?"

I stare at him, trying not to laugh as my face heats again.

It bothers me that he can be so unaffected and in control when I'm a giant puddle, slopping around on the bed, trying not to say something stupid.

"I'm going to have an early night," I tell him, not wanting to end the conversation but sensing where it's going and needing to keep in safe territory. I know that look in his eye right now, and it confuses me. We said we'd forget about the restroom. We're friends, nothing more.

So why does it feel like we are *everything* when it's just him and me like this?

I used to spend hours into the night with him—Megan too at times, but I always knew the boundaries. I always protected us, and he did too. He knew just as well as I did.

It feels different now, and it's terrifying.

Something's shifted.

I focus back on the screen and find him watching me. He rubs his hand across his mouth and gets up from the sofa as if he can't sit still. "Try and sleep, yeah. I'll be here if you can't."

"Thanks, Ell." I pause for a beat. "You're a good friend." My throat aches as I say it, and I instantly kick myself for it.

Why did I say that?

It came out forced as if the words didn't belong in my mouth.

We crossed the line that night. It's obvious.

Panic shreds me as I lie mute on the bed, and I know he's feeling the confusion too. It's in the frown that draws his brows into a distorted line.

It's in our transfixed gaze.

We're in uncharted territory.

"We're fucked, princess, you know that, right?"

My heart splinters, searing everything in its orbit.

Fuck.

"Night, Ell. I'll call you tomorrow."

I hang up.

Elliot

MONDAY MORNING COMES at me hard.

I barely got a wink of sleep last night, and when I did, it didn't last long. Four years ago, I didn't even know that Lucy

Morgan existed, and now I'm up in the night, worried if she's sleeping okay.

She didn't call me this morning, and when lunch came and went, and I still didn't hear anything, I presumed she was getting on alright. But I still wasn't satisfied.

"Jasmine," I speak into the intercom.

She replies a moment later. "Yes, Ell."

"Can I borrow you a sec?"

"Of course."

Minutes later, she steps into my office. Jasmine has worked for us for two years now. She's good at her job and took on roles Mason and I used to do ourselves. Between her and George, we're pretty damn lucky.

"I need you to find me a florist."

"You don't want to use our usual?" She frowns.

I shake my head. "I need one based in New York, somewhere reputable."

"Of course." She grins at me, doing nothing to hide the fact she knows entirely too much. "What sort of arrangement?"

I check my watch. "What time's the meeting with Phillips?"

"Ahh, it's a long one. He's pencilled in two through to five. I can cancel, still? He cancelled the last two. Dick."

"No. Don't cancel." I drum my fingers on my desk.

I want to pick the flowers myself.

"Send me whatever you find, and I'll take my laptop with me. I can order them from the meeting."

"Of course! Is Luce settling in okay?" Jasmine asks, drawing my gaze up. She's backing out of my office, chewing on her lip as her smile grows huge and ridiculous.

I tip my chin. "She's settling in just fine."

She nods and turns. "Tell her I say hi."

I recline back into my chair and scrub my hands over my face. Ever since the night of the showcase, things have been off. It's only been a week, and maybe it's still too soon to expect it to go back to normal.

Maybe it will all settle down now that she's in New York.

Seems impossible when I can barely travel a foot without thinking about her.

I went to The Nightingale last night and ended up leaving with a hard-on.

That's never fucking happened.

I've always felt a little more protective over Lucy. Ever since we met, the girls became a solid fixture in our friendship group, but Luce was different from day one. She wore her heart on her sleeve and told me to go fuck myself when I tried it on with her—although it's Luce, she was unbelievably polite and let me down with her typical class. I know why she didn't want me then, though, and it's the same reason she'd never go there with me now.

She knows how I am.

If nothing else, it made me respect her.

She says she isn't independent and all that girly bullshit she spouts, but truth is, she's more independent than any woman I've ever met. She has a standard, one which I'm not even sure she understands—Miller is the perfect example of that—and she doesn't settle for less—again, Miller.

And me.

And rightfully fucking so.

I just don't know what this feeling is or what to do with

it. Rational thought gets thrown out the window when we talk.

I know it will be playing on her mind.

Everything plays on her mind.

"Fuck it."

Elliot: If you knew this would happen when you begged me to touch you in that restroom would you have stopped it?

Princess: Knew what would happen?

Elliot: Not in the mood Princess

Princess: ELLIOT

Princess: I'm at work!!

Princess: What do you want me to say?

Elliot: I want the truth

Princess: Can I call?

Elliot: NO. You'll give me those come fuck me eyes and I'll be fucked for it again

Princess: Come fuck me eyes – howling

Elliot: Luce

Princess: I'd never take a thing back with you Elliot. NOT A THING. Okay? You wanna chat later? I'm at work still. Might be late today xxx

I start to type and then stop before typing again and stopping.

Princess: Outta your head Handsome

My phone knocks on the hardwood of my desk, and then my head follows.

"Well, shit."

I give myself ten minutes, then I go to my meeting, my head jumbled and my laptop tucked under my arm with a list of florists in my pocket.

12

Lucy

I STROLL DOWN THE QUIETENING PAVEMENT AT A SNAIL'S pace. I'm shattered. Beyond tired with aching feet and my head mentally drained.

Working at Venty's wasn't easy. We'd be on our feet from open till close, with fittings around London and delivering garments to clients, but never have I had a day like the one I've just endured. My boss, Monica, was off sick today, so I'm putting the shittyness down to that.

It'll get easier—that's what I told myself on the fifth hour. No one else told me that. No one asked me how I was settling in or if I needed to be shown around.

They weren't mean, but they weren't nice either.

Just busy.

Luckily, I knew what I was doing with most of the jobs they gave me, and the schedule helped, but that didn't stop the worry from creeping in. What if I screwed something up? It isn't Jean anymore. It's big executive owners that will rub me out quicker than I can apologise.

I push open the door of my hotel, and my feet come to a stop on the etched marble. My eyes drift closed as I inhale the pungent scent of fresh flowers. They smother me, wrapping me up and making me feel weightless. The heady aroma is so unlike the usual clinical smell of the hotel, and it makes a small smile lift my lips as I stand motionless in the middle of the entrance.

"Miss Morgan?"

I open my eyes and start forward without knowing which direction the voice came from, worried I look like a fool standing in the middle of the doorway sniffing the air. I scan from left to right before my eyes land on the young man standing behind the main desk.

Rolling my lips, I move towards him. "Sorry, did you say my name?"

He gives me a huge smile. "I did."

"Sorry," I repeat. "I was blindsided by that incredible smell." I look around but don't spot any flowers.

"Yes, your flowers," he tells me, pulling a rose out from under the desk. It's not wrapped in anything. Just a single rose with all the thorns and velvety crimson petals.

"Oh. Thank you." I frown, taken aback. "Sorry, do you know who this is from?"

"You're most welcome, and yes, I do." He nods, still smiling.

When he doesn't elaborate, I ask, "Who?"

"I'm afraid that would go against our confidentiality policy, Miss Morgan. I hope you enjoy your evening. If we can help with anything at all, please let us know." He busies himself at the computer, and I stand with an awkward smile on my face. I can feel my cheeks burning, but I don't even care.

I turn and walk to the elevators, feeling like the world is watching me with my rose clutched in my hand.

How strange.

Dipping my head, I sniff the rose as the elevator carries me to my floor, and as the doors slide open, I'm assaulted by the liquefying, heady smell all over again.

It's not this rose. It's beautiful, but it's *not* this rose.

I go to my door and swipe my card, wondering who could have sent it to me.

Maxwell maybe?

Or does the guy at reception have a thing for me? I chuckle at that, but it dies on my lips as I push open my hotel room door.

My jaw drops.

"Oh my god." I cover my mouth with my hand, my eyes wide as I try to fix my gaze on one spot in the room.

"What the hell?"

Bouquets of flowers fill my room.

On the sideboard, the dressing table, coffee table, and even the floor. So many colours of every flower you can think of littered around the small space. The smell of lavender and lilies is overpowering, and it warms me from the inside out, making my shitty day a whole lot lighter.

I step toward the bed, where a large, rounded box is sat in the middle of the duvet with a smaller parcel gift wrapped beside it. I lift the lid of the bigger box and gasp.

It's filled with roses—red roses, just like the one I was given at reception.

I slip the card from the inside of the lid and tear it open.

Not a thing, Princess.
Happy first day of living your dream.
I'm so proud of you.
Elliot xx

My eyes burn, and I cast my gaze to the ceiling to try and cut it out.

I read it again.

Not a thing.

He wouldn't have stopped it either. That's what he's telling me.

What does that mean?

I place the card on the bed and sit down to open the smaller box.

Removing the lid, I try to control my laugh as it mixes with my surprise. Wrapped up in silk are two shiny silver balls, a remote control nestled between them.

"That motherfucker sent me balls." I laugh, feeling crazy as I look around at the flowers which clutter the room, the box clutched in my hand.

I'm not sure I can even make it to the bathroom if I tried.

What am I going to do with them all?

I want to call him, but it's gone seven here, and I don't want to wake him if he is already in bed.

Princess: Are you up?

Princess: Thank you for the flowers

Princess: I love them

I don't get a response.

With time to kill before I can get to bed, I start to arrange the flowers so that I can move around my room. When that doesn't work, and I conclude that I have far too many—no matter how beautiful they are—I should spread some love.

I grasp up two bouquets—because it's as much as I can manage—and head out of my room and into the city.

People stare at me as I struggle through the street with the ostentatious arrangements, and I smile the whole time, knowing that they'd be mortified if they saw my hotel room.

This isn't the half of it.

I still have no idea what I'll do with all the flowers, but the fact Elliot sent them makes my stomach do crazy things.

I find a busy corner and don't overthink it. Placing the flowers at my feet, I look around and try to figure out who needs a little pick-me-up.

I sure as hell needed one after my first day.

For a good five minutes, no one makes eye contact with me. In fact, they go out of their way to avoid me.

I contemplate what the hell I'm doing.

Maybe I'm high on plant fumes.

I just want to make someone smile today—just like Elliot has done for me.

"Excuse me," someone says, huffing as they scuff their leg against one of the boxes. The woman trips but carries on.

I mutter a sorry and cringe as I pull the box back an inch, feeling like I'm in the way.

I lift my eyes to see the woman stalk off down the street.

Everyone is in such a rush.

I pull a rose from the box and run after her. "Excuse me."

She doesn't turn. No one does. But I can't stop now; that would be even more mortifying than this shit show I'm currently living at my own hands.

"Excuse me," I say again, close enough to touch her arm.

She spins and removes her earphone, frowning down at me in annoyance.

"I'm so sorry I tripped you with my box. Here." I hold out the rose to her, feeling unbelievably silly and small as she casts her eyes over it.

"I don't want that."

"Oh."

"Why would you presume I did?" she asks, her feet settling on the pavement as she gives me her full attention. "You're British?"

I smile. "I am. And I had some flowers delivered for my first day at my new job and thought I'd give some away."

She looks over my shoulder and then down at me, scrutinising me with her hardened gaze. "You'll never make it in this city."

And then she turns and walks away.

My heart jolts at her hurtful words, and although I know better than to listen to someone who doesn't know me, I can't help but feel a pang of insecurity over hers.

Today was hard, but nothing I didn't expect. I want to do well. I know I can do well. But am I naive to think I can do it in a city I don't know?

New York City.

I head back to the boxes of flowers. People look down at

them as they skirt around them, probably wondering why they are left in such an awkward spot.

I start to pick them up.

This was a stupid idea.

I should've stayed in my room and not bothered with bringing them out here.

The flowers seem heavier as I walk back through downtown Manhattan, and I consider ditching them when my feet remind me of the day they've had. Of course, I don't, and when I spot a sign for a chapel on the next street, I put them through a little more work.

"Never heard of a dead person saying no to flowers." I smile as I turn on the balls of my feet and head in the opposite direction of my hotel.

St Paul's Chapel sits on a small imprint just a short walk from my hotel. I spotted the building when I was out with Maxwell on Sunday, but we were on our way back from a day-long tour, and neither one of us was feeling up to stopping.

It seems almost deserted at this time of evening, and I slip through the open gates and make my way around the path of the small graveyard.

I quickly realise I won't be laying my flowers. These graves are centuries old and are fenced to stop what I imagine is the likes of me from getting too close to them. It makes me wonder who is buried beneath my feet.

I walk towards the building that stands proud beyond the tombstones—a chapel. It's not a huge building, but the impressive tower gives it enough of a neck to contend with the buildings it's surrounded by.

It's the brickwork and pretty grounds that are so unlike the other buildings that draw your eye.

When I spotted the chapel with Maxwell, I was caught up in the excitement of the Zara I spotted opposite. I didn't take enough notice, but I knew I wanted to come back.

I round the walkways, looking at the different stones and the wording on each. Some are weathered and broken, the words barely readable.

I come to a stop in front of a giant bell. It sits on a stand at the top of the pathways, and I lean in to read the inscription.

"The bell of hope."

I spin to find a man sitting on a bench.

"I'm sorry," I mutter awkwardly.

It's obvious he's been watching me by the way his wrinkled face smiles at me. It's an easy smile.

"What for?"

"I don't know. I… I don't know." I smile, feeling stupid.

"The bell of hope was a gift. Sent from London," he informs me.

"Really?" I smile and turn to look at the bell again.

"Forged in adversity—11.September.2001."

Recognition clicks, and I find myself looking up and across the graveyard to where the World Trade Center once stood beyond.

I place the flowers at my feet and trace the words on the bell.

"THE ENDURING LINKS BETWEEN THE CITY OF LONDON AND NEW YORK CITY."

"It's so…."

"Grand."

I peer over my shoulder at the elderly gentleman, then step back and towards the bench he's sitting on. "I'm from London."

"I thought as much."

I smile and look down at my feet. "Do you mind?" I ask, pointing to the bench.

"Of course."

"It's surprisingly peaceful in here. Away from the hustle and bustle on the streets."

He hums in reply, and I wonder if he would prefer peace. Maybe he was only being polite, and I should leave him be.

"What's with the flowers?" he asks.

"Well," I start, laughing under my breath as I look down at the arrangements. "It was my first day at my new job today, and I had a delivery of a million flowers sent to my hotel room whilst I was out."

"A million." He eyes me sceptically, but his top lip curls with the wisps of his grey moustache.

"Fine. A lot of flowers."

"An admirer?" He pops an inquisitive brow.

"A friend."

He leans into me like elderly people do. As if they're about to tell you a secret. "You know, you lost all credibility when you came at me with a million flowers."

I laugh, not expecting his reply, and he sits back, rearranging his stick on the chair beside him. I can tell my reaction to his smartness has tickled him.

"My name is Lucy," I tell him.

"Ralph." He nods back.

"Do you come out here often? The building is beautiful."

"Every day."

"Every day?" I repeat, surprised. "To the chapel?"

"I do. My late wife is here."

"Oh, I'm so sorry." I frown, looking around at the stones. I'm certain they're centuries old.

"Not in here," Ralph answers my wandering thoughts, lifting his stick and pointing through the trees. "I wasn't one of the lucky ones. They never found my Elsie."

I lock my jaw and frown harder, blinking away the burning in the backs of my eyes. "That's awful. I'm so sorry."

"I don't know. I sometimes wonder if it was her way of saying *fuck you, Ralph.*"

My eyes forgo all politeness. They shoot wide in shock. "Uh… you…"

"We were sweethearts and very much in love. Doesn't mean we didn't have our moments. In fact, they were my *favourite* moments. Elsie was my wild girl. She never wanted to settle here in New York. She dreamed of everything beyond." He looks back at me, a warm look in his stare. "Made sure I knew of it too."

"You didn't want to leave New York?"

He shook his head. "I grew up here. Ended up working in film. All my plans were for later in life."

My heart hurts for the stranger by my side. How life can be so cruel. "What did you dream of?"

"I don't know. You could say it always changed. I guess finding stability was important to me for a long time. Children. Happiness. Just a life fulfilled." He dips his head, a sadness washing over him that I feel semiresponsible for. "I got one out of the four, and I choose to believe that Elsie is living out hers in another life."

My throat aches, and I wonder which of the four he found.

I hope for children, but I don't ask, and the sheer class the man carries tells me he possesses the stability of a wealthy man.

How devastating.

"Was New York always a dream for you?" he asks.

"Yes," I reply simply. "I dreamt of working here since I was a little girl. I never believed it was possible, and it seemed to grow smaller as I got older."

"Smaller?"

I nod. "For a long time, I was afraid to take that step—make the move. I didn't want to up and change my life. I was happy at home, and I had all my friends and family around me."

"I had many of the same conversations with Elsie. You did well, then. You made it."

"I guess I did." I smile. "It's only my first week, and my job is proving to be nothing like I expected. I'll find my feet eventually."

"New jobs are like new homes. You'll soon become part of the furniture."

"I hope so." I chuckle. "And I still have to find an apartment here in the city."

"You don't have anywhere to live?"

"No, I do. I'm staying at The Four Seasons until something comes up. I came with only a couple days' notice, and my friends are a little overprotective and want to make sure I'm staying somewhere safe."

"It's a big city to be alone in."

"It is."

"You'll do fine here."

The little bit of faith I lost when that horrible woman tore me down in the street returns. "Ralph." Reaching down, I pick up one of the bouquets of flowers. "Would you like these?"

13

Lucy

It's Tuesday, and my day is currently going far better than yesterday. When I arrived at work this morning, I got my head down and tried not to overthink things. The two girls in my office, Jenna and Bella, are much less manic today, and when lunchtime came around, they asked if I wanted anything from the deli down the street.

I took it as a good sign.

The issue, if you can call it an issue, is the two women and one guy situated in the office opposite ours.

Chelsea, Tanner, and Lessy.

They don't like me. I can feel it. I'm not sure what I've done to upset them so much, but they aren't even pretending to be polite. Which leaves me reluctant to ask them for anything.

I knock on the glass door and step into their office. "Hi. I just need—"

"We can't help today. It's too busy."

I frown and clench my teeth, feeling uncomfortable. "You don't even know what I need."

Chelsea rolls her eyes and huffs. "You need your design board signed off, right?" She looks me up and down, and I sharpen my gaze on her. Bitch. "We aren't here to babysit the *designers*. Ask Monica."

"Right." I turn and walk out of their office, my blood boiling.

I want to be polite, and I won't snap back. No matter how badly I want to rip her a new one, I have to keep my head and make a good impression in and around the office.

Chelsea can go fuck herself quietly in the insignificant corner I've reserved for her in my mind.

AT FOUR O'CLOCK, I get a spare few minutes alone and check my phone.

I have a load of messages from Mum, the girls, and some Instagram notifications, which I quickly scroll through.

My stomach clenches tight when I see Elliot's name.

Those damn inappropriate thoughts.

I laugh and click on the image he's shared with me. It's from last night as I walked back to the hotel. The sun is disappearing at my back, and I have a rose pulled to my nose as I look into the camera. I captioned it *Outta my head,* followed by a red heart.

You're fucking beautiful, Luce. I hope you had a good first day. Sorry I missed your text I was asleep before my head hit the pillow. Call me next time.

I look over my shoulder as I exit out of the app, then

pull up his messages from this morning. I read them when I first woke up but was in too much of a rush to reply.

Elliot: You're welcome... what about the balls?

I grin and start to type.

Princess: Good evening!! Will you be up later? I should be home by five my time

Elliot: I'll be up

Excitement flits through me, and I suddenly look forward to the last hour at work. I had messages from the girls and Mum, which I should get back to, and I make a mental note to call them all on the way home.

"Lucy." I spin and pocket my phone. Jenna follows my hand and smiles. "You don't have to hide that from me, just Monica."

"Right." I nod.

"We're going out on Friday for some drinks. We do it most weeks. Monica wants you to come."

"Oh." I should go out with them. It's important to me to make friends here. "Sure. I'd love to."

"Just let her know. Someone will let you know where we're meeting." She disappears again, and I let the excitement in my gut free as I bounce on the spot.

This is what I wanted to happen when I came here. Yesterday made me doubt my decision more than I cared to admit, but bar Chelsea and her bitch squad, I can handle this.

I can absolutely do this.

The rest of the day flies by, and by four forty, I'm slipping out of the doors of Almendo with a spring in my step. I call Mum and send a message to the group chat to tell the girls I'm all good and will catch up properly soon.

As soon as I get to my room, I slip off my heels and FaceTime Elliot.

"Hey, pretty girl."

"Hi." I smile.

"Good day?" he asks, sitting up in the bed. He's bare chested, and his tight abs peek out from the top of the duvet. His hair is pushed back and off his face, and his eyes seem tired.

"I had a much better day." I frown, taking him in. "Did I wake you?"

"No, I was watching a film."

"I feel bad keeping you up. You're going to get exhausted chatting to me every night."

"Who said I was going to chat to you every night?"

Shit. I spin the camera around and show him the flowers, diverting the conversation before he gets a look at my panicked face. "Look, you're everywhere."

He chuckles. "Fuck. I didn't realise there would be so many. I wasn't sure what you'd like, and once I started, I couldn't stop."

"It was so thoughtful. I love them."

I walk into my bathroom and start to wash my face.

"Tell me about your day," he tells me.

"Well," I pump my cleanser. "One of the girls in my office invited me out to drinks on Friday."

"Yeah?" he says, genuinely happy.

"Uh-huh. I was convinced they didn't like me yesterday. I think people are just super busy here. Like even in the street, everyone moves at this pace. You can spot me a mile away."

"I can imagine," he says, rubbing at his jaw as if his smile hurts him being there.

I don't tell him about Chelsea, Tanner, or Lessy. Those fuckers aren't getting any more headspace.

"I still haven't properly met Monica yet. She's literally never around."

"Your manager?"

"Yep." I spritz my toner and swipe it around my face. "She's the one I'm most nervous about meeting."

"Why?"

"She's like… one of the savviest fashion designers in the world," I state as if it's obvious. I know I've mentioned her before.

"What's that you're using now? You didn't use that last time."

I hold up the pot. "It's exfoliator."

He seems genuinely interested, and it makes me smile. "What made you send me gifts anyway? You once told me you weren't a flowers kind of man."

"I've never said that."

He has.

"It was your first day, and we couldn't celebrate like we would if you were at home." He watches me in horror as I put on my sheet mask.

"The fuck is that now?"

I laugh and walk out to the bedroom, dropping back on the little sofa. "It's a mask." I pick up a white rose and pick at the petals one by one. "I love the flowers; I wish you could smell them. They're intoxicating."

"Women are weird."

"Well, that's rude. And pretty condescending for a man who seems to spend so much time with the female species."

"I didn't say I didn't like weird."

"Oh, you do, do you? A kink of yours?" I laugh, puffing away the mask as it falls across my lips and into my mouth. So sexy. "You must love me then."

"You are top-shelf weird."

"And you're an asshole."

"Top-shelf asshole, though."

"True." I smile, and he grins back.

We both go quiet for a minute, not needing to fill the silence that settles over us.

Elliot does anyway. "Can you go take that thing off your face? I can't take you seriously."

"Fine." I tut as I stand and walk to the bathroom again. I peel the mask off five minutes too soon and pump out some moisturiser. I drop back down on the sofa and grab my laptop. I want to ask him about the messages he sent yesterday, but I feel like it's random to bring it up now. It's all I've been able to think about in my small breaks at work.

We've slipped into this odd dynamic of skirting around the topic. I know he's thinking about it, though. He wouldn't have messaged me yesterday if he wasn't.

"Talk to me," he prompts.

I dip my head and purse my lips. "What makes you think I have something to say?"

"I just know. You go into your own little world when you get in your head." He tightens his gaze on me, and I know he knows what I'm thinking. "You can tell me anything, you know that."

Shit.

I go with the truth because it's the only way to move forward. I need to know what it all means. "I was thinking about your note."

He tips his chin, tightening his eyes on me. "What about it?"

"You said *not a thing*—"

"So did you."

I nod and swallow, feeling my body heat. "What does it mean?"

His hand rubs across his mouth and toys with his bottom lip. "I don't know, Luce." He huffs. "Do you?"

I shake my head no. "Ever since that night…." I wish I didn't remove all my makeup before bringing this up with him. My face feels like it's on fire. "I feel like something's changed. You say such… I don't know, your words… the things you say." I roll my eyes at my lack of vocabulary. "You're so bad sometimes," I rush out.

"Bad." He chuckles before he sobers. He wets his bottom lip, and my gaze transfixes on the motion. Everything gets a little warmer. "Luce, you've not even had a little bit of my bad yet."

"That's exactly what I'm talking about. *Yet.* You have to add a yet. Like you're going to give me more of it."

"Do you want more of it?"

Holy mother of balls. "I don't know. Do I?"

"I'm not sure how much I can give from three thousand miles away."

"True." But if there wasn't the distance. I sigh and sink into the cushions at my back. "What do you think would have happened if I didn't come to New York and the restroom thing still happened?"

His face transforms into a knowing smirk, and it makes my stomach flip and bottom out. "Luce."

Oh boy. "You think something would have happened?"

"Do I think I'd have been able to keep my hands off you after I touched you in that restroom?" He waits, knowing I don't have the answer. "Fuck. I'd have tried, but it wouldn't have done shit. You know how it is with us."

I do, but that didn't stop him messing around with Harriet straight after. "I don't regret it. I meant what I said, but it does rock me a little. I don't know what we're supposed to do from here." I run a hand through my hair and watch as his jaw works.

It's his only tell that he's bothered. He's always so relaxed and unaffected. "How about we go with it," he suggests.

"Go with it?"

"No pressure. Just us, like always."

So very Elliot. "I don't think I can do normal with you anymore; I think about what happened all the time." I wring my hands in my lap, trying not to bring them up to cover my face.

This is too much.

He is too much.

"You don't think you can do normal? Are you forgetting that you were walking around in a face blanket five minutes ago?"

"Face blanket." I laugh, dropping my head back. "It's a sheet mask, and it's really cold."

"Would you fuck me, princess?"

My face drops along with my jaw. "I—"

"That's a yes."

All the air whooshes out of me. "Why do you do this to me? You have to warn me."

"You want me to warn you when I'm going to be *bad?*" he taunts, using my own words.

"Yes! You come at me, and it messes with me."

"Alright." He rolls his lips and lies back on the pillow, tucking his hand behind his head, getting comfy. "Luce?"

"Yes, Elliot."

"I'm about to fuck you with my words." He grins and watches the screen with a tilt to his chin, looking down his nose at me.

It's too flirty.

Too good.

"How about we play a game? I'm going to ease you into this."

"What's the game?" I ask, apprehensive about where he's going with this.

"Twenty questions. Nothing's off the table. Mine are going to be filthy as fuck, and I want you to be honest with me."

"Okay."

"You first," he prompts.

"Ummm…" He said he was going to go filthy, so I need to level with him. Something he might think of… "What's the dirtiest thing you've ever done to me in your head?"

Elliot's face stills before it drops. He opens his mouth to say something, then closes it again. "Fuck, Luce."

I chuckle and hop over the sofa, then climb onto the bed.

"What makes you think I've done dirty things to you in my head?"

Oh, crap. I've exposed myself.

"Well, I know what my first question will be. Let me think, the dirtiest thing."

My body tingles as anticipation sets goose bumps skittering up my arms. I momentarily regret my question, not being able to hack waiting on his answer.

"Do you remember that night at The Pearl? It was Halloween, and you were wearing that catsuit."

"Uh-huh."

"Well, that night, I almost caved. You were on fire; everyone saw it. Aldridge had to talk me out of throwing you over my shoulder and taking you the fuck home. You were on the dance floor at one point, dancing to 'Sex' by Cheat Codes. Your hips were moving, and I couldn't not watch. You had me."

I pull my bottom lip into my mouth and smile as I fight to dip my head away from the camera.

"I slid up behind you and gave you your drink. You were right there, back to my front and all I wanted to do was put my hands on your body. Let all the other eyes in the club know you were mine. I imagined what you might feel like under my touch. How it would feel to strip that suit from your damp skin and ruin every inch of you."

"You said Charlie stopped you?" I say with fake annoyance and a scarlet flare I can feel coating my cheeks by the second.

"He did." Elliot smirks, back in the now. "And rightfully so. Who knows what I would have done to you that night."

"You sound so sure of yourself, Mr Montgomery. What makes you think I'd have been up for it?"

"You were giving me a look."

"A look?"

"Yes. You wanted my hands on you just as much as I did. I've always seen the way you look at me. I'm surprised we lasted as long as we did before breaking in that restroom."

Before breaking. Is that what we did? We broke? I look to my lap and inhale a shaky breath before lifting my eyes to him. "It's your turn."

He watches me deep in thought, his gaze penetrating past any boundary I could put between us, but it doesn't make me feel uncomfortable. His eyes on me make me feel safe to be the most sacred version of myself.

"How would you feel if I told you that was a lie?"

"It was?" I try to hide the dejection in my voice.

"Hmm," he groans as he settles back in bed further, a tic in his sharp jaw. "I've done way worse, but I don't think you'd look at me the same way if I told you."

I roll my lips. "Was that your question?"

"No."

"Yes, it was." I decide.

"It's my game, and I make the rules," he tells me. "I have a good one anyway, and it's important."

"Okay…" Nerves clutch at my stomach, the unknown in his possible questioning messing with my temporary calm.

"Did Miller make you come?"

My shoulders drop. Of course, that's what he wants to know. "Why is that so important to you?"

"Is that a trick question?"

I pause, gnawing at my bottom lip.

"Surely you would answer if he had. You said you'd be honest."

"No."

"No?"

I bulldoze right over his curiosity and think on my feet. "Who was with you the night I called? You told me you had imagined me while she sucked you off. Who was it?"

He rubs his hand over his mouth, shaking his head. "Harriet," he grits out.

I got what I asked for.

It's not his fault that I don't like the answer.

"She gets how I am, Luce. It's the only reason we do what we do. She knows what I need in a relationship."

"Which is?"

"Sex. I run a multimillion-pound company; I don't have time for anything else."

His bluntness doesn't come from a place of malice, but that doesn't stop it from burning through my thin skin and scorching my chest.

"She wasn't enough for you, though?" I ask, feeling ballsy and wanting something to cling onto.

"Nothing's been enough."

"Meaning?"

"Meaning, the minute I watched you come apart all over my fingers, I've been fucked for any other woman."

"But you've tried?" I frown, rolling my lips.

"You make it sound like I'm out on the prowl." He gives me a hard stare, and a fucked-up part of me loves it. "Right now, I'm on the phone with you, and I have absolutely no desire to go out and mess around. Don't ask me to tell you what that means."

"Okay."

"Okay?"

"Yeah. Okay." I watch him watch me, wanting to reach out and touch him, roll into his arms and sleep into the night. "Your turn."

"Tell me what you were just thinking about."

Easy. "I was thinking how much I wish I was there with you."

"Yeah?"

"I miss having someone to snuggle up to. I feel like I lost Miller and then came straight here to New York. I don't know… It feels weird being on my own so completely."

"You miss big spooning me?"

"I'll never enjoy that." I chuckle. "You're lucky you're warm. It's the only reason you get the big spoon from me."

"You're lying."

"Not many men would admit to enjoying being the little spoon, you know."

"Anyone who knows me knows I don't have good bed etiquette. It's common knowledge. Give me dessert, and I'll eat it without the fucking spoon."

"How have you gone from spooning to eating *dessert*?"

He goes to smile but gets caught out by a yawn that he tries to stifle. "Ell, you need to go to bed."

"What will you do if I hang up?"

I look around the room, racking my brains for something I can use as an excuse. My eyes land on one of the many arrangements of flowers, and I instantly think of Ralph. I check the time on my phone. "I'm going to go for a walk."

"Isn't it getting dark there?"

"Not yet. Well, just."

"Can you text me when you're home?"

I can't help my smile. "Of course."

"We can carry on our questions tomorrow. It's my turn, by the way."

"No, it isn't. You asked me what I was thinking."

"That wasn't a question."

I give him a bored look. "Seriously? You want me to school you right now?"

"Don't get smart with me, princess. Does things to me." He runs his hand through his hair, and I get a little bit lost in all that is Elliot. "It wasn't something I wanted to know; it was something I needed to know. There's a difference."

"So, knowing if Miller brought me to orgasm." I give him a pointed look. "That was a want or need?"

"That was research. For your benefit, I might add."

Everything south flutters, arousal igniting from his words. "Go to sleep. Sex fiend."

"Good night, princess."

"Good night, Elliot."

14

Elliot

"I'm fucking around with Luce."

Mason looks up from his computer as I walk into his office. His dark brow pulls low, and I know he's heard me. "Fucking around how?" he questions.

"I've spoken to her every day since she left. Pretty much every night."

"You're in two different time zones, though."

"Yeah, I'm fucking fucked."

He shakes his head at me as I slump down onto his sofa on the far side of his office. My head hits the soft cushion, and I close my eyes. "Order us in some lunch, will you?"

I hear him tut before he lifts the phone. "Jasmine, could you have something brought up for lunch, please? Something for yourself and George, and if you could have something sent to L&M for Nina also." There's a pause, and I smile. "Thank you."

"When did you become so nice?" I ask once he hangs up.

"Shut the fuck up," he mutters. "The hell are you doing to Lucy? Nina will come for you if you hurt her."

"No, she wouldn't. I'm pretty sure your wife likes me more than you. She gives me the eye all the time."

When a stapler hurtles towards my head, I duck and hold my hands up. "Calm down."

"Why are you here?"

"I want your opinion."

His brows drop lower. "On the Lucy thing?"

I tip my head in response. "She's too fucking good for me, yet I know I could have her. I've already done too much."

"What like?"

I push back into the seat and spread my arms wide across the back of it, pushing my feet into the ground. "Any other woman, I'd tell you, but not Luce."

His bottom lip protrudes as he nods, seeming happy with that answer. "So what do you want me to tell you? That you're good enough? That I think you should bone my son's auntie? My wife's best friend."

"That's exactly what I want you to tell me."

He stands and walks to the opposite sofa, resting on the back of it. "She's in New York."

I shrug. "I could be there by dinner, balls deep by—"

He regards me with a hard stare, and it unnerves me more than it should, being that he's my best friend of thirty-plus years.

Mase knows who I am better than anyone does. My

emotional onslaught over his opinion tells me more about my feelings than I care to admit.

"No. I don't think you should." My stomach sinks to my ass. "Not because you're not good enough for her. That's just bullshit, and you need to get over the mindset that you're this notorious cunt. Have some balls and be a man about not wanting to fuck around anymore. But don't go jetting off to New York and mess with the girl's feelings before you're sure it's what you want. Have you thought long term? What happens if shit gets serious?"

"I never think long term," I reply honestly.

"She's just got there and started a new job. Her dream job. The least you could do is give her a chance to find her way before you sweep her off her feet with your cock."

"Always did have a way with words."

"Learnt from the best," he shoots back.

I scrub my hands over my face and groan. "Fuck it, you're right."

It's just not what I wanted to hear.

"Has she mentioned a Maxwell to you?" he asks after a beat and with an interest that has me sitting a little straighter.

Maxwell. "The guy she met on the plane?"

Mason nods. "He showed her around her first day. I was listening when Nina was on the phone with her."

"She mentioned him the once, said he was a friend." And now I'm wondering if I asked enough questions.

A look passes between us—an unspoken conversation and acknowledgement.

"I want to know who he is," Mason voices, and never in my life have I been happier to have such a controlling prick as a best friend. He's doing what I shouldn't. "I've already got Vin on it. He asked Scott to get back to me."

"You'll let me know," I tell him.

He dips his head in answer, and then the door opens.

"Hello, gents! Are we all in here for lunch today?" George asks in his usual singsong tone.

"No. I have work to do, so I can leave early this evening."

I look at Mason and snigger. "Come on, George. You can eat in my office. Leave this grumpy prick to eat his lunch alone." I give Mason a smirk. He knows I'm fucking with him. He has to drive over an hour home every day to get to the estate. I understand his need to get back to his family.

"Elliot," Mason calls.

I turn as we reach the door

"Just give it a bit of time."

If anyone knows anything about time and healing, it's him. I nod and head back to my office.

Maybe things need to slow down a little.

The rain lashes down on my windshield as I pull in through the gates at my home. I wait out the heavy shower from the warm confinements of my car, my eyes falling over the double-fronted house I've spent the past sixteen years of my life in.

When Mason and I left home for university, we bought this place together. It was more for him than me at the time. A place he could escape to. He would have lived anywhere at the time, so long as it was away from the estate. I never thought I'd end up holding on to the house for as long as I have, and truth be told, I've grown quite fond of it.

I ended up buying Mason out when he purchased his penthouse apartment.

I wonder if he always knew he'd end up back at Lowerwick. I sure as shit never thought I'd see the day. But when he bought the penthouse, did he know he would end up going home?

Nina changed him.

Fuck, Nina changed all of us.

I pull my phone from the centre console and consider turning it on because *that's* where I'm fucking at… ten thirty on a Wednesday night, and I'm only now getting in from a two and a half-hour gym session, all so I don't come home and call *her*.

When did I become so dependent on hearing from her every day?

When did I become such a simp?

It's been what? A week since she left.

I used to see Luce a couple times a week at most. We'd all go out for dinner or go for drinks, and then we'd pick a place and finish off the night. There were occasions where I'd call after work to see if Meg was in, the idea Luce would be on her own messing with me too hard to ignore.

Maybe Miller was always the barrier between us. Although, I'm not sure I really believe that. There were plenty of times we could have pushed the boundaries. It just never happened.

Fuck, she's in my head.

I pull open my door with a grunt and climb out, jogging up my steps and slipping my key into the lock. Inside, I shake off the rain that has my hair sticking to my forehead and pull my T-shirt from over my head, leaving it soaking wet on the tiles.

A calm comes over me as I settle on the spot, my eyes absorbing the main entrance of the house.

Silence.

I've always liked it—maybe never really noticed it. But today, when Mason told me I should take a step back, give Luce a chance to find her feet, I didn't want to come home.

I wanted the noise. The thoughts in my mind that have been running without a care this past week. Not these fucked-up, heavy dwellings taking root.

Nobody teaches you how to deal with those.

My feet carry me to the kitchen, but I don't turn on the lights, moving around the island with ease to my fridge. I grab a bottle of water, unscrewing the cap and downing half the contents.

I pull my phone from my gym shorts and finally turn it on. It chimes like a fucking bell tower as message after message comes through at once.

Princess: Bruhhhhh! Freezing my peachy little ass off over here today

Princess: I just got asked if I know the queen

Princess: I was awkward and weird and said "yes but I've never met her." They looked at me as if I was stupid af

Princess: I'll be home by 5

I have messages from the guys and one from Nina, asking me if I can pick Ellis up from nursery on Friday.

Ever since my conversation with Mason this morning, I've been thinking about everything that's happened since the night in the restaurant. The way Lucy and I speak every day. Me sending her flowers. The balls. The texts. The filthy fucking words I've spoken to her. I know she's been walking in the evenings, but her exploring the city seems like an afterthought while I sleep. She isn't even making friends at her new job like we expected her to.

I can't be the reason she doesn't find her feet in the city.

I won't have it.

Once I've finished my water, I take a shower and shoot her a quick text before I go to bed.

I feel angry. Pissed at myself and the world; because I want her pointless as shit texts. They're all I found myself looking forward to these last few days, and it feels wrong to shut her down.

Elliot: Just got in. Will call tomorrow x

But I need to give her the best shot at finding her dream in New York.

I need *that* a whole lot more than any need I could have for her.

Lucy

My phone chimes midmeeting, and I cringe internally, trying to not make it obvious that it came from my cardigan pocket. Thankfully, Monica seems to miss it, and I slowly sneak my phone out and look at the screen.

Maxwell: Can you meet me here tomorrow? 7:30.

He's attached a location on the text for a bar named Ginny's.

Crap. I forgot about meeting him.

I've been glued to my phone all morning, waiting on any sign of life from Elliot after his text yesterday.

I side-eye Tanner, who is sitting on my right, and smile when he frowns incredulously at me.

So dramatic.

This entire week I've gone out of my way to get them on my side, but they've made it impossible. Which in turn, makes it impossible for me to do my job properly. Every night I walk out the doors and tell myself tomorrow will be better, but it's hard to keep a positive head and vibe when they refuse to work with me. Everything I need has to be delivered via Bella or Jenna, and I know it's wearing thin on both of them. Bella told me Lessy was set to get the designer role I'm now occupying, and I get it. They're pissed for her. But I only want to be a part of their team. This is my dream job too, and I worked my ass off to be here.

Time. I have to give it time.

"Uh, Lucy, are you texting?" Chelsea sniggers.

I snap my eyes to her as she sits like the ice queen on the other side of the desk. We're in a conference room, and the desk puts a good two metres between us.

It could never be enough.

"Lucy?" Monica questions as all eyes turn on me.

Fuck Chelsea and fuck time. If I roll over every time they take a shot, I'll never win.

"Yes, I was texting. I'm sorry, I should have picked it up after the meeting. I'm actually waiting on a delivery from downstairs. It's my fabrics that were left off the order on Tuesday."

Monica's eyes flash to Chelsea, wide and accusing. "They haven't come in yet? It's Thursday."

I watch as Chelsea's face drops then reddens, her anger fizzling on the surface of her flawless cheeks. "It was late yesterday when we realised they didn't go down with Ben. I'm sorry, Monica."

It was late yesterday when I decided to pull my head out of my ass long enough to make the order Lucy needed.

Dick.

Monica drops her tablet to the table with a thump, and I flinch. I swallow the tension that forms in my throat. "Come on, guys. I need you to do better than that."

Placing my phone in my lap, I sit for a moment in silence.

I feel Tanner leaning in close to my shoulder, but I don't dare turn around.

"Well done. Real teamwork from you there."

My eyes close, and I take a deep inhale.

Sorry, Max, I double booked myself and have to go out with Chelsea, Tanner, and Lessy…

Sorry, Monica, I double booked myself, and your employees are a bunch of fucking assholes. I'll be meeting my friend instead…

They didn't even make it hard for me.

It's just after six fifteen when I spot Ralph struggling from his car. I take off down the path wrapped up in my new thick woollen coat. My nose feels numb from the chill that whips between the buildings, and as I reach Ralph, he quickly takes my arm to find his balance.

"You know, my Elsie will be wondering who this pretty blonde is stalking me at the cemetery."

"Oh, stop. I know you like the company."

We make our way up to the bench where I've placed today's bouquet of flowers.

"The house hasn't smelt so florally in years." He grins, lowering himself to the wood seat. "Have you had a good day at the office?"

"It's been… okay. I'm getting used to the dynamic, and I'm learning who will help me and who won't now. I've dealt with far worse than Chelsea and her bitch squad in my time."

"Bitch squad," he muses, watching me with a wicked smile.

I laugh and lean back on the wooden slats. "Will you tell me more about your films, Ralph? I need my mind cleansed with one of your stories after today. Oh, I want to know what Elsie did when you proposed at the premiere. Graham cut us short last night," I say, referring to his driver.

He chuckles at my enthusiasm and gets right into it, rubbing his hands together to keep them warm. "Well, she loved it, of course. It was very her. She always loved the glitz and glam of the film world but still remained grounded—I could never get her to give up her work. She was watched by everyone. Eyes trailing her wherever she went, and photographers shouting for her to give them her attention. She was very beautiful. She used to tell me off whenever we'd go, lecturing me to look at the camera so that she could frame a proper picture of us in our *glad rags,* as you Brits might say."

"You wouldn't look at the camera?" I beam at him, not being able to help the emotion on my face.

"Elsie was my rock. I wasn't supposed to become a film director, Lucy. Not really. It was what my father wanted of me, my mother was so proud, and then my friends thought it had the label to get them into the swanky bars—it did, of course. It was something I had to learn to love."

I smile sadly at him, although he doesn't see, too lost in the moment.

"No, when I was at premieres or anything equally terrible, I'd be drawn to her. I used to tell her she was my lighthouse seeing me in."

"So if you hated them so much, why did you propose at one?"

He dips his head and smiles. Or maybe it's a smirk. It's definitely a little cheeky.

"She was watched by *everyone*. What better way to tell them all she belonged to me than to look into the camera lens and tie her to me for life?"

"You didn't look at her when you proposed?!" I chuckle.

"Not until she grabbed my cheeks and pulled me to her." He stares at the wood between us with a huge grin on his face. My entire chest warms as he relives the moment.

"You did good," I tell him, leaning in and squeezing his gloved hand.

"I have that picture. The only one where I'm looking at the camera, and she's looking at me."

"Wow." Goose bumps cover my arms beneath my coat, and I roll my lips as I swallow back the lump in my throat. "Will you bring it? Next time you come here? I'd love to see it."

He sits back a little, looking at me with deep fascination. "Yes. Yes, of course, I will."

We people watch for a good few minutes, and Ralph asks me about today's arrangement of flowers. He's had four bouquets so far this week and seems to love the small gifts I bring along with me each day.

"Do you have a lighthouse, Lucy?" he asks after a while.

"A lighthouse?" I frown, although I know exactly what he means. I just need a second to think about the question.

"An Elsie," Ralph confirms.

I dip my head thinking about the support I have at home. "I wouldn't call it a lighthouse. More like a village."

"Ah, I see. And the young man sending you *a million* flowers? Elliot, isn't it?"

"You don't give up, do you? I'll have you know I haven't spoken to him since Tuesday. I have nothing more to report."

"Two days?" He smiles as if it's no time at all. It feels like a lifetime. "I have a soft spot for this Elliot boy. He checks in and makes sure you're home safe. I like that."

"He's a good guy." I nod. "Although, I think he's ghosting me right now."

"Ghosting?" he retorts. "If anyone should be ghosting, I'd like it to be my wife."

I chuckle, and it warms me to the bones. "No, I mean he's avoiding me," I explain, still laughing.

"Right… right, okay. Why do you think this?"

"I normally would have heard from him by today, that's all." The fact it's quarter past eleven at home, and he hasn't sent so much as a text. Something feels off. I can sense it in my gut.

"No, I think you're being a little dramatic. It's been two days."

"You're supposed to be team me, Ralph!"

"Listen. Us men, we're stupid. We need things spelt out to us—can't tell our asses from our elbows, most of the time." He elbows me in the side, and I grin back at him. "Elliot doesn't know what's going on. He's a man. He's probably working. Trust me, Elsie was always pulling my head out of the studio at crazy hours of the night."

"He told me he would call me today. He almost always does, and I felt like maybe something shifted the last time we spoke."

"Asses and elbows, Lucy."

"You have an answer for everything, Ralph. It's a talent."

"Give the boy some time. He'll call."

15

Lucy

It's Friday night, and I should be well on my way to the bar Maxwell told me to meet him at. Instead, I'm sitting in the hotel's restaurant, sipping another cosmo while I try to work up the courage to go out.

I made it through my first week in New York, and I should be celebrating.

I pull up the girls' group chat.

Luce: Girls, talk me off a ledge. I'm being a dick about going out tonight

Megan: Don't be a dick and get off the ledge

Luce: Gee thanks mate

Megan: Who are you going out with?

Luce: His name's Maxwell. He showed me around on my first day here

Scar: I get the nerves Luce. Have you had a drink?

I snap a picture of my half-full glass, and a full one lined up waiting in the background.

Scar: Not working?

Luce: I've not let them touch the sides

Nina: I was wondering what the fuck you were up to for a minute Scar

Luce: ??

Nina: We're down at Rosestone. She was smiling at her phone being all goofy and happy

They're all together tonight?

Luce: Send Frey and Glen my love

Scar: I can't text and be happy now?

Nina: Don't be so dramatic. You know why I was asking...

Megan: OKAY! Spill it bitches and don't leave out a juicy drop

Scar: No

Nina: Scar's had flowers delivered to work every day for the last week

Nina: No name

Nina: We've been doing some creeping on socials and have narrowed it down to three possible suspects from the hospital

Luce: WHO???

Scar: Ridiculous. This was supposed to be us helping Luce

Luce: It's working

Nina: Don't lie to us. You not feeling it tonight?

Luce: Not really. I'm tired but full of energy. These cocktails are definitely giving me a buzz

Megan: Why don't you go out for an hour

Megan: You don't have to stay late

Nina: What she said

Luce: Yeah. I plan to go. I'll have this last cosmo and head to the bar

Scar: Elliot wants to know how you're getting there

Scar: And said to share your location

Scar: And that 'Maxwell doesn't sound like the girls from work'

Nina: Double fuck

I roll my eyes and then drop them to my glass. I waited for his call yesterday, but it never came. Normally I'd call first, but I presumed he was busy. Or maybe he didn't want to speak to me. After the way our twenty questions went the last time we spoke, I guess I expected him to call.

As confusing as it is, the fair thing to do would be to believe he's been busy.

Luce: Yes, Sir.

I frown at the screen, waiting like a dog to a bone.

Scar: I'm serious, Lucy. Do it now. E x

Scar: How are you getting there?

Elliot.

I switch out of the app and share my location.

Luce: I'm getting a taxi. Location shared.

My phone alerts me of a message, and I click out of the group chat again to open it.

Elliot: I've not had anything. Share it again. Who is this Maxwell?

That's because I didn't share it with you.

Nina: Got it. I'm tracking your ass all night, baby!

Scar: I'm pretty sure Elliot is offended

Nina: I heard the man growl. Hahaha

Megan: If I had a dick, I'd probably be hard

I laugh out loud despite being sat alone at the restaurant bar.

I imagine them at the Montgomerys' estate, laughing and drinking all together. My eyes sting with tears as I read over their messages.

I blow out a breath and blink away the wetness, quickly realising the cocktails have started to take effect.

Luce: I miss you guys so much

Nina: We miss you too! Go out and have a good night. You deserve it!

Scar: You got this!

When I arrive at Ginny's, I find Maxwell sitting at the bar. He didn't spot me as I walked through the entrance, so I slowly make my way over to him, using the moment to shamelessly get a good look at him. He's sporting a beer, his hair freshly buzzed, and his sweater is a deep navy. His muscles strain the thick fabric. He looks at ease—just a guy in a bar having a pint.

I make myself known and touch his shoulder but quickly jump back when his body tenses.

"Oh, sorry!" I apologise, awkwardly holding a hand up. "It's me."

I give him a sheepish smile as his shoulders relax again. Maxwell's face settles, his eyes creasing as he gives me a full smile.

"Well, hello," he murmurs, turning fully as he stands to kiss my cheek.

"Did I startle you?" I say, amused.

"You did. I didn't think you were going to show."

I dip my chin, feeling shitty for being so late. "I'm sorry. It's not that I didn't want to come. I'm terrible in social situations," I admit, hoping I can be honest after the state I was in on the plane.

"It's fine. Let's get you a drink. What do you fancy?"

"I'll have a glass of wine, please. White."

Maxwell orders our drinks, then turns and glances around the mostly full bar. "I'm not sure we're going to get a table this late. I should've booked. Do you mind eating at the bar, or would you prefer to go someplace else?"

Feeling comfortable at the bar we are at, I slide up onto the barstool next to him. "Here's just fine."

"Good," he nods as if that was what he was hoping I'd say. He looks at me as he slides back onto his barstool. "You look beautiful tonight," he tells me. "How's your first week been?"

"Mostly good, and thank you." I tilt my head to the side, acknowledging his compliment. "Almendo is busy. Mad busy, actually, but I expected it. Back home, I worked in a shop with only one other person and a Saturday girl. It's nothing like that here."

"Have you been out and about much?"

"A little." I look at my hands and smile. "There's the chapel just across from my hotel. St Pauls. I tend to go there in the evenings. Still wandering around in a safe little bubble at the minute, though."

"People tend to keep to themselves in the city. You'll be

fine after a month or so, and it'll feel like home before you know it."

I don't tell Maxwell about my work colleagues or the woman who spoke down to me just a few days ago. Mostly because I don't want to embarrass myself.

"I hope so."

"It'll happen. Just you wait." He tips his glass to me before taking a sip. "You can't not fall in love with the city."

I give him a pointed look, and his lip twitches slightly. "Hmm, enough about me. Tell me something about you." I lean my arm on the bar and really look at him.

"What do you want to know?"

"Anything. Have you always lived in the city?"

He shakes his head, placing his glass back on the bar top. "I used to live in Boston."

"Why did you move?"

His gaze flicks to me, not giving me a ton of eye contact but enough to show me he doesn't like this topic. "I didn't have a lot waiting for me when I left the Navy. I lost my mum while I was away. Decided to start fresh here instead of going back to Boston when I got out."

"I'm so sorry, Maxwell—"

He shakes his head at me. "It's fine," he assures me, although I can see from the way his jaw works it isn't fine.

"A year, you said you've been out, right?"

"That's right."

"Do you miss it?"

"Boston or the Navy?"

"Both." I shrug, hoping to wade us into safer territory.

"I miss neither. Both were…" He regards me with a

hard stare, but I don't think he's fully with me. His mind is someplace else.

"What about now? Do you like New York?" I ask, trying to give him an out.

"It's where I need to be for work. And it does seem to play house to some of the most beautiful women in the world."

I roll my eyes playfully as I sip my wine. "Do you go out much here?"

"A lot. I like the buzz that never seems to switch off when the night ends."

"It really does have a buzz, and it's different to London. I'm hoping I'll settle better when I find an apartment. The hotel has a constant energy of people in the halls or someone using the lift at silly hours."

"You're not sleeping?"

"I get some sleep."

"You'll learn to function on less. I barely get three hours a night these days."

I stare at him in shock as he has another drink of his beer. "Three hours? Who functions on three hours!"

"It's what you get used to." He smiles at me and licks the froth from his upper lip. "I'm usually up late working or away on a job. Every couple of weeks, I tend to snap. I have to sleep for an entire weekend to catch up." He shrugs as if he knows he has terrible sleeping habits.

"That's crazy. I need my full eight hours—no exceptions—or I can't function. It's like nothing connects in my brain, and I'm a ball of mush."

"I don't like to rely on anything but myself to get me through the day. It's why I don't drink coffee."

"Do you eat?" I say with a stupid smile.

"Don't be smart." He chuckles, downing the last of his drink and lifting it in the direction of the barman to signal another. "Do you want another?"

"No, thank you." I frown as I look from my mostly full glass to his empty one.

He drank that damn fast.

"So…" Maxwell peers at me over his crossed arms, and I can't help the grin that forms on my face with the way he looks at me.

"What?" I ask, my cheeks starting to ache.

"You haven't mentioned a boyfriend on the last two occasions I've seen you…." I shake my head at him and look at my lap. "You're single?"

"I am single." I breathe through the dull ache that punctures my ribs. I decide to be honest. "But, there is this guy."

"Is his name Maxwell?"

I laugh and push his arm. "His name is..." Why don't I want to say it? Elliot's name is on the tip of my tongue, but it feels wrong to tell Maxwell about what we have when I'm not even sure what it is myself. "His name is Miller."

I swallow hard, trying to force the lie back into my throat as my brows meet.

"He's your ex?"

Shit.

"Yeah. It actually ended right before I came out here. I guess we're both pretty confused still."

The truth in my lies makes me feel all the more shitty. I should've just been honest.

Elliot deserves better than that.

"What went wrong?"

"I came here. Although, we were on two different paths long before that. He's the sort of man that's hard to keep hold of."

"You're out of his league?" He frowns, the unconvinced look on his face contradicting his words. "I don't believe that."

"Not out of my league," I confirm, thinking about what he's said. There's no doubt in my mind that Elliot is an elite form of man. He's kind, caring—at least to me and the ones he loves—and looks after himself. He's funny. He's not out of my league. "We're in different leagues. That's the problem."

"He still wants you?"

"I don't know," I answer honestly.

I know that we've been speaking more than usual since I left London, but I've seen how Elliot Montgomery operates. He has a different flavour of the month whenever he feels like it, and although I don't think I'm a flavour, I do know that he's an in-the-moment guy. It's two different mindsets and two different goals.

I want a picture-perfect happy ending, with kids and a white wedding in the country.

Elliot wants a happy ending. Simple.

"He's an idiot," Maxwell tells me, reaching out to take his drink from the barman.

His comment is supposed to compliment me. He's telling me that Elliot's an idiot because of *his* own perception of me. But that doesn't stop me from wanting to set him straight. I've lied on the spot and feel like an ass for it. "Elliot is one of the most incredible men I know. He's not an idiot."

The tips of Maxwell's brows tease together as he looks at me in confusion. "*Elliot?*"

My stomach drops, but at the same time, relief consumes me.

I shake my head and take a large sip of my drink. I don't know why I even lied in the first place. "Elliot is—"

"Alec!" Maxwell cuts me off midsentence, waving at someone over my shoulder. I turn on the barstool and spot a short, blond-haired man headed in our direction, a woman who I can't quite make out trailing behind him. "How are you, my friend? It's been a fucking week."

The guy slaps his hand into Maxwell's, their matching smiles knowing. "I'm good, I'm good."

The guy looks from Maxwell to me and then back to Maxwell again, a silent exchange passing between them. "Come to Russo's tonight. Corkscrew is playing from ten."

"I plan to head over after here. You want a drink?" Maxwell offers.

"I'll get them," Alec insists, inserting himself between Maxwell and another guy at the bar. "What time did you finish up on Tuesday?"

I tune the two men out, easing back on my stool to get a better look at the woman at the guy, Alec's, back. She looks bored and maybe a little distant. Her hair is dark brown and curled to one side. She's slightly taller than Alec and is built with lines and angles I'd die for. Her arms are toned to perfection. The girl clearly works out. She's beautiful. "Hey!" I greet, holding out my hand. "I love your makeup tonight. It's stunning."

She takes me in for a split second, giving me a once-over before a smile dances across her face. "Thank you. You're here with Max?" she questions, flicking her eyes to the two men.

"Yes, I actually just moved here. I met Maxwell on the plane, and he kindly offered to show me around."

She nods, then gives me a smile that doesn't quite meet her eyes. "I'm Polly."

"Lucy."

"Where were you flying from?" she asks, her eyes growing a fraction sharper.

"London. I'm British."

"I can hear that." She smiles at me, and it feels real this time, a little warmer.

"Are you having a drink?" Just as the words leave my lips, Alec turns with a pint of beer and hands it to Polly. She thanks him, then looks back to me, popping a brow as she takes a sip.

"Alec, this is Lucy. She's a friend of Maxwell's. And, Lucy, this is my boyfriend, Alec."

Maxwell stands and throws an arm over my shoulder. "Yes, I met Lucy last week on my flight home."

"It's nice to meet you, Lucy," Alec tells me, nodding his head at me as if he's only now noticing me. "Apologies, I didn't realise you were here with Max before."

I raise my glass in his and Maxwell's direction. "Just a thank-you drink for showing me around."

"Will you come to Corkscrew with us?" Alec asks, looking at Maxwell even though the question was undoubtedly for me.

Maxwell looks to me for confirmation, but I don't have it right away.

Do I want to go?

I was quite happy staying at Ginny's.

"They have decent music." Maxwell shrugs.

I look to Polly, feeling like all eyes are on me, and just as she goes to say something, her head shifting to the side, Maxwell butts in. "If you don't like it, I'll walk you back to the hotel. No pressure."

I roll my lips, feeling like it would be rude not to go when Maxwell spent the whole of last Saturday showing me around. "Okay, I'll come."

"Perfect. Cheers, guys," Alec toasts.

16

Lucy

I'M ON THE DANCE FLOOR AT RUSSO'S WHEN POLLY LATCHES onto my arm and drags me to the entrance. She's matched me drink for drink all night, yet she looks completely sober.

"Lucy, I have—"

"What?" I call out, pointing to my ear.

Stepping closer, she leans in and raises her voice. "I have to leave."

My shoulders drop. "What? Why?"

I don't want Polly to leave. Maxwell and Alec have spent the night chatting in techy slang, and I've been left to drink wine and dance with Polly. She seemed reluctant at first, but with the conversation stuck on work for the men, having a female to chat with probably came as a welcomed distraction for her.

"I'll leave with you," I tell her, turning on my heel to go and get my things. It's been a long day, and I've drunk more than I should have. I know I'm at my limit.

Polly grasps my wrist to stop me. "No, you can't. I'm sorry, Lucy, there's someplace I need to be." She stares at me intently. "Grab a taxi if you're ready to leave. Maxwell will see you home safe." She nods, pulling her bottom lip between her teeth as she checks her phone screen. She seems distracted, and I wonder what's so important to pull her away.

"I'm fine." I wave her off, swaying on my feet and feeling the full effects of the alcohol. "I hope everything's okay."

The last thing I need is anyone worrying about me.

I should go home.

Polly says goodbye, and leaves, telling me she hopes we can all meet again soon. It feels real and very normal, I guess. The guys may have been stuck in work mode all night, but isn't that just men? I think of Ralph and his asses and elbows comment.

Men are just fucking idiots sometimes.

Or something like that.

I turn and walk back into the club. My eyes scan the bar area where Maxwell and Alec had been sitting before but are now nowhere to be seen. Suddenly everything seems foreign to me: the bar, the music, the people who I've been dancing around all night.

My heart starts to beat faster in my chest.

I spot my jacket on the back of the bar chair and walk towards it.

Where's Maxwell gone?

Did he leave?

Pulling out my phone, I text him.

Lucy: Where are you?

The message delivers, but when it doesn't mark as read after a few minutes and with my rising anxiety of being in the club alone with way over my sensible limit of alcohol coursing through me, I decide to leave.

Out on the street, I pull up Maps and find that my hotel is only a fifteen-minute walk. I close my eyes and pull in a deep inhale. I'm not that far from the hotel. I'm okay.

Needing the fresh air to sober me up a little, I turn right on the sidewalk and follow the pin.

Vendors filled with hot dogs and late-night windows selling pizza by the slice line my journey, making me feel safe as I stroll home. The night air feels thick and full, and instead of feeling the effects of the alcohol wear off, it seems to only heighten everything.

I pass a diner selling breakfast and come to a stop, a wide smile gracing my face when the smell of pancakes assaults me. Why don't we have this at home?

My stomach growls, and then I think of something.

I step into the diner and walk to the counter. "Can I get two pancakes, please?" I dig into my purse and pull out some cash.

They cook them fresh and add the toppings I ask for.

With a huge smile on my face, I leave the shop, dipping into my bag to find my phone again.

Princess: Why when I see pancakes do I think of you?

Princess: I just got these

Princess: I got two

Princess: One for me and one for you

I snap a picture of the pancakes and send it to him. The picture is blurry, and I get syrup all over my screen.

"Ball bags."

Princess: You're probably sleeping. I had a good night.

Princess: I miss you, Ell.

My phone starts to ring moments later, and Elliot's voice echoes down the line as I connect the call.

"Hello, Luce? Can you hear me?"

"Elliot! I can hear you, can you hear me? You're awake still? Why are you up?"

"I just got in. We ended up having a few drinks tonight."

"Hmmm. I'm a little tipsy myself."

"Are you at home?" he asks, the urgency in his tone making me smile.

"No, I'm walking back now."

"Who with?"

"Luce," I say with a smirk on my face. "She's a fucking queen, you know."

"Lucy," he snaps. "Pull a taxi. Why are you walking? It's not London."

"London is just as dangerous as any city."

"You know London. There's a difference."

"Don't be a dad."

"If I were your dad, I'd have you over my knee, spanking your ass."

"Ooh, daddy kink, huh? You'd love that, wouldn't you?" I smirk, taking another bite of my pancake. "These are delicious. I wish you could taste them."

"How far are you from home, baby?"

I pause with the fork in my mouth, my body growing hot. *Baby*. "Like five minutes maybe." I pull the phone from my ear and check the map, realising I've missed the street I should've taken. "Crap."

"What?"

"Nothing, just making a detour."

"Are there no taxis?"

"Tons. If there was just one, I'd get in, but with so many, whipping around like madmen." I watch as the street buzzes. "I'm happier walking. It's super busy out. I feel safe."

"That doesn't even make sense, Luce."

"I'm fine, I promise. And I'm on the phone with you. You can walk me home."

Baby.

"What happened to the guy you were out with? Maxwell?"

"He straight up disappeared. I was out with him and his friends—"

"His friends?"

"Yeah. Polly and Alec—Polly's lovely. And then when Polly left, and I went back to find the guys, they were gone. I didn't want to stick around not knowing the bar."

I hear Elliot huff in aggravation. "Luce."

"What?"

"I can't stand not being able to walk you home."

"I can see my hotel. I'll call you once I'm in my room."

"No, don't hang up. Stay on the phone until you're inside."

"Such a worrywart. Which is odd, considering you've not called in three whole days… You found a new bitch to put you to sleep or something?" I chuckle at myself as I walk towards the entrance of the hotel.

"Morgan, I will get on a plane and come spank that sweet ass."

"What do I have to do? Tell me."

His deep raspy chuckle has me smiling, and for the first time all night, I feel a little more like me.

"I danced to some rocking music tonight, you know."

"Yeah?" he hums, the sound of glass clinking on his line letting me know he's getting a drink. "Tell me about it."

I smile, knowing he really does want to know. "Polly's a superhero. She drank just as much as me and was totally fine."

"What were you drinking?"

"Wine."

Elliot whistles. "Lethal for you."

"Right, and Polly was drinking beer. What a woman." I admire to myself.

"Nina was steaming tonight," Elliot tells me. "I think she needed a night off. Time to let her hair down with the girls."

"Oh, don't. I'll get all emotional."

"Why?"

"I miss her. I miss you all."

"Come home then."

I push into the hotel and allow the warmth of the reception to settle around me, relaxing my tensed muscles. "Don't tempt me, Mr Montgomery."

Stepping into the elevator, I smile as he does exactly that.

"Tempt you… hmm, that should be easy. Are you in your room yet?"

"Why do you sound so filthy?" I look around the empty lift as if the cameras might catch me doing something I shouldn't be. "You're not even asking anything hot, and I'm getting all worked up."

"Worked up?" he purrs, and I know he's in a whole ass mood. "Baby, if you're wet, just say you're wet."

I sway on the spot and lean over to bin the pancakes in the hallway.

I knew it.

Slotting my card in the lock, I push into my room. "Alright, I'm home… and I'm wet," I add, biting my lip.

"Good girl." His tone drops even deeper, full of something that calls to the slow-building ache at my core.

I walk to my en suite and grab a wet wipe to remove my makeup. "Wanna play a game, big boy?"

He chuckles down the line. "Who sounds filthy now?"

"I never said it was filthy."

"Is it?"

"Yes, but that's beside the point. You'd have to have a dirty mind to get to that conclusion, comprende?"

"No. Fucking. Comprende. Admit it, you're a filthy little slut, aren't you, princess?"

I tilt my head to the side, loving this too much. "For you… I could be."

"Fuck, yes, you could."

I fall to the bed and start to FaceTime him, throwing my makeup wipe onto the nightstand.

"You got something you want to show me?" he smirks as the screen switches, revealing the finest specimen of a man I've ever seen.

Elliot is wearing a white T-shirt. It fits tight across his chest and makes his skin glow deliciously.

"No. I just want to play this game," I tell him, sitting up on the bed.

I look at him through the camera, and his lip curls. "What's that fucking look?" He laughs, but it's quickly silenced as I lift the balls from the satin-lined box and let them hang heavy from my pointer finger.

"Did you pick these out for me yourself?"

He nods his head yes, his throat working on a swallow.

"Do you want to play the game?" I question.

He clears his throat then asks, "What's the game?"

My tongue peeks out to wet my lips, but I don't retract it fully. Tilting my neck back and exposing my throat, I hover the silver balls above my mouth and utter, "Who can last the longest."

I dip the balls into my mouth, letting them sink deep before I suck them slowly, drawing them out from between my lips.

I moan around them.

Elliot is silent on the other end of the phone. I know I've probably shocked him, but with the way our calls have been going, the way he looks at me and gives me cheeky comments—which I know mean more than either of us let on—he should've been expecting this.

"How much did you say you'd had to drink?"

I smile and look down at him through the phone. "Take your top off."

Reaching over his head, he bunches the material at the back of his neck and pulls the white T-shirt off.

"This is fucking dangerous," he tells me, his eyes eating me up through the phone.

"We're just celebrating my first week! We'll take turns.

Anything you're told to do, you do, and if you don't do it, you'll forfeit your next question."

"You asked me to take my top off—"

"It's your turn." I nod, staring him down.

He scrubs his face as he watches me, reaching south and out of my line of sight. Although, I can see by the way his forearm strains that he's rearranging himself.

"Are you okay?" he asks. "And I mean *really* okay?"

"That's your question?" I rear back, knowing what a sex fiend he is. "Wait, you're supposed to have me do something!" I shake the balls. "Of all the things you could have asked—"

He gives a subtle shake of his head, cutting me off as he says, "It's the most important."

He's so fucking good at this. Why is that making him hotter? "I'm good. I promise I'm good, okay?"

He nods, then tips his chin. "Alright. Your turn."

I roll my lips. "I want you to lie on the bed, hold your phone so that I can see your body."

"Not my face?" He tuts, sounding hurt. "I'm wounded, princess."

"It's the game!" I grin.

I'm not losing.

"I know what the game is. I'm wondering if *you've* forgotten."

Elliot lies back on the bed, his chest bare and his abs taut, rippling as he gets comfortable. He has a pair of shorts slung low around his hips and a deep *V* that directs my hungry gaze to his gloriously hard cock. It lies heavy under the material of his shorts, but the sheer thickness of it has the fabric moulding to him deliciously.

He grasps himself, squeezing his hardened length as he flexes his entire body. "I want your mouth to do everything your eyes are promising." He squeezes himself again, then lets go. "I want you on your knees. Put the phone somewhere I can see."

I immediately rise to my knees, then I lean across and stand my phone on the discarded pillows.

It's my turn, and I know I'm about to veer far from the path I've always trusted. The path of a friendship. Gone. "Take your cock out. But no touching."

I hear him groan, and I wish I could see his face. It's not fair when he can see all of me, but I also want to win. If Elliot goes where I think he will, where I want to go—knees either side of that masterpiece of a face—I'll lose.

I lift my hand and palm my breast through my thin silk shirt, knowing it will get me off the slowest and drive him wild.

Hooking a thumb into the waistband of his shorts, he drags them down with the phone held steady in his other hand. "How the fuck am I naked before you?"

I laugh lightly, pushing my hair over my shoulders. "You asked me stupid questions."

His cock springs free, and I ravish my eyes over his manhood with no shame. My lips roll before I can catch myself, and I don't fight the urge to lean in a little closer.

Jesus Christ.

He's perfect.

I suck on my bottom lip until it throbs, my nipples pebbling. "Elliot—"

"Stop touching yourself," he demands, cutting me off just like I did him.

"We'll go around in circles if neither one of us can touch ourselves." I remove my hand and place it on my thigh, just below my skirt.

"Fuck, I want you, Luce."

I tilt my head back, smiling at the ceiling as his words urge me on. "You can touch yourself, but it won't feel like me," I tease, my voice low and purposefully sinful.

He gives me a guttural growl that makes my pussy clench and I feel a rush of pleasure at my centre.

"I'm dripping wet, Elliot. Make it feel like me. Sit up and spit on your dick. Make sure I can see."

"I knew you were a filthy girl."

He sits up.

His abs tense as he takes his cock in his hand, angling it so when he releases the spit from between his lips, it strings down and meets the thick head, coating his silky skin and running over his fist.

He gives himself a slow, lazy pull, then looks back up at the phone. His jaw hangs slack, his eyes only a couple shades off the bottom of the ocean.

And it's that look in his eye that I was trying to hide from.

I swallow hard, unable to snap away from his demanding stare.

"You're about to get fucked. You know that, right?"

My hands itch to move from my sides, to slide them over my stomach and under my skirt.

The way he studies me as if he's learning something new every time his gaze catches mine makes me ache in places I never knew it was possible to ache.

"You look beautiful without all that makeup on, you

know. Beautiful with it too, but I love to see the you that no one else does. The way your face heats."

Dipping my head, I stare at the duvet that's bunched around my squirming knees before lifting my eyes. He knows no boundaries, and he knows I love it. The things he says, the way he can make me nervous and red faced with the slip of his tongue.

"Tell me, were your cheeks that pink when I had my fingers snug inside that sweet little cunt of yours?"

My breathing gets heavy, my chest noticeably working.

"My bet is they were, but we weren't like this. I couldn't see you bare faced and fucked." He licks at his lips, watching me like a hawk surveying his prey.

I look up at him through my lashes, begging him to give me an inch. "I can't handle this. I need touch, Ell, but I want your hands. I want you."

"You could handle it; I know you could. And I'm not there to touch you, princess, but know that if I was, it wouldn't be my hands deep inside of you."

"No?" I moan, my brow flinching as I rock forward on my toes, looking for friction that isn't there.

"No, you'd be as you are now. Only my tongue would be cleaning up the sticky sweet mess between your legs. I'd have you work those hips over my mouth until you have nothing left to give me. I want you dripping down my throat, baby. Inside and out. And then and only then, if my need is satisfied, I'll let you up."

"I'm going to lose."

"You're going to lose," he rasps out in agreement, giving himself another pump. "Take off your skirt."

I do as I'm told, sliding from the bed as quick as I can to pull off the garment.

I unbutton my silk shirt, letting it hang open, then I climb back onto the bed, angling my hips to the side in an attempt to keep my modesty.

"Luce."

I look up, dragging my hand deliberately up my thigh. My sensitive flesh heats as if the tips of my fingers are sheathed in seared embers.

"You'll show me. You'll show me it all."

My nipples glide over the silk that scarcely covers them as my back bows and my lips part. I suck in a rush of air as if his words have a pull. And they undoubtedly do.

I want to show him everything.

The good.

And the bad.

And me.

"Look at me."

I open my eyes. "It's not your turn."

"Then why are you doing what I say?"

When I don't say a word, he continues. "Take your fingers in your mouth. Make them wet for me, and then I want you to spread your knees wide and touch yourself."

No man has ever been this way with me. It's like he knows what I need and how to command my pleasure with his words.

Then again, I've never been this way with a man.

Maybe our friendship has laid a bed of trust beneath our feet, so when we completely cross the line, it's with knowing.

A little cautiousness.

Unbound desire.

A different level entirely.

I wet my fingers, drawing them past my lips just like I did with the balls.

"Good girl. Now spread your pussy and show me how you do you."

My fingers brush my clit, and it has me trembling on the spot, my body threatening to surrender unforgivably. I try to keep my eyes open, but I can't help the heaviness that comes over me. It's as if everything is on edge, ready to reach the pinnacle before free-falling.

I can't lose this. I want to make him come before I do, but that seems impossible when I'm so close to coming myself.

I focus back on the phone and find him watching me, his back against the headboard and his hard cock in his hand. It's an image I don't ever want to forget.

"Tell me how wet you are."

"You want me to show you?" I ask with a seductive hum.

Elliot's jaw flexes at the thought, his forearm bulging as he grips himself.

"I would dip inside," I tell him, doing it anyway. My fingers sink into my sex before quickly slipping out and back up to my clit. The lights above me shine down, illuminating the arousal that coats my fingers. The obvious slickness is visible on the phone screen, and I know Elliot's seeing what I am. "But in my mind," I continue, dipping my head to my shoulder as I slip back inside and rotate my hips. "You're already there. Inside me. I can feel you filling me, Elliot. Every inch of your thick cock stretching me, taunting me, fucking me until I cry out."

Elliot moans, working himself faster. “Lucy.”

A shiver runs through me.

I’ve got him. “You’d fill me up; I know you would. Wouldn’t you? You’d fill me up, Elliot?”

He twists his wrist, pumping his dick with relentless vigour. “I’d fill you up so good we’d both be dripping down my balls. Then I’d have you on your knees licking them fucking clean.”

“Elliot,” I fall forward, grinding into the bed as I ride my hand.

“Me… too, baby.”

I lift my head, panting and flushed as everything tenses blissfully inside of me. I watch as cum paints Elliot’s abs and drips down his fingers. My hips grind down harder, thrusting over my hand as my own orgasm tears through me. My limbs shake. My face burns. My core throbs. It feels so damn good, and I can’t stop.

Not until my eyes roll and Elliot pulls me from the moment.

“Princess,” I hear the smirk in his voice.

I lift my head from between the pillows, still shaking. He’s cleaned up and looking perfect. Not a hair out of place.

“I win.” He grins, darting his tongue out and wetting his bottom lip.

I roll to my back, leaving the phone where it is as my chest heaves. “Whatever.” I smile.

17

Lucy

MAXWELL CALLS ME JUST AFTER TEN A.M. THE NEXT morning. I'm halfway through eating an apple when I notice his name lighting up my phone, making my hangover come to life all over again. Memories of dancing around the bar last night flash through my mind, and I smile on the inside. Maxwell wasn't up for dancing, and that's fine, but I hoped to get to know him a little at least. He's currently my only friend here in New York.

"Hi, Maxwell."

"Lucy. You didn't answer last night. I was worried."

"You called me?"

"I did," he tells me, sincerity in his voice. "I called lots. I stepped out with Alec for a cigarette, and when we came back, you were gone. Was everything okay?"

"I was waiting at the table. You weren't there, so I thought I'd leave. I thought you'd left too."

"I wouldn't leave without you. Fuck, I'm sorry, Lucy."

"Don't apologise." I frown and think about all he's said. Did I wait long to see if he'd come back? Maybe not. "I had a lot to drink, and I probably wasn't waiting as long as it felt at the table."

"Did you at least have a good night?"

"It was good. Polly and Alec seem lovely. Thank you for inviting me." I smile.

"I feel like it was ambushed by the two of them, and I let it happen. Do you think we could have a do-over? Maybe I could book a table, and we could actually have some food?"

No.

Crap, no, I don't want to do that.

I want to be his friend, and he isn't suggesting more, but food—one on one with another man. After last night and the feelings I'm starting to develop for Elliot, I don't think I can.

I wouldn't like it if the shoe was on the other foot. "I'm not sure, Maxwell. I have a lot on over the next couple weeks with finding an apartment and work."

"Do you need any help with moving or finding a new place?"

Probably… "Nope. I have it all planned out."

"Maybe after you've moved and are settled, I can pop by, and we can have a do-over? You probably think I'm a complete douchebag."

"I don't think that," I say through a defeated smile, dropping my heavy head into my hand. "And, of course, a do-over sounds great."

I'll deal with him when it comes to it. It's not a right-now problem, and I can tell he's not going to drop it.

"I hope you don't think I was being off with you last

night. I haven't seen Alec in days, and he had a bunch of work stuff to catch me up on. I'll show you a good time when we go out again."

"Of course, please don't worry about it or me."

"I'll see you soon, Lucy. Just call if you need anything."

"I will. Thank you, Maxwell."

I'M LATE GETTING to the chapel this evening. My hangover seemed to get worse and worse as the day went on, and I've slept the majority of my Sunday away. I find Ralph already sitting on the bench when I arrive, and I quickly make my way to him.

"Lucy, I thought you might've stood me up." He eyes the pizza box by his side.

"Oh, you sure know the way to a girl's heart. Give me that."

I sit down beside him and smile on the inside when he hands me one of two china plates. He lifts the lid of the pizza box, and my mouth waters as the steam hits me in the face. "Barbecue chicken with bacon and extra cheese. I thought extra everything was a safe bet."

"You were so right."

"Dig in," he tells me with no rush to make a start himself.

"Thank you," I say, looking at him with a genuine smile before sliding out a slice.

"Have you had any news on an apartment yet, Lucy?"

I shake my head and finished my mouthful. "I have a couple I need to view, but nothing has been walking distance to work and suitable in Elliot and my friends' eyes."

"I like how you separated the two. Elliot *and* my friends," he notes, popping a bushy grey brow at me. "I have a proposition for you, Lucy, and forgive me for being so forward, but you've shown me nothing but kindness since the day I met you, and you've seemed to have breathed a little bit of life back into me. I'm very happy I got to meet you when I did."

I fan my eyes with one hand while holding my slice of pizza in the other. "Ralph. You'll make me cry," I say with an awkward laugh slipping past my lips.

I sit up straighter, my stomach churning with the way he's set up the conversation.

"Don't cry. You'll set me off." He pats my knee and picks up a slice of pizza for himself. "How about this. I'd like you to consider living in my home whilst you're here in New York. You have eleven months left on your internship, and September will mark twenty years since my Elsie passed. I think it's time I left the city and moved on. I need to take a leaf out of your book and pull myself together, live out our dream of retiring to our Hamptons house."

"What, wait. You're leaving?" My heart sinks. I love coming out to the chapel; it's one of the only things I look forward to besides my calls to Elliot.

"I knew it was time long ago, but I've never wanted to let go. I'm much like you with my love of routine. I mean, look at us both."

It's true. From the conversations I've had with Ralph and the fact he's here every evening without fail because he feels less alone and closer to Elsie. He doesn't want to be alone, and I carry the same fears. "You're kind—too kind, but I can't live in your home, Ralph—"

"You can and you will. Please. And if you try to offer me money whilst sleeping under my roof, you'd only be offending me. You'd make a dead woman very angry also."

"You can't bring Elsie into this," I retort.

He takes a bite of his pizza, smug. "It's safe and will make Elliot happy. And…" He looks across at me as if he knows he's got me. "It's a ten to fifteen-minute walk to Soho on your legs."

"It's a fifteen-minute walk to my work?"

"And it's extremely safe, Lucy. I'd feel much happier seeing you out of the hotel. It's not feasible to stay there, surely."

"I don't know what to say."

He smiles and wipes his mouth with a napkin. "That's the thing with friendship, sometimes, you don't have to say anything at all."

He gives me a look that conveys all that we *could* say.

I crossed Ralph's path because he needed me too, and I already knew the value of his company from the very first moment I met him on this very bench.

A very special friendship indeed.

Elliot

I RAP my knuckles on Mason's office door before walking in. He looks up from his monitor, his phone held to his ear as he holds up a finger and turns to look over his shoulder. His eyes quickly flash back to me.

Before I can say a word, Nina walks out of his office bathroom. Her face is flushed, and her eyes go wide, shortly followed by a devilish smile.

Mason covers the phone with one hand and leans away from it. "Fuck off, Montgomery."

Nina pulls her tank the rest of the way down her torso and comes to me, kissing me on the cheek.

"It's fine," she says in a hushed tone, waving Mason off. "You guys are out for lunch."

She turns back to me and gives me a look that says we all know what's just happened, and it doesn't need to be discussed. "I was just leaving."

"You good, Pix?" I ask, dropping my arm around her shoulder. "He in a mood?" I mumble, quiet enough that Mason won't hear.

"Not anymore." She waggles her brow.

I take her in, appreciating the healthy glow that surrounds the contours of her face. My best friend's wife is beautiful. Simple as that.

"Stop staring at me like a creeper." She sucker punches me in the stomach, and I fold. I lift my eyes and glare when Mason sniggers in approval. "You heard much from Luce?" she asks.

"A little." I shrug, righting myself. I don't know how much Lucy would want me to share.

"She seems happy. It's good."

I try not to wear the smirk that's threatening to break. "I agree. She does seem *happy*."

"Hmmm," Nina hums.

"What?"

"Nothing." She rounds the desk, and Mase turns, leaving no room for her to decide for herself how it will go. Still, she tries to go in for a quick kiss, but the second their lips touch, the room calms, a brief moment of something that feels fated, and in the next second it deepens, and he stands, sliding his hands over her face and into her hair.

"I think I might get the Caesar today."

They break apart, with only Nina smiling.

"Let's go, asshole," Mason grumbles, grabbing his jacket and pocketing his phone. "You okay to pick Ellis and Ave up today, angel? Scar is working late."

"Yep. I'm good, you get going. Charles is probably waiting." She ushers us out and towards the elevator.

"I'm going to cut the grass tonight, don't you or Scarlet go doing it."

"Alright, bossman. I'll have Ellis ready when you get in."

Mase nods, and we step in through the steel doors.

"You cut the grass now?" I ask after a beat, trying not to laugh.

"Me and Ellis cut the grass," he huffs. "You know what they're like about paying people to do the shit we can. And Ellis loves it on the ride on."

"Fair."

A comfortable silence settles as we descend, and my mind drifts to Lucy, wondering what she might be up to.

She'll be at work.

"Look at my wife's face for five seconds too long again, and I'll do worse than a fist to your gut."

I crack up, laughing despite his serious face. I know he isn't mad about it. "What you gonna do, bossman?"

“I’ll run your fucking face over with my lawn mower.”

“Alright, *Dad*.”

“Cunt,” he retorts, striding out of the elevator and towards the exit of The Montwell.

“You love that she loves me really,” I shout, making heads turn, including Masons.

He shakes his head in disbelief and carries on ahead.

When we get to the restaurant, Charles is in fact waiting for us. He’s sat in a private room with paperwork scattered around him. He’s calm and controlled, sipping his coffee while reading the document in his hand.

“Fuckers are late,” he remarks, looking up with a smile.

I pull out a chair and sit back while Mason goes to stand at the window. “Lowell was boning his wife.”

Mason looks over at me, and I smirk. I enjoy winding him up too much.

“You all good?” Charlie asks, his question directed at Mason. He nods and then comes to sit down, his jaw clenched and his hands clasped.

“What is it?” Charlie asks, watching him closely.

Confused, I glance at Mason.

He sighs. “I’m worried the surgery Nina had is stopping her from getting pregnant.”

Fuck. I look at my best friend of thirty-four years and then back to Charlie, who’s wearing a matching expression to mine.

The fuck do we say to that?

When it’s obvious I’m not going to say anything, Charlie jumps in.

“You’ve not been trying all that long, though, right? And the doctors gave her the all clear?”

I don't say a word. Last I heard, they were waiting, so this is news to me.

"That's what Nina said, and she's so fucking stubborn over it, but it happened so fast with Ellis. And look at the Waverley situation. Dr Sarnmer said that my mother conceived both me and Scarlet quickly. It just feels off that it's not happening for us." He scrubs at his face, and I know this will be the reason for his outburst before.

It's bothering him.

I look at Charlie and shrug.

He sits forward, silently asking for Mason's attention. "You can't compare between Ellis and Ave—it's different. You've got ways to investigate this if you need to. Give it some time, and then get specialist help when Nina's ready."

"Yeah, I know." He scrubs at his face again, shaking it off.

"Enjoy the office sex," I tell him, clasping a hand on his back and making him laugh. "I know I would be."

"I am, boys, I fucking am." He finally grins, readjusting his cuff links.

"Let's eat. I have some shit to run by you both." Charlie nods at the menu on the table and then goes back to his work whilst me and Mason order.

Twenty minutes later, we're eating our lunch, and Charlie is filling us in on the charity event he needs us to attend.

"I've already donated and secured the tickets, so you don't have much of a choice. I think it would be good publicity if you want to take over the Reynolds account. Would help if you happened to make a substantial but anonymous donation on the night, of course." He wipes his hands in his napkin and waits.

"Seems decent," I tell him, nodding.

"I agree. It would be a good move considering Hemmings is looking to outbid us." Mason runs his pointer finger across his top lip, deep in thought. "Can't do no harm."

"Done," Charlie says, final. "I got tickets for the girls also. I presume Luce won't be making a guest appearance at such short notice, but I purchased an extra ticket anyway."

"I'll have Nina ask her. We could fly her home easy," says Mason.

The thought of seeing Lucy as soon as the end of the month makes something spark inside of me. I right myself in the seat. "I'll ask her. Better yet, I'll go and get her myself."

"Or we could ask her first," Charlie suggests with a frown.

"She'll come if I ask her to."

I grin, thinking about the way she was with me just the night before.

"You didn't listen, did you?" Mason sits stoically beside me, not an ounce of shock or emotion in his words.

I look at him, my face dropping.

"I'm missing something." Charlie realises. "What is it?"

"Elliot's *fucking around with Lucy*," he says, mimicking my outburst from just last week.

"That's nothing new." Charlie fixes me with a nonchalant stare.

"Exactly," I agree. "Lowell just doesn't like the fact his wife and her bestie think I'm hot."

"Jesus fucking ego," Mase sniggers. "You haven't taken it further then; that's what you're saying?" He looks at me, sure as fuck.

"That's none of your business."

"The fuck it is."

"You really are a prick today, fuck off," I snap.

"Alright, lads," Charlie interjects, a hint of amusement in his tone.

"If you do plan to take it further, make sure you know what you're getting yourself into. You know how Luce is. She wouldn't...." Mason's brows twitch as they draw together, but that's about all the remorse he shows.

"She wouldn't what?" I ask, a bitter taste of disloyalty coating my tongue.

"You've said it yourself. She isn't your type."

"I'm not *her* type." I lift my drink and mutter into the glass, "Get it fucking right."

Notorious.

The word rattles around my brain as if it's all that occupies it.

"Elliot wouldn't hurt Lucy."

Charlie's comment comes out of left field, and I shoot him a look around my glass.

"Would you?" It's meant as a question, but it's laced with confidence. The same confidence he wears in a courtroom.

Charlie Aldridge doesn't say a word he doesn't mean. Period.

I place my coffee down. "Not intentionally. Never."

He nods, then chances a look at Mase. "Don't be a dick about it. It's none of your business."

"Alright." Mason holds his hands up in mock surrender. "But don't expect me to be there with a mop and bucket when it all goes to shit. And if you drag my wife into your mess, it'll become my business real fucking fast."

"Loud and clear."

I love the guy to my right to the death, but he's a real prick sometimes.

"You two are bitching today." Charlie smiles. "Entertaining if not a little concerning. All's good in the office, though?"

"Fine." Mason and I both say in unison, both looking at each other before our lips curl.

18

Lucy

It's been the longest Monday in the history of Mondays. After Ralph told me about the house on Saturday and how he wanted to get things moving as quickly as possible, I knew he needed me to agree to the proposition more for his benefit than my own.

As soon as his driver arrived to pick him up from the chapel, he had him make the calls necessary and said that I should be ready by Tuesday to move in.

I told him there wasn't any rush and that he should take his time, but he was certain he wanted to make the move now. I sensed his need to speed things along was more out of anticipation than anything else. And I can understand that.

My family was a little taken aback by my news, but once I told Elliot the house was in the West Village and a short walk from my work, he seemed to come around to the idea. No doubt he now knows more about Ralph Mendes than I do, but I also know his obsessive need to know that Ralph is legit comes from a good place.

I haven't had a chance to Google the West Village or Ralph for that matter, but I trust him—maybe that makes me a little foolish, but Elliot and Mason wouldn't let me live in a crazy person's house, and I trust their judgement as much as my own.

In my excitement and with Ralph pushing things along, I stupidly told the hotel I would be checking out by tomorrow morning and wouldn't be back after I leave for work. In my head, I thought I'd spend my time yesterday packing, but I ended up calling the realtors I was supposed to be meeting this week, and then Elliot called and… and that was the end of packing.

Which leaves me with a couple hours tonight to get all my things moved over to Ralph's home.

Idiocy at its finest.

The minute I set foot in my hotel room from work, I start to pack up all my things, stuffing everything I brought to New York into the boxes I had sent over from home. They're mostly full, but because I didn't have time to get more boxes, and the suitcase I arrived with doesn't seem to go back together the same way, I have to improvise.

Elliot calls me at six p.m., and I'm a wild mess of panic.

"I shouldn't have said yes to tomorrow. I'm so stupid. I still have your flowers here."

"Luce, breathe. I have people in the area who can come and help you."

"No. I will get it done." I can't think of anything worse than having someone I don't know moving me into a new home. It would be awkward. I'd waste more time trying to not do or say embarrassing shit. "I could give Maxwell a call. He said he'd be happy to help."

"The dick who left you on Friday night?" Elliot questions, his voice full of displeasure. "No. I don't like him."

"He's a nice guy, Elliot. He called on Saturday morning to apologise."

"Let me call my friend. He and his wife would be happy to help."

"I'd rather call Maxwell. Don't be annoyed, please. I just want to get this day over with."

I hear him huff, and I roll my lips.

"You're jealous?" A slow grin masks my face.

"Jealous, princess?" His voice grows raspy with the deep rumbling laugh that comes from deep in his chest. It rolls right through me and into my bones. "You'd know it if I was jealous."

"So you don't mind?"

"Call whoever you want."

My shoulders slump. "You sound annoyed."

There's a pause. "I'm not annoyed, but I told you I'd come over and help. I don't know why you have to be so stubborn."

"Because that's completely irrational. Why would I have you fly thousands of miles to help me move a dozen boxes?" I go to the bathroom and grab my toiletries. "Come on, you know it's ridiculous."

"Yeah, because I'd move a dozen boxes then leave, Luce…."

My brows jump in realisation. "Oh." I giggle. "Ohhhhh."

"Fucking oh." He tuts, and I continue to laugh.

"Elliot," I drawl, fanning myself.

Thankfully he can't see me.

"If I let this conversation continue, I won't get anything moved tonight."

"There was a reason I called," he carries on.

"What's that?" I ask, a smile creeping onto my face, even though I have no idea what he has to say.

"Charlie has a charity dinner. It's on the twenty-eighth of the month. He got you a ticket."

I watch in the mirror as my features tighten. "In London?"

He hesitates. "Yeah."

"I can't come home," I tell him, feeling bad when I shouldn't. "At least not that soon? I've just got here."

I'm still trying to find my feet, and if I go home now, I'll never want to leave. I know me. I'm not ready to go home. Not yet.

"Why don't you wait. See how you feel after you've moved. You might need the break."

I drop my head, running my finger across the cool ceramic tile. "Ell, I won't come back. Not yet, it feels too soon. I'm sorry."

He huffs in annoyance. "Don't apologise."

What I would give to see him. Mum and Dad. Ellis and Ave. The girls. But the other side of that is the painstaking task of leaving them all again. It was hard enough the first time.

"It's not that I don't want to come home, and with everything that has happened since I left, I want to see *you* especially." I bite my lip, my cheeks growing flush as I open up a little for him, hoping it will pacify him. "I'm nervous, excited about how it will be when I see you in person."

"You worried you'll jump me?"

"Or that you'll jump me," I accuse. "You were just as invested on Friday night, Mr Montgomery."

"What? No, I wasn't," he says sarcastically.

"Uh-huh, don't bullshit me. I heard you getting all hot for me."

He chuckles. "I know exactly how it will go when I see you."

"You do?" I grin.

"I do. I won't be waiting long either," he trails off, not finishing fully, and I know he's pushing for me to come home still.

"I'll come back, I promise. Just not as soon as this month."

"Alright." he sighs, and we both fall silent.

I feel sad that I can't see him, that he isn't here helping me move. The same as Mum and Dad. It's things I've always had help with. The big things. But this is exactly what I wanted, and it's giving me my independence. It's all I've wanted for years. Oddly, it's brought me closer to Elliot in what feels like the most incredible way, and I think the reason I'm so hesitant about going home, or having him here now as easily as he could be, is because he will have to leave.

We can't do this like we want to right now, and that makes this whole situation really difficult.

"Outta your head," he mutters, sounding deep in his own thoughts.

"I should get packing. I'm going to give Maxwell a call, okay?"

"You're not asking me, are you, Luce?"

"No?" I say, lacking all the sincerity he had.

"I need you safe and your things over in that house before it's too dark out. Can you do that for me?"

My chest warms, and I smile sadly at myself in the mirror. "Yeah, I can do that."

"Alright." I hear him shuffle around. "I'm getting some sleep. Call me if you need me, yeah? I'm here."

"Good night, Elliot."

"Good night, Luce."

I stand for a solid five minutes, wasting time I don't have while I try not to get upset. I don't want to call Maxwell. He will help me, he said he would, but it's not who I want to unpack this new chapter of my life with. It feels personal. It's a memory that will belong to someone else now, and it makes me doubt my decision to ask for help at all.

Unfortunately, I know I can't do this alone tonight.

Lucy: Hey, Max. I got a house! Could really use a hand moving if you're around? Please.

Maxwell: On my way.

On my way, just like that. No questions asked.

I've never known anyone to be as straight to the point as he is. I call down to reception and let them know that Maxwell will be coming up. He arrives twenty minutes later.

"You don't have much stuff," Maxwell notes, picking up the first lot of boxes. "We can probably get these in a taxi. I can ride over and drop them off while you pack the rest?"

"Yeah?" I smile. "I still haven't hailed a taxi. It's the stationary ones I jump in."

He smiles at that before turning to walk towards the door. "We can practice tonight."

"Thank you so much for coming over. I know I told you I could do it myself, but then everything happened so fast with Ralph, and I had to pack up fast."

"I don't mind. Can I tape this one?" he asks, closing up one of the boxes.

"Yes, that one is ready." I throw him the tape, and he makes quick work of sealing the box. "You said you work late. I didn't pull you away from anything important, did I?"

"I'm always working on something important," he tells me with a smile. "Alec said he and Polly would come and help, too. I told him I'd let him know, but I don't think you'll need any help, to be honest." He scratches his brow as he looks around my room.

"That's so lovely of them! Do you have Polly's number? I'd love to meet up with her."

Maxwell looks across at me, the skin on his forehead bunched up until he catches me watching him. "No, I don't actually have it. I've only actually met her a couple of times."

"That's okay," I tell him, "I will get it the next time I see them."

He nods his head. "I'm sorry about Friday night, Lucy. One minute you were there on the dance floor, and the next minute you were gone. You shouldn't be walking home on your own."

"I know, but Polly left, and when I came to find you and Alec, you weren't there. It felt like I was waiting at the table for a while, but obviously not. I feel silly thinking about it now."

"Don't. Just know that I wouldn't leave you in the club on your own."

"Okay." I smile, picking up a box at my feet and following him out the door.

"Let's get these moved, and then we can call up the others and get a beer."

"It's a Monday!" I proclaim. "I have work in the morning."

"You have to celebrate, and it's not like you can unpack until the old guy leaves tomorrow." He looks over at me as we wait for the lift, taking in my pensive look.

"Don't tell me you can't hack it, Luce."

I smile and roll my eyes, knowing I could use the drink to settle this nervous energy hanging over my head.

We load the taxi with as many boxes as we can fit in, then Maxwell heads off with them to Ralph's while I go back upstairs and pack up the rest of my things.

Polly and Alec couldn't come out with us tonight. Which makes sense considering it's a Monday, and we all have work in the morning.

"It's okay for you!" I groan, walking from the hotel elevator and into the corridor. "You get to sit at a desk all day tomorrow. I have to look at designs, patterns, and people. Ugh, Chelsea. It's going to be awful."

"Don't be so dramatic. You needed to chill out." Maxwell laughs, pushing on my back and steering me in the direction of my door. "Do you feel chilled?"

"I feel drunk."

"Just as good in my book."

I have to say it was nice to go out this evening. It was much quieter than Friday, and I would've only sat in my hotel room and felt lonely with how empty it now is. Once Maxwell got back from the first trip, he loaded up the last of the boxes and made me take a shower and get ready to go out. It meant I didn't get to go to the new house yet, but Maxwell assured me it would be a nice surprise when I finish work tomorrow. He promised me it would be worth it.

So, I stayed behind and laid out my work clothes, had a super quick shower, and then we headed out for dinner, and I did my absolute best not to think about all the clustered thoughts plaguing my mind about the next day.

Maxwell seemed to open up a little more this time, and for some reason, I felt myself warming to him as I did on the plane the first day I met him.

"Thank you for seeing me home, Maxwell. Will you get a taxi?"

"No, I can walk. Pass me your phone."

I frown as I try to unlock my door. "Why?"

He takes the key card and does it for me. "So I can set your alarm."

"I'm not that bad." I push his side and give him a smile. "I've had a great night. It's so nice to have a friend here, so thank you."

"Of course. Let me know if you need anything else, yeah."

"I will."

I watch as he rounds the corner and takes off down the steps. A smile slips into place as I push on the door and walk inside.

Tuesday morning is a breeze. I drank wine last night, and although I did feel a little spacey when my head hit the pillow, I couldn't have been as bad as I thought I was. Work's busy, and I get stuck straight in when I arrive. We're working on a walk that will be taking place in Italy next month, and ever since Monica pulled us into the meeting and picked the team, it's been a buzz in and around the office.

Jean would be so proud of me for being a part of this campaign.

At lunch, I slip off down the street and find a coffee-house. I order a sandwich and check my messages.

The girls and Elliot have all replied to the picture I sent them last night of my packed-up hotel room. I was lying on the bed, my legs laid out on the duvet.

I pull up Elliot's message first.

Elliot: Be better if your face was in this Princess

Elliot: Let me see you

I try to call him.

"Luce."

"Hey! I'm on lunch. Are you free?"

"I'm in a meeting still." His voice drifts and sounds further away. "Excuse me a moment."

"Oh, no, it's okay. I will call back later."

"It's fine. What's up?"

"Nothing, this is what I mean. I was just calling."

"You missing me?"

"No," I drawl. "Why are you still in the office anyway? It's late there."

"It's just past five. I was wrapping things up when you called. Lowell will handle it for me."

"He's giving you the evil eye through the windows, isn't he?"

"Yep," he tells me. I can just picture him standing watching Mason with a calculated smile on his face.

"Are you using me?" I exclaim.

"I'd never."

"Hmmm."

"How did last night go? You got all your stuff moved, I presume? How's the house?"

My fingers curl around my coffee cup, and I take a sip. "I did," I mumble, licking the bitter taste from my lips. "But I still have to unpack later, and I haven't actually seen the house yet. I called Maxwell in the end, and he came to help me move it all over."

"Maxwell. Tell me about him."

"What do you want to know?"

"What does he do?"

"He's in tech. Used to be a Navy SEAL."

"He likes you?"

"I should hope so." I laugh. "He just gave up his night to help me."

"You know what I mean."

My eyes scan the tables full of people that surround me, feeling like everyone in the small shop can hear our conversation. "He's a friend, Elliot. I speak to you every night, all night long. I need someone here."

"I know that."

"Then why are you asking me that? I feel like it's

because you don't like the idea of me having a man around me, but…."

"But what?" he repeats when I trail off. "Finish what you were going to say."

"It's not like you aren't surrounded by women at work and day-to-day. You love women, Ell. They're what you're good at. It's never even crossed my mind to look at Maxwell in any other way but as a friend."

"I know how men work, Luce, and I know what it's like to stumble across *you*. If you think he hasn't thought about fucking you, you're sorely mistaken."

"You sound like a dick."

"I am."

I run my tongue across my teeth, feeling myself get annoyed at him.

"And if you want, we can call it right here and now."

"Call what here and now?" I frown.

"Whatever this is."

My brows shoot high, my face burning up. "What do you mean?"

"You want me to spell it out for you?"

"I don't know." I should know, but my mind is blank.

"You're mine now. And if you want, I'll be yours, princess. You just need to say the words."

"Yours?"

"Mine," he confirms. "Don't overthink this."

"What does mine mean?" I ask, utterly lost, slightly hot, and maybe a little horny. The way he makes me feel is untamed. Unmatched. He's ruining me.

And I'm in a damn coffee shop.

"It means Maximus gets to live."

"And if I'm not yours—"

"You are."

"Metaphorically speaking."

"I guess we can fuck whoever we want."

My heart pounds so hard I have to close my eyes to focus. Exclusive? Is that what he's insinuating? Elliot wouldn't mean that; he doesn't do exclusive anything. "I don't sleep with anyone I'm not in a relationship with, you know that."

"You did Miller. And that random Ted guy."

"Both of them I knew in some way. Miller became well… Miller. Ted is the exception."

"And me, what am I? Because I'm sure I remember you riding your hand until you moaned my name the other night."

"I'm in a coffee shop," I whisper, shrinking down in my seat.

"What am I?"

"You're Elliot." I huff out. "You're different."

"Different how?"

"I don't know. I know you better than any man I've been with."

"So you'd sleep with me without being in a relationship with me?"

My brows draw in, heat spreading across my chest. "No."

"No?" he asks, affronted.

I shake my head, trying to word it so that he understands. "It's about the connection in that moment. The feelings. Not the relationship."

"Okay. So I have to make you feel something."

"You already have. Will you stop!" I hiss, looking behind me. "I'll ring you later."

"I like you like this. You're giving me more than you realise."

"Do you ever have a bad day?" I snap, hearing him laugh as I hang up.

The man is impossible.

Gathering my hair up off my shoulders, I spin it into a bun and tie it into place with a hair band. I finish my lunch and then head back to the office, where I try to get some work done, all while Elliot Montgomery's words filter through my constantly running thoughts.

19

Lucy

Is THERE ANYTHING MORE EMBARRASSING THAN BEING A tourist? Or at least looking like a tourist. I'm walking down Charles Street with my head down and my eyes glued to my phone. The pin I'm following tells me I'm close, and the anticipation of almost being at the house has an exciting ball of fire boiling in my stomach. I'm eager to see where Ralph lives. Where he and Elsie made their incredible memories.

Where *I* will now live.

I look up, and my brows pull in slightly, noticing that I need to cross the road. Checking both ways, I slip my phone into my pocket aimlessly and ogle the brownstone houses before me.

"Holy shit."

I come to a stop on the pavement and look up at number 63 with my heart in my mouth.

I'm speechless.

All the expectations I had about Ralph's home were wrong. So so wrong. This is like something straight out of a movie.

For starters, there are ten windows.

I count three floors, but like the other houses on the street, it's raised with a door on the underside of the steps. I peek around at the little black iron gate and fencing that box the area in. There are two windows on the ground floor, and with the quirky little side door, it makes it look like there's a tiny apartment under the house.

I store my questions away for later and hurry up the steps to the double-fronted door.

I knock and wait, looking around at the identical homes on the street.

The door swings open, and Ralph greets me with the warmest smile. "Lucy!"

"Hello." I smile wide.

"Come on in, my dear."

"Ralph, your home..." I step through the front door and swallow my words. Black-and-white chequered flooring carry my feet for three steps forward until my eyes catch on the entrance room, and I come to a stop.

"Probably wasted on me, after all these years," Ralph tells me, drawing my eye back to him.

"Yeah," I say with a shocked laugh. "My god, it's beautiful. Nothing like what I imagined."

"What did you imagine?"

"I don't know. One up, one down."

"Ah, no, no. You have four floors, and the apartment below us which is empty. Not much light down there."

"The little door on the side of the steps?"

"Yes, it's actually where the maids used to live," he tells me, taking my coat. "Back in the day, of course. Most of them were turned into apartments or basements."

"Wow." I drop my bag down on the floor in the hallway and step into the entrance room. I cast my eyes up at the high ceilings, the coving and pillars. Intricate, unique designs that scream money. This place is beautiful. "This is your home!"

Ralph chuckles behind me as I continue under the arch and into what I'd have to call a sitting room. It's all open plan, so I can already see the main living area beyond this one. Both have large open fireplaces.

"You have two living spaces. They seem so different but still so connected."

"I have four living spaces, actually. Or should I say you do? This is the parlour floor as we call it—mostly for show. Let me show you the main living space."

The main living space. Is he joking? I can't even tell at this point. This is like discovering Elliot and Mason's estates all over again. The girls are going to freak out.

It takes Ralph a good few minutes to manoeuvre up the stairs, and by the time we reach the top step, he's a little out of breath. "Elsie made me fork out on a two-story house for our retirement." He looks up, and I follow his line of sight between the multiple staircases that lead to the very top floor.

Holy fuck.

I can't live here.

He bangs his closed fist on the bannister. "These are the only thing I won't miss about this house."

I try for a smile but panic claws at my throat as I walk behind Ralph and down the landing.

"You've gone quiet on me," he observes, looking over his shoulder.

"It's a lot. It's very big."

"It is. But it has a lot of life and love, too. You'll like it here, I'm sure of it."

I nod, feeling overwhelmed.

Ralph shows me the bedrooms, which are just as grand as the rest of the house. The bathrooms are sleek and modern, with quartz countertops and different marble and slate patterns varying in each.

"Did you renovate it recently?" I ponder, running my hand down the panelled bedroom wall. There's a fireplace in here with a wood surround which seems to complement the oak floors.

"I only finished what Elsie started. There was a lot she wanted to do. When we bought this place, I was at the peak of my career. I had all the money yet no time to do the things we wanted. It's funny, we tend to think we'll have time to enjoy the good one day, yet what we don't realise is that the good is already in this very today."

"That's true and a very good reminder."

He dips his head and points to a door leading off the bedroom with his stick. "I had everything cleared out in here and the rest of the floor. The things I didn't want to take with me are upstairs. I hope that's okay."

"Of course it is okay!"

"That's a wardrobe," he tells me when I don't make a move to open the door he pointed to right away.

I walk over and look inside, my jaw dropping for the millionth time today.

"If you don't mind, I'll leave you to explore the rest of the house on your own. I have a love-hate relationship with those bastard stairs."

I chuckle and scan the room again before following him out. "Would you like to eat with me this evening, Ralph? One last knees-up before you leave? I can cook, or we could order in."

He turns as he reaches the top step, a full smile on his face that he does nothing to hide. "There's an Italian restaurant not far from here. Let me put an order in. It's a favourite of mine, but I don't tend to order when it's just me. Too much waste."

I grin right back, a lump forming in my throat at the joy on his face. "Perfect."

Elliot

I INVITED my parents to dinner. It's not something I do enough, and when I pull my car up to the gates of my home. I remember why. My mum and dad are great parents, which means they care, which also means they want to know everything there is to know about me and my life.

I already know my mother will quiz me on where I've been, who I've been with. It's always the same. And my father, he'll ask me about the company. It's the one thing he's never quite let go of.

They're already inside and waiting for me when I walk

in the door, and the smell of my mother's infamous steak pie assaults me instantaneously.

"Mum. Dad," I greet them, stepping into the kitchen and smiling over at my mother, who's busy at the sink.

"Hello, darling. You're late today."

"I had a meeting. Sorry," I tell her as I move to stand behind her and pull her back into me for a hug. I kiss her head. "You made my favourite."

"I did. This kitchen isn't used enough." She elbows me and shrugs me off. "Are you eating enough?"

"Freya," my dad groans.

"Don't Freya me. He's my boy."

"I'm eating, Mum, I promise."

I look across to my dad, who's sitting at the kitchen island peeling carrots. "Your meeting," he mutters, tipping his chin in question.

My mother tuts behind me.

"The developers from the Stanley site. They've had some funding issues."

"No surprise."

"Right."

"Has it been sorted?"

I nod. "We're getting it done."

"Good." He continues to peel the carrot, and my lips form into a grim line.

I can't imagine not doing something I loved anymore. Real estate wasn't always my plan, and if Mason didn't take on the company, I can't say I would've taken it on by myself. Over the years, I fell in love with the business. I saw what it meant to our fathers when we made the decision to take it on and the way we have developed it in such a short space of time, I know my dad is proud of me, but I also see how it bothers him that he isn't hustling at it anymore.

My mother places a hand on my back as she leans over and places an ice-cold pint of beer in front of me. "Did I hear right from Nina? You're going to the Hamilton gala."

"Thank you," I tell her, lifting the glass to have a sip. "And yes, I am. Charlie's doing a speech or something."

"Wonderful. It always was a favourite of ours, wasn't it, Glen?" She looks across at Dad, and he smiles at her. "Are you taking a date?"

My lip twitches. They're too predictable. "No, Mum. No date."

"You do realise I'd get off your case if you gave me something? Anything. Even a bread crumb. I don't believe a man as handsome as my son is still single at the age of thirty-four. There must be someone."

My mind instantly wanders to Lucy.

We're having fun right now. She's in New York and doesn't have any plans to come home.

It is what it is.

"If I were you," My father warns her. "I wouldn't ask the boy any more questions. I can guarantee you won't like the answers you get."

I smile despite the tugging in my chest. My mum bore witness to many of my one-night stands fleeing from our family home, but she doesn't know about the women that go that one step further. My father once walked into my office to find it completely trashed by my receptionist. She got the sack—obviously, and my father added another colour to the image I allow the world to paint me in.

Fuck them.

I am who I am.

My mum knows what she needs to know.

"Shall we eat?" my mum asks with a clap of her hands.

My parents leave just before nine p.m., and I quickly shower. Lucy doesn't finish work for a couple of hours, so I don't expect her to call for a while. The time difference between us is messing with any attempt I have to get her home for the gala.

Fuck. My mother would lose her head if I went with Lucy.

The woman is as obsessed with her as I am.

I've turned into a wet blanket these past couple of weeks, and I know it's confusing Lucy.

Worse… it's confusing me.

I've always known what I want, and for me to tell Lucy that she's mine and I'll be hers if she asks. What the fuck *does* that mean? The words slipped free in the moment in the hope they would tie her to me in some screwed-up way. I'm afraid she will find someone else—I know that's the reason. But I also don't know if I want to be tied down.

What if I don't make her happy?

It's all she wants.

I already know I'm not the man she should be giving her time to. Yet I'm too selfish to stop. Too far gone to know how to, even if I wanted to.

She's the woman of my wildest dreams, and I'm the broken fragments of yesterday's nightmare.

Unwilling and not ready to let her go.

When I didn't hear from Lucy by six p.m. her time, I decided to go down to my home gym and work out. I don't use it often because there's no buzz. I prefer to be around people at the gym.

I'm on the treadmill, sweat dripping from every inch of me when she finally calls.

I hit the stop button and step off. My chest heaves, and I stare at her picture for a beat before I answer, trying to clear my earlier thoughts.

"Ahh, I thought I missed you, and you were asleep! You're working out?" She watches me with intrigue, and I frown as I clench my jaw.

Why am I so annoyed with myself?

Annoyed with her?

"Yeah, I needed to blow off some steam."

"What steam?" she asks unapologetically. I'd ask her the same thing.

"I had my parents over for dinner."

"Ahhh," she smiles. "Explains it. What was it this week?"

"Just Mum, wondering if you're going to get your ass home and come to this gala with me."

"That's low. You can't bring your mum into this."

"Will it make you come home? I don't want to go on my own."

I want to stop myself from saying it, but now that I'm talking to her, it feels right. She should be home with us. At the gala and on my arm.

"Elliot," she croons.

"Hmm?"

"I'd tell you to get out of your head, but I have a feeling you need to be there." She gives me a smile. One that's meant to ease a turmoil she knows she's in the dark about.

Still, she doesn't push.

"I'm all moved in, and I know I need to give you a tour, but I locked the door the second Ralph left, and I'm now hiding in my room." I smile, loving her dramatics. "Honestly, this place is incredible."

"Good. I want that tour tomorrow, though, okay? You're safe there, Luce. We made sure of it."

"I know," she murmurs, dropping her eyes, and I can tell she is caught up in her own head. "Do you want to watch a movie? I'm about to unpack my clothes and need something to keep my mind from wandering. I'm thinking *Beauty and the Beast* tonight."

"I need to shower first."

"That's okay, we can watch that movie first."

Fuck.

Rational thought seems to redirect straight to my dick.

"You coming with me, are you, princess?"

"I wish," she says, her tongue lodged provocatively in the side of her cheek. "Don't tease me."

I pull my tee off from over my head, watching as her eyes hungrily scour me. "I'd never. And you started it."

"Can I be super honest with you?" she says, her cheeks already blushed.

It makes me pause. Something about the way she says it makes my heart pump harder. It's as if my body is the calm before a beat drop and every fibre of me knows shit's about to get wild.

I tip my chin in answer.

"Sometimes, I wonder what it would be like," she starts, rushing her words. "Like, if I was right there with you now, what would it be like? Would we touch? Would we be how we used to be? Would we be just friends? What would we say? Would we talk like this, open and honest? Do you ever wonder what it would be like if I never left? If I came home. Do you ever wonder what we are, even now, right here?"

"Do you?"

She comes back to me, surfacing from her heavy thoughts and taking a breath. She tilts her head a fraction. "Clearly." She chuckles.

I roll my lips and lick them. "I guess I do think about all of those things."

Her brows lift in surprise. "You do?"

"You're all I fucking think about these days, Morgan." I gesture to my torso, swiping my hand across my sweat-covered chest. "I had to go workout after Mum and Dad left because I didn't hear from you. I had to take my mind off you."

"Did it work?"

"Did I stop thinking about you?"

She nods her head yes.

"No."

Her smile makes my heart somersault in my chest. "I like that."

"I try not to think about the what-ifs. I know that's hard for you to do, but I can't promise it will be a certain way when I see you next. And looking back is pointless. You're in New York, Luce. It did something that probably wouldn't have happened had you stayed."

"Do you think this was always inevitable? Us."

"Honestly?"

"Always."

"No. For a long time I wrote you off, and not because there wasn't an attraction—you know how it was in the beginning, and then we fucked around last year. But you look for something I'll never be. I didn't consider we'd be at this point, ever."

She looks down, hiding from me when all I want to do is grasp her face and see into her beautiful mind. "This point," she mutters.

"Yeah, Luce, this point. And don't ask me what it means because I don't know. I don't think you know either, do you?"

"No, not really." She smiles. "Sometimes I think it's obvious to me, and I'm on the cusp of understanding it all."

"But then you look into my eyes and get lost in my allure. Right?"

"Something like that." She laughs. "Or you say something filthy, and it sends me into this horny frenzy."

I watch as her face blushes again, and it makes my stomach twist. Not a feeling I'm used to. "What are you thinking, sweet girl?"

She looks up and into the phone, biting her lower lip. "I've never been the way I am with you with anyone else. This connection… and we've never even touched—"

"I've touched."

"You know what I mean. The way I was the other night on the phone. I've never been so into it. I'm not sure I've ever felt more me with a man."

I can't help the pleased smirk that tips up my lips. I let it sit freely on my face for her to see. "I like that answer," I rasp out.

Her lips twist as she stares at the ground. "Go shower. I'll get changed, and we can watch a film before you fall asleep."

"Alright, princess."

20

Elliot

It's the night of the gala. The gang are all here, cooped up in my kitchen and drinking my bar dry—I wouldn't have it any other way.

Other than Lucy. I'd have that situation a different way entirely.

"She should be here." Nina sulks, pulling herself up onto the counter next to me despite her beaded gown that looks like it should restrict her. She's not long arrived with Mason, and the sadness in her eyes as she looks around my kitchen sits heavy on my chest. After Mason's confessions at lunch the other week and the shitty feeling marinating inside of *me* over Lucy's absence, I know she's probably struggling.

"You're not wrong. A lot's changed." I swig back the remnants of my scotch.

Megan and Scarlet are dancing around the kitchen island, wineglasses poised above their heads as they chant the lyrics to Beyonce's "Irreplaceable" like women scorned.

"I feel selfish to want her home as much as I do," Nina admits.

I turn my head to look at her fully.

"She's doing so good without us. I feel proud and sad all in one."

She's doing so good without us.

"Why are you frowning?" Nina asks, her own brows creasing.

I try to gather my thoughts as her words settle. "I…" Fuck. "How often do you speak to her?" I question.

She shrugs as she thinks. "Maybe a couple times a week on the phone, and most days we text. It's hard with the time difference."

I nod, dropping my stare to the crystal base of my tumbler.

"Why?"

"We speak a lot," I admit, feeling guilt seep into me. "Daily."

Nina's quiet beside me, her thumb stroking over the rim of her own empty glass. "I guessed as much. It's not a shock to any of us. You know that, right?" She bumps my shoulder with her own. "Don't you remember that bet Mason made with me in Bora Bora? He was so sure nothing would happen, but I always knew."

"How?"

"Call it a woman's intuition. The way you looked at her and the small things you'd do that I don't think even you noticed yourself."

"Like what?"

She smiles at me. "Do you remember the first night I

stayed at Mase's with you all? You took me back to his when he went out to Lowerwick to see his dad."

I nod.

"We were all in bed the next morning: Luce, Megan, and me and you came in with breakfast for us."

I frown, trying to remember.

"You brought us toast, in nothing but your tighty-whities and that handsome smile you steal names with."

"I always knew you fancied me more than him," I tease.

"Shut up." She laughs. "You gave Megan the tray, bypassed me, and handed Luce the toast."

"What?" I rear back, a half laugh blending with my words and making them rasp. "That's all you've got?"

"No. I have years of it, but do I really need to go on? You know as well as I do how you are with her."

"And then there's all the things you don't know."

"Oh, really," she drawls out. "Like?"

"Top secret." I give her the smile she referred to moments ago.

"Luce will tell me."

"I'm sure she won't." I pop a brow, hammering my statement home.

"We'll see. Either way, I find it kinda sweet that you're so clueless over it all. The way everyone else can see it but you."

I swallow harshly, running my tongue over my teeth. "I see it." And I do. I guess I've always seen it—contrary to what everyone thinks. "But I also see her, what she wants, what she needs. Where I am, who I am."

"Who are you?" Nina asks as if she already knows where my mind is. It pulls my attention back to her.

"I'm notorious."

"Notoriously what?" she snaps, her eyes pinching in.

I tip my head, giving her a knowing look. "Come on, Nina, I don't need my ego stroked, and you're not dumb."

"I'm serious." She frowns, her annoyance at me building. "Notoriously funny, kind, caring, bold. You're one of the most thoughtful and giving people I've ever met, Elliot. You care about Lucy—it's painfully obvious to me and everyone else, and it doesn't stop there. The way you treat my son—who I know looks up to you—Mason, me, the girls. Megan told me how you were over there on Thursday to help her put her new desk together. You didn't have to do that. You didn't, but you did. You treat everyone around you with such love and respect," She grasps my forearm, her tone absolute. "Even the women you take to bed at the end of a night. They don't ask for anything beyond the motive, yet you see to it. Because you know there's a misted perception to your life and the way you choose to live it. A sticky label you get slapped on the chest with after them knowing you for all of two minutes. That's not on you. *It's on them.*"

"Two minutes," I tsk, making her pause before her face cracks and she laughs.

"My point is…" she sobers. "It doesn't mean shit. They don't know you like we do. You are notorious, but not in the way *you* think you are."

I scrub at my face. It's like everything I've lived to fight against is being unravelled at my feet. And by a tiny five-foot-nothing pixie at that. "I still don't deserve her."

"That's your opinion."

I laugh at that, shaking my head. "A pretty important and crucial one if anything is going to happen."

"Not really," she says, full of confidence.

"No?" I snigger, not understanding the happy smile dancing across her face.

She shakes her head. "Love is love. It doesn't give a shit about your opinion, Ell."

"Love," I repeat, my face growing blisteringly hot.

"Love." She chuckles, with pity in her laughing eyes. "We'll come back to that when you're ready."

She's still smiling like a fool.

But I'm still not over her original comment about Luce. *She's doing so good without us.* Although, is she? Lucy isn't doing anything without me. I'm at the end of the phone, morning, day, and night.

"I've never seen you this quiet. It worries me."

"I'm fine," I tell her.

"Hmm, okay, I'll let it go. But only because I've given you too much to think about as it is."

I look down at her, rolling my eyes and dragging her under my arm in an embrace. She wraps her arms around me, and I kiss the top of her head.

"If you hold back because of the opinions of people who don't truly know you, you'll end up resenting yourself, not them. They aren't there at the end of the day, and they certainly aren't important. Fuck them, okay?"

"Car's here," Mason claps, drawing both Nina and my own eyes up.

"Let's go," I tell her.

Nina slides to the tiled floor and readjusts her dress. I shut off everything I need to downstairs, then step out and into the waiting car.

Lucy

After turning down the invitation to the gala, then feeling utterly gutted over missing out, I texted Maxwell and asked him if he wanted to meet for drinks tonight. I knew I'd be sitting at home, sad about not being out with my friends if I didn't do something. And then there would be the pictures. I've only ever been to two events for Charlie, and both blew me away. The suave of it all. The passion for the charities and organisations being spoken about. It always amazed me how he could stand up on stage and speak to a crowded room when he rarely had a word to say to the rest of us.

When Nina sent me a picture of them ready in their gowns and tuxes, it was enough to make my eyes well. She would've sent it to make me feel less left out, but it did the opposite.

I miss them.

Thankfully, Maxwell was up for going out, which means at four o'clock on a Saturday, I'm at a bar drinking every cocktail I can find on the menu.

"You should slow down," Maxwell tells me, a slight shine in his own eyes.

"I'm fine." I wave him off. "What's the point of getting day drunk if you aren't going to drink?"

"The morning."

"I'll deal with the bitch when she gets here."

He gives me a grin and eats a handful of nuts. "You like the house?"

"I do. You never told me how incredible it was going to be. I feel so safe and content there."

"When I got to the house and saw it, I knew I wanted it to be a surprise for you. They had a removal van there taking Ralph's things. I just knew it would be better in the light of day."

"You were right. I was gobsmacked when I arrived."

He nods, clearly pleased. "Hey, the apartment below, is it renovated?"

"Uh, I think so… Ralph just said it's dark and dingy."

"Hmm. Alec and Polly are looking for a place. Is it up for sale or rent at the minute or just empty?"

I rest my arms on the table, leaning in. "Just empty. How come they're looking for a place?"

"There was a fire at Alec's apartment building two nights ago. They don't have anywhere to go right now."

"What? Polly and Alec?" He says it as if it's nothing. As if he's reading off his shopping list. "That's awful. Do you know what happened? What caused the fire?"

"Arson," he grits out. "Fuckers."

"Oh my god, that's terrifying." I sit up a little straighter, my blood turning cold. "You didn't mention it before. Are they okay?"

"From what I've heard, they're fine. Alec's a hard man to get hold of."

"You think they would want to live in the apartment? I could call Ralph?"

"Would you? They're likely to go anywhere right now, and I've seen how clean your new place is." He pulls out his phone and starts to type.

"Of course. I'll get hold of Ralph as soon as I get home."

Maxwell looks up from his phone, giving me a warm smile. He seems spaced out, and I wonder if maybe the fire has been playing on his mind this whole time, and he didn't say anything.

"Do they need help at all?" I nod to his phone. "We could help."

It would give me something to do besides sinking cosmopolitans as a distraction technique.

"Nah, I tried to help yesterday. They have it sorted."

We order basket meals and eat them at the bar, and I order a Coke to drink instead of any more alcohol. I want to go home. The news that someone intentionally set their apartment building on fire has made me feel sick to my stomach. And I know that this sort of thing probably happens all the time in such a big city—I live in a super safe area (apparently), but it doesn't make it any less scary. For the first time since I got to New York, I feel unsafe.

WE'RE sat watching football on the wide screen when Maxwell's phone rings.

I watch him as he answers. He doesn't say much other than the standard greetings, and when his body tenses, a flush of heat rushes me. "Yeah, she said she would speak to the owner." I roll my lips, waiting. "I'd say so. And it's a quiet street… Yeah, okay, let me know."

Once he hangs up, I step forward a little. "Was that Alec?"

"Yeah, he said to say thank you."

I nod, glad that I might have helped. Polly seemed like a super nice girl, and the thought that she could live so close to me makes me feel surprisingly happy.

"You don't have a lift in your house, do you? Only stairs?"

"Uh-huh, there's stairs in the main house and also a hidden stairway that leads to every landing from the apartment. It's creepy, and I haven't been down them since Ralph showed me. I've locked the door for now. It won't be an issue for Polly and Alec, but I expect to have a nomination for *rear of the year* by the end of my internship." I laugh, finding myself funny.

"Rear of the what?"

"Nothing," I say, feeling insensitive. "You never said about the fire before. I'm sorry if I made the night all about me."

"You didn't. Alec is a private person, and I wasn't going to bring it up. Don't sweat it."

I look to the bar and then back to our table, where my full drink sits. Day drinking seems like the last thing I really want to be doing right now.

"Come on, let's get you home."

My eyes snap to Maxwell. "We don't have to leave."

"Do you want to stay?" he asks, tilting his head to the side.

I look at him sheepishly and shrug.

He shakes his head and laughs. "Go home, run a bath, and wait for your friends to call. They'll be having a shit time without you."

"Thank you, Max," I tell him, appreciating his understanding.

Maxwell walks me back to my house, making sure he sees me to my door.

"Thank you for this afternoon, I had a great time."

"Me too. Are you around tomorrow? We could get breakfast."

Crap. I have a list as long as my arm to get through tomorrow, and I want to catch up with the girls and Elliot. I feel like I used Maxwell today because if my friends weren't busy, I wouldn't have gone out.

I'm a horrible person.

"I can't tomorrow."

"Right," he frowns and kicks the frame with his toe.

"I'm sorry, Max," I groan. "I feel like I should be honest. I really like you, and you're a super great person, and you've been unbelievably kind to me since I moved here, but—"

"Miller."

I snap my mouth closed, shocked. "You remember that?" I didn't think he listened to a word I said that first night he took me out.

"I do."

"It isn't anything serious right now."

"But he could be?"

"Maybe." I shrug, feeling my heart swell.

I hope so.

"It's complicated."

Maxwell rubs a hand over his buzz cut, taking a step back. "You're a lovely girl, Luce. A good, honest girl." He nods and smiles. "I like that."

"I hope you don't feel like I led you on at all. When I got here, I didn't really know what was going on at home.

Things have changed—fast. But I'd really love to have you as a friend here."

"Of course. You have my number." He backs away. "Don't be a stranger, yeah?"

"I won't." I step forward as he walks away, feeling good as I watch him disappear down the street.

Once inside, I pull off my coat and walk to the kitchen in search of a bottle of wine. It's been a week of living at Ralph's, and it already feels like a safe space.

It's so homely and wholesome.

I smile to myself as I stand at the kitchen counter. Now I'm home for the night, I feel ready to put on my comfiest pyjamas and sit out on the terrace on the second floor. It's only six thirty, and my subconscious mind is counting down the hours to the end of the gala. It finishes at midnight, so not long.

Once I've poured myself a glass of red wine, I run a bath, adding more bubbles than necessary. Then I slip in and let the heat of the water soothe me. I last five minutes before I reach for my phone.

First, I try Nina, not wanting to come across as needy by calling Elliot, but she doesn't answer.

I want to call him.

We've spoken every night on the phone this week, and it's equally terrifying as it is exciting. I always knew this side of Elliot existed, and it's not shocking to me. If anything, it's completely normal, and it's the same things he's always said and done.

What's changed is the way *I'm* behaving. The way *I'm* allowing him in that little bit deeper and egging *him* on.

We haven't just crossed the line this time. We've

unwritten it. As if it never belonged there to begin with. And as I lie in this steaming hot bath, I can't help but think about the conversation we had the night before.

"I can't wait to kiss you." He grins at me like a kid in a sweet shop, his head dropped to the side as his eyes grow heavier by the second. "It's a fucking travesty that I haven't felt those sweet lips against my mouth already."

"You think I'd let you kiss me?"

"Yes. And if you didn't, I'd steal them anyway. They belong to me now."

I smile. "You've felt them before."

"When?" He frowns in question.

"Remember in the hospital with Nina? You had pancakes and—"

"I fed you," he rasps out, finishing for me.

I nod, thinking back to the way his finger curled over my tongue as I took the syrup covered batter from him.

"It was the first time I saw you crack. You knew what it did to me, and you played up to it. You licked my finger as if it was my dick." He bites his bottom lip as his smile spreads. "It's making me hard just thinking about it."

I surface from the water and drag my hands over my face, wiping away the water. Without thought or trepidation, I call Elliot. It's been a long day, and I'm desperate to hear his voice, have him tell me all about the night, or just absorb any scrap of information he wants to give me.

I stand from the bath and step out as I wrap a towel around my body. I put the phone on speakerphone and walk out into my bedroom. It rings five times, and I'm about ready to give up when he finally picks up.

There's a rustling sound, then laughing.

"Princess?"

I frown at the female voice. It's not one I know. "Hello? Ell?"

"I'm sorry, *Ell* isn't available to take your call right now."

"Oh," I reply, and I feel my brows knit further as if they are trying to pinpoint something. "Umm."

"HE IS BUSY!" She laughs with someone and my chest aches.

The phone becomes muffled again, and then I hear a woman call out clear as day, "Harriet, babe! Come dance with us."

My eyes fill, blurring with every second that ticks by on the screen.

"I'll tell him you called." She hangs up, leaving me standing in the middle of my bedroom, dripping wet and feeling like the biggest fool on earth.

Harriet? The woman from his office. Why would he entertain her after everything he has said to me? And why is she answering his phone?

Question after question muddles through my mind, my stomach growing tighter and tighter with the hysteria I work myself up into. And I have no right. Not when he isn't mine, not officially.

Not at all.

Is he?

"Oh, God." I sit on the edge of my bed, my phone slipping to the floor as my shoulder slump in realisation.

I like him.

I really, really like him.

It's never felt this way before, and I've never felt betrayed over the women he's slept with. Why do I feel betrayed? He hasn't done anything wrong.

Has he?

I should have gone to the gala.

Maybe he's annoyed with me.

I knew he didn't want me to go out with Maxwell tonight. Is this his way of getting back at me?

I stand, leaving my phone where it landed. I grab my wine from the bathroom and go downstairs to the terrace with a blanket. It's not particularly warm enough out here at this time of year, but it's the perfect spot to clear my thoughts.

I need clarity.

For over an hour, I sit and pick apart every conversation between Elliot and me, trying to figure out if I took what he said wrong. Maybe I got the wrong idea, or maybe he didn't mean to lead me on the way he did.

He's been there every night, just a phone call away.

We've grown closer. That's not something he can deny, but now he has Harriet answering the phone? A woman I know is unbelievably beautiful and smart, and he's slept with. It feels shit. And without a label, I don't feel like I have a leg to stand on when I try to rationalise my jealousy.

How does this work?

How do I pursue a relationship—or whatever this is—without feeling shitty over the women he acquaints himself with? They won't ever go away—I know this. They love him.

They're enamoured by him, just like I am.

God… I'm just another one of them, aren't I?

Why did I want to be special to him?

Who do I think I am?

I always had good reason for keeping Elliot Montgomery on the other side of the line, and now I'm afraid that it can't be fixed. It's gone, I know that.

Am I too far gone?

Is that why I feel like this?

"Fucking shit, Luce. Just call him!" I snap, placing down my wine. I go up to my bedroom and find my phone.

I tap my foot as the call continues to ring, but eventually, it cuts to voice mail. Feeling completely rotten on the inside, I climb into bed with the rest of my wine bottle, pull the sheets high, and cry.

Elliot

"Come here, Megamus."

"Not if you're not going to stand on your own!" Megan snaps at me, her face laughing even though her words bite.

We take the last three steps to her floor, and I pull her into my chest, trying not to bear my weight on her.

"Ell! You're too damn heavy for it," she tries to get her words out, but they are muffled. It sets me off.

"Don't be so grouchy."

She pushes me to the side, and I cross my arms with a smirk on my face as I wait for her to unlock the door.

"I used to think you came here for Luce," she teases.

"I wanted to make sure all my girls got home safe," I tell her, bopping her nose.

"Whatever," she says, a knowing look on her face as she pushes open the apartment door.

I stroll in like always.

"Hey, will you come to Bora Bora? I want us all there," I tell her, knowing that getting Nina on board at the gala was key.

I know they'll come.

"I'll see if I can get the time off. I obviously want to, though."

"Obviously." I smile. "What are we cooking?"

"Nothing. I'm going to bed."

I tut and watch from the fridge as she disappears into her bedroom. "You're a disappointment!"

After a three-course meal, I'm not all that hungry, but I also know that it is almost a tradition to have a feast before bed. At least in this house, it is.

Megan is just being lazy.

I scour the fridge for everything she has, and then I take what I find and go to her room.

"Cheese?" I flick on her light with a smile as I kick open the door.

"Ell, I have work late tomorrow."

"Then sleep all day."

She sighs, rearranging her pillows as she sits up. I stretch out on the end of the bed and lay out the cheese, crackers and grapes I found.

"You're a fucking idiot, you know that?"

I slip a grape into my mouth and smile. "Luce called me. Think it's too late to call her back?"

"It's two thirty in the morning. It will be like nine thirty there. I'd say she'll be up."

"She was going out with that asshole she met on the plane."

"Why is he an asshole?"

"He looked at her."

Megan nods in understanding as her eyes drift closed. "Fair."

"Wanna know all our secrets?"

"No."

"She's kinky." I pick up a piece of cheese. "Did you know that? Luce is a proper naughty girl." I smile.

She cracks open an eye. "Really?"

I nod as if that's all I have to say on the matter. It's not like Lucy wouldn't tell her friends, she tells them fucking everything. I've been privy to far too many of their girly conversations.

"I'm kinda proud of that little snippet of information." She closes her eyes again. "But, Ell."

"Hmm."

"Shut the fuck up before you get yourself in trouble for telling me something you shouldn't, and go to bed."

I grin as I stand, then bend down and kiss her head. "Can I stay?"

She rolls over and looks at me. "You think I thought you actually wanted to see me home?"

"Was that English?"

"Fuck off."

I laugh. "I did want to see you home, you know I did." I also wanted something familiar. Something that wasn't fully me and a little bit of *her*.

"I know. And yes, of course, you can stay. Always."

"Night, Megs. And thank you."

"Good night."

I leave her room and dump the food in the kitchen, knowing Megan will have me clean up every scrap of mess I make in the morning. Then, I walk to the other end of the apartment and into Lucy's bedroom.

It's painted a simple shade of beige, with black and white furnishings. The bed sits in the middle of the room, and the wardrobe is at an angle in one of the corners. Everything is as it should be. Megan hasn't changed a thing, and I know that will be for Lucy's benefit. She would've wanted a backup plan. A what-if plan.

I smile as I face-plant the bed, pushing my arms up under her pillow as I become immersed in everything her. It's not enough, not even close. I need the real thing.

I need Luce.

I pull my phone from my jacket pocket.

She called me hours ago, and I didn't notice until I was on my way home in the car. I didn't plan to stay as late at the gala as I did, but for the first time in a long time, I actually enjoyed being out with all my friends. Even Mason took his head out of Nina's ass long enough to enjoy his night. The only thing missing was Luce.

I try calling her, but she doesn't answer. I decide to leave her a voice mail.

"Luce, I missed your call. I'm sorry. I hope you had a good night with your friends." I readjust my head on the pillow and breathe her in. "I kept looking around the gala tonight, wondering where you were. I pictured what you'd be wearing. I thought gold at first, but then I thought about how you wouldn't want the attention on you, and you'd go for something solid. Black. Conservative but sexy as fuck with your hair down and curled. They played Norah Jones, and I knew it was the song you'd have me up on the dance floor for. I sat it out with Megs while Charlie took Scar. We all miss you. But definitely me the most. I miss you, Luce. You're enjoying New York, aren't you? You'd tell me if you weren't…." I frown, my jaw aching as my teeth clench. "Sometimes I wonder if I'm giving you the chance to explore it all like you wanted to, like you deserve to. Am I holding you back? I feel like I am. I feel like when the days done, you come home and fall into me, but only because I'm not letting you live in any other moment. That was the deal, right? You living your life without restraint." I pause, reminiscing on the night of the ball. "You'll be thirty-two in ninety-seven days. I worked it out at dinner. That's soon." I chuckle, already knowing I'm about to delete the entire thing. "I shouldn't want you to fail, should I? The idea you could meet someone else, and it be real. The idea that you could find yourself and not need me anymore—our pact." I snigger, pulling the phone away from my ear as I erase the message.

"It fucks me up inside," I say to no one. "Good night, princess."

I drop my phone to her sideboard, clean my teeth, and undress, then I lie in her bed without her, thinking of all the times we lay here together and didn't touch once.

I'm selfish.

I should send her the message, let her see the truth in my words for herself. She's so afraid to be on her own, and I've used that. I haven't let her go like Nina, and the others have, and I don't want to.

She feels so in reach, yet she's never been further away.

21

Elliot

"You got bread crumbs on the cheddar!"

My eyes peel open. "Huh?"

"Don't mess with my cheese! You know this."

I reach blindly, feeling the sharp line of her nose. "Megs, go away."

"You need to get up." She tuts. "You told Ellis you'd take him out on the boat and over to your mums today."

Shit. "I did."

I swing my legs over the bed and stand, stretching. "What time is it?"

"Just gone ten. You're going to be late."

Balls.

Ellis has these eyes. He'll look at me, and I'll be spending the day trying to make it up to him.

"I need to shower," I say to myself.

"You do," Megan agrees. "Nina and Mase know you

were out, and you probably shouldn't drive yet anyway. You were proper sideways last night."

"I wasn't that bad."

"I made breakfast. It's in the oven. I'm going to get some fresh air, try and shake off this hangover."

"Have you got your key?"

She shakes her keys in my face. "Go shower and eat. Don't drive for a bit, okay?"

"Yes, Mum."

She stops at the door and pokes her head back in. "Did you speak to Luce last night?"

I close one eye as my brows pull in. I run over the night before. The message I recorded but didn't send. "She didn't answer."

"She was in the group chat this morning, but I didn't say you were here. I wasn't sure you'd want her to know what a sap you are."

"She was in the chat this morning?" I frown. "What time was it?"

"Early. Half sevenish, maybe. She said she went to bed at like eight last night so was up."

"I thought she was going out last night?"

Megan shrugs. "Guess she was home early."

She leaves, and I work out the time difference. It would have been around two a.m. I consider sending her a message but think better of it. If I wake her up after she was up in the night, she will be knackered for work in the morning.

I shower and eat the breakfast that Megan made me, and then I get an Uber back to my house.

It's gone midday when I finally arrive at the estate. I spot Ellis sitting on the terrace with Scarlet and Waverly playing with chalks, and I know I'm in trouble when Ellis refuses to look up as I pull up to the circular drive.

I jump out of my car and take the steps two at a time, checking out what they are colouring in. Scarlet—I presume — has drawn a giant fish. It's not the shitty figure-eight style of fish I used to add to my drawings in primary school, though. It's a decent fish, with gills and—"

"You're late!" Ellis accuses, standing up on his little feet. The little guy is almost three and has a better vocabulary than some grown men I know.

"Sorry, mate, Uncle Elliot had a little too much beer last night."

His dark brows lift. It's unnerving. "I not going now. I drawing with Ave."

"You sure?" I ask with a smile.

He nods and sits back down, crossing his legs.

"Alright, I'll be inside with Mum and Dad if you change your mind, okay?"

Scarlet looks up at me as I step her way. "Why do you look so fresh?" she groans, her face screwing up as the sun peeks through the clouds.

I bend at the knee and kiss Waverly's soft mousy hair, careful to avoid her flowery garland. She's sat between Scarlet's legs, her hands slapping the cold concrete. "I don't feel fresh," I tell Scarlet, giving her a wink before disappearing inside.

I hear Nina before I see her, and I follow her voice to the

utility room that leads off the kitchen. She's sat up on the tumble dryer laughing at something while Mason is on his knees with piles of washing around him. A smile just as big sits on his face.

"They didn't know."

"They did," Mason scoffs, looking up at me as I enter the room fully. "My son is pissed at you."

"Yeah, that won't last long."

I go to the cupboard and pick out Ellis's all in one waterproofs, then bend and search for his wellies in the rack. "Last night was decent," I say.

"Right," Nina agrees, a smirk on her face which she directs towards her husband.

I get the feeling I'm missing something.

"Lowell, I will come up there and nail you into that tumble dryer quicker than you can say *not in front of Elliot* if you don't stop looking at me like that," Mason warns as he carries on sorting the washing.

Nina grins wide, knowing he isn't lying. He'd totally fuck her on the tumble dryer.

"What a lousy threat," she taunts before turning to look at me. "Have you spoken to Luce today? She seemed a bit off on the phone earlier. She spoke to the kids, but that was it, rushed off the phone when I tried to speak to her."

"I think she had a shitty night's sleep."

"She isn't the only one," Mason groans.

"Yeah, it was stupid o'clock in New York when she called. Let me know if you speak to her today and tell her to call me back, please."

"Uncle Ell."

A smile spreads wide across my face, and I turn. "Yes, Ellis?"

"We go out on lake?"

"I didn't think you wanted to go?" I tell him, watching as Mason's eyes lift to me in warning.

"Frey said she make me crumble."

"That crumble is mine, boy."

I pick him up and stand him on the counter. "Get in your waterproofs, and I'll think about it."

His face transforms with excitement. "You go really fast over bumpy bits gain?"

This time it's Nina's eyes burning into the side of my head. I lean in and whisper into Ellis's ear as he shuffles his arms into the all-in-one suit. "Mum will go postal if you carry on, and then neither of us will get crumble."

"No, Mummy and Auntie Scar went to the post office after school. To post the letter for Lance."

I shake my head and laugh at how perfect that came out of his mouth. "Alright, down you get."

Mason doesn't say a word as I usher his son out the door. He knows I wouldn't let anything happen to him.

We walk across fields and to the other side of the meadow to the lake. I put Ellis in his life jacket then set him in the boat. "Go sit on the seat until I get in, mate."

"Okay!" he toddles off down the slippery boat, his hands balled into fists.

I pull out my phone and call Luce as I work on untying the rope.

She answers on the second ring. "Hi."

"You're up." I smile.

"Yeah, I've been up for a while," she tells me, her tone softer than usual.

"Did you have a good night? The girls said you were up early. I thought you were going out with your friends."

"I did. I ended up coming home early." She pauses. "We started at lunch, so…yeah…."

I rub at the back of my neck, frowning over at Ellis, who gives me an equally perplexed look. "Everything okay, Luce?"

Silence. Nothing but a heaviness that travels through the phone and falls on my shoulders.

"I just get a feeling that you're not okay. You were up in the night."

She blows out a ragged breath. "I'm fine, Ell. Did you all have a good night?"

"Yeah, it was good." I roll my lips, my eyes still glued to Ellis. "We missed you, though. Wasn't the same without you."

"It wasn't?" she asks.

"No. I mean, It didn't suck completely. I won't lie to you, we had more fun than we have in months—"

"Good. That's good. Are the kids okay?"

My brows pull in. "I was about to say that it won't ever be the same, not when you're not there. We all missed you."

"Maybe another time," she mutters, and the way she says it makes the hairs on my arms raise.

"Yeah—"

"Uncle Elliot!"

"Hold on, Luce." I move the phone away from my mouth and put one foot in the boat. "Ellis has me out on the —shit!" My foot slips on the muddy bank, sending my front foot, the one planted in the boat, forward. "Fuck! Fuck! Fuck!"

"Elliot! Did you just say Ellis? Is he there? What's wrong?"

The gap between the boat and the bank gets wider and wider, and I try to reach forward to throw myself onto the boat, but it's no use, my foot slides up the bank, and before I allow my crotch to be split in two, I collapse sideways and into the water.

"Uncle Elliot!" Ellis cries, reaching for me with his little arms as I surface.

The water isn't overly deep, but it's enough to soak me right through. I look at my phone, which is lit up for all of five seconds before it flashes black, then white and then to nothing.

"Hand? Hand?" Ellis reaches.

"It's okay, mate." I stand, pulling the boat back to the bank. "I'm okay. Are you okay?"

He nods, his lip curling.

"What's funny?"

He shakes his head.

"Tell me, or no crumble."

"Your arms were flappy." He starts to flail his arms around.

"We aren't telling anyone about this." I point at him.

"You said fuck." My eyes close in mortification. "Tree times."

"We aren't telling anyone about this," I reiterate.

Ellis nods, watching me quietly as I climb in. I start the boat and drive it around to my parents' estate, letting Ellis think he's steering the entire time. It's not far, and it would be more convenient to walk the fields between the two properties, but where's the fun in that? Ellis loves this little bit of us time. In the summer, we plan to teach him to swim out here.

As we approach my parents' dock, I see my mother rushing down the garden. She's panicked and throwing her hands about.

"They're here, they're okay," she says into the phone.

Leaning down, she takes Ellis from me when I lift him out to her. "What happened? Lucy phoned Nina in a panic." She eyes my soaking wet clothes. "You fell in?" she exclaims.

"Elliot said fuck. Tree times."

My mother looks at Ellis's two fingers then back at me with wide eyes.

"I slipped getting in the boat. My phone went with me."

"Right. Let's get you boys warmed up." She holds out her phone as she turns to walk away. "Call Nina and let her know you're okay, please."

I take the phone and call Nina. She doesn't make a big deal about it, but I know she would've been worried when they couldn't get hold of me. Part of me is pissed at Lucy for worrying them, but she wasn't to know. It probably sounded bad from her point of view.

I shower and change into some old sweatpants and a tee, then I go and find Ellis. He is in the kitchen, sitting on the kitchen island with a chocolate-covered spoon.

Walking past him and my mum, I dip my finger in the cake mix she is spreading and kiss her cheek. "Thank you for sorting Ellis."

"You have to be more careful of your language around

him," she tells me, not deviating from her task. "He's advanced for his age, and you need to remember that."

"I was going down, Mum. And Mase has said worse for sure." I walk to the Rayburn and place my phone on top of a tea towel. "Will this dry it out?"

Mum peers over her shoulder, a frown marring her already wrinkled face. "It might. You could try rice if not."

I nod, checking the cupboards for snacks. "Shall we go watch a film, Ell?" I ask Ellis, knowing his dad hates the nickname. "You can pick today."

"Yes!"

"Can I borrow your phone, Mum? I need to call Luce back."

"It's wherever you left it," she tells me, watching as I leave the kitchen with Ellis in my arms. She wants to ask questions, but I don't let her.

I take Ellis to the cinema room and settle him on the oversized sofa. "What do you want to watch today?"

He shrugs. "Don't know."

"There must be something you want to watch?" He looks up at me dazed, and I can tell he's tired. "How about we have a look through, see what there is?"

He nods and scoots up the sofa as I sit down. We end up settling on *Spiderman*, and for the first thirty minutes, the little guy is glued to the screen. Then his head bops, and he climbs into my lap.

I lay us down, letting him sprawl out over my chest.

"Auntie Lucy's in York," he tells me, pointing at the TV.

"She is." I smile, feeling proud of how smart he is.

"She doesn't pick me up on Thursday anymore."

"No, but she misses you lots, and it won't be for long, and she will come home again."

"We used to go for secrets."

"Go for secrets?" I frown.

"At the ice cream shop."

I chuckle, hugging his precious frame tighter. I could listen to his jumbled words all day.

"Does she go for secrets without me now?"

"No! She would never. It's your thing, bud."

He seems to accept that and snuggles deeper into me, his little hands fisting my tee tight at my sides. My own eyes start to grow heavy, and by the time he's asleep on me, I'm drifting off, too.

"Elliot. Elliot." I feel a hand on my shoulder. "Ell."

My eyes open to find my mum standing at the back of the sofa. A warm smile slides over her face, and she nods at Ellis. "Such a sweet little angel." I see her eyes grow shiny, and I know she is thinking about Ellis's grandmother—her best friend.

"What time is it?" I ask.

"Just gone three. Your phone's working." She passes it to me, and I thank her. "Don't let him sleep much longer, or he won't sleep tonight."

I nod, letting Ellis's warmth, along with the sleepy haze I'm in wrap around me.

Afternoon naps are the shit.

I unlock my phone and breathe a sigh of relief to see it working.

Elliot: Hey beautiful.

Princess: Hi

Elliot: I'm at mum and dads, with a sleeping Ellis on me. Wanna know what's missing?

Princess: ??

Elliot: You.

I see three dots bounce, then stop, then start again. My brows draw in as I wait.

Elliot: Outta your head

Princess: Can I ask you a question?

Elliot: Always

Princess: I'm sorry I'm asking this. You know I never question you and I feel so stupid over it.

Her next message comes straight in.

Princess: Did you go home with Harriet last night?

My stomach bottoms out, making Ellis on my chest feel like a lead weight.

"What?"

I go to type, and my phone flashes off.

"Shit!"

Where the hell is this coming from?

Why would she think that?

My throat feels too tight, and I lie stoic on the sofa, my annoyance growing by the second.

She thinks I slept with Harriet.

I snigger, chewing on my lip. Of all the people who could label me, and after everything that's happened over the last month.

Surely she knows.

Needing to speak to her, I slowly sit up and ease Ellis awake before taking him to see my mum.

She takes him and smooths down his back as she watches me closely. "What's the matter?"

"Nothing. Just something I need to sort out."

"With?"

"Nothing, Mum," I snap, walking from the kitchen with purpose and feeling like a prick for it.

I grab my mother's phone from the sideboard and take the steps out into the small courtyard that sits between the dining room and library.

I call Lucy, my body tense and full of energy.

"Hello."

"What the fuck, Luce."

"Please don't be mad."

"You think I slept with someone last night?"

"I don't know."

"I didn't," I snap. Pinching my brow, I try to chill the fuck out. "I wouldn't."

Of all the times I've fucked around with women—with Harriet, this is what it gets me. Nina told me I'm not notorious in the way that I think I am.

The irony that I'm standing here not twenty-four hours later having this conversation.

"Elliot, I've been thinking."

My body runs hot, the hairs on my arms and neck standing on end.

Maybe another time.

Her words from this morning slap me in the face.

My jaw flexes as my teeth clamp tight. "Hit me with it," I bite out.

"I think maybe we should slow down. I don't know if we can do this. The distance thing makes it impossible and—"

"I said I would come out wherever. You can come home."

"I know, but it's…."

She's doing so good without us.

"Tell me what you want, Luce. Tell me, and I'll make it happen."

I hear her sniff, and it makes my heart crack.

I'm hurting her.

She's doing so good without us.

"I don't want you to do anything. I'd never want to change you." She pauses, taking a breath. "When she answered your phone, Elliot. I knew you wouldn't. I don't think you slept with her. But I wasn't okay with it. The fact she was with you, and I wasn't. I felt horrible, and I don't want to feel like that again."

I rear back. "When who answered my phone?"

"Harriet. Last night."

"What?"

What is she talking about?

"Lucy, what the fuck are you talking about?"

"Please, don't get mad at me."

I grasp the back of my neck, refraining myself from screaming the words down the phone. "Okay, but I need you to give me a little more than what you are. I wasn't with Harriet last night!"

"Was she at the gala?"

"Yes. But I didn't speak to her."

"She answered your phone. She told me you were busy."

My jaw clenches. I think back to the night before, wondering how the fuck she would've got my phone.

Then it clicks.

"Luce, she's being a fucking bitch. She's trying to upset you. I was with the guys last night, ask them."

"I don't need to."

"I left my jacket on the back of my chair, and she must have got hold of it. It's the only explanation I have."

"Elliot, please, you don't have to explain. You aren't mine, and I shouldn't be so jealous over this."

"What?" What is she saying? "Luce, you might be upset, but you are fucking me off with what you're saying."

I hear her cry, and I stand frozen to the spot, eyes burning with no idea what to say or do.

I can't get to her quick enough.

She's doing so good without us.

"Luce."

"Can I call you back?"

My shoulders drop in defeat. "Don't hang up on me, baby."

The phone clicks off, and I refrain from launching it into the concrete at my feet.

I want to be mad at her, but I know what Harriet can be like. I know exactly how she would have made it seem.

Needing to get home so I can fix my phone, I go back inside and collect Ellis's things. "Will you and Dad take the boat back to Lowerwick for me? I'm going to take your car and leave it up there."

"What's the rush?" My mother asks.

"No rush." I look down at Ellis who's watching me. "I have a headache and want to get home."

"Stay. You can sleep it off here tonight. It's a long drive back."

"I'll be fine, Mum." I lean in and kiss her cheek. "I promise."

She nods and smiles at me, leaning in and saying goodbye to Ellis.

22

Elliot

I PULL UP AT LOWERWICK AND FIND MASON SITTING ON THE steps with Waverly. She lives to be outside. She's so much like Scarlet with the way she loves the estate and nature.

Mason stands as I step out of my parents' car. He walks over with Waverly in his arms. "Everything okay?" he asks, taking Ellis's waterproofs while I get him from his car seat.

"Yeah. Fine."

"You're back early."

I round the car and pass him, walking up the steps and into the house. "I need to go get my phone fixed."

"Not on a Sunday, you're not," he deadpans. "We have a couple old ones kicking about, let me see where they are." He walks off down the hall. "You staying for food?" he calls over his shoulder.

"No."

He nods, already expecting my answer. Ellis disappears up the stairs and I follow Mason into his home office.

"Nina's on the phone to Luce."

I snigger and throw my gaze toward the bay window. Probably telling her everything she didn't say to me. "Harriet answered my phone last night. Told Luce I was with her."

Mason looks up at me in confusion. "Who the fuck is Harriet?" He lets Waverly down to play on the carpet as she starts squirming in his arms.

"Nelson's granddaughter."

His eyes pinch in at the corners. "You left with Megan and Charles."

"I did."

"So, what's the problem?"

I shrug, although I do know the problem. Last night was the first night in a long time that me and Lucy didn't talk.

She left London to find her independence, and all I've done is get in the way.

"We have something, me and Luce."

Mason laughs. It's open and mocking but not meant in a dickish way. "Is this the part where I act shocked?"

"How did you know with Nina? How did you know…."

"How did I know Nina was it for me?"

I nod.

"I didn't." He stares back at me. "I thought she was a prostitute."

I roll my eyes and give up on getting anything useful from him.

"Wait a second. I'm fucking with you."

A beat passes, and then he steps around his desk and hands me the phone. "She became my obsession. It's like everything you think you don't want in life falls in your lap and demands focus until it becomes all you want. All you can focus on."

I take the phone from him and round the chair to sit down. "But there wasn't a solid moment when you knew for sure."

He rubs at his chin, his mind ticking as he leans back on the desk. "I guess there were lots. But I had this gut feeling when you texted me that pixie."

"That first night?" I ask, surprised.

He shrugs. "I don't fucking know, Montgomery. It was years ago now. It wasn't just one moment; it was every moment. Good and bad. More and more pieces."

I sigh and scrub a hand down my face. "I just don't know if now's the time to do this with her. She needs to focus on her job. I feel like I'm holding her back."

"She'd let you hold her back." I look up at him, hating that he's agreeing and isn't going to bullshit me. "She became dependent on whatever shit the two of you have going on long before she left. She isn't calling Nina, which makes me wonder who she is calling." He pops a brow.

"She doesn't really have anyone in New York," I admit.

He nods, a strained smile pulling at his mouth. "Which is perfect for you."

"I'm a prick for wanting that, aren't I?"

"I'd be the same."

We sit in silence for a moment.

"Nina said something the other night, and I agreed with her. You're different now. Not just since Luce left—before that too. You aren't out like you used to be before we met the girls."

"Yeah, they spent the last three years cockblocking the fuck out of me, that's why."

"True." He chuckles, standing. "Luce is a smart girl, and she knows how it is between the two of you. I trust you, Montgomery, no matter how stupid that might be." I snigger and lift my eyes to his. "Just go with it, see what happens."

Just go with it.

That's all I ever do, and this time I don't think it's going to work out for me.

I GET HOME EARLY EVENING. Feeling like crap from the night before, I plug the phone Mason gave me into the charger and take a shower.

After weeks of texts and calls, I know I have to be real about what's happening between Luce and me. She deserves more than I can give her, and with her internship being so new, we can't keep doing it my way. We have to have a conversation about tomorrow. And the next day. And the day after that.

I've never lived by a plan, and it feels fucking stupid.

Why would I want to plan something when our lives change with every second?

Lucy

I'M LYING on my bed asleep when Elliot calls me. It's late, which means it's even later at home. It's been the longest day, and my emotions have been at an all-time low since I arrived in New York.

When I told my family about the internship, and they were so excited for me, I wanted to do them proud. Elliot wanted this for me, and I'm glad I listened to him, but in the process, we somehow pushed ourselves into this messy area that I don't want to leave.

It feels impossible.

But I don't see a way back.

I sit up and let it ring out, choosing to quickly fix my face in the bathroom mirror before speaking to him.

I call him back once I'm sat downstairs in the lounge, choosing to FaceTime like he had. Anticipation stirs inside of me, making my limbs become restless beneath me. I know he will be annoyed that I implied he slept with Harriet, and I need to apologise to him for that.

He answers, and I wait while the screen catches up.

His beautiful face fills my phone, and he instantly gives me a small smile.

"Hi."

"Hey, Luce," he mutters, his voice tired and like velvet slipping over my skin.

"It's late there," I say, my throat tight and burning.

His deep blue eyes are glued to me. They make me want to run away until I can find a way back into their abyss. "I was at the gym."

I roll my lips, not knowing where to start.

"Luce," he calls.

I lift my head to look at him, his eyes looking sad.

"You've been crying?"

It's not a question.

He knows.

"Not since this morning." I lie.

He looks to his lap and then back up at me, and I hate the look he gives me. I feel like I should know what's coming, and maybe I do.

"I'm sorry you felt the way you did last night. It isn't fair you were put in that situation."

"I was jealous. It wasn't your fault," I tell him.

"No, but it wasn't your fault either."

"I think with moving and then seeing you all out for the gala, it felt like everything I've been holding in hit at once." I feel my eyes well, and I blink my tears away. "I felt left out more than ever. I miss you all, and then Harriet answered the phone—"

"Luce… I'm letting you go."

My face drops. Nothing forms in my mind, and I stare blankly at the screen. It's impossible to form a coherent thought when my body feels like it's splitting in two.

"I want you to try doing this alone. Without me."

"No," I say without thinking as panic crawls up my throat like a choke hold.

"It's not because of anyone else. I'm not mad at you—"

"Elliot, don't be so stu—"

"But you left to do something for you, and all I've done is make it impossible."

What is he saying? Doesn't he see that he has been the one who's made it possible? I shake my head, my nails pinching into my palm, piercing the sensitive skin. I shake my head. "I don't understand."

"If I don't do this, you won't ever know what it's like to live this dream the way you intended to. You'll regret it."

"You're making out like I'm not happy here. I was fine up until last night."

He runs a hand through his hair, his gaze not leaving me and very obviously conflicted. "I know that, and this works for me—"

"Then why change it!" My voice cracks and I frown in annoyance. I already know I'm going to cry, but I fight it.

"Because you won't ever know what it's like to be alone if you don't try."

"I am alone!"

He tilts his head with a look.

"So, what, you're not going to speak to me anymore?" I snap the words, and they snap straight back, slapping me in the chest full force. I grind my teeth. "You told me to come to New York, Elliot. You said I should be here and pushed and pushed."

"You should be there."

"Then why are you abandoning me?"

"I'm not." He shakes his head, his face screwing up in pain. "Don't say that."

"Then what? You want to be friends again? Go back to the way it was so you can fuck around like before?"

His nostrils flare, and I stare him down, feeling like a horrible bitch for the words I just threw at him.

"Why have you done this?" I choke out.

"Luce—"

"Weeks and weeks of pulling me in, and now you just want to drop me." I knew it. I told myself it was possible, but I never believed it would happen. "I'm in New York, I still need you guys."

"We're here, Luce."

I snigger and shake my head, a tear rolling free.

"I stand by our pact—"

My chin wobbles. "Why bother—"

"But you have to stand by it too." He stops when a sob slips past my lips, then breaks me completely when he whispers, "Baby...."

I look up at the phone, a tear dripping from my nose.

"Enjoy this. Please. Fall in love with the city. Almendo's. Yourself. I'm going to be right here waiting. What's a year?"

I stare at him in disbelief.

"I'll still come out and see you, and of course, we can still talk." He laughs. As if it's a joke.

"No," I mutter, shaking my head.

"You're mad at me," he states. "I'm not trying to hurt you, Lucy."

"Well, then you failed," I cry.

"I don't do this. I never—"

"Don't do what?"

"Plan. Spend my time agonising over what I'm doing and how it affects other people. I live and let live."

"So you're doing this because it's inconvenient for you."

He tuts, his own annoyance seeping through. "I'm doing this for *you*."

"That's bullshit. If you wanted to carry this on, you would. You don't want this, and you're using me leaving as an excuse."

"I'm not. I just want you to experience this like you wanted to."

All I wanted to do was make them proud. Now I'm in a city I don't truly know, and he wants to cut me off.

"I'm going to go." I sniff, wiping at my face.

"Will you do something for me?" he asks, his eyes shining—wild and lost.

"What?"

"Call the girls. I know you don't want to speak to me right now, but I can't stand the idea of you being upset."

He's all I want right now.

How does he not know that?

"Goodbye, Elliot."

"Luce—"

I hang up the phone and immediately break down. My shoulders shake as I fall forward on the sofa.

I want to go home.

I want to go back to how things were.

Back before I fell in love with him.

MONDAY MORNING HURTS WORSE than I could have imagined. I barely slept last night. Everything Elliot said to me replayed like a broken record in my mind, evoking all the emotions that I felt in the moment over and over again.

I wondered if he was awake. I wondered how someone can go from caring so much, being at the other end of the phone and sharing intimate moments with them, to then just stop and say no more. I wondered if he felt the way I did. I wondered if he was already with someone else.

That one hurt the most.

I've felt so strong for weeks. Living in New York has been

an eye-opener, but I've been doing it. I'm surviving. Despite the way I let things twist me up inside, I did what I said I would do.

Why does he think he's getting in the way of that?

It feels like an excuse. When I said I wanted to do this alone, I meant it. I want that independence. But that doesn't mean I want to cut off my lifelines. Elliot knows how much I need him.

Surely living in this city alone is enough for them all?

Are they not proud of me?

Are they all sitting at home, thinking I'm not doing it right because I'm building something with Elliot?

I pull myself out of bed and head to work early. I arrive at eight and find my desk filled with a list of to-dos.

The girls arrive just before nine, and I go out of my way to avoid having to chat with them over coffee, pretending I'm too busy to stop. I'm pretty sure I have bags under my eyes, and if anyone asks me if I'm okay, I might ball my eyes out.

I work through lunch, not wanting to stop and think.

By the time five thirty rolls around, my feet are throbbing, and my stomach is growling at me. I leave the office and walk down the street, not paying any mind to anyone around me.

I don't have anything waiting for me back at the house, and I don't want to sit on my own all night. The girls are probably busy, although I don't feel like checking in with them. It hurts, but London seems like a side, and I'm not on it.

I walk to the nearest shop and buy a sandwich and a bunch of flowers, knowing I won't be able to lay them. Then

I walk to the chapel. One of the only places I don't feel alone.

I don't check my phone until hours later when I get home. Nina has called and texted me, but I don't reply in case I wake her up. Elliot has sent a message, but I don't even open it, knowing I need to sleep. I'll call my mum first thing. She will be able to make me feel better without even trying.

I'VE CALLED into work sick for the second day running.

Two days since the phone call with Elliot, and everything feels like it's getting worse. The sadness inside of me seems to outshine the day's existence, and all I want is to go home.

But what I want more than that is to be stronger. To stop feeling like an anxious mess whenever my life's routine changes.

I didn't get out of bed yesterday other than to eat, and when I did, I carried it back to my bed. I'm ignoring my friends, and I know they will worry. But I also know that Elliot will tell someone what happened. He doesn't keep anything to himself. He would've told Mason, and Mason would have told Nina.

Nina: Right. Last chance or I'm flying out

Luce: I'm okay

Luce: Promise

Luce: Give me a day or two. Please.

Nina: No you're worrying me. Why won't you talk to me!

I don't reply to her most recent message, hoping she reads it back and knows that I mean what I say. Because I will be fine. I'm always fine. It just takes a couple days of bone-aching reality. At least, I think it's real. It's like all the bad thoughts stolen from my best days unload in one giant pile in my brain.

Brain tip day.

Pickup time: Unknown.

But I *will* be fine.

IT'S FRIDAY NIGHT, and I'm on my way home from another afternoon and evening at the chapel. It's become my go-to spot when I need to get out of the house, and I know Ralph would appreciate me visiting.

I'm pretty sure the majority of New York will be out, partying and feeling alive on this Friday night, but I can't think of anything worse.

I feel alone.

Which is a me problem because I have an entire family at home who have been calling me all week.

My steps are unhurried as I walk down my street and towards the house. The whole street is super quiet, and that makes it hard because I want to love it here. And I have loved New York so far, but the last few days have been the hardest by a mile.

I'm scared.

Sick to my stomach to even go to the shop on the corner when last week I walked in with all the confidence in the world.

Rounding the steps to the house, I spot someone in the gated area below, and instead of making eye contact, I pull my bag from my shoulder and quickly look for my key. Just as I wrap my fingers around the cool metal, someone says my name.

I lift my head at the familiar voice and slowly smile, my first genuine smile in days. "Maxwell."

23

Lucy

"Hey!" he says, smiling as he walks up the steps with a box in his hands. "How are you?"

I swallow, pulling my jacket tighter. "I'm okay." I nod.

He looks at me, really looks at me. Then he nods over his shoulder, his lips twisting up in a coy but knowing smile. "Alec and Polly are moving in."

I look past him, my shoulders relaxing as what he's said registers. "Ralph agreed?" I say, surprised. I've not heard anything from Maxwell in weeks, and Ralph never mentioned anything when I'd spoken to him on the phone a couple of days ago.

"Yeah, the realtor called this morning to let them know. Thank you for talking to him."

I smile, and it's even wider than before. "Of course."

"We're nearly done if you want to get some food with us?"

I swallow, a frown forming as I nod in agreement. "That would be lovely. Thank you."

Maxwell being here, showing up out of the blue, it takes me back to the moment I met him on the plane.

"Alright, give us twenty to move these last few boxes, and I'll come up and get you."

"Okay." I turn, unlocking my door as I speak over my shoulder. "I'm going to take a quick shower," I tell him.

"See you in a bit."

As soon as I'm in the house, I sink back against the door and slide to the ground. "I'm okay," I whisper to myself, closing my eyes as a tear falls down my cheek, an actual smile—a real one—slips into place. "I'm going to be fine."

One week post-Elliot call

Nina: Luce I miss you. I was hoping to fly out maybe at the end of the month. Let me know so I can plan it around work xxxx

Meg: Nina's worried, Luce. You good?

Scar: Hey! Wanna do a group call tonight??

Elliot: Are you free tonight?

Elliot: Luce call me.

Elliot: I took Ellis ice skating today after he saw pictures of The Rink at Rockefeller Center. He wanted to know what it was all about. He misses you.

Shit. The girls have obviously been talking. I've thrown myself into work this week, and it's been a godsend. I'm not ignoring my family and friends. I just need a minute to work out how I feel.

I text Nina.

Luce: I'm good I promise. Just been busy but I'll call tomorrow.

Two weeks post-Elliot call

Mum: Hello darling. Missing you today. I popped in to see Jean at the shop and she gushed about how well you're doing. She said Almendo has been nominated for an award? You never told us. Call me soon please. Mum xxx

Nina: Black or red?

Two images sit below Nina's text. She's wearing two different dresses and looks phenomenal in both. I wonder where she's going.

Luce: Red

Luce: With your hair down and straight

Elliot: Answer your phone Luce

One month post-Elliot call

Nina: You've called me three times in three weeks. I know you said work is busy but I know it's Elliot. I've booked a flight. Will be with you in two weeks bitch.

Fuck.

Luce: What about work?

Nina: What about us? Stop avoiding me! Can I call?

Luce: I'm in work

Nina: Don't shut me out. It's me.

Polly: We're heading out tonight. Are you coming?

My eyes well as I read Nina's most recent message. It's just gone two, and I'm on my lunch break.

I make the decision to call her.

"Luce!"

"Hey." I force a smile, even though she can't see me.

"How are you? How's work been this week?"

"Works been fine. How are the kids?"

"Ugh." She huffs, making my chest ache at the normalcy of it. "Ellis has just gone down. Not sure about Ave. They're okay, though. Ellis is talking about you constantly. They probably find it odd given you were such a big part of their routine."

"I miss them."

"Well, *we* miss you! I don't think we've ever been this long without talking properly. I know you have this walk coming up with the company, but I also know you're struggling. I can feel it. Is that weird?"

"I guess not." I smile, loving and hating how well she knows me.

"We did spend our entire lives joined at the hip."

I roll my lips as a wave of tears threatens. The urge to off-load my life onto her is strong.

It's always terrifying pulling someone into your circle. They go from the safety of having a perception of you—the Instagram reel—to uncovering the you who truly walks this earth. They see your struggles and adversity. The ups and the downs. The mistakes and the selfishness. I wish I could protect them from it. Stop them from bearing witness to the girl behind the rose-tinted glasses.

But then, who would pull us back from all the shit?

Who'd save us if it wasn't for our saviours?

"Luce, I'm worried. I just need to know you're okay."

"I'm okay."

"But you're struggling?"

I toy with my lips, not knowing what to say. "I feel better now. The last couple of weeks were hard."

Different.

"Well, that's good. I can't wait to see you. Meg is trying to get time off, but it's not looking good. Scar is going to stay back with Ellis and Ave."

"It will be really good to see you. Do you remember Max—"

"Shit! Shh…" She tuts. "Ellis is up… Mase!" She calls out then there's silence. "Damn it. Just a sec, Luce."

I smile as I hear Ellis's little sleepy voice paired with his sniffles.

"Back into bed, baby."

"I go down to Ave room, Mummy."

"No, Ave is learning to sleep on her own."

"But she is so far way."

"Come on, back into bed. You have nursery tomorr—"

The phone disconnects, and I pull it from my ear and check the screen. Something about the call makes me feel a little bit lighter than I have in weeks, and it makes the prospect of Nina coming to New York that much more exciting.

I need her.

Five weeks post-Elliot call

Elliot: I've called you seventeen times in the last month. How many times have you called me Luce?

Elliot: I just want to give you a chance to do this on your own

Princess: What do you think I'm doing?

Elliot: Being a mad bitch

Elliot: Don't be shocked. It's true

Princess: I don't want to fight about it

Elliot: If I call will you answer?

Princess: Not right now. I'm with friends.

Elliot: Where?

Elliot: Share your location

Elliot: Luce

"One cosmopolitan for the lady."

I look up from the phone as Maxwell hands me his homemade cocktail. "Thank you, Max." I take the drink, my phone feeling like a lead weight in my lap. "I feel like we should be helping them," I say, looking through the terrace windows and into the kitchen where Alec and Polly are washing up our dinner dishes. The terrace spans the entire back of the house, with bifold doors that are currently only half-open.

"You cooked. They clean. It's the rules."

"And what did you do?" I ask, my top lip curling as I bring the salted rim of the glass to my lips.

"I washed the kidney beans."

"Washed the kidney beans," I repeat with a chuckle. "Of course, you did. Sorry, Nigella."

He shakes his head laughing, then drops his eyes to his

beer as his features warm. "You must be excited to see Nina. Was that who you were texting?"

"No," I mutter, thinking back to Elliot's messages.

He's barely texted for the past two weeks, but he calls almost every night. I want to answer, but I also know that if I do, I'll let him pick me straight back up. Which gives him too much of an opportunity to drop me again. There was truth in his words, as much as I didn't want to see it at the time. He was wrong to think he was getting in the way of me living out my dream—he was very wrong about that. But me not living my dream the way I intended to, without restraint, without slipping into routines, and confiding myself to a hotel room for the majority of my nights, he was right about that.

He just failed to see all the ways he made me stronger.

"No, that was my friend, Elliot. And yes, I am excited. I've never been away from her for this long. Or my family."

"Only another ten months, and you'll be home. Long gone from this place," he says nonchalantly, clearly trying to make me feel better.

"That's odd, right?" I say, looking around the room as I rest my head on my hand. "This has been such a life-changing experience already. I met Ralph, and you guys, who I already know will be friends for life, and yet one day, this will all just be a memory. A story I'll tell people about the time I took a year-long internship in New York. A small scene in maybe my most pivotal chapter yet…."

Maxwell smiles over at me. "You sure know how to get deep inside that pretty head of yours."

Outta your head.

I crave the words as fiercely as I crave the rasp they'd be spoken with.

"It's a talent," I say as I knock back the rest of my cocktail.

"It won't be as insignificant as you think," he tells me, and the way he says it has me lowering my glass to my lap again. "You're pure, Luce. Sweet, kind, and ruthlessly transparent. You wear your heart on your sleeve, yet you have this grit and determination cloaked around you like armour—and you know it. *That's* a talent. We might not be in the middle of a war, but I've seen grown men lie in their beds weeping while they've missed home, and then when they wake up, I've watched as they've taken it out with them onto the battlefield. It's dangerous to act with emotion, but it's human nature. You have a self-awareness that's hard to come by."

"Indecisiveness will get you killed," I recite the words he once spoke to me.

"Exactly that." He points the neck of his beer bottle at me.

"I'm not sure my self-awareness is as sharp as you think it is. I'm the most indecisive person I know."

"You're here, aren't you? It's where that indecisiveness is coming from that's important. Is it weakness?" He looks at me dead in the eye, telling me that isn't it without saying the words. "Or is it the need to be who you know you are?"

"I've never thought about it like that." But he's right. I've always known why I want what I do. My doubt comes from the way it could make me feel. The way it could make the people around me feel.

It's why I cling to routine.

"Guys," Polly pokes her head around the door, gauging the mood in the room as she interrupts. "Sorry, do you want custard or ice cream with the brownies?"

"Custard with brownies?" I question incredulously. "You're having a giraffe, surely?"

"Having a giraffe." Maxwell chuckles. "You Brits have an idiom for everything."

"We do," I agree, standing from the sofa and trailing after Polly into the kitchen. "Ice cream for me, please."

"And me." Maxwell joins me at the kitchen island. His arm slips around my neck and settles high across my chest, then he pulls me into a hug from behind as if he's done it a million times before.

"You okay to drop a monitor down to Felix later? I told him it would be with him by the end of the day," Alec asks, his question clearly directed at Maxwell as he scrolls on his phone.

"Sure," Max replies into the top of my head. "I'll drop it on my way home."

"Felix," I admire. "I've always loved that name. It's on my baby name list, actually."

"It's not his real name," Max tells me with a hint of amusement in his voice. "He's a Carl, but fucking hates it. Felix is his late father's name, I think."

"He looks like a fucking Carl too," Alec adds, with a chuckle, pocketing his phone.

"Wait." Polly shakes her head to halt the conversation, blatant confusion washing the pink hue from her cheeks. "Felix isn't Felix's real name?"

"Nah, we just call him it to keep him sweet." I watch as

Alec rests his hands on the kitchen island, his eyes on his girlfriend in deep fascination.

"I won't be able to look at him the same way ever again," she says, turning her back to dig the ice cream out of the fridge freezer.

"Just don't go calling him Carl. He doesn't fucking like it."

"Noted," she sings, placing the desserts on the counter. "Let's eat!"

Eight weeks post-Elliot call

Nina: You won the award?? Okay this is totally worth blowing me off for hahaha! SO PROUD!

Luce: I did! I'm sorry you couldn't come out. We have to rearrange it. I desperately need to see you.

Nina: Love you always! Go celebrate!

Polly: Congrats girl! We knew you'd do it!

Mum: We are so proud of you darling. Not even three months in and you're bossing it! Mum xxxxxxxx

Luce: Thanks Mum! I can't believe it. I'll call later xxxx

Elliot: I'm so fucking proud of you baby

My heart jolts as I read his message, the alcohol not seeping deep enough to numb it completely.

Princess: Thank you x

Princess: I miss you

Elliot: You do?

Always.

"To Lucy." My eyes lift to Maxwell, who stands beside me at the table. "For absolutely smashing it and making Chelsea's face look as sour as spoilt milk!"

"Sit down!" I hiss, pulling on his coat until he falls heavy into the seat next to me. "You're embarrassing me."

"Everyone should know." He leans in and kisses my neck, and I ease away, smiling.

Something registers in my brain—the smell of his cologne and the bitter stench of beer triggering a memory.

We'd been at the house. Maxwell stayed late after Polly and Alec had left. We fell asleep on the sofa watching a movie, and when I woke up, Maxwell was carrying me to my bed.

He placed me down on the mattress and kissed my forehead, but just as he turned to leave, I grabbed his hand.

"Will you stay?"

"Do you want me to stay?"

"I don't want to be alone. I feel so alone."

He pulled back the comforter and slid into the bed, the heat from his body welcomed and so, so foreign.

I'd not had company for so long.

"It's safe here. You shouldn't be so afraid to be alone. The security of the street and house was one of the reasons Alec was so keen to move in."

I smiled, my eyes growing heavy.

"Luce."

"Hmmm."

I lifted my head. His face was right there.

He kissed me.

Maxwell kissed me, and it felt like the most incredible, fulfilling, fucked-up, traitorous kiss I'd ever received.

"I should get you home."

I snap back to the here and now. My eyes easing into focus only to find Maxwell entranced on me, the bar bustling with music all around us.

I nod, sliding from the seat.

Ten weeks post-Elliot call

"Luce?"

"Up here!" I call from my bedroom, sliding on my robe with a smile. "You're home early?"

Maxwell appears in the doorway, his shoulder falling to rest against the wood. "We finished for the week. Both of us were ready to get home."

"Everything went okay?" I ask, noting his tired eyes.

"I am now I'm back." He pushes off the frame and walks towards me, kissing the corner of my mouth when he reaches me. "How's things been here?"

"Quiet," I tell him, slipping into my wardrobe so I can change.

"Has Polly been up at all?" he asks, following me.

"Nope. I saw her when I was leaving on Wednesday, but otherwise she's been busy."

"Hmm, Alec couldn't get hold of her yesterday." He straightens his jeans in the mirror then turns to leave. "Get dressed, we'll go out for dinner."

I reach for his wrist. "Can we get a takeaway instead? I was going to put my comfies on. It's been the longest week."

His eyes fall to my grip on him, and he steps closer,

sliding his hands over my waist. "Of course. Do you want to pick a movie?"

I shake my head no. "You can pick."

"I always have to pick," he mutters, leaning in and kissing my shoulder. "How about we sack off the movie and dinner? Just climb straight into bed." His nose trails up my neck, making my skin pebble.

"You don't want to eat now?"

"I'm hungry for something else."

I work on a swallow, closing my eyes as his lips continue their way up my neck and to my mouth.

He guides me from the wardrobe and over to the bed.

"Max, you know I can't—"

"Still?" he questions, pulling back.

When Maxwell first tried sleeping with me, I told him I was on birth control and that it was causing me to bleed irregularly. At the time, it felt too soon for me to be entertaining another man after what I shared with Elliot. Now, it feels like an excuse.

I needed a friend, yet it's as if I blinked, and Maxwell became something I wasn't ready for, and now we have this messy relationship between us because of that.

"I'm sorry," I tell him, placing my palm on his chest.

"You don't need to apologise." He eases his hand through my hair, running his fingers over my scalp. "But if you're going to… at least do it on your knees."

He pushes me towards the ground, my heart in my throat. It's not that I don't want to do this, it's….

Or maybe that's exactly it?

Nina: Help… I know I'm annoying.

I stare at the message and the four images of Nina smiling as she stands in the dresses. Another tear slips down my temple and into my pillow.

Luce: Black

Seems fitting.

Nina: You okay? You've been quiet

Nina: Have you heard from Elliot lately?

I've not heard from Elliot in over a month other than him texting to congratulate me on the award Almendo won. He stopped calling eventually, and I know it's his way of making sure I do this right.

Somehow, though, I think I got it all wrong.

Eleven weeks post-Elliot call

"Hi," I call out, walking through the house and into the kitchen. I find Maxwell at the cooker stirring something on the range. "What's this?" I frown, inhaling the delicious aromas.

He places the wooden spoon on the side and walks across to me. "I wanted to do something nice for you. You seemed sad this morning, and I know you got upset last night."

I roll my lips and try to figure out what to say to that. "I did."

"You don't have to worry about it, okay? I know it's not your fault."

Not my fault. Is he for real? It's the same conversation week in, week out. "Max, you called me a frigid bitch."

"Luce," he drawls, stepping closer and wrapping an arm around my waist. "Think about it from my standpoint. Weeks and weeks, and still the doctors can't get it right? I'm a fucking man, babe. And my time with you is limited. That is unless…I can make you stay."

My brows dip as he pulls me to him, my head slipping past his shoulder as he holds me against his hard body.

That's never been part of the plan.

Eight more months, and I'll be home.

Long gone from this place.

"I'm out with Polly tonight for food, remember?" I pull away, feeling off with his insincere—practically nonexistent—apology. "What?"

"I told you about it." I walk to the fridge and reach for a bottle of wine, pouring myself a small glass.

"You didn't. You're seriously going out when I've done all this?"

"I *did* tell you, Max," I bite out, slamming the fridge door shut harder than necessary. I close my eyes, instantly feeling shitty for taking the tone I have. "Sorry. Look, thank you for cooking, I appreciate it. But I told you I was out for food this evening. I plan to pop to the cemetery then—"

I frown as Maxwell tuts, cutting me off.

"Alright, whatever. Go to the fucking cemetery." He turns his back and continues to stir the dinner.

Not wanting to argue with him—something that's been happening more and more these last couple weeks—I leave the kitchen and make my way up the stairs to change.

I flinch, pausing midstep as the telling sound of a saucepan smashes against a wall.

Twelve weeks post-Elliot call

Megan: It's early as shit but HAPPY FUCKING BIRTHDAY queen!!

Nina: The kids want to call! Answer your phone birthday girl!

Mase: Have a good one Luce

Mum: Happy birthday darling! Let us know when you're up xxxx

Polly: Happy Birthday Lucy

Elliot: Not a thing

Not a thing.

Maxwell: I'm sorry I can't be there. I'll make this up to you, okay

Maxwell: Call me when you get this.

My cosmopolitan is ice cold against my hand, but I welcome the sharp sting as it cools the burning that wraps from my wrist around to my thumb.

Dropping my phone to the bar, I consider who to reply to.

Home or Maxwell.

I swipe up, discarding the message screen as I take a large gulp of my drink. Maybe I could go to the chapel. It's been days since I've been.

Maybe I should go home.

I shake my head. Birthdays are important to my family. We don't get away with not celebrating together. Mum wanted to fly out, but I told her no. Nina wanted me to fly home, and I said no. I feel bad. It's like I'm depriving them of something.

Days like today, I wonder if maybe going home is

exactly what I should do. But then I get brain tip, things start to get better, and I go again.

Routine.

My bittersweet carousel.

I sigh and look at my lap, feeling ready to up and leave, when the warmth of two hands slip over my eyes.

My body tenses.

Goose bumps scatter up my arms, sending my back straight as the air shifts. And then I smell him, his heady scent bleeding into the very depths of me.

"Outta your head, princess."

I grab his wrists, pulling them away and looking at his hands before I spin. My jaw drops, and without thinking, I jump down from the stool and leap into his arms, hoping the devastatingly handsome smile he's wearing embeds itself somewhere inside my soul and never leaves me again.

My legs hook at his back, and he holds me, spinning me around twice in the middle of the bar. "Happy birthday, Luce."

"You're here."

"I am." He chuckles.

I pull back, looking at his face again. "You came to New York." My hand reaches subconsciously to run through his short, silky blond waves.

He leans into my touch, his eyes closing. "Hmmm. It's a miracle I lasted this long."

A laugh breaks through, and I lock my legs tighter.

Elliot licks his lips and drops his heavy gaze to my mouth. "You look perfect tonight."

My eyes flick around his face, trying to figure out if he's

real. I'm trying to hold back tears, and it's messing with my ability to speak. "How did you know where I was?"

It's as if the universe knew I needed him.

"Nina." He grins. "You shared your location."

I slide my legs to the floor. My hands linger on his arms, and I don't let go, but neither does he. His hands are plastered against my lower back, smoothing over and over as if he can't get enough.

My cheeks blush.

This was all I wanted.

Him here.

In New York....

"Do you want a drink?" I ask, my heart rate rocketing as what feels like the weight of the world lands on my shoulders.

He smiles right back at me. God, I've missed his light. "If you don't have plans… could I take you out? I have a reservat—"

"Yes."

"Yeah?" He smirks, his jaw razor sharp.

"Take me out, Elliot."

His face settles, the hard angles I love turning to the soft contours I adore. He watches me. Pain, guilt, and too much of everything, reflecting onto me. "Fuck, I missed you."

He swoops in, his lips dusting the corner of my lip in a kiss that could be played off as nothing.

It is far from nothing.

It's the butterflies in my stomach.

It's the energy in the room.

It is the organ in my chest, beating loud enough to wake up my sad little soul.

"You miss me, princess?" he whispers.

I nod, my brows pulling in as everything we've endured over the last three months slaps me in the face all over again. I get the image of me on my sofa, his words breaking me. I wish he never did it. I wish we could go back in time. "You're an idiot," I mutter.

"No, I'm a *fucking* idiot." He slides his palm from my shoulder to my neck, slipping around to hold my nape. He pulls me to him, kissing my brow quickly before pulling away. "Come on, I want to take you someplace special before I take you home."

"Elliot, we need to—"

"Just…" He rolls his lips, and the look on his face tells me he knows. Or he thinks he knows. Truth is, I don't think he has any idea. "Luce, for one night, please. It's your birthday. Forget about everything else and do this thing with me."

"I can't—"

He steps closer, pulling me so close I have to tilt my head back to look at him. I'm weak to him. And maybe it's because I know I deserve this. I do deserve this. "Please, baby," he whispers.

I swallow, conflicted when the answer is simple.

I shouldn't do this.

24

Elliot

I CAN SEE THE HESITATION IN HER EYES. IT'S PAIN INDUCED and my own fault. She should have slapped me around the face when she spun around. It's what I expected.

She might have had her fair share of stubbornness over these last few months, but I did it. I told her to do it.

"Dinner. Just me and you, please?"

She hasn't taken her eyes off me, and I can tell she's lost in thought. I don't want to force her out of her own head, but I know she doesn't need to be there.

"Do I need to give you one of your birthday presents to sweeten you up first," I question, pulling on a strand of her blonde hair. "I promise we will talk later."

"You brought me a present?"

"Presents," I correct. Reaching into my pocket, I pull out one of the envelopes. "That's a good one," I tell her, tipping my chin at it as she flips it over.

"What is it?" she grins, her face getting giddy and child-like. "Why did you get me presents?"

"Just open it, Morgan."

She tears into the paper, pulling out the three small slips. "Tickets?" She laughs, reading the pieces of card. She holds them to her chest, her eyes shining. "You're so stupid, I love it."

"Three movie passes." I reach out and catch the blonde curl shielding her face from me, tucking it behind her ear. "You get to pick, but they can't be the same movie."

"I already know exactly what I'm going to pick." She puts them into her bag, and I watch on, hopeful as she pulls it up onto her shoulder.

"Does this mean you're coming to dinner with me?"

"Of course, I'll come to dinner with you, Ell."

Well, thank fuck for that. I smile down at her, the knot in my stomach easing as I reach for her hand.

"Shit!" she hisses, snatching it away.

I reach for it again so I can see. "What's wrong?"

She shakes it out, flexing it. "Nothing. I jammed my hand in the door this morning. It's been killing me ever since."

"Stop shaking it so I can see."

"It's fine, let's just go to dinner." She walks out through the bar in a rush, and I start after her.

She's still pissed at me, and I know it's going to take more than dinner to get her back on my side. I hurt her even if I didn't want to, and I stand by it. Leaving her to do this alone was the right thing to do.

Out on the street, I quickly catch up with her, and I struggle to keep the smile off my face when I do.

"What?" she frowns, mad-bitch face in place as she looks between me and the throngs of people in front of us.

"Where are you going exactly?"

She comes to a stop, causing people to step around her. Of course, she apologises.

"I have no idea."

I HOLD open the door to the rooftop so that Lucy can walk through. When we arrived at the nightclub, I could tell she was unsure. The music was vibrating at our feet, and bodies were already packed tight together on the dance floor.

I flew in late after a delay at the airport, and it set my plans back by hours. Luckily, I know enough people in New York to pull everything off.

"I didn't know if you'd want to go out or…."

She observes the fairy-lit rooftop and the single table in the middle of the space. "So, you did both?"

The tips of my fingers on her hip guide her forward. She's wearing a black dress tonight. It's strapless and fitted and has no business fucking with me the way it does. "I thought we could eat first before we celebrate."

I want tonight to be special for her.

I want every day to be special for her.

"This is beautiful," she tells me as she walks toward the table. I pull her chair out for her to sit down.

"Are you warm enough?" I move the outdoor heater closer until it towers over her. "I got you a blanket just in case."

When she doesn't say anything, I look in her direction,

finding her already focused on me with an amused smirk twisting up her lips.

"What?"

"I'm fine. Now come sit down."

I sit in the chair opposite her and place my forearms on the table, an awkward feeling settling over me as I survey the distance between us. I pull my chair in a little, and she laughs.

"What?"

"What is up with you?" She chuckles, her face illuminated by the glowing lights overhead. She sounds a little nervous. "You look like me with the balls. You've not got them stuck up your ass, have you?"

"Wine?"

I watch as Lucy's shoulders jolt and her face drops.

"Please," I tell the waiter. I smile over at Lucy as her cheeks colour. "Luce?"

She looks up and nods. "Thank you."

This time I'm the one laughing as the waiter walks away.

"How mortifying. Can we leave?"

"No chance. And for the record, there isn't anything in my ass now, and there won't be anything in my ass ever."

She shakes her head and eyes her lap, mumbling something I can't quite hear.

"What was that?"

"Nothing."

I tilt my head, loving the naughty glint in her eye. I've never had this side of her before. She used to shut me down any chance she got. I was flirty, and she loved it, but since that night in the restaurant, she gives it right back.

I don't even think she can control it anymore.

This is different.

Us.

"The power you wield with those fuck-me eyes, princess."

"Excuse me?" she asks, foreign offence with a hand to her chest.

"You know exactly what I'm talking about."

"I don't."

"No? Then why didn't you ever look at me like this before?"

"You think I want to fuck you now?" she whispers, looking over her shoulder this time.

"Do you?"

The little vixen fucks me with her eyes, and I have to take a sip of my wine to drown the inappropriate words I was about to spew.

"I have an entire evening planned. How about we shelve this conversation?"

"You can't handle it?"

I point at her. "You won't handle it."

"We'll see."

I blow out a breath, needing to cool it before I do something I'll regret. "What do you want to eat? You can have anything you want." I try to change the subject.

"Anything?"

I lift my head from the menu to find her eyes still on me. I nod, swallowing down the adrenaline fighting to the surface.

She makes me feel unhinged.

"Can we skip straight to dessert? I want cake."

"I tap up a Michelin star chef for the night, and you want cake."

She bites her lip and nods her head. "Chocolate cake."

"I—" Fuck it. If she wants cake. "Sure. Why not?" I call the waiter over and ask him for the best chocolate cake he can get his hands on.

She sips her wine, watching me over the rim of her glass. "I still can't believe you're here."

"You thought I'd miss your birthday?"

"I was surprised Mum and Dad were so agreeable when they told me it was fine I wasn't coming home. I guess I should've known."

"We wouldn't have let you be alone. You know that." The need to explain myself weighs heavy on me. "I am sorry for what happened, Luce. The way it happened more than anything. I didn't want to hurt you, and I hope you know I only did it for you." I itch to reach out and pick up her hand. "I wanted you to have some time without me getting in your way. And look at what you've achieved. That award was for something you've been working on."

She nods, her face growing conflicted. I can tell she's listening to me, but her mind has gone elsewhere.

I smooth a hand down my chest and lean back, doubting if now is the time to talk about it. Maybe I should have let her have her say down in the restaurant like she wanted. "Do you want your present from Ellis?"

Her eyes light up, and it sparks stupid, irrational jealousy deep inside me.

He's just a kid.

I pull out the envelope and place it in the middle of the table. "He wrapped it himself."

Lucy slides out the terribly wrapped, small parcel. It's a little smaller than the size of her palm. She treats it like it's a bomb that's about to explode, gently picking at the edges of the paper.

"You won't break it."

She looks up, and I catch the glint in her eyes.

"Already?"

"I miss them so much."

I sigh, leaning forward and reaching for her arm. I brush my thumb over her wrist, wishing I could be closer. "I know you do."

She opens the present, a huge smile transforming her face when she finds the bracelet in the paper. But then her smile drops. "Wait. This is Nina's."

"What?"

"This is Nina's bangle. Mason bought it for her when they first met."

"Let me see." I hold out my hand, and she passes it to me.

I inspect the bracelet, noticing some words engraved on the inside. "That little shit!"

"Nina will die." She laughs. "Oh, bless him. He's the sweetest little boy."

"Sweetest little boy? He stole this."

"From his mother," Lucy deadpans.

"So. He told me he went shopping with Nina to get it."

"He's three years old. And he wanted to treat me." She grins.

"I can't believe he lied to me."

"And all to make his Auntie Luce happy…." She arches

a brow, tipping her head to the side. "If we ever needed to settle who the favourite is..."

"We know it's me."

She shakes her head, her eyes fixed on me with the warmest look in her gaze. Something feels different, and I can't put my finger on what. The way her eyes consume me as if she needs something. As if she is asking for something.

"Are you—"

"Oh my god, the cake!"

I turn to find two waiters carrying a huge, three-tier chocolate cake to the table.

"It's huge," Lucy shrieks with pure, unfiltered glee in her voice.

"I will just get the knife to cut it," one of the waiters tells me.

I start to sing her "Happy Birthday," and the other waiter weirdly sticks around and joins in. Lucy stands and blows out the candles, then swipes her finger through the chocolate icing.

"Hmmm. That's good," she tells me, pointing to the cake.

Thankfully, the waiter chooses to disappear.

Lucy uses her spoon to scoop up a piece of the gooey chocolate. I watch with intense fascination as she brings it to her mouth.

"Did you know you have fuck-me eyes… for my cake?"

I catch her gaze.

For the cake. Yeah, as if.

I tip my chin. "Come here, birthday girl."

She looks up at me through her brow, the spoon lodged in the cake.

She takes another bite. "Should I bring this?" She holds up her chocolaty spoon.

"Why else would I be asking you?"

"Well..." She stands, walking around the table to stand beside me. She places the plate down beside mine, then brings the spoon to my mouth. "I thought you said you'd eat your dessert without the spoon. Open."

She slips the spoon past my lips, her eyes flicking between my eyes and mouth.

"Good?" she whispers.

I wonder if she is thinking about pancakes. Late nights. Us. "Too good."

She smiles a warm smile, pursing her pouty lips before turning to walk back to her chair. She doesn't flinch when my arm bands around her waist. I pull her back to my lap.

"I'm sorry," I rasp against her ear.

Her head turns, her nose dusting my jaw. I catch her smile. "What for?"

"It's been too long. I don't feel like being a gentleman tonight."

I watch as she swallows thickly, her gaze lifting until it locks with mine. "Does that mean I can be someone else tonight?"

"Someone else?"

She nods.

"Why would you want to be someone else, Luce?"

Pain flashes in her eyes, and I wonder if it's because of what happened between us. What I did.

"Princess, you can be anyone you want to be. But I need you to always be real with me."

She shakes her head and sits up on my lap. "No. No,

tonight I want to pretend. I want to be the Lucy I was before I got here." I frown, not understanding.

Her hand moves to rest on my shoulder, and I wrap my arm around her back, slotting us together.

"Whatever you want, Luce."

Because I'd do fucking anything for this woman.

"One night. Me. You. And nothing else."

My eyes are glued to her. I try to dissect the look she gives me, but I don't find anything fast. She stands from my lap and holds her hand out to me. "I want to dance."

I stare at her hand until I see the hesitation register in her eyes. I stand, lacing my fingers with hers and not leaving any room for it. "Then we dance."

We enter the club from the back doors and find it just as full as it was when we first arrived—if not busier. Lucy immediately squeezes my hand tight, and I lean into her, keeping her back to my chest as I move us forward.

"I've got you."

"I need a drink!" she yells, twisting her neck to look into my eyes.

She's feeling anxious. I can see it in her wide gaze, and she wants me to see.

She needs me.

I usher us to the bar, keeping her snug to my front until we reach it. I place my arms on either side of her as I rest against the polished edge.

She looks everywhere around her, not focusing on one thing and not giving me the attention I want.

"Baby, breathe," I whisper against her ear, not knowing if she will fully hear me.

Her head drops back to my chest, and I wrap my arm around her waist, taking any weight she wants to give me.

"You smell divine," she tells me.

Her height puts her tilted head between my pecs. I look down at her and raise a brow. "Edible?"

Her grin tells me she'd take the fucking lot of me.

I feel her unease slip away as she closes her eyes and starts to sway to the music.

The coldhearted bastard in me wants to pick her up and take her home. It's been months since I've seen her, and to finally have her with me again—this time in my arms—it feels good.

"Luce," I groan into the top of her head, my fingers poised on her perfectly rounded hips.

She turns to face me, looking up as I lock her in again. "So, you missed me a little bit, huh?"

"Just a little smidge." I shrug.

"A smidge?"

I nod, our eyes saying more than our mouths in the moment. We can't look away, or at least I can't. She has the most hypnotising eyes—wild blues with a thick black band that conceals that illusioned ocean.

"Wanna know a secret?" she hums, moving so close I should inch back.

I don't.

Our noses brush, and she smiles as her body eases away from me. "I missed our calls the most." She nods her head, her eyes dropping to my lips. "I missed your voice at the end of my day more than anything else."

Fuck.

"What can I get you?"

She turns again at the sound of the barman's voice, and I lean into her as I order my drink, our bodies now flush. For a moment, we don't acknowledge the move, although we're both aware of it. But then Lucy does a little shuffle, and it's not a shuffle to shrug me off. It's a hip shuffle. It's a look how quickly I can get your dick up shuffle.

"Luce," I warn.

"Yes," she drawls out.

I look down at her. "Let's not start something we can't finish."

"We both know I can finish."

I snigger. "You're sucking the gentleman out of me by the minute."

"I am?" she sings, flipping her hair over her shoulder and letting it fall down her back. "I'm ever so sorry, you'll have to excuse"—she rolls her hips, grinding her ass over my dick—"me."

My head falls back, and I try to conceal the rumble that fights its way from my chest.

This time when I step back into her, I do it with force. My hand slips up her thigh and around to the side of her ass. "I'm a goner," I whisper into her ear. "You ruin me, baby. I had fucking plans tonight."

Her body shakes in my hold, and I watch as goose bumps shoot up her arms. Her reaction only fuels my need. Knowing she wants this as badly as I do sparks an already growing obsession.

"Come with me."

I ditch our drinks and move her to walk in front of me. I guide her with my hands on her waist.

Once we reach the dance floor, I pull her close to me. She comes willingly, placing her hands on my upper arms as she looks up at me with a sweet smile.

"Is your plan to seduce me with your dancing?" she asks.

"I've already seduced you, princess. This is me warming you up." I lean into her, making her back bend. "Stretching you out so that you can keep up later."

She laughs as I glide my nose up her cheek. "So thoughtful."

"I aim to please."

"Stop giving me your lines." She makes a move to slip out of my hold, throwing up her arm as she spins around. I catch her waist and haul her back against me, this time my front to her back. "I want my Elliot."

"I am your Elliot."

She looks up at me with a wicked smile.

Her hips start to move to the music, and I mould to her, enjoying the position it puts us in a little too much.

Everything about her is as I remember, and it makes the last three months of torture feel unnecessary. I shouldn't have worried about her. She's exactly as I remember her to be.

She turns as the song ends, and another one begins, and my dick strains in my trousers, desperately wanting to drag her back into me. Instead, she moulds to my front, slipping her hand around my neck and grinding her pelvis against my erection. Her mouth drops open, the desire in her gaze crystal clear and on display for the world to see. It's for me, though. That look, it's mine. "You're so fucking sexy like this."

"I am?" she speaks so close to my mouth I feel the breathy words against my lips.

We both know what's about to happen, and we're both delaying it. I've never kissed this woman, but it's something I've thought about a lot. We talked about it once, but I wonder if she's imagined it like I have.

I skim my hand up the back of her leg, my fingers brushing her lace underwear before teasing along the crease under her ass.

I lick my lip and then drop my eyes to hers. "I want these lips on me, baby. Wet and messy. Sucking me in—"

She grinds harder, moaning as my hand squeezes the sensitive flesh at her inner thigh. She knows my words have double meaning, and I crave more of her reaction to them.

"Luce," I rasp out.

She rolls her hips, and I meet her with the friction she wants. Her eyes are heavy, and her nose and lips skim everywhere but my lips. "Princess." I use my thumb to lift her chin, splaying my fingers around her jaw and throat. Her gaze finally locks.

My lips part.

And then I smile.

She doesn't give me anything back, her face bearing an almost pained look as she hovers right in front of me.

"Outta your head."

Our lips brush.

The music blares around us, but it's as if we are the only two people in the room. It's just us in this moment, standing still in the middle of the thrashing bodies.

I drag my thumb across her bottom lip, my eyes lost and glued to the pouty flesh when she quickly moves in and kisses me.

I freeze for a second, not expecting her to take control. But then, she pulls away, and before she can open her eyes, I take *her*—my way.

My lips seal over her mouth, and it's not as perfect as her sweet kiss. It's a hard kiss, with hunger at the root of it, driving us as far as we can go as we plaster our bodies together. It's not enough, though. My hands slide to the backs of her legs, and I lift her up and wrap her legs around my waist. Her hands slide over my face, scratching through my hair and dragging back over my stubble.

It drives me wild.

I lock her legs at my back myself and then push her hands off my face. "Get out of my way, Morgan," I groan playfully.

I suck on her lip until she hisses, then kiss the spot to soothe the sting. My tongue licks through her mouth, and she catches it with her own, commanding me to give her more.

Sensing the lack of control from both of us, I walk us to the side of the dance floor.

I pin her to the wall, shifting my hips until my cock nestles into the soaked line of her pussy. "Fucking snug," I breathe out, pulling away and looking down at where my jean-clad erection strains against the tight lace of her underwear.

Lucy looks back up at the same time as I do, and the idea she was seeing what I was—

"That smirk will be the death of me," she rushes out,

pulling my mouth back to hers by my T-shirt. "Don't stop kissing me," she orders.

"Your pussy." She bites my lip, making my eyes water and voice drop dangerously low. "Is fucking dripping," I finish on a growl.

"Prove it." She hikes her legs up higher, working her hips and sliding back down my length despite there being layers between us. "Don't move," she mutters in a rush, panicked even.

She starts to rub herself over me as if her life depends on it, and like the good boy that I am, I don't fucking move.

"Oh my god."

She's going to come. Right here, grinding against my dick in the middle of this club.

Her head hits the wall, and she looks down her nose at me, her mouth growing slack. I lean in, careful not to move our position while she works herself over me. I kiss along the underside of her jawline.

My lips dust her ear. "Come for me."

"Elliot." The words shake as her body tenses, her legs going stiff at my back.

I push her deeper into the wall, and my cock jerks, desperate to be properly freed.

"Take me home. Take me home, Elliot." The words rush past her lips as her pussy pulses. I can fucking feel it. "Please."

She slows her movements, and I know that if she was barefaced, her cheeks would be the perfect shade of pink. Her head falls forward and hits my chest, and then I feel her smile against my left pec.

I unhook her legs and drop her to the ground. Stepping

back, I look down at her. "If I take you home, I won't be able to stop. I can't lose control with you, Luce."

She palms the back of my neck, bringing her lips to rest against mine. "Control? It's already gone. Fuck control. Fuck everyone else and their opinions." She licks along my lips. "Fuck me, Elliot, and don't hold back. Please!"

You'd have to be a fucking saint to deny this woman.

"That's what you want? What you really want?"

"Is it not what you want?" She frowns, and I see the doubt settling in, her stance growing defensive as she crosses her arms over her body.

I pull her to me, and she comes to me with ease.

Pushing her hair back from her shoulders, I try to fight my smile. "There's still room for me to fuck up, Luce, that's all. I'm trying here."

Her face softens, and I see her melt little by little until she drops her arms to her side and brings herself nose to nose with me.

The air shifts, and I swallow hard as something twisted happens in my gut.

The fuck.

"Hey. Outta your head, handsome."

She kisses me like before. It's soft and gentle and apparently my newfound obsession.

"Take. Me. Home."

25

Elliot

There isn't any hesitation left as we stumble through her front door. I try to get a look at her home, but she pulls on my shirt and up the stairs to her bedroom. It's a decent size and has a walk-in closet and en suite bathroom.

"Naked."

I watch, amused, as Lucy starts on my belt buckle. She tugs my trousers down my legs then immediately pulls off my shoes. As she stands and grips my shirt, I grab her wrists. Twisting them in my hold, I pin her chest first against the door.

"What do you think you're doing?"

"Your body—"

"Hmm." I brushing my nose along the smooth skin at her neck, placing a kiss just below her ear. "What about it?"

"I want to see it. All of it. Bared of the mask you give to all the others. Give me it all, Elliot, please."

I plant my hand beside her head, my jaw tight. "Tell me

something first," I rasp the words, my teeth exposed and rippling across her cheek. "When was the first time you imagined what I might look like *bared*?"

She twists her head, catching my gaze as she swallows guiltily.

Fuck.

"Bend over and don't fucking move."

I readjust myself and watch with anticipation as she takes a step backwards and further into me. Her wrists are still poised in my hands, and I move them to sit high on the wall. I take a slight step back to make room for her, then wait.

Her hips bend, growing wider as her ass stretches, and all I can think out is how I need *her* bared.

Spread out beneath me and fucked.

"Don't move your hands."

I let her go and start on my buttons. My pelvis is the only part of my body touching her, and it lines my dick up perfectly with her ass. My shirt floats to the ground, and I step away from her. Picking up her iPad, I search through her songs.

"Elliot."

"Shh."

Her hips wiggle, and I give her a slap across her ass.

"Oww!" She giggles.

I side-eye her, loving how this feels between us.

I'm going to have her.

Luce.

After all this time, I'm finally going to have her.

"I'm making a playlist."

"Multiple songs?" she ponders. "Here was me thinking it'll only take three minutes."

My palm comes down again, the slap making me hiss in unison with her moan. "Every time you sass me, I'm gaining a hole. First up is that mouth. Carry on, and I'll have your ass, Princess."

"My ass is already reserved."

Something feral unleashes inside me. Ditching the playlist with four songs added, I hit play and step back up behind her.

"What did you say?" I ask, gliding my hands over her hips and up to her waist. My fingers knead into her back, itching to feel her skin.

"I said, my ass is already reserved." She hits every syllable with confidence.

I lean into her again, and her head lurches forward and hits the wall. "By who?"

She twists her neck to look at me over her shoulder, her eyes dropping down my body. "Who do you think?"

"Prince fucking Charming?"

She gives me a killer smile that detonates my own and has my cheeks aching with the fight I try to put up against it. "When I know, I'll know. For now, it's my ace."

"Your ace?" I snigger, pinching the material of her dress at her hips and pulling upwards. "Wanna see my spade?"

The material drags painfully slow over her thighs, and with every inch of her skin that's exposed, my cock grows that little bit harder.

"Can you feel it?"

"I'm not sure I can."

My palm connects again, and I pull the dress the rest of the way over her hips, leaving it at her waist. I see the scarlet sting that I've left and quickly reach out to palm the sore spots.

"Tell me to stop," I whisper, looking to the ceiling.

"Never." The little devil circles her hips, grinding herself against me.

A groan erupts from my throat, my restraint thinning by the second with the way she goads me.

"Ace." I dust my thumb over the crack of her ass.

Goose bumps prickle all over her back, her spine snaking as her body rolls like a wave and into my groin.

I slide off my boxers, then slip the band of her thong in each hand as I move my hold higher up her waist.

"Spade." My cock slides along her silky-smooth skin. Right where my thumb had been moments before.

"Elliot."

Her *ace.*

My spade.

Fuck it, I'll give her them all.

I tear the material from her waist, making her gasp as it lands in two scraps at her feet.

"Arms up."

She obliges, lifting her arms so I can pull her dress over her head. I blink hard as I stand and look at her like this, her arms raised high, her long back bare—that curved waist wrapping around to her full ass.

"Luce," I breathe.

She turns slightly, killing me with a glimpse at her tits.

"Don't turn around," I tell her, wanting to keep her like this, in this exact position.

My fingers dust down her arms as I step behind her,

moulding us together. She sucks in a breath, letting it out with a gasp when my knuckles tease over the sides of her full breasts. "You're fucking perfect."

I spin her around, pushing her back and against the wall as I drop to my knees at her feet.

"Yes," she elates.

I move quickly, a smirk on my face as I lift her knee and place her leg over my shoulder. I spread her pussy open, and her fingers instantly lock to my scalp, pulling at the strands of my hair.

"Club," I utter with a smile before running my tongue through the slick flesh between her lips.

She groans, rolling her hips against my mouth.

I don't know if she tastes as good as I think she does. Like a man dying of thirst, that first drop will always hit different. I've craved this woman for too long for it to be anything but incredible.

I swirl my tongue over her opening in slow circles, teasing her and not dipping inside. Her body becomes hot, her leg brushing my ear as her hips start to build a leisurely roll.

"Elliot, please."

I pull my mouth away, then place a soft kiss on her groin. "What do you want, Princess?"

"Everything. Make me forget. I need…"

Forget?

Her hips search for friction as she writhes in my hold. She meets my chin, coating it in her excitement, and I instantly nuzzle into her leg.

I can't get enough of her, kissing and sucking on her skin.

"Look at how wet you are for me." I stare at her centre before reaching out and swiping two fingers through her folds, coating them in the translucent liquid.

"Yes," she moans as I brush her clit. "I need…."

"Don't tell me what you need."

My head drops low, and I flatten my tongue, dragging it through her heat. I draw her clit between my lips and pull, tugging and sucking on the little bundle of nerves. Her hips buck. I dip low again, this time dipping my tongue inside. Her breathy moans make my cock drip with need.

Her legs begin to shake, and I catch hold of her other leg and pull it over my other shoulder, so she's held up with my hands on her ass. It takes away her ability to grind her face against me, and although I loved the way she let loose on my face without holding back, I know I can get her there all on my own.

"You taste fucking divine." I groan, running my nose through her slit. I pull my head back then blow against her clit. It's swollen and pulsing. Begging me for more.

I get lost in her, fucking her with my tongue and eating up everything she gives me.

"Your whimpers shouldn't be adorable," I rasp, dropping even lower. "Not when my tongue is rimming your asshole." I slide forward, lapping up the cum that pools at her entrance. "Certainly not when I'm sucking on your saturated cunt." I smile against her as she shakes. I place a hungry wet kiss on her pussy before I bury my face completely, not focusing on a specific spot as she works like a champ to ride my face. I help her, my fingers biting in the flesh on her ass as I devour every inch of her, pulling her forward and back onto my mouth.

"Oh my… Elliot."

I growl, the sound vibrating off my chest and falling from my lips to hers. It sends her over the edge, her pussy convulsing around my mouth and covering my lips and chin in her cum.

I don't give her much of a chance to come down from the high, removing her legs from my shoulders and wrapping them around my waist. I take her to the bed and lay her down, and she quickly reaches for my dick, working it in her small hand and not paying me any mind. I lean back and grab up my trousers, fishing out the gift box.

Instead of letting her unwrap it, I pull the necklace from the box.

She wraps her hungry mouth around my cock, and I hiss, fumbling with the box. She's fucking perfect. Pushing back her hair, I slip the necklace around her neck. She eyes me as she sucks on the head, driving me wild. I can barely figure out the clasp, but when I finally do, she eases up and pulls away, her hand reaching blindly for her neck before she looks down at the jewel adorning her.

"Diamond."

While she sits staring in wonder, I slide my hands under her knees and pull her down the bed. I kneel between her legs and tear open the condom.

Her eyes follow the foil packet, and I freeze with it between my teeth.

She opens and closes her mouth to say what, I'm not sure. And after a solid five seconds pass and neither of us has moved, I still don't know, but in a moment of pure fucking insanity, I toss the condom to the floor.

I grab her hips and pull her to me. Then, I line myself up.

"Elliot," she warns.

I drop my head to hers. "Heart."

I slide into her heat, my spine stiffening with the resistance I'm met with.

"Outta your head, baby, please, get outta your head."

She opens her eyes and looks into my deepest parts, her gaze pinning my soul to the spot.

I circle my hips and tell her, "Let me in, princess. I promise I won't hurt you."

I know what she needs, and I'm not afraid to give it to her.

Lucy needs connection. Reality. She isn't a woman you fuck around with. She demands more, and it's what makes her so damn sexy. That defiance to find pleasure in empty places.

Giving her my eyes, I let her see it all. I tell her everything I can convey in a look, and then I gently drop my lips to hers, coaxing her mouth with my own in a slow, deep kiss.

"You're perfect." I kiss her. "Beautiful." Kiss. "Smart." Kiss. "Mine."

I drive forwards as our lips catch, sinking the rest of the way into her as she relaxes around me. My head burrows into her neck, and I fight the urge to roar out in pleasure.

Soft sounds leave her throat, and I turn my head to kiss there too.

"Baby," I whisper.

She brings us nose to nose, her eyes shining.

I smile. "You're so damn perfect."

We continue to stare, and I want to say so much more—she wants to say so much more.

I can feel it.

Fuck, I can feel it.

"I—"

"Lucy!"

Her body recoils, jumping as her pussy clamps tightly around me, and she freezes beneath me.

I frown in confusion as the door bangs downstairs.

I look down at this girl who holds all the cards in my hand and watch as her eyes fill with tears.

"Elliot. I'm so sorry."

26

Lucy

I ROLL ELLIOT OFF ME AND JUMP FROM THE BED IN A PANIC. I grab up everything in the room that's his and turn to face him. "Get in the wardrobe."

I watch as his face falls. I watch as I break him, and I know I can't fix what's about to happen.

"Elliot, please, I beg you."

"No." He shakes his head in disgust, his face screwing up in pain as realisation sets in.

"I don't want to hurt him. I don't want to hurt either of you. Elliot, please, do this for me. I'll come home," I whisper.

"Are you fucking serious right now?"

I place the clothes in his arms and pull him to the wardrobe. "Please. I'm sorry." I close the door and wipe the tears from my face as I try to control my shaking hands.

I pick up my ripped underwear and stuff them into my drawer. Then I grab my dressing gown and slide it on.

Maxwell walks into the room.

"Hey." He looks me up and down. "You didn't answer your phone."

I swallow. "I was napping."

"I thought you were out."

I nod, not truly hearing him past the pain haunting me. The pain I saw in the eyes of the man I love just moments ago.

"Luce, it's your birthday, I don't want to fall out with you today. I'm sorry about this morning. I told Alec I can't go with him tonight." He steps forward and cups my face. I flinch. "You know I didn't mean any of what happened this morning, don't you?"

I nod, knowing it would never have happened if I hadn't been so persistent.

"You know I would've gone to the cemetery. You didn't give me a chance to wake up. And that girl is a friend of Alec—"

She wasn't, but I nod, cutting him off.

"I'm going to go shower. Why don't you get dressed? I'm taking you out someplace special."

"It's gone midnight," I choke out, making him frown.

"Don't be mad at me, Luce. You know how it makes me."

"I'm not mad." I shake my head vehemently. "Go shower, and we can go out."

He leans in and kisses my lips, and I want to die. I want to disappear from this moment and forget about its existence. "You're tired, that's all."

Maxwell shuts the bathroom door, and I go straight to

the wardrobe. Elliot bulldozes right past me before I can fully open it, and it knocks the wind right out of me.

"Elliot."

He keeps going, pulling on his shirt and securing the buttons. I realise his trousers are already on. His jacket clutched in his hand.

"Elliot, please," I whisper with purpose.

I follow him down the two flights of stairs, and he heads straight for the door. I grab his arm in a desperate attempt to keep him with me. "Don't leave me here. Please, Elliot, don't leave me. I had no one else. Let me make this right. I'll talk to him."

"No!" He roars, making me flinch as he finally looks at me.

I see the glint in his eye, the pain and hurt I've put there.

"I'm so sorry," I shake my head, a tear slipping free as I pull on his arm. "Don't leave me here."

He shrugs me off, and I cling to him, pulling at his collar as he tries to force my hands from him. "Stop!"

"Don't go," I sob, wrapping his jacket in my fist.

He steps through the door, and I fall forward onto my knees. I lose all grip and land hard.

Elliot stops on the threshold and looks down at me. I watch his throat bob, his indecision clear in his eyes before they blur.

And then he leaves.

I HAVE SO much to fix. So much to put right, yet I don't know where to start. Maxwell has been here for me since I moved to New York; I can't ignore that fact. But the pain and remorse that eats at me over what I've just done to Elliot hurts worse than anything else.

If I thought running after Elliot was the answer, then I would, but I know *he'd* need answers, and I don't have any.

At least not any that I want to admit to.

I'm embarrassed.

I didn't know Maxwell would come home. He was supposed to be away with Alec for the night on a job. And although it is as cut and dry as me cheating on one man with another, it's also not.

Not even close.

We both know I won't be here this time next year, and we both know he sleeps with other women. When I denied Maxwell for the third time, he started to become a different person from the one I met on the plane. The good guy is somewhere in there, and I even get glimpses of him on good days, but he's mostly lost to late-night runs with Alec and not-so-secret hookups. And the fucked-up thing about it… I've never cared.

He turned up when I needed a friend. He makes me feel safe here, and he knows how grateful I am for that. In return, I give him small pieces.

Little by little.

More and more of me.

"You okay?" he asks as he smooths a hand down my back.

I turn and nod. "I should go shower."

"Are you going to be mad at me all night?" I stop on my way to the door. "I don't see much point in taking you out if you're going to be in a mood."

I turn, needing to be honest with him. I don't know how he would react if he knew about Elliot, and that scares me.

My fingers instinctively wrap around my other hand, the dull ache still there.

I start with that. "You hurt me, Max."

He frowns, pointing to the door. "That's what's wrong?"

"I wanted to go to the cemetery, but it wasn't a big deal. I was going to go on my own—"

"You were trying to guilt me, Lucy."

I shake my head. "I wasn't. I was happy going alone."

He sniggers. "You don't even know when you're doing it."

I swallow, wondering if subconsciously I did try to push guilt onto him. "I didn't mean to make you feel that way," I tell him. "It was the only thing I wanted to do today."

"Why are you doing that?" he snaps.

"What?"

"You. That. Throwing going *alone* at me. *It was the only thing you wanted to do*. Are you trying to make me feel like shit?"

I walk towards the bedroom, wanting desperately to be alone. The irony isn't lost on me. "I'm going to bed."

"Luce."

I sigh, not knowing how much more I can take in one night. "What?"

"Just forget about it today, okay? Get some sleep, and I'll take you out tomorrow. I'm just annoyed I'm not going with Alec. It was a big job I blew off for you."

With the guilt of what I've done festering within me, I nod my head and disappear into the bedroom.

I call Elliot five times, but unsurprisingly, he doesn't answer.

Tomorrow morning, I'm going home.

"Lucy. Lucy."

My eyes snap open to find Maxwell standing over me.

"Lucy, get up. Alec's in the hospital."

I sit up in the bed, fear making my heart pound. "What? What's happened?"

Maxwell throws me a hoodie, and I slide my arms in. "I don't know, he was followed home and Polly's missing. He's in the hospital now."

"What?"

"Get up."

I dash around the bedroom to get ready, then rush down the stairs. Out on the street, Maxwell waves down a taxi, and I stand beside him with my heart in my throat, my brain not quite caught up as I fully rouse from sleep.

Polly's missing?

Elliot.

Oh God, Elliot.

What have I done?

Maxwell looks down at me once we're seated in the taxi. His face instantly softens. "Come here."

He pulls me under his arm, and I fall into him, knowing I don't deserve his pity.

We arrive at the hospital and are shown to a waiting room, where Maxwell leaves me almost immediately. "I'll be back," he utters, and I watch his back as he disappears through the doors.

I wrap my arms around my body as the room falls silent. My eyes scan the seats, the water machine and plant in the corner of the room. I move to sit down, feeling like I'm having an out-of-body experience.

After a few minutes, a police officer enters the room, knocking the doors into the wall as he throws them open in an obvious rage. I sit up straighter as adrenaline pulses through me.

"Sorry," he gives me a tight smile as he realises he isn't alone, regaining some composure as he steps further into the room.

"Fuck," he mutters under his breath, locking his hands on the back of his head.

I can tell he's just arrived by the way his chest works and the despair at being placed in the waiting room.

Just as he takes a seat opposite me, the doors open again, and a man in dark-blue scrubs walks in.

The policeman stands straight back up.

"Murley Wright's next of kin?"

"Yes," he tells him.

"She's waking up. You can see her now."

They leave the room, and I smile to myself, knowing his turmoil might be over soon.

I wait for fifteen minutes, then decide to go and find Maxwell.

I want to go home.

I have to find Elliot.

I walk down the corridor, trying to be respectful with my gaze as I look around for him.

I notice a room in the middle of the corridor. I'm only drawn to it because it's heavily guarded on the outside, the blinds pulled tight on the windows.

I wonder if there could be someone dangerous inside.

Why else would they have guards on the door?

Just as I pass, the door eases open, and I can't help myself as I peer through the thin gap. I see the policeman from before and frown, and then see someone else, right before the door is wrenched closed.

I shake my head, clearly mistaken.

I'm tired and shaken from the night before.

There's no way that was Polly.

"Excuse me," I say to one of the guards. "Could you tell me who's in that room? It's just my friend Polly might be missing and—"

"This is a police matter. Please, move along immediately."

I frown at his tone, stepping back and walking forward a couple of steps. At the other end of the corridor, I spot Maxwell being shown into a cubicle. I quickly make my way to him.

"I'll have it ready for Felix. Go back to—"

"Hi," I say, poking my head into the cubicle. "Are you okay?"

Alec is sitting on the edge of the bed, his legs dangling. He looks to be okay bar a nasty cut that sits just below his eye.

"I'm okay. You didn't need to come down here." He looks at Maxwell, annoyed.

Maxwell started working full-time with Alec when he moved into the house. They've spent the past month working all the hours in the day, and it's one of the main reasons that Maxwell's been so snappy. He's stressed and tired. I can see it in his face. Hear it in the way he speaks to me.

"I wanted to come," I assure him. "Where's Polly?"

Alec's jaw clenches, and he looks to the floor. "I don't know. She wasn't home when I left earlier."

I frown, rolling my lips. "What? How don't you know?"

"Come on, we should go."

Maxwell takes my hand and tries to guide me from the cubicle, but I frown and pull away.

"When did you last see her?" I question.

"She left me a note." Alec looks across at me. "She went home to see her mum. She does this sometimes."

Maxwell turns to me. "I need to stick around here for a bit. Will you be okay getting home?"

"Alec was just followed," I tell him.

"You're safe, Luce, it's the morning, and you can call me if you need me."

It is the morning and daylight outside. Which means Elliot will be up. I nod. "Okay."

Pulling out my phone, I leave the hospital and text Polly.

Lucy: Polly call me

Lucy: I'm worried and need to know you're okay

I'm on my way back to the house when she replies, and I frown at my phone as I read the message.

Polly: I'm out at my mum's place. I'm okay

Why didn't she tell me she was leaving?

Knowing she's safe, I pull up Elliot's number and try calling him again.

Elliot

My phone rings for the tenth time in a matter of hours. I'm climbing from my car having just arrived back from the airport, and I know I should check the messages piling up in my inbox.

The look on Lucy's face as I left last night still guts me, but what's worse is this anger I have raging inside of me. It makes me want to smash the phone to pieces so that I never have to look at the messages.

My suitcase feels heavier as I carry it into the house. I go straight to my bedroom and walk-in closet, where I pull on a pair of shorts and a white T-shirt. The last thing I want to do is lie around my house feeling like a cunt all weekend.

I should be in New York.

With her.

Leaving my phone on my bedside table, I pick up my keys and slip on my trainers and cap, and then I head back to my car.

L&M Fitness suite is a twenty-four-hour gym that stands as a powerhouse in the middle of London's financial district. It was renovated around two years ago and has fast become the go-to spot for fitness fanatics.

For me, it's close to my work, home and has the added benefit of Nina working on the third floor.

Usually.

Today, I could do without it, and being that it's gone eight on a Sunday evening, I presumed I'd be safe from her.

"Elliot!"

Nina frowns as Ellis runs for me. She has Waverly rested on her hip as she approaches me, and I know she's mentally trying to figure out what's going on.

Despite my mood, I pick Ellis up under the arms and throw him high before I catch him again. "There's my main man."

"You went on an aeroplane."

"I did. I went on *our* aeroplane," I tell him.

"I want to go gain."

I smile for the first time in twenty-four hours. Memories of travelling with the Lowells too sweet to ignore. "Yeah, we will soon."

"What are you doing here?" Nina asks as she steps closer.

"Did you see Auntie Luce?" Ellis bulldozes right over her, and for the first time, I wish the little guy would keep his mouth shut.

"No, she was busy," I say, keeping my eyes tuned in on Nina. She must take the hint and reaches for Ellis.

"Want to talk about it?" she questions, not meeting my eyes as she places her son down on his feet.

I shake my head, then nod towards the gym upstairs. "Lowell up there?"

"Sure is. Tell him we won't wait. I'll take a taxi to the hospital with the kids. Scar can drive us back, and Mase can drive home once you're done."

"I'd rather be alone, Nina. Lowell can leave with you."

"Not how this works with us, and you know it." She

pushes up on her tiptoes and kisses my cheek. "You look sad, Ell. I'm sorry," she mutters quietly so no one will hear.

I watch as she picks up the children's bags and ushers them out the door, wondering what she sees to think I'm sad.

Because all I feel is fucking anger.

It's been a week since I got back from New York, and the calls haven't stopped. I was sure she'd be home by now. That's what she said. *I'll come home.*

As if that could fix this.

"Knock knock."

Nina's head pops around my office door, her face assessing and full of pity.

"What is it?"

"What do you think?" she asks, coming to sit in the chair opposite my desk.

I don't stop working on my computer. "I don't know. Checking up on me again?" I have no doubt she's reporting everything back to Lucy.

I didn't tell Nina about what happened, and I didn't plan to tell Mason, but when I punched him in the face at the gym during our sparring session, adding a little too much behind it, he took me to the floor and told me to spit it out.

I told him pretty much everything.

"Are you okay? You haven't been over, and Ellis is asking about you."

"I don't think I'm the best company for him right now."

"Don't talk such rubbish. Ellis would make you feel a million times better, and you know that's the truth. You're wallowing in this self-pity." She holds up a hand to stop me. "And rightfully so. I don't blame you. Luce isn't returning my calls, and I have no idea what she is playing at."

"She's probably busy," I mumble absentmindedly.

"What?"

I look across at Nina, then drop my hand with a sigh. "I said she's probably busy."

"Don't be an asshole. I still love her more than you."

"I'm not being an asshole. I'm speaking facts."

"You're being an asshole. All week, in fact. Jasmine said you've been snappy."

I give her a look that says fuck off before I tell you to fuck off and get punched in the face.

"Come to dinner tonight, please?"

"No."

"Elliot!"

"Nina, I'm not in the mood."

"Right." She stands and rounds the chair, muttering under her breath. "Damn stubborn, impossible man!" She storms out of my office, and I know I haven't heard the last of this.

Which is why when my phone chimes not fifteen minutes later with a text, I'm not surprised to find Mason's name lighting up my screen.

Mase: George is clearing our schedule. We leave for Bora on Friday.

I consider it for a moment, not expecting the message.

It's been a while since we've managed to get away together.

I snigger to myself.

Elliot: If it gets me out of dinner tonight

Bora Bora would be a distraction right now. I could get out on the water, maybe even stay out at Mum and Dad's place….

Elliot: I'm in

27

Elliot

"Breathe Me" by Sia.

It's Wednesday, and I'm in the middle of a meeting when I feel my phone start to vibrate in my pocket. It's like clockwork. She calls me every day—morning, at lunch, and at night. I don't answer, and she doesn't leave me any voice mails.

I'll speak to her soon because I know I need to, but I can't bring myself to listen to what she has to say yet.

She hurt me.

Simple.

I thought we had something, and I was wrong. Speaking to her now will only make me even angrier at her, and it won't solve the situation.

The call rings out and then starts again seconds later, making me huff. I continue to explain the point on the screen.

"Excuse me for interrupting, Mr Montgomery, but I have an urgent call for you." My eyes shift to George, who's stood in the doorway.

He knows not to interrupt my meetings.

"How urgent?"

"I could get Mr Lowell. But I believe you should take this."

I roll my eyes, knowing George's beliefs probably don't match up to my own. "Bear with me, please," I tell the room, nodding at Jasmine to take over before I walk out into the reception area.

George closes the conference room door and hands me the phone.

"Who is it?" I ask him, but I already know.

"Lucy. She's having—"

"Fuck's sake." Why would she call me at work? If I wanted to talk to her, I would. And I will. But when *I'm* ready.

"What?" I snap down the line, my jaw cracking as I pull the wire to the phone over the desk.

I hear her take a heaving breath through the line and everything inside of me jars.

I plant my free hand down on the desk and lower my tone, a frown marring my brow. "Lucy?"

She continues to breathe rapidly, and I can tell she can't catch a full breath. "Elliot."

"Luce," I snap.

"Can't. Breathe."

"Lucy?" I panic, face distorting as my gaze lifts to George. I run my hand through my hair. "Where are you? Is anyone with you?"

"I think she's having a panic attack." George mouths at me.

"No. No. Elliot, my heart."

I close my eyes and try to ease the adrenaline making my own heart pump. "You're having a panic attack, Luce. You're okay. You can breathe. Are you on your own?"

"Yes."

Fuck. "Where are you?"

She seems to get worse, and I don't catch her reply.

"Put your back to a wall. Can you do that? Feet flat on the floor, and I want you to listen to me. Luce, can you hear me?"

"Yes."

"I'm going to count to five, and you're going to do it with me. In your head until you can do it out loud, okay?" I pull the phone from my ear and ask George, "What do I do?"

He skirts around the desk and starts typing on his computer.

"One. Two. Three. Four. Five." I do it slowly, trying to help her but not having a fucking clue where to start. "One. Two. Three. Four. Five."

I listen as her breathing doesn't change.

My hand scrubs at my face as an ache grows in my chest, my heart thrashing a million miles a minute now.

"I don't know what to do," I mutter to George at a loss.

"Keep talking to her. Tell her something."

Something for me to fixate on.

"Did you open my note? Do you have it there? Something to fixate on?"

I wait but get nothing.

"Luce!" I bite out.

"No. No, it's under my bed in a box."

Fuck.

I can't speak those truths right now.

I sigh and lower my tone. "You're okay, Luce, you can breathe. You can breathe," I plead with her to take a steady breath as I close my eyes. "Listen to me, okay? Listen to my breathing. Take a breath in and slowly let it out. Like this."

I inhale, then slowly exhale into the phone. "Do it with me, baby."

I listen as she pulls in a breath and lets it out.

"That!" I snap open my eyes. "Again, keep doing that."

I do it with her.

"You're amazing. You're okay, Luce. I'm right here."

I listen as the minutes tick by and her breathing starts to even out, her panting turning into soft weeps.

I swallow around the ache in my throat and ask, "Luce?"

"Yeah."

Fuck.

She's okay.

She's okay.

I look to George and nod, my skin prickling as relief settles over me and a different type of adrenaline rushes through my veins.

"I'm okay," she repeats my internal thought, her voice cracking as she continues to cry.

Silence stretches between us, and it only brings everything back. From the moment I touched down in New York to the moment I was lost inside of her.

"Elliot…I'm so sorry. I didn't want to hurt—"

I push the phone towards George, and he takes it before I turn.

"Elliot…" he calls to my back.

I walk down the corridor, clenching my eyes tight as stars build behind them. I pull my tie free, feeling like I can't breathe and needing to be away from everyone.

Elliot: Cancel the meeting

Jasmine: I will reschedule

Jasmine: Do you need anything?

I step into my office and shut the door. My eyes close in reverence as I fight to find my calm.

Fight to find a way out of the hell she's dragged me back into.

The ache in my throat gets tighter and tighter until it burns so bad it makes my eyes sting.

After a week of nothing, I feel everything unleash.

I pick up the plant in the corner of my office and hurl it into the glass wall.

"Fuck you!" I roar, watching as it shatters the floor-to-ceiling pane.

My chest heaves, and I grab up the coat stand. I slam it into my desk, knocking everything to the ground before my foot connects with the monitor and then again, and again.

"Fuck!"

I feel rage like never before. I want to hurt something, make it broken and battered, no matter how unjust it is.

"Elliot."

"Get out," I bellow, and shame fills me, knowing everyone will hear me. I face the only solid wall with my hands on my hips. "Leave me alone, Lowell," I warn.

"Go home for the day. Lucy—"

"Don't." My voice cracks, and I snap my mouth closed, my jaw cracking with the force. "Don't fucking talk about her."

"Mate—"

"She found someone else." I slam my fist into the wall, cracking the plaster. "While I was waiting here every day, trying to give her what I thought she needed!" I hit the same spot, my knuckles splitting as the plaster gives way. "She was fucking somebody else!" I keep going, my eyes blurring as the wall is splattered red. "I didn't think about anything but her." I wince as something snaps in my hand. "I didn't go out. I didn't sleep and barely ate." I turn, my chest rising and falling fast as I fucking cry.

Mase stands with his hands joined at the back of his head. He runs his tongue over his teeth at a loss, but his agitation is clear. "Don't do this to yourself."

"I hate her. I fucking hate her."

Mase pulls me into an embrace, clasping the back of my head as I eye the mess on my office floor.

"No, you don't."

Lucy

EMBARRASSED DOESN'T EVEN COME CLOSE to how I feel. Not only did George hear me having a panic attack down the phone, but he also would have heard everything that came after. Or what didn't come after.

It wasn't the time to have a conversation with Elliot, but

not saying anything when I had him on the phone felt wrong.

I wish I had a better coping mechanism. I wish I'd called Nina, or Mum, or even Maxwell. Anyone who could have talked me around.

Something had me choosing Elliot, though. In that moment, he was all I could think about, and there has to be a reason for that.

I know it only happened because Maxwell is coming home today. He went on a last-minute job for Alec last week, and I know when he gets back, I have to talk to him. With him coming home, Elliot still not returning my calls, and Polly still out at her mum's, I felt completely off when I left for work this morning. Then, when I arrived and found three of my projects wiped from the files on my computer, something broke inside of me.

Files don't just disappear.

I went for a walk to calm down, and the further I walked, the worse I seemed to get. Before I could even think about getting on top of my thought process, I was lost to it.

I couldn't breathe.

I drop my eyes to the kitchen island as my phone lights up with a call. Nina. I've replied to one of her texts in the last week, and she's left me three voice mails which I've refused to listen to.

I'm that embarrassed by my actions, I can't even listen to what she has to say to me.

"Hi."

"Hi? Luce, hi?"

"I'm so sorry, Nina."

She huffs, and I close my eyes as I drop my head.

"Will you give me a chance to explain? Cause I can. At least to you, I can. Elliot won't speak to me."

"Elliot is a fucking mess."

I knew on the phone he wasn't okay, but to have someone confirm it hurts even worse.

"Luce, he isn't okay. Mase hasn't ever seen him like this. We're worried. He started off quiet when he got home, and then today has just been the breaking point."

My chest grows tight as hot tears well in my eyes, quickly dripping down my face. "Nina, I've screwed up so bad."

"Tell me what happened."

"We were getting closer and closer. Then at the gala—"

"Harriet."

"Right, and he called it all off. Told me he wouldn't get in my way and would give me a chance to experience the city. I felt so alone. I didn't want to be here, and I was having more bad days than good. I ran into Maxwell." I swallow and look to my hands, knowing it's selfish but true. "I needed a friend, and he was there."

"So, Maxwell is just a friend?"

I clench my jaw and stare at my lap as more tears fall. "No."

"Luce—"

"It's complicated. We aren't in a relationship. Not really. He's even been with other women. It's only this past month that he's been a little more… protective."

"In what way?"

"He doesn't like the attention I get when we're out. He'll say things as if to tell me he doesn't want me putting myself out there. He's been stressed with work; he doesn't mean to come across so—"

"Toxic?"

"He's been good to me, Nina."

"He sleeps with other women."

"And I slept with another man."

"And you think that's okay? Do you think this is healthy?"

"I think sometimes in life we have to do whatever we have to, to get through. I don't know why you'd judge me." My voice cracks, and I stare at the ceiling. "I felt like I was on a different side to you all when Elliot dropped me, and I feel it now. I fucked up, and I'm sorry. I'm so sorry and hate myself for it, and I will fix it. But I need you to be you… I need you, Nina."

Silence stretches between us as tears stream down my cheeks.

I don't know how this happened, how I got to a point where I'd ever feel so disconnected from my salvations.

"I'm not judging you, Luce."

"It felt that way." I sniff.

"All I'll ever want is the best for you. You've come a long way since the likes of Hugh fucked you around."

"It's different with Max. He knows this is temporary. I know it's only temporary."

"You live together?" She asks sceptically.

"It made sense. It puts him closer to work with Alec." I shake my head at a loss, knowing she won't understand. I wouldn't understand. "Nina, I didn't want to hurt him. Elliot means so much to me…." I cover my mouth with my hand as my voice cracks. "I don't know what to do. He won't talk to me. We slept together, and it was so much more, and I don't know what to do to make him okay."

"Wait. You slept with *Elliot*?"

"He didn't say?"

"He didn't say you slept together! Mason is with him at his place tonight, and I'm hoping he will open up to him."

"It's such a mess."

She blows out a breath, and I sit and wish I was with her. "It is, but I know you can fix this. Both of you."

"I have eight months left on my internship. I can't even come home."

"Can you take some time off?"

The idea of going home terrifies me. Which tells me I'm afraid to face my family for a reason. Maxwell might not want to label our relationship, but that's exactly what it is—a relationship. I've done things with him. I share a bed with him at night and kiss him goodbye when he leaves for work.

Somewhere along the way, I've lied to myself, and worse than that, I've believed it. I can say it until I'm blue in the face, but Maxwell is something to me.

"I don't know. I don't know if Elliot would even entertain hearing me out. He was so hurt."

"He was, but it's Elliot. He won't stay mad at you. You need to be honest about who Maxwell is. And maybe have a conversation with Maxwell."

She says it as if it's easy.

"I'm going to speak to Max when he gets back from his trip. He's been out of the city this week for work. And Elliot, I have no idea how I get through to him."

She sighs. "We're going to Bora Bora on Friday, and I wanted us all there—"

"Elliot's going?"

"He said he would. I was really hoping you would too."

Could I go away with them?

It would mean I could speak to Elliot, and I wouldn't have to face my parents or his. Although I'd like to think he wouldn't tell his mum our business, I know how close he is with his parents.

"I'd have to speak to work."

"It's late notice, but I think it would be good right now. And you just had the walk, right? Is it a busy time in the office?"

"It's always busy in the office, but Monica knows I've had a shitty couple of weeks." I dip my head. "I'm pretty sure Chelsea made a complaint about me the other day, and then work went missing from my computer this morning."

"Are you fucking kidding me? Why would she complain about you?"

"I've just been struggling. I've been emotional and not on my *A* game."

"Fuck her!"

I snigger, a smile pulling at my lips before I sober. "I'm sorry, Nina."

"What are you sorry for?"

"I don't want to disappoint you."

"Are you kidding me?"

"I know it's hard with Mason being connected to Ell; it's one of the reasons I never wanted to start anything."

"Luce, you could never disappoint me. I might not understand the decisions you make but believe me when I tell you, I will always stand by you. This is going to work itself out. It has to. It's us. We don't let shit get between our group."

I pinch my lip between my fingers, feeling like there's already a wedge in the middle of our pack.

"No more avoiding me!" she snaps, a lightness to her tone.

"Yeah, okay."

I'd give anything to hug her. To go out for the evening and just dance and sing and be stupid.

When did life get so serious?

"Speak to work and let me know."

"I will. And thank you. I really need you right now—this holiday with you."

"We all do. It's been too long."

When I get home from work the next day, I find Max asleep in the bedroom. He works late into the night, so this isn't a rarity. But with everything that happened with Alec last week, he's been working more than ever.

I take a quick shower, trying to be as quiet as I can be before cooking us dinner. Maxwell joins me once it's ready, and we sit at the kitchen island to eat our food.

"Good day?"

I nod, slurping the pasta into my mouth. "Have you heard from Polly?"

He shakes his head, and my shoulders drop. "Me neither. Not since Monday."

"I'm sure she's fine."

"Why isn't Alec bothered? I presume they argued, and that's why she left."

"It's none of my business, and I like to keep it that way. Don't worry about them."

"It feels wrong, Max. I don't know… I am worried."

He sighs, dropping his fork and looking at me fully. "Polly will come home! She's always been flighty, and you've not known her long."

I frown and give a light nod, although I know he hasn't known her all that long either.

"Look, Luce, it's been a hell of a week, and I just need to sit with you and eat this lovely food. Can we do that? No arguments."

"I was hoping to speak to you this evening."

He looks at me with his tongue tucked behind his teeth.

"I'm going away with my friends," I tell him, feeling too much of a coward to bring up what I've done.

"Where?" His frown is sharp, quickly forming and sticking in place as he watches me.

"The French Polynesia—Bora Bora."

"What? When?"

I swallow, wiping my hands on my thighs. "Friday. I'm so ready to see them all. It's been such a long time."

"I was going to take you away."

I snap my eyes to his. "What?"

"I was going to take you away. It's kind of ruined now."

"Oh…"

"Who's going?"

"To Bora Bora?"

He nods as if of course that's what he means.

"Um, everyone, I think. Nina, Mase, all the guys and girls."

"Miller?"

My heart flips, then sinks to my ass. He's never mentioned Miller in all the time we've lived together. I didn't think he'd even remember the stupid white lie I told him. "No. Miller won't be there."

He nods, continuing to eat. "Good."

I gently release a lungful of air and sit forward to eat my own food.

"I'll come with you."

I still, suddenly losing all interest in my meal. "What about work?"

"I can work from anywhere at the minute. It will be good to get away, and you've ruined my surprise now." He looks at me with a smile, and I force one back. "You'll have to go shopping for us. Take my card tomorrow. Treat yourself."

I frown, trying to stop the tears from forming in my eyes as I nod. "Sure." I fight to keep the word whole.

"You okay? You seem quiet."

"I miss home," I tell him honestly. "And I'm really worried about Polly."

He takes my hand and squeezes it, reminding me that he is here for me. From the first time I touched down in New York, he's been intuitive to my moods. And even when I couldn't give him more than friendship in the beginning, he still showed up when I needed someone.

And yet right now, I wish I could tell him that I don't want him to come away with me.

I wish I could tell him about Elliot but living in a different country and sitting opposite someone I'm not sure I truly know anymore, I'm scared.

What sort of person does that make *me*? The type to

pick someone up and drop them the minute another man shows up?

That's not me.

Maxwell can't come to Bora Bora.

Elliot doesn't deserve that.

Which means I don't go to Bora Bora.

28

Elliot

THE LOWELL HOUSEHOLD IS UP IN ARMS WHEN WE ARRIVE ON Friday morning. I look behind me at Charlie and Megan as Mason's voice bellows through the hall.

"No, you've done this on purpose! Why wouldn't you say something yesterday?"

"You know what would happen if I did. I want us all together, Mase. We need it." Nina's voice is pleading, and we walk towards the voices.

"You don't know what you're fucking around in, angel. It won't end well."

"What won't," I ask, stepping into the kitchen.

Mason stands with his hands on his hips, his face grim and his lips flat. "Tell him," he snaps at his wife.

"Mase!" Nina hisses.

"I'm not blindsiding him. Tell him."

I frown and look between them. "What is it?"

Nina grits her teeth, looking to the floor before rolling on the heel of her trainers.

Mason huffs and shakes his head. "Lucy's coming to Bora Bora. She's bringing Maxwell."

I hear Charlie tut behind me, and Megan snaps, "What?"

Fuck. I roll my lips and nod. "Alright." I blow out a breath, my heart hammering against my rib cage.

If only I could control that shit.

"I didn't want to tell you and you not come," Nina says, her head still dipped. She won't meet my eyes. "Luce said she wouldn't come, but I told her she had to. I'm worried about her, and I just want to see her. She was adamant she wasn't going to come because of Maxwell, but I knew she had to."

"So she knows I'm coming, and she's happy to come. With him."

Mason looks down at his wife, then back to me. "She thinks you already pulled out when she agreed to come by herself. Nina lied to her."

My brows rise in surprise. "So, she changed her mind. Once she knew I wouldn't be there."

That hurts a bit.

"No, she fought me on it. I made her come, Elliot. I did anything I had to to get her on that plane."

I nod, laughing under my breath as I feel all the eyes in the room glued to me. "Well, let me make that easy for you. I won't go. You can see Luce, and I can avoid an absolute fuckfest of a week."

"No! Please, Ell, you have to come."

Mason shakes his head and rolls his eyes at her. "I'll sort

the flight details, don't stress changing anything," he tells me, stepping past me and walking down the hall.

"Mase!" Nina storms after him, leaving Charlie, Megan, and me in the kitchen.

"You're really not going to come?" Megan asks, her features heavy with disappointment.

"Would you go?" I reply.

She shrugs and pulls herself up onto the kitchen island. "This is shit."

"You didn't know she was coming with Maxwell?" Charlie asks Megan.

She shakes her head. "We've barely spoken in weeks."

"Nina isn't wrong," My nostrils flare, and I stand up straight. "Lucy should go. I think you all need to see her."

Silence falls over us, and I welcome it. I was looking forward to getting away with my friends. I needed it. But I can't go if Lucy will be there with him.

I'd kill him.

I'd kill her.

Nina steps back into the kitchen after a few minutes. "Can I talk to you, please?" she asks me.

I walk with her from the kitchen and out onto the terrace. She links our arms and hugs my side. "I'm sorry."

Nothing can stop my smile as I look down at her.

"I know you won't come with us, but can I tell you some things?"

"You can talk until I tell you to shut up."

"Deal." She grins.

"I really want Maxwell to come this weekend. I was actually glad when Lucy said he wanted to come."

I try to keep my face free of emotions.

"She's a clinger—we know this. Always searching for her happy ever after and not letting them go when she should. But from what she's told me, I don't get why she's with him at all. Miller was nice. Hugh wasn't great, but she didn't live with him…."

"You want to meet him," I say in understanding.

"I want to know who he is. I want to see how she is."

I nod. "It's okay. I get it."

"I thought the two of you could talk it out. I didn't think it through, and I'm sorry for that. I was being selfish."

"Stop apologising."

"What will you do? We'll be gone for a week. I don't want to go without you, and Mase is pissed with me."

"I'm sure I can find something to keep me busy." I give her a forced smile, already knowing I won't be doing anything.

"She's going to come home at the end of her internship, she told me. She said that Maxwell knows it's only temporary."

I don't answer Nina, but I do inhale her words as if I'm starved.

"I know she hurt you, but I get the feeling he isn't what you think he is to her." She gently brushes her fingers over my still swollen hand. "It doesn't make it okay. I know that. But I think you should talk to her. Give her a call or send a text. I plan to give her a giant shake when I see her."

I feel her eyes on me as we continue to walk around the terrace to the front of the house.

"I'm a fine one to talk, but if I've learnt anything in life, it's that sometimes we have to face the bad shit it throws at us. It's easy to ignore, but it's still going to be there at the end of the day."

I come to a stop, pushing my hands into my pockets as I turn and look down at her. "Sometimes, yes." I give her a look, knowing she will understand exactly what I mean. "And sometimes, it fucks you so hard, all you can do is ignore it." Leaning down, I place a kiss on her head. "Have a good time, yeah? I had Oscar get the skis ready for Ellis. I want him out on the water."

I walk down the steps to my car, opening the boot.

"Grab these cases, Lowell."

"This isn't right!" She jogs down the steps and takes Megan's case, then Charlie's. "I'm so sorry."

I close the boot and then climb into my car, opening my window.

"Me too, Pix," I tell her, throwing her a strained smile before tearing off down the driveway.

Lucy

Never have I been in the company of my people and felt like I don't belong. And maybe it isn't me, maybe it's the man standing beside me that makes this feel so wrong.

I close my eyes to try and block out the twisting feeling in my stomach.

My friends haven't got off the plane yet, but I can see them from my spot on the tarmac. Nina's hustling around with the bags in tow, and Mason is giving orders to everyone around him. I spot Megan and then Charlie.

Why do I feel so nervous to see them all?

Why did I even agree to come?

It would've been so much easier to stay in New York.

They all know about Elliot and me. Everyone but Max.

"You're nervous," he says, sliding his hand into mine.

I realise he's been watching me and force a smile. "I'm okay."

I consider what it would be like to go back to New York without him. Would I feel like I did in the week that Elliot stopped speaking to me? The horrible week alone before Maxwell showed back up.

For a time, he was all I had to rely on.

"I haven't seen them all in so long."

Maxwell nods and looks towards the windows. "They brought the kids?"

I nod, a smile playing on my lips. "Yeah, they go everywhere with them."

Ellis stomps to the top of the steps, and Mason grabs his little hand. He doesn't see me standing by the car, and I have to step forward toward the steps to gain his attention.

Once he spots me, every doubt and worry in my mind drifts away.

"Auntie Luce!"

He charges me once he reaches the bottom step, hurtling into my arms and holding on to me for dear life.

"Ah, I missed you so much, Ellis, baby!"

"Ave here too!"

Scarlet climbs down the steps with Waverly in her arms. Nina follows with Megan, their driver Vinny, and Charlie.

I smile as I take them all in, quickly standing straight with Ellis in my arms.

"Hey!" Megan pulls me into a hug, squishing Ellis in the process. "God, I've missed your face."

"I missed you too!"

"Luce! I'm so glad you're here!" Scarlet gushes, coming to kiss my cheek.

"Me too! It's going to be the best week," I say, forcing the words and barely believing them.

We stand looking at one another, and I know they're trying to figure out all the parts I haven't told them.

Mason takes a step toward us, and I give him a tentative smile. He meets my eyes, his lips set in a grim line before he takes a sleepy Waverly from Scarlet's arms and moves to speak to someone at the door of the plane.

Something inside me jars.

Charlie takes my upper arms and gives me a genuine smile. "Ignore him. It's good to see you, Luce." He turns to Maxwell, who's stood just behind me and holds out his hand. "Charlie Aldridge."

I watch as Maxwell takes his hand, his eyes climbing up Charlie's athletic frame. "Maxwell."

"Pleasure to meet you, Maxwell."

Charlie carries on to the cars, and I turn to the girls. "This is Max," I say, nerves making my hand shake as I smooth out the hem of my dress.

"Hi!" Megan grins, shaking his hand.

Nina and Scarlet both offer the same politeness, and then we awkwardly make our way to the cars that are lined up.

With Maxwell here, I feel the need to babysit him—not that he would ask that of me, but he's my guest, and I don't want to leave him on his own. The girls all file into one car with the kids, and I want to be in there with them.

"Go."

I turn and look at Maxwell. He's pulled out his phone, and his eyes are glued to it. "Huh?"

"Go spend time with your friends. It's why we're here, isn't it?"

"I don't want to leave you alone…It's not far to the house." I eye Mason getting into the car with Charlie. Vinny has the only other empty car, which would be the car we'd ride in. There's no way Mason will want Max in with him.

I should have thought about this.

It was too easy for Nina to talk me into it.

"You don't think I can look after myself? I have a call to make. I'll ride with the old guy. " He nods towards Vinny.

I stare at the side of his head, trying to see if he means what he says. I don't want anything to be misconstrued and turned into an argument later.

"You're sure?"

He nods before flashing his eyes up from his phone in answer.

"I'll see you at the house then."

"Luce, I'm fine."

I nod and smile at him. "Thank you."

I quickly rush to the girl's car before they drive away, and my eyes lift to Nina as I slide in.

"Hey, you." She smiles.

I settle in the seat and blow out a breath as I pick up Waverly's small hand. "Hey, girls."

"Here." Megan hands me a glass of something bubbly,

her face screwed up in an awkward contortion. "You'll be alright."

I take a sip and look around at them all. I have so much to say, so much to ask, yet with Ellis in the car with us, I know it has to wait.

"Happy holiday, whores!" Megan toasts, clearly not concerned for little ears.

We arrive in Bora Bora just after three in the afternoon, and the sun is still burning hot. Both the Lowells and Mongomerys own properties out here, and although Mason's is closer to the village and we've never used Elliot's parents', I know that it is just as grand and boasts beautiful views.

The house sits on the cliff tops, with glass windows stretching its entire face. There's an infinity pool and terrace for lounging, and then two more terraces for dining on.

"Holy shit," Maxwell steps up beside me, taking in the building before him in awe. He turns to me and smiles. "This is all private?"

It really is something special.

"Yeah. Family only." My eyes close, and I bite my tongue as Mason strolls in past us.

"What's his fucking problem?"

"Shhh," I snap. "Seriously, you do not want to piss off that man. Think rottweiler on steroids and then make it vicious." I shake my head and huff.

I can't go home now. That would mean telling Mason to call his people to have him turn the plane around, and that's just… worse. So much worse. I have to make the next week work.

And then I can only hope Elliot will be ready to talk when I get home.

We set up in our rooms and make ourselves comfortable. Mine and Maxwell's room is at the other end of the lodge. I'm not used to sharing with anyone other than the girls when we come away, and the idea I might be missing out on their antics makes me sad.

"Do you guys come out here often?" Maxwell asks while I unpack my suitcase.

"I've been twice, but as a family it was always their go-to." I look over my shoulder at him, finding him at the double doors that lead to the terrace, looking out over the ocean.

"They have some money," he remarks. "The Lowells."

The Lowells do have money, and maybe at times, it shows. Mason has had his share of moments since I've known him, throwing his money around to get what he wants. And Elliot lives life exactly how he wants to, with no limits.

"The other guy." I look up to find him turned around and facing me. "Who is he?"

"The other guy?" I swallow.

"Yeah, the one who actually said hello to me."

"Charlie." I smile. "He's a friend of the family. A lawyer."

"You didn't tell me that."

I hold up a floral bralette to my chest. "You didn't ask."

"What's *your* relationship with him?"

The top bunches in my lap, and I lift my gaze to his.

"My relationship?" I frown. "Charlie is a friend. A very, very good friend."

His face tightens, and I can tell he doesn't like that answer.

I don't know if it's the bubbly I had in the car or the fact my girls are just down the hall, but for the first time in a long time, I want to call him out.

"Why do you think it's okay for you to be friendly with women, but I can't be with men?" My eyes don't leave his, and the way his glare down at me tells me that he knew what I was about to say before I uttered the words. "I don't want to start an argument. But we made it very clear what we wanted from this," I gesture between us. "Before you moved in."

"You want to sleep with him?"

I recoil. "What? No."

"Then what's the problem? Why would you say that if you didn't want to fuck around?"

"Max—"

"And when you give me fuck all, it's a bit of a kick in the teeth, Lucy. I don't know what you expect, but if I'm not getting it from you, then I'm going to get it from somewhere." He places his hands on his hips as I rise to my feet, not liking the stance he has above me. "You said yourself that we knew what this was when I moved in."

"My point was, I'm allowed to have friends, as do you. I feel like it's been a problem recently."

He rolls his eyes and turns away from me. "You're being dramatic. I didn't even say anything about Charlie."

My shoulders drop, and I sigh, not knowing why I

brought the conversation up. "It was written all over your face, Max."

"All of this over a *look*," his tone bites, eating away at my fire.

A fire that's not been there for a long time.

"I said I didn't want an argument. I don't want to do this on the first night."

"Unbelievable."

"I'm sorry, okay. It doesn't even matter." And it doesn't. It hasn't ever concerned me that Maxwell messes around with other women. Our relationship, if you can even call it that, is just that.

A relationship.

It's two people connected by a level of trust. I know what he trusts me to know, and he knows what I allow him to. It's not love, or lust or anything to cry over when it ends —which it will. I plan to come home after my internship finishes.

He'll remain a friend.

It's probably the most emotionless relationship I've ever been in.

He helps me by being a pillar, and I help him by being there at the end of a day. Takeouts, and nights with our friends, it was good.

It got me through.

There have been times when I would've crumbled in the last three months, but he never let me. Between him and Ralph and the odd call from Mum or Nina, I've managed to live this wild dream.

"You need this break too, Max. I want you to enjoy it."

He nods his head and pulls me into a hug. "Sorry."

"Don't be. Just enjoy it here. It's one of the most beautiful places on earth."

"I'm going to shower before dinner. What time do we need to be down there?"

"Six."

29

Lucy

My feet hit the uneven sand as I jog from one side of the beach to the other. With the sun on my face and the warm air seeping in and out of my lungs with each breath, I feel the weight of the world slip away. I feel relaxed and sated on the island, and a million miles away from New York, my job, and even my home.

This was exactly what I needed, and if Nina hadn't pushed me, I wouldn't have come. I'd have stayed home all because I didn't want to bring Maxwell.

I meant what I told him last night. He really does need a break away from home.

I come to a stop at the shoreline, my chest heaving as the waves roll against my ankles. I watch as my feet get eaten by the wet sand.

My mind drifts to dinner the night before, and the reason I wanted to clear my head this morning.

Mason was as cold as he was when we first arrived, not

paying Maxwell or me any mind as if we weren't even there. I wish I could brush it off and give his mood right back, but I can't. I feel sick to my stomach to think he might be disappointed or mad at me. It only makes me wonder how Elliot is. He hasn't answered his phone or texted me back in over a week, and with Mason's frosty demeanour and everything Nina's told me, it's clear to me that he isn't okay.

My gaze dances along the cliffs and up to the lodge that sits close to the edge. It seems so small from down here, and I can just about make out two people on the terrace.

It's Nina and Mase. I can see Mason's tall frame towering over Nina's small body. He's hugging her, his hands slipping around and holding her stomach.

If I can have what they have one day, that level of love…

I laugh under my breath and continue my run up the beach. I always hoped Miller would be something more, like I did with all my exes. It never worked out for me.

That happiness I see between the lovers around me…It seems unattainable.

Or maybe I'm just trying too hard.

"ALRIGHT, spill it, bitch! We want to know everything."

To my surprise, Charlie, Mason, and Maxwell all went into the town this afternoon. Mason took Ellis and Waverly to get ice cream, and Charlie needed to see an old friend. Maxwell said he would catch a ride with them and then have a nose around the town.

My jaw almost hit the floor when Mason came to let

him know they were leaving, and there's no doubt that it had something to do with the woman sitting opposite me.

"It's been so long since we have all been together and alone. Childless too!" Megan grins, sitting forward in her seat and picking up her cocktail. "This is just perfect, right? Talk, please." She gestures toward me, and it has me smiling right along with her.

"Where do I even start?"

"Maxwell," Scarlet interjects, nodding her head as she sips through her straw. "Start there."

"Maxwell kinda showed up right when I needed him."

"When?"

I look around at the girls, finding them all hanging on the next word out of my mouth. "Maybe I should start with Elliot."

"I'm a little nervous to hear that part," Scarlet tells me honestly.

And I'm terrified to tell them. "We started something, you knew that. It was right before I left." I rush out the words, but none of them look surprised. It makes me a little more comfortable talking about it. "We did things at the showcase, that's when all this started. He told me to go to New York. He was in my ear, telling me it was the best thing for me and that I'd regret not going. All the while, he had control of those balls." I take a large gulp of my cocktail to calm myself down.

"So, I left, went to New York, started at Almendo, and spoke to Elliot every day. We grew into something else entirely. I'm sorry I never told you more, but at the time, it felt like something special that I didn't want to share." I drop my head and bite my lip. "If I'm honest, it was nice to not tell anyone. It felt… I don't know… different."

Scarlet's voice breaks the unnecessary silence that falls over them all. I need them to talk back. I can't tell them this and have them judge me. Not them. "Different because of New York, or different with Ell?"

My eyes flick between them all, filling with tears and blurring my vision. "Elliot," I mutter, swallowing around the lump in my throat. "He was so sweet with me. He was there every night, knowing I'd need someone."

"Did anything happen?" Megan asks.

"It got pretty deep on the phone, and we FaceTimed a lot." I give them a look that they quickly make sense of. "Then things went to shit fast. He got a little distant, and I know he was worried I wasn't living the 'New York dream' like he thought I should be. He thought it was his fault. I got angry at him when he told me he wouldn't be calling me anymore."

"This was after you'd done all the FaceTiming and stuff," Scarlet asks.

I nod. "Yeah."

"Well, I get your annoyance. No one deserves to be made to feel a certain way and then have that cut off."

A tear slips down my cheek, and I wipe it away as I reach out to grasp her hand. She knows firsthand how that feels. When Lance first got arrested, Scarlet spiralled fast. To see someone as strong and resilient as her crumble was the hardest thing to witness.

She might not talk about him, but I know she misses him.

"I felt alone, and I called into work sick for a couple days in a row. It's probably the worst I'd been in a long time, and for some reason, I didn't want to call home and tell you all I was struggling. It made me feel weak as if I was failing for needing the support."

"That's ridiculous, Luce," Nina mutters, emotion making her voice rasp. "We were so proud of you, and because you didn't call, I thought you were doing great. I felt like I should limit how much I called so that I didn't mess with your headspace."

I frown and look at my lap. "I was doing fine—amazing even, until Elliot put a stop to us. But I guess he felt how you did, and that's why he did it. I know he never meant to hurt me at the time. He was trying to do the right thing."

"He doesn't give the sweet side often. He probably felt a little out of his depths himself," Megan says, her eyes staring at the table, clearly thinking out loud.

Although, I don't think Elliot was ever out of his depth. I think he knew exactly what he was doing and exactly what he wanted.

I just couldn't hold on to him.

"Maxwell ended up outside of my apartment one evening. Polly and Alec, friends of ours, were moving into the apartment below Ralph's house."

Nina's eyes home in on me as if she knows this half of the story will be new to her.

"I didn't feel like I had anyone else at the time." I wince as I say it. "I know how stupid that was."

"Hmmm," Megan groans, while Nina looks across at me with glassy eyes.

"I felt a level of safety around Max. He's an ex–Navy

SEAL, knows the city, and was kind to me when I arrived. It felt like fate when he turned up on my doorstep."

I flinch as someone tuts from the poolside.

"Fate," he bites out.

We all turn to find Elliot just a couple of feet away. He's in a pair of black shorts and a cap flipped backwards.

My heart aches.

He's so fucking beautiful it actually makes my soul hurt.

"How perfect that you could finally find that one. Your soul mate, is it?" he challenges me with his stare, his anger rolling off him in waves.

With slow strides, he pulls up a chair and spins it, straddling the leather as he looks around at the girls.

"Elliot—"

"Shh."

Nina starts, but he cuts her off.

"She's telling her love story; we all want to hear it." His eyes come back to me. "Tell us."

"Can we talk?" my voice is small, and I clear it, hating the way I sound. "Alone."

"No," he replies, giving me a sideways glance before looking out to the sea. "No, we cannot."

I keep my eyes on him for a solid five seconds before I drop my gaze. "Right." Being so close to him, so close I could reach out and touch him, run my fingers through his hair and pull his head into my neck. I frown as tears threaten again. "I'm gonna go take a walk," I stumble to my feet, and Nina stands.

I rush off towards my bedroom.

"What am I going to do? When Maxwell comes back, and Elliot's here." I hold my hands on my head, pacing the length of Megan and Scarlet's room.

He hates me.

"Calm down," Nina tells me. "It's going to be okay."

"This won't end well," I tell them, dropping my hands to my lap as I fall back to sit on the bed.

"Tell us everything that happened with Elliot. Then we can figure out what he's playing at," Megan snaps. "I didn't like his tone. Asshole."

"I slept with him," I admit, staring at the ground. "I slept with him whilst I had this thing with Maxwell, and he came home. I told Elliot to get in my wardrobe. I hid him."

The girls stand quiet. All but Nina, she sits with her hand rubbing small circles on my back.

"You put Elliot Montgomery in a wardrobe?" Megan questions in utter disbelief. "Have you lost your damn mind?"

"Megan," Nina scolds.

"What? I'm not being a bitch. But Maxwell is… he's…."

I look up at her, a frown marring my brow when deep down, I know exactly what she is thinking.

"He's so different. Like, a little far out compared to us. Maybe it's because he's American, but I've seen more chemistry between an apple and an orange. It just shocks me. It's Elliot." She looks at me and frowns. "He actually stayed in the wardrobe?"

I nod. "He read the situation for what it was."

"He never would've outed you to Maxwell," Nina murmurs, shaking her head.

"And he won't now."

I look up at where Scarlet stands, and she gives me a soft smile. "He wouldn't. You know that."

"This is a mess," I wipe at my face, knowing I need to clean myself up. "I need to go and find him, talk to him."

I stand and leave the room, checking every room before I go outside. I find him lying out on a sun lounger. His long torso is bare and ripped, with little beads of sweat already coating his tanned skin.

"Please, speak to me, Elliot," I beg.

He lifts his head, his eyes dropping down my dress. "I have nothing to say to you."

"Then why are you here?"

He sits up, my words hitting all wrong. "Let's get one thing straight and fast. I. Do. Not. Want. To. Speak. To. You." His lips form a grim line, and I take a step back. "This is *my* family. I have every right to be here," he snaps, staring me dead in the eye. Everything goes quiet, and something passes between us. Anger, hurt, everything we've not said.

"I didn't mean why are you here because you don't belong or owe me anything, but you told Nina—"

"Uncle Elliot!"

We both look across the terrace to where Ellis climbs the steps.

"That." He points across the pool. "That is why I'm here. Don't twist it up in your head into something it isn't. We're done."

He stands from the lounger and meets Ellis in the middle of the patio.

I spot Maxwell striding up the steps behind them, and in

a moment of panic, I rush inside. I'm met with the brick wall that is Mason Lowell, though.

"Where are you going?" Mason asks, his hands righting me and setting me on my feet.

"Elliot's here."

"So?"

"So! Mason, I can't do this with them."

His eyes watch me accusingly before flicking over my shoulder. "You don't get a choice." He looks back at me. "This is hard for him. Being here with you and that prick."

"I told Nina I wouldn't come. I would never have willingly put us in this situation!"

"Well, now it's happening, and it's on you. You can't run away and hide, Luce. You fucked up." He nods his head in the direction of the terrace.

I spot Ellis, Elliot, and Charlie standing by the pool and Maxwell sat off to the side still trying to get Wi-Fi on his phone.

"Fucking go over there and fix this mess."

"Who do I go to?" I ask.

Mason frowns down at me, his face screwed up in wonder. "Who do you go to… I'd probably go with your boyfriend if I was you."

He sniggers and walks past me, joining Elliot and Charlie. I swallow and look to the sky, hoping I'll find something written in it that will help me through the next few minutes.

As I turn around to walk over to Maxwell, he stands and looks over at Elliot and the guys. I know he's about to introduce himself. I can see it in his stance, the way he holds himself as he takes steps towards them.

"Max!" I smile, grinding my teeth as I quickly walk to him. I reach him as he reaches the guys.

"Hey," he says, throwing his arm over my shoulder. He turns his head and nods at Elliot.

"Maxwell, this is Elliot Montgomery." I wring my hands together, my chest burning. "My friend from back home."

"Good to meet you," Maxwell says, and just as his hand lifts toward Elliot, there's an almighty scream ringing out, making us all freeze.

It comes from the lodge, and Mason moves first, then Elliot, followed by Charlie.

I walk after them into the lodge and find Nina, Scarlet, and Megan standing in the living area.

"What is it?" Mason snaps.

I'm pretty sure if he was a dog, his hackles would be up.

Nina looks at Megan and then at Scarlet with wide eyes. She goes to open her mouth when Megan blurts, "There was a lizard."

At the same time as Scarlet says. "I stubbed my toe."

They look at each other, and I frown.

"I stubbed my toe. Looking at the lizard. I ran from it fast." Scarlet is the smartest of us all; the fact those words have just left her mouth leaves me in utter disbelief.

"Are you fucking serious? You almost gave me a heart attack."

"Calm down, bossman," Nina soothes, taking his hand and walking him from the room.

Elliot follows them back out onto the terrace.

"Are you okay?" Maxwell asks Scarlet.

"Fine now." She nods, picking up Waverly and taking Ellis's hand. "Luce, will you give me a hand bathing the kids before dinner? Megan, I need you to go down to the staff's hut and ask them to have dinner ready for six. The phones have been down since the storm. Take Elliot with you, and he can carry back the canopies."

"I won't be long," I tell Maxwell. "See you at dinner, yeah?"

"Sure. I'm going to go have a nap anyway." Maxwell leans in and kisses my cheek before disappearing down the corridor.

Scarlet walks ahead of me, and I go to follow, quickly leaning around the door to see Elliot sitting back on the lounger again.

"This entire week is going to be a giant fuckup. I can feel it."

"We've got your back." Megan throws me a wink, giving me a soft smile before walking out of the door.

Elliot and Mason didn't come to dinner last night. If ever there was any doubt in my mind that they didn't want us here, that pretty much confirmed it. They said they had business in the town, but we all knew it was absolute bullshit. Thankfully, Charlie stayed and chatted with Maxwell.

Ellis spent the whole meal asking where his daddy was, and Nina sat with a hard face for the majority of the night.

Everything feels wrong. Me being here is causing a rift between us all, and it's not fair.

"I'm going to go home." I drop the book I'm pretending to read and look across at the girls. They are sat out on loungers next to me.

"Shut up," Nina mumbles, not even flinching.

Scarlet and Megan don't say a word, and I know it's because they can feel it too.

Maxwell has stayed home at the pool today, he couldn't get a signal down here, and with the internet being out for the first day of our stay, he was desperate to get back online.

"I'm serious," I tell her. "It's not right me being here with Max. You'd all have a nicer time if we headed home."

"You aren't going home."

"I am, Nina."

She sits up in a rush, pushing her sunglasses up and levelling me with a stare. "Ignore them. Especially Mase. You need this break, Luce, and you need time with us." Her lips purse as she looks at the girls. "We've been so worried about you, and I'm not letting you leave yet. I need to see you, spend time with you. Let them do them and enjoy this with us!"

"I don't want to hurt anyone." My words come out in an almost inaudible whisper as my emotions rise. "It's hell to be around Elliot and have him ignore me. And I don't blame him." I pull my sun hat low and wipe the corner of my eye. "He has every right to feel the way he does."

"But it hurts. It's hurting the both of you," Scarlet adds.

I nod, rolling my lips. I want to be honest with them about how I feel, but it terrifies me. If I'm honest with them, then I have to say it out loud. And that means being honest with myself.

"I want to scream at him to hear me out, but what do I even say?" I frown. "That I don't feel anything for Maxwell. Would that make it any better?"

I see the sympathy in my friend's eyes, and it makes me feel like shit inside. I'm ruining their holiday.

I'm hurting *him*.

"I think..." I close my eyes, letting the lie go because I *know*. I've known it for a long time. Maybe before I even started to fall. "I love him."

Can you do that?

Fall in love with someone you're already in love with?

We sit in silence as tears run down my face.

"Then why Max?" Scarlet utters softly.

I shrug, frowning as my face screws up in pain. "I don't know." My chin wobbles, and Nina comes to me. "I don't know anymore," I sob. "I want to come home."

"Luce."

"I just want to come home. I want to forget about New York and go back to before."

"Shit," Megan cusses.

"Luce?" I hear Mason's voice and spin around.

He, Elliot, and Charlie stand a few feet away, a volleyball clenched tight in Elliot's hands as he watches me.

His face is like stone, and I quickly hide my tear-lined cheeks under my hat.

"We're heading back," Nina tells them, picking up my things and grabbing my hand. "Can you sort the kids?"

"Sure," Mason tells her.

We walk back up the beach and up the steps to the lodge. The girls do their best to lift me up, telling me random shit things, knowing talking about Elliot or the situation will only make things worse.

We put on a movie and end up passed out on the bed, not waking up until there's a knock at the door.

Nina gets up first and answers it, and I slowly sit up, rubbing at my eyes as they find focus.

"Shit fuck. What time is it?" Megan groans, rolling over.

Mason walks past Nina and looks at us sprawled out on the bed. "Unbelievable," he says with a smile, his hands on his hips.

Nina slips her arms around his waist, hugging him with her eyes closed.

"We're going out tonight. All of us." He looks at me, telling me he means *all* of us. "We need it."

"Hmmm." Nina groans. "What about the babies?"

"Vinny will stay behind."

"I can stay home," Scarlet voices, but Mason shuts her down.

"You need the break too, Scar. Cars will be here at eight."

"What time is it now?" Nina asks.

"Five."

What? "We slept for hours," I say.

"Jet lag is real." He kisses Nina's head and goes to leave. "Luce, can I have a quick word?"

I nod, shimmying down the bed and following him out the door.

He gives me a tight-lipped smile as he faces me.

"I'm sorry for the way I've treated you—"

"Mason, you don't—"

"Yes, I do. You don't deserve it. I've been a prick, and for that, I'm sorry." He dips his head, catching my eyes and meaning his every word. "That being said, he's fucking hurting, and he's already better than he was last week. When he got home...." His nostrils flare, and he crosses his arms. "I've never seen him that way in my life."

"I never meant to hurt him."

"I know. But you did."

"I don't know how to fix it."

He tightens his eyes on me. "Don't you?"

"You think I should leavc?"

"What?"

"Go home. You think I should leave?"

"Fuck, no. Luce, for Christ's sake." He pulls me into a hug, wrapping his muscular arms around my neck. His chin rests on my head, and I feel him pull in a long breath. "What do you want? Cause I keep thinking I know. That I see it, but then you come out with this shit."

I swallow, glad he's bear-hugging me and can't see my face.

When I don't answer after a beat, he pulls away and exposes me. I look up at him, knowing the answer will be clear to him.

"Thought so."

"I don't know what to do."

"Be honest." He lets me go and walks off down the corridor. "With everyone," he adds just before he rounds the corner.

I drop back to the wall and take a second, needing to compose my thoughts.

What the hell am I doing?

30

Lucy

"Tell me you're trying to kill off two men without telling me you're trying to kill off two men." Megan eyes me as if I'm the next ticket popping out at the deli stand. "You look insane!"

I look in the mirror and readjust my black vinyl-effect miniskirt. It sits high on my waist, dropping down a couple inches past my ass. My thigh-high black suede boots create a gap between the two, my tanned skin glowing under the artificial lights in the bedroom—my top matches in colour, cropped with a high neckline and long sleeves.

I push my hair over my shoulder, but the bouncy curls that Megan's spent the last hour creating fall right back into place.

I turn and look down at her. She's barefoot, wearing a black dress and her dark hair poker straight.

"Put your lippy on and come get another drink with me. I need all the alcohol in the world to get through tonight."

Nina and Scarlet went to get ready in Nina's room, and I can already hear the guys outside on the patio from Megan's room.

I pick up my empty glass and walk to the terrace while I wait for her. I spot the guys sitting around the firepit right below us.

Charlie's speaking fast, clearly a little tipsy and loose, and Mason and Elliot are laughing at whatever he's saying —I hear the word spank and zone out. I don't need to know what Charlie Aldridge gets up to after dark.

I've heard the rumours.

I don't see Maxwell at first, but the light from his phone quickly directs me to him. He's stood poolside, speaking on the phone.

My eyes drift back to the guys, and I smile as I watch Charlie laugh out loud. He doesn't do this with many people, and I feel like an imposter watching him be so at ease without knowing he's being watched.

I rest my arms on the metal bar that runs around the terrace and take in the sun as it dips below the horizon.

I can't help this nagging feeling in my gut. Like the longer I spend here with my friends, the clearer everything becomes.

Maxwell is a good person.

He's helped me these last few months.

But he isn't my people.

He isn't my person.

I feel Elliot's eyes on me and shift my gaze to him. And the look on his devastatingly handsome face knocks the air right out of me.

It's hungry.

This man, he wants me.

He seems almost boyish as he sits assessing me, his legs thrown wide and his hand nursing a glass of something I can't identify between his fingertips. But that look on his face, the way his eyes pin me down, and the way his thumb dusts the side of the tumbler… This man wants to ruin me.

Piece by piece.

I don't know how long we stare at one another. Maybe it's a matter of seconds, or perhaps it's longer. But the longer it goes on, the faster my heart races, the more my—

Crap.

"Fuck!" Mason snaps, looking to my broken glass beside him on the ground and then up at me. "Luce!"

"I'm so sorry!"

Megan rushes to the terrace and looks over the railing, then back at me.

"Tell me you're trying to kill two men without telling me you're trying to kill two men…." Her lips twisted up in amusement. "Or just throw champagne flutes at their heads." She cackles her witchy laugh and slaps my butt, sending me in the direction of the door. "Let's get you another drink!"

We find Nina and Scarlet in the kitchen eating from a giant platter. Megan and I get a cocktail from the minibar, then join them.

"I love that we all got the unwritten memo tonight," Nina says as she looks between us all and our outfits.

We're all in black.

"You bitches look good." Scarlet grins, pulling up her freshly washed, perfectly curled, lavender hair and tying it into a messy ponytail. "I think I'm wearing my DMs, though. The walk back is always a killer."

"We can get the cars to pick us up," I tell her.

Scarlet smiles around a mouthful of meat. "We walk. Always. It's like my favourite part of the night."

"You're not cliff jumping," Nina warns her.

She shakes her head. "I wouldn't do it drunk," she assures us. "But we'll probably end up at the beach, right?"

"Depends how messy we get." I shrug, inhaling my cocktail as if it's water.

"I am so excited to go dancing!" Megan buzzes, walking to the music console and plugging in her phone.

A remix of "Dancing in the Moonlight" plays out, and we all follow her into the lounge, our bodies swaying to the beat and the last of my inhibitions float away. I throw my arm in the air as Nina pulls me to her side, smiling at me as we sing the words.

The guys must hear the music and appear at the folding doors. They observe us from the patio for a single second before they join us.

We laugh, sing, and dance.

And when my eyes drift to Elliot, who's got Scarlet all but off the ground as he spins her, I get this feeling deep in my gut for the first time since seeing him yesterday. It's hopeful.

I have hope.

Maxwell seems to stumble from the taxi, and I wonder how much of his afternoon he's spent drinking. When we get inside the club, he heads straight for the restrooms, and I know I won't be seeing him for a while. Other than at dinner and when I've crawled into bed at night, I've barely spent any time with him.

He spends all day working on his phone, and for me, that's not what a holiday is about.

The girls and I disappear to the dance floor the minute we get our drinks, and that's where we stay.

After an hour of nonstop dancing, I have to sneak away to take a breather. I go to the restroom and fix my makeup and hair.

I'm on my way back to the dance floor, pushing my way through the tightly packed bodies, when I spot Maxwell with his mouth ghosting up the side of a blonde's neck.

I watch him as his hands roam her body, and I feel nothing—other than embarrassment.

Most women would go over there and cause a scene, but I don't want to.

Maybe it's what I want to see.

I get knocked by two women and fall into someone's back. The man looks over his shoulder at me, and I apologise, instantly snapping out of my trance.

Not wanting to dance anymore and needing a drink, I walk towards the bar and slip in at the very end, putting myself against the wall.

My fingers grip the edge of the bar, and I lean back, needing the distance it creates in front of me. Bodies push into me from all angles, and I close my eyes, feeling stuck and as if my space is getting smaller and smaller.

I feel the panic rising in my gut, the alcohol in my stomach growing hot.

Images of Maxwell and the woman flash in my mind.

I should go and find the others.

Breathe, Luce.

I should never have left the dance floor alone.

I turn and suck in a sharp breath.

Elliot is standing right there, his arm pinned on the bar top and his body firm as he gets knocked from behind.

He doesn't look at me, his eyes locked on something behind me.

"Vodka cranberry," he says, reeling off my order.

"Elliot."

He looks down at me, his jaw ticcing as he moves to rest his other hand on the wall above my head, boxing me in. I don't think he's going to answer me and then, "What?"

I swallow and try to think of the words that are needed, but the barman comes back with my drink.

I turn and take it, quickly paying and drinking down the contents.

When I turn around again, Elliot is shaking his head at me, a hard look on his face.

My chest works hard, and I know he can see it. The way my eyes bounce around his face.

This charged energy between us is unlike anything I've ever felt.

Is this how it is for everyone?

Is it just him?

The Elliot Montgomery effect.

"Your boyfriend's a cunt."

I nod my head, not knowing what else to say.

He steps back, and it feels like a reluctant move. As if he has to force himself away from me.

I walk in front of him through the crowd, but I want to turn around. I want to speak to him, tell him everything I haven't had the chance to yet. But the fear of him shutting me down keeps my feet falling one after the other, closer and closer to our table.

Would he hear me out if I tried?

Am I naive to think this is fixable?

My mind is a muddle, and I'm not fully concentrating when two guys come tumbling through the throngs of people. Their fists are flying at one another, and they fight to stay on their feet as women and men grab at their limbs to try and break it up.

I put my hands out, anticipating the inevitable as they continue in my path.

It happens fast.

They fall towards me, and I squeeze my eyes shut as I wince.

My feet lift from the ground, and I snap open my eyes as I'm enveloped in warmth. Elliot's arm is hooked around my waist, holding me to his body as he steps backwards and away from the people who are now brawling on the ground.

Once we're clear of the mess and locked in the confinements of the less wild patrons, he places my feet on the ground.

His hand doesn't move, and neither do I.

We stand still, and I don't believe either of us want this moment to end. Our bodies are one, the closeness so familiar and yet sorely missed. He shifts me, and I'd think it was thoughtless, but then I feel his rock-hard cock against my back. "These boots." I feel his hot breath rasp against my ear, and goose bumps sheath me.

His fingers dig into the sliver of skin at my waist, and my head drops back to his chest, desperate for his hands to explore further.

His tongue traces my ear, and my lips part. "Outta my motherfucking head," he whispers, his mouth dragging over my cheek. "I don't want you there."

I turn in his arms fast, looking up into his eyes to search for the lie.

His eyes scan my face, and his chin lifts a fraction of an inch before he pulls back. The hand on my waist works to turn me away from him again, and then he's pushing me in the direction of the others.

Elliot

We walked home.

Well, Scarlet, Megan, and I walked home. We went to the beach and ended up soaked right through, thanks to the girls.

They choose to go through the main entrance of the house while I slip around the back, wanting the peace and quiet of the ocean in my ears before I end my night.

Mason, Nina, Charlie, and Lucy left in the cars when Maxwell couldn't be found in the club. I could tell it bothered Lucy not knowing where he was, and I couldn't understand it. The prick spent the majority of the night with another woman.

It's ironic, really, that she can spend the best part of three years telling people we'd never be compatible because of the way *I* work, yet she will fuck a guy who's happy to openly screw her over.

I'm removing my wet shirt, not expecting anyone to be up when I spot Mason and Charlie sitting at the firepit with the little prick. I come to a stop in front of the house. My eyes gravitate to the right, towards the bifold doors, and I catch Lucy watching me from the kitchen island. She's wearing a bikini, her hair wet and pulled over one shoulder. She's chopping something up, but her eyes are firmly fixed on me.

She looked fucking incredible tonight, and at one point, I almost caved. I almost gave her the chance to open her pretty fucking lips and tell me how sorry she was.

And then she left to go find *him*.

My tongue swipes over my teeth, and I stuff my hands in my wet trouser pockets.

I stroll over to the firepit.

Maxwell follows me with his eyes as I round the flames and sit opposite him.

I'd like to think I've made it quite clear I don't like him. We've not spoken a word since I got here.

"You're fucking wet, Montgomery," Mason hisses, pushing my knee away as I sit down next to him.

"The girls fucked me over," I tell him, tipping my chin up at Maxwell. "Why do you think it's okay to disrespect Lucy like you did tonight?"

Mason and Charlie stare him down just as hard as I do. They knew I wasn't looking for a peace offering here.

The piece of shit smiles around his glass, swaying in his seat. He's been on something all night. "You know how Lucy is."

He leans back in the seat, looking for her through the window. His eyes roam her body, and I fight the urge to smash his face into the firepit. "Just look at those sweet tits." He looks back at us, not gauging our moods as he continues. "She knows what she gets, and I know what I get—which isn't a fucking lot." He pauses and points as if he's just remembering something. "The girl can suck a dick; I'll give her that."

"Watch your fucking mouth," Mason snaps, sitting forward in his seat.

Maxwell eyes him, running his hand over his buzzed head.

"She isn't going to call me out," he tells us as if it's obvious. "She's too afraid to be on her own. And while she can't give me any, I'm sure as shit going to find it elsewhere." He shrugs, finishing his drink and pointing it at Charlie as he sways. "Sue me. Lawyer."

"Alright, I think we're done," Charlie says, sensing my mood and giving me a look as he stands.

Maxwell throws his arms out wide with a smile. "What? I've not offended you, have I?"

"She doesn't *give* you any?" I ask, my eyes wild as I sit disgusted by his entire being. "The fuck does that mean?" I grit out the words, not giving a shit what it might start.

"I don't know, I'm no doctor. She's been bleeding for months, and I don't get a day off because of it. Or a day on." He laughs again, and Mason's knee starts to bounce. "She's on some kind of birth control that's fucking with her."

I don't speak.

Mostly because I don't have any words.

"Are you saying you've never slept with Lucy?" Mason seems to find his tongue, and I want to kill him just as bad as I want the answer to his question.

Maxwell frowns as if it's a stupid question. "You make it sound so fucking sad."

My heart jackhammers.

"Like I said, the girl can suck a dick."

I want to kill him.

I could kill him.

I could throw him from this motherfucking cliff, and my friends would cover me for a lifetime. Fuck, I think even Charlie is ready to lay into Maxwell's face at this point.

I stand, and they don't stop me, but instead of doing what I want to do, I do what I should do.

She's still standing at the kitchen island when I walk through the doors, and I close them behind me.

Her eyes dart up and then drop down my naked torso. She frowns and goes back to chopping up the strawberries on the counter.

I'm still so fucking angry at her.

I walk through the lounge and over to the island, resting my hands on the worktop, giving myself the opportunity to properly take her in.

Her hair is wet, and her makeup is wiped clean from her face. Her tits look sweet as fucking sin in her black bikini, and I stare at them without a single ounce of guilt. She looks just as perfect as she did in the bar, although now, I know that she hasn't had a cock inside her since me.

He hasn't touched her.

I'd be lying if I said it didn't make me happy.

“Are we calling off our pact?” I ask, breaking the formidable silence hanging between us.

Her gaze lifts, confusion and hurt painting her face. “Uh, if you want to. I guess.”

She swallows harshly, and I tighten my gaze on her. Reaching out, I pick up a strawberry. I hold it between my fingers, and she watches as I slowly squish it. The red juices run down my fingers and between my knuckles, dripping onto my wrist and then the counter.

I turn my mouth down and shrug. I lift my hand and lick up the mess. “Do you *want* to call it off? What was your plan here?”

“I presumed it was off the table since I left. You mentioned it before, and I thought maybe we’d just postpone it.” Her chest rises and falls as she continues to watch me. “I didn’t think… after you came to New York.”

“New York.” I nod, a smile pulling at my lips which she does nothing to reciprocate. “I’m curious as to why you’d lie.”

“Lie?”

“Hmm, because if you still wanted to go ahead with it before I came to New York, surely you wouldn’t have gone and put yourself on a contraceptive.”

Her cheeks redden, and it fuels my fire.

“Do you remember when I stayed over at your place, and you needed me to go out in the night for supplies?” I start to round the counter. “I phoned you up because I didn’t know what to get you.”

“Elliot,” she warns.

“You told me to put the tampons back because you don’t use them—I mean, now I’ve been inside of you, I get it.”

"You'll never get it, don't try to understand things you never will," she says in a panic.

I lean down beside her body, resting my arm on the kitchen island. I pick up a strawberry and suck it between my lips before I eat it. "Tell me, *Luce*, has anything changed from that night?"

She stares at the chopping board, and I shift my eyes to the window. I give Mason a look, and he nods his head in understanding.

My hand curls around the smooth skin on the inside of her knee and her lips part as I drag my fingers up the inside of her thigh.

"Because today at the pool, I was watching you, and at the beach, all the damn time actually—but especially in this tight little bikini. And do you want to know what I think?"

She drops her head back as my hand cups her bikini covered pussy from behind. My chest brushes her arm, and the skin-on-skin contact has my cock twitching behind my slacks. I use my nose to nuzzle her hair clear of her ear. "I think you're a liar."

I pick up another strawberry and hold it to her mouth. She looks at me with uncertainty, and I glare back, not being able to help the feelings still surging through me. "Eat it."

I feel her clit throbbing as I run my hand between her legs, forwards and back, slow sweeps as my fingers tease her. She bites into the strawberry, and I feel her excitement leak from her, creating a wet spot on her bikini bottoms.

She moans around what's left of the strawberry, darting her tongue out to pick up the juices from my pointer finger.

"That tastes good?" I ask.

She nods her head, chewing down on the piece of fruit and looking up at me. "Elliot, anyone could—"

"Cut the fucking strawberries."

I'm half-cut, and maybe I'll regret this in the morning, but it's not fucking likely.

I want to know.

I stand behind her and shift her hips apart, knocking her foot out a step and widening her stance.

I turn my back to her and manoeuvre myself, kneeling on the ground backwards behind her. My hands wrap around her thighs as I ease my head back and between her legs.

Her thighs clamp around my head as she panics, her gaze jumping to the guys sitting on the patio just beyond the doors. "Elliot."

"I have a point to prove." I bite her plump pussy through her swimwear, and she releases her hold on me. "A lie to expose."

"No. You're only exposing *me*."

"I am." I reach across and hook a finger in the opposite side of her bikini, *exposing her*. "So stop me."

My eyes hold hers, shit I don't want to delve into passes between us, and then I drop them to her glistening cunt.

I tut, nudging open her lips with my nose and mouth.

"How did I know you'd be dripping wet with desire"—I suck on her parted pussy, flicking my tongue over her clit—"and nothing else?"

"You can't do this," she hisses.

My eyes meet hers again, and I swirl my lips over her slick flesh, smirking against her as I show her exactly what I can't do.

Lucy

My hands clench tight on the work surface, and I drop the knife. I knew he was going to touch me when he stepped up behind me, but when his hair tickled my thighs and his head pushed between my legs, I thought I might explode on the spot.

His mouth covers my pussy, and I suck in a sharp inhale. My eyes snap to the patio, but still, nobody looks in our direction.

My hands flatten on the worktop, too afraid to reach for him when it's what I need—my hands on him. Touching him and consuming him in any way he'll let me.

With my intelligence all but shattered, I let him do what he wants. I lose all my dignity and stand at the kitchen counter while he kneels at my feet and fucks me with his mouth. It shouldn't be hot, but it is, and I can't seem to focus on the rights or wrongs while the ache building in my core grows.

"Elliot," I moan.

He flattens his tongue and works me from bottom to top, drawing my clit between his lips and soothing it with gentle licks. Our eyes meet as he pushes inside of me, manipulating my hips in a rocking motion onto his tongue. The sound of my arousal meeting his wet mouth, coating him, it makes my stomach clench. My body flushes, and I cry out, grasping his head in both hands as I grind down and get lost in the moment.

His growl is feral and draws my eyes open. My heels lift

as he ravishes me. His mouth sucking and lapping. He's wild, and he doesn't care. He wouldn't stop if someone walked in here, and I don't want him to. I'm so close. So so close.

"Elliot," I whisper, waiting for him to look at me.

He opens his eyes, dark and dangerous and full of pain. My brows pinch together as my jaw hangs slack. I'm going to come, and he continues to mould his mouth to me, working his head from side to side. But my hips stop their pursuit as our gaze's lock and I still.

With his head held in my hands, I slowly smooth my thumb across his brow, completely lost in him.

My head tilts as I trace his temple, and a look passes, one that he holds for longer than he'd probably like. Because I see it. I see what he tries to mask from the world.

"You never could hide from me, Ell."

He pulls my hand away hastily and sucks my pussy almost violently. Hard enough to bruise. I slide my hands back in his hair and pull hard.

"I'm sorry," I cry, riding wave after wave of pleasure. His nose brushes my pubic bone, his mouth dragging heavy as he laps and rids me of everything I give him. "I'm sorry," I moan. "Baby." My eyes roll as I continue to come on his mouth. It's relentless and makes my toes curl against the cool tiles. "I didn't… I didn't… I don't want him… I only want you."

I feel his mouth vibrate against me with a growl, and then he eases up, pulling my sensitive flesh slowly between his lips in hungry kisses as he brings me back down to earth.

He drags my bikini bottoms back into place and stands without making eye contact.

I turn on shaky legs, quickly grasping the counter at my back. He's facing the sink, and it's obvious he's avoiding having to look at me. "Ell, I don't want him. I want you."

He reaches for my discarded swim towel on the stool, and I watch as he wipes at his chin and faces me.

The agony he fronts me with makes my insides burn.

I don't want it to be real because I did this.

I hurt him.

"Talk to me."

"No," he snaps, making me jump. "I don't have anything else to say to you tonight."

"I—"

"What? You what, Lucy? You're sorry? Because that doesn't seem to be working for me." His nostrils flare, and he shakes his head. "Maybe I'm sorry."

He tosses me the towel and walks down the hall to the bedrooms. I close my eyes just before the door slams shut.

I still flinch.

31

Lucy

"Auntie Luce, I can see up your nose."

My eyes drift open, and I find Ellis leaning over the back of the outdoor furniture. After what happened with Elliot last night, I couldn't face going to my room and sleeping next to Maxwell, so I chose to sleep out here.

My eyes feel tired and puffy, and I know I probably look a mess. "Do I have anything up there?" I ask.

Ellis gets a closer inspection, using his pointer finger to pull back the tip of my nose. "Lots of boogers."

I chuckle and grab his arms, pulling him over the seat and setting him on my stomach. "You're getting cheekier by the day."

"We going ski today!" He bounces on my stomach in excitement.

"Are we?"

He nods his head, smiling wide. "I show Dad how it's done."

I chuckle at his serious little face. "Who told you to say that?"

"Mumma." He grins, pulling his hands to his mouth. "Uncle Elliot broke his hand."

"When?" I frown.

"The other day. And Daddy had a sleepover." He pulls on the string in my hoodie, and it pulls right through. His eyes widen in panic, and then his lips start to curl.

"What did you do, Ellis!" I groan playfully, gathering up the string.

"Mean to, Luce," he tells me.

"Right, that's it. You're making me pancakes for breakfast!"

"Yes!" he cheers, throwing his hands in the air.

I lift him in my arms and walk towards the kitchen, tickling him under his knees and making him giggle.

As we step into the lounge, I find Charlie and Maxwell standing at the back of the sofa. Charlie quickly masks his emotions when he spots us, but Maxwell isn't so fast, and it's clear to me the conversation they were having wasn't a friendly one.

"What's going on?" I ask, looking between them both.

Charlie looks at Maxwell.

"I've got to get back to New York," he tells me.

"What? Why?"

"Alec needs me for a job. I can't not go." He looks to the ground, then back up at me, remorse blatant on his face. "I'm sorry, Luce."

"Surely work can wait?" I mutter, readjusting Ellis on my hip. "We've been here for three days. Not even three full ones."

And I don't want to leave.

Yesterday I did, but not now.

"You're staying here." Charlie gives me an apologetic look. "With us."

"I—"

"It's fine. Stay," Maxwell interjects. "I won't be around for a couple days at home anyway." He rounds the sofas and leans in to kiss my cheek, pulling me in for a quick hug. "I'll see you in a couple of days. I need to hit the road, but I'll call you when I land."

"How are you getting to the airport?"

"I've called for a car. Should be here any minute now," Charlie tells me.

I frown as I watch Maxwell pick up his suitcase and walk towards the doors.

"See you later, yeah."

And then he leaves.

I stand in the middle of the lounge, completely at a loss as to what's just happened.

"Pancakes!" Ellis wiggles down from my arms, and I silently follow him to the kitchen.

Thankfully, Charlie takes over the cooking while I sit on the stool and get a little lost in my head.

How can he just leave?

I get Alec's business is only now taking off, but to up and leave in the midst of a holiday?

Should I leave with him?

After a few minutes of silence, Charlie rests both his hands wide on the counter, staring down at the worktop between us. He holds a thoughtful look on his face, and after a beat, he lifts his eyes to mine.

"I don't like him, Luce."

My jaw locks.

His eyes plead for my understanding, and being that it's Charles telling me this—the most honest, respectful man I know, I soften.

"He's a good guy, Charlie. He's been there for me."

Charlie nods, although his face remains grim.

"I'm a good guy," Ellis glees, climbing to his knees on the seat.

"You're the best, buddy." Charlie smiles, setting him back on the seat properly.

I toy with my fork, not eating like I know I should. "I planned to ask Maxwell to move out when we got back."

Charlie's brows shoot high. "You did?"

"I wanted to." I shrug. "I have a lot to tell him. Whether or not I would've had the balls to actually do it—"

"I think you would have. This week will be good for you."

"Maybe." I smile at him sadly.

"Eat your pancakes," he tells me, leaning down to kiss the top of Ellis's head. "We've got a busy day ahead of us, right, Master Ellis?"

WE WALK DOWN the coastal path to the beach after we've all finished breakfast. The guys get the Jet Ski's into the water while we get Ellis into his life vest. Waverly stayed behind with Vinny today. She loves the outdoors but is far too young to ride with anyone.

Elliot, Charlie, Mason, and Megan all climb onto the skis, leaving me, Nina, and Scarlet to ride on the backs.

Scarlet jumps onto Charlie's—which was my first choice as far as safety goes.

Mason whistles at Nina. "Mrs Lowell, come wrap those legs around me, thank you."

"You need to take Ellis, Mase," Nina frowns.

"Ellis, do you want to ride with Auntie Megs?" he shouts.

"Yes!"

I flick my eyes around at them all, wondering if they think I'm stupid.

"He's not riding with *you*!" Elliot tells Megan. "Ellis, come here."

Ellis wades in until one of the guys who was helping to move the skis lifts him up and onto the front of Megan's.

"Megan," Elliot warns, flipping his cap around and staring her down. "Don't you dare."

Megan hits the throttle, throwing up water and heading out of the cove. Nina and Mason follow close behind, chuckling as they go.

"Scar, get over here," Elliot says, making my heart sink.

"Umm…" Scarlet looks from me to Elliot and back again. "I… I—"

Charlie shoots off with Scar screaming and clinging on for dear life.

I shake my head as they all get further and further away, leaving Elliot and me alone.

He twists to look back at me, his jaw like stone, as he nods for me to get on.

"I can wait… we don't have to."

"Get on, Luce."

Nerves swim in my stomach as I walk over and climb on behind him. I shuffle forward on the seat until my body fits with his, and he waits patiently for me to get into position. I wrap my arms around his torso and take a deep breath. The feel of his body pressed tightly to mine, his chest warm under my palms, it feels too good.

"Fucking meddling pricks."

I close my eyes as my stomach bottoms out. We fly out of the cove and speed out to sea, bouncing across the surface of the water. I squeeze Elliot tight, not being able to do anything else but hold on.

We quickly catch up with the others, and I watch Ellis with his hands on the body of the Jet Ski as Megan swings it around in circles. He's having the time of his life, and it makes my heart warm.

The guys try to race around and act like typical men, all while we scream like a bunch of girls on the back—I wish we could be better.

Elliot looks over his shoulder at me at one point, and I swear I catch a hint of a smile.

I'm sure he's doing it on purpose.

We come to a stop on the water, and Ellis calls out to Scarlet. She dives in and swims over to him, taking him from Megan when she lifts him down.

Megan, now being free of the small child, shoots off to the left of the cliffs.

"I'll stay here with these two," Charlie tells us, nodding at Ellis, who's clinging to Scarlet's back as she swims around.

Nina swaps and sits in front of Mase.

Elliot twists in the seat. "You want to drive?"

"I don't know how."

"It's easy."

He reaches for my hand, and I stand, stepping on the side of the Jet Ski as Elliot shuffles back. His hands grasp my hips, and I suck in a breath, memories from the night before flooding back. He lifts me with ease, placing me in the driving seat.

I reach for the handles, getting a feel for the position. "What do I do?" I ask, turning to ask Elliot.

He grasps the handles with me, using them to pull himself forward and flush to my back. It makes his biceps bulge against my barely defined ones.

It makes me feel dainty and reminds me that he's all man.

My lips part, and I know my cheeks are pink.

"This is the throttle." He twists the handle. "Brakes. And this button here will—"

I grasp his hand when I spot the light-yellowish bruising on his knuckles. I pull it closer so I can inspect it better, looking down at the scabs that are almost all flaked off.

My thumb runs over the shiny skin. "What happened?"

I turn my head, finding his face right there, our noses almost touching as he watches me. Our eyes meet, and I search for the parts I know are there, buried deep by my betrayal.

"What happened?" I ask again, knowing he's almost there.

He looks to his hand and then back into my eyes. "You had a panic attack."

My brows pinch together as my body aches.

He did this because of me? Because I called him?

"Does it hurt still?" I ask, watching my thumb trace his knuckles. I can't look at his face right now.

"It'll always hurt when it comes to you."

I snap my eyes up, sucking in a breath as he reaches out and pushes my hair off my shoulder. My throat works on a swallow, and I know he sees it, his eyes trained on the motion. I think he's going to say something. Shit, I should say something. But then he shocks me, hooking his pinkie under my necklace as he lifts it.

"Did you wear this while you were sucking him off?"

Oh my god.

"I haven't," I rush out.

His eyes jump from mine to the necklace and back again. I can see him fighting with himself. He wants to be mad at me because he is, it's clear. But I also don't think he knows how.

"Do you want it back?" I ask, feeling awkward and waiting for him to pull away.

His eyes spark at the idea. "Yes."

I nod, quickly undoing it and placing it in his hand. I feel a pang of pain that travels right down to the tips of my fingers as I pull away empty-handed.

He looks at it for a second, flipping it over in his palm. And then, in a moment of gut-wrenching absurdity, he drops it into the sea.

My heart lurches as it plops in the water, and I gasp. I want to jump in, sink with it so I can wear it for an eternity. But like every other pivotal moment in my life, I look to the closest person to me for an answer, approval, any guidance they'll give me.

I get nothing from the man staring back at me, and

when I finally cut my eyes to my necklace in a panic, I see it glisten in the clear blue water before fading into the infinite black.

My eyes tear up as I sit, too stunned to speak.

That was the first piece of jewellery any man had ever given me. And he's just thrown it away as if it's trash.

I look forward again as a tear threatens to fall, not wanting him to see.

I'm in shock.

He shifts behind me and grabs the handles. "Like I said—"

I tune him out, not being able to hear him over the beating of my heart.

Nothing seems real. I can see it. The sea, the cliffs in the distance, and the others riding around on the skis, but I can't hear them. I can't focus. I can barely breathe.

My chest starts to ache, and my eyes widen.

My arm snaps out and knocks Elliot's grip on the handle, freeing me from his confinement.

I stand from the Jet Ski and dive into the water.

Elliot

I SIT and watch as she surfaces, swiping her hair as she smooths it out. She looks around the water frantically, and I think she's looking for the others, but then she makes eyes for the beach and starts swimming towards the shoreline.

My nostrils flare as I watch her swim away from me.

"Lucy," I bite out, swinging around the Jet Ski and pulling up alongside her. "Give me your hand, now."

She continues to swim, and I don't miss the devastated look on her face.

It amps up my own anger, but it's not directed at her. I'm angry at myself. No, fuck that. I'm angry at both of us.

"Now," I tell her, shaking the hand I have held out to back up my demand.

"Leave me alone," she mutters.

I watch her strokes, slow and pitiful against the current.

"Get on the Jet Ski!" I yell in frustration, circling her too close and causing the water to slap against her.

Fuck.

She comes to a stop and watches me with wide eyes.

"Are you insane!"

I see her tears slip free, and I stare right back. My jaw locks painfully tight, reminding me that my heart isn't the only thing that aches.

I stand prone on the Jet Ski as she swipes at her face and continues her way back to the shore.

"Fuck!" I roar, going hard on the throttle and flying across the water. I pass a pissed-looking Nina as I head towards the point. I don't need to look over my shoulder to know where she's going.

Megan circles around and picks up Mason, who had jumped into the water. They follow behind me as I round the point and head for the small cove that leads to my family's home.

The Jet Ski flies onto the sand, and I cut the engine.

"You think Ellis needs to see you out there acting like billy big balls!" Mason snaps, pulling up alongside me.

I look across at Megan and him, then flip my hat and

cover my eyes. My face remains hard, and I know they get the message.

"Are we jumping?" Megan asks, looking at the point over her shoulder.

I throw my leg over the Jet Ski and start towards the steps.

"Yes!" I hear her hiss.

"I'll go check the rocks."

Mason heads back out while Megan and I climb the steps to the top of the cliff top.

Scarlet and Megan are the only two who ever want to come up here to jump. Lucy is always too afraid, and Nina uses Ellis as an excuse.

"What happened before? Want to talk about it?"

I ignore her.

"She genuinely doesn't want to hurt you, Elliot. She—"

"You think I don't know that?" I snap, rolling my eyes.

"She doesn't know how to make it right, not without hurting anyone more than she already has."

"Megan," I warn.

"I'll shut up. I'm just saying. She knows she hurt you, and she knows it will take time to fix. She didn't ask to be on your Jet Ski today and her being here with dickface wasn't completely on her. You need to listen to what she has to say because if I'm being honest, you're both being a little backwards about it now."

"Why even start with *I'll shut up*?"

"I'm done."

We get to the top of the cliff, and I spot Mase at the bottom. He waves his arms no and shouts up, "It's shallow as fuck, Montgomery."

I look at the water and see the rocks littered on the bed. We've been coming out here since we were kids, jumping these cliffs and fucking about. We know when it's safe and when it isn't.

My eyes hit the horizon, and I relax my shoulders. "I'll see you back at the lodge in a bit."

"You don't want a ride back with us?"

"I'll walk back across the path."

She hesitates at my back for a minute, and I gear up for more of her girly bullshit.

"I'll see you in a bit then."

I turn, catching her pity-filled stare. "Thanks, Megs."

I end up sitting out on the cliff top for nearly two hours before deciding to go back. The air seems to shift as I walk the path to the lodge, and I can tell with the wind picking up that we're probably due another storm.

When I get to the lodge, I find Mason, Charlie, and Vinny on the patio having a drink.

I contemplate not joining them but decide against it when Mason waves me over.

"We're eating in the dining room tonight. Scar's looking for you, she wants to have a black-tie sit-down whilst we're here."

"You think I brought a suit to the middle of the Pacific fucking Ocean?"

He grins around his glass, his brows lifting in amusement. "No, but she did. She planned it all."

I can think of nothing worse than sitting down at the table with a bunch of angry women tonight. I'm counting on Nina coming for my head. "Why black tie?"

Mason takes a swig of his beer and lounges back on the seat. "It's the anniversary—"

"Elliot!" Scarlet calls my name, and I can tell she's been looking for me. "There you are! Come here, please." She ushers me over with her hand.

The guys all give me a sympathetic smile, and I shake my head as I follow the little lavender-haired menace.

I'M WEARING A TUX. There wasn't much choice in the matter after Scarlet went to so much effort to surprise us with the sweet gesture. You don't tell Scarlet Lowell no—it's more of the logistics of saying the words as opposed to the choice. She'll look at you, much like the way Ellis looks at me when he wants something, and the words don't come.

I pull on my jacket and make my way down the corridor towards the kitchen.

I'm halfway down the hallway when I hear a door open and shut behind me. I glance over my shoulder, my steps faltering.

Lucy is coming from her room. She stands at the door, watching me as I take one slowed step before halting completely and turning to face her. She's wearing a black, what looks like velvet gown, that slips elegantly off her shoulders and frames her breasts perfectly. It hugs her slim waist and drops over her curvy hips with a slit that leads my eyes entirely too high on her thigh.

"Good swim?" I ask, a frown forming on my brow despite my question.

Her eyes tighten on me, and I fight the nervous smile that threatens to show.

I don't feel fucking smiley right now.

My stomach rolls as I stand on the spot and clench my fists, and for the first time in maybe ever, I don't know what to do with a woman.

The fact that woman is Luce, the only person I've ever felt comfortable enough to give it all to, kind of fucks me up a little inside.

"When you're ready to listen to me without being a dick, I'll be waiting." She starts towards me, her heels hitting the floor with force. She doesn't readjust her dress once; she just walks like a motherfucking queen right past me and into the dining room.

I head to the bar area and pour myself a glass of something strong before following her in.

Thankfully, I'm sitting at the other end of the table from her. I take my seat, pleased she can't get under my skin from over here. Charlie is to my right, and then I have three empty places next to me. Ellis has a name card to my left, and I presume the other empty seats will be for the rest of the Lowell tribe.

It doesn't shock me that they're late. Since they moved in with Scarlet, the five of them can't be on time for anything.

"Can I just say"—Megan taps her glass although no one is talking—"I look absolutely phenomenal tonight."

It breaks the awkward tension between the four of us, and I smirk into my glass as I take a sip.

"You both look absolutely stunning, ladies," Charlie tells them, raising his glass in a toast to them.

They clink glasses then look at me. I lean in and follow suit, my eyes avoiding all contact with Lucy.

"Sorry, sorry, sorry!" Scarlet comes rushing into the room with Waverly in her arms. Vinny follows with Mason and Ellis right behind him. Nina trails in last, readjusting something on her skirt. "We aren't late, are we?"

"You know you are," Charlie chuckles.

Scarlet takes her seat and looks around at us all. "You guys look incredible. We need a photo later!"

Our food comes out, and we eat and chat about anything and everything. It's comfortable, and it's not. I don't look at Lucy, and I don't feel her eyes on me like I normally would.

She's pissed at me, and it annoys me that it has me doubting throwing her necklace in the water.

Why would she want it now?

New York was a shit show. Neither of us needs a reminder of it.

"Did you all go cliff jumping today?" Vinny asks, lifting a hand to cover his mouth as he swallows his food.

"Just Megan and Elliot," Scarlet sulks.

"We couldn't—"

"We're planning to go out tomorrow but with everyone," Scarlet cuts me off, grinning at everyone. "We all have to get back up there. It's been years."

"Everyone will jump?" I snigger, sounding more bitter than I feel.

Multiple eyes flick to me.

"Yes?" Scarlet replies with a frown.

Naturally, my eyes go to Lucy. "You plan to jump, princess? I can't see it."

Her eyes remain on the table, and I can tell by the way her lip twitches that she's annoyed at me.

"If I want to jump, I'll jump," she mutters eventually, the table silent.

I rear back in mock surprise. "A decision." I swig down my scotch, feeling it take full effect. "Lookout. Pigs might actually fly."

"You got the pig part right."

She isn't wrong, and I don't know why I've called her out as I have. It definitely doesn't make me feel any better.

I push back my chair and go to get another drink, Mason's eyes burning into my back with every step I take.

We're halfway through dessert, and I can confirm that if Ellis wasn't sitting by my side, I'd have left an hour ago.

I'm not sure what was expected tonight, but with everything that happened out on the water, you'd think it would be obvious.

Lucy won't look at me, and I refuse to look at her. I feel like a kid in school again, pretending my crush doesn't exist because I don't want the whole school to know she was the reason I got a hard-on in drama class.

There's energy in the room, and it's going to blow up any minute now. I can feel it.

"So..." Nina announces, and I drag my eyes up. She looks to Mason, and he beams down at her. My heart rate seems to pick up, and I can sense the mood in the room shifting—my own mood shifting.

"Oh my god," Lucy mutters, dropping her fork down.

"We have some news."

"Oh, guys!" Megan cries, covering her mouth.

Nina laughs. "You don't even know what it is yet!"

"You're having a baby," both girls say in unison, looking between each other before they both stand and go to Nina.

"Fuck," I mutter, not being able to keep the smile off my face.

"Uncle Elliot!"

I look down at Ellis as everyone crowds around Nina and Mase. "Sorry, buddy."

He looks back at me and smiles so wide, his little eyes water when in reality, I'm not even sure he knows what it all means.

I sit him on my lap and whisper into his ear, "You'll be a great big brother, champ! Congratulations." I hold out my fist, and he bumps it with his.

Everyone sits back down, and I place Ellis in his seat, clasping Mason on his back and nodding with a wide smile at Nina. They know how happy I am for them.

"You've been drinking!" Megan gasps.

"I know. I stopped last night when we worked out my dates. It's why we left early." She laughs, but I can see the worry on her face. "I had no idea! It's the first month I said screw it and stopped tracking everything."

"We're over the moon for you, guys," Charlie tells them.

Scarlet stands and swipes at the corner of her eye. I'm guessing she knew judging on the way she reacted so calmly compared to the other two girls.

"Thank you all so much for being here with us this weekend," she says to us all. "Nina and Mase, you've brought us so much happiness tonight, and on a day that always hurts so hard."

I watch as Mason looks to the table and clears his throat. He nods at his sister and gives her a tight smile.

My mind races, trying to figure out what I've missed.

"Mum and Dad would have been overjoyed to see us out here, especially with you girls." She looks at Lucy and Megan, giving them a warm look. "And to think they are watching down, seeing this news being shared among us all, it makes me think they'd be super happy and proud. And I know I moved the Antlis ball to an entirely different date and season due to our terrible British weather always screwing us up, but I couldn't not celebrate what would be the third anniversary of something we all started together."

The ball.

My gaze shifts to find her staring straight back.

"Two incredible years, three insanely successful events with over ten million pounds raised for a charity so dear to our hearts. I can't thank you all enough for your support over the years."

Two years.

That's all I hear.

Lucy's eyes snap away, her chest working as she reaches blindly at her neck for something that's no longer there.

I look at my drink.

"So, if we could all raise our glasses. I'd like to make a toast." Scarlet lifts her champagne flute, and we all follow, my arm lifting on autopilot. "To Mum and Dad, *and,*" She dips her head in Nina and Mase's direction. "To Mum and Dad to be."

Everyone chuckles, but I fail at putting on a facade.

Something feral has my eyes locking back on Lucy's. She tries in vain to avoid it, but there's nothing stopping the energy settling between us.

"Luce, I wanna see you live your life."

"I am."

"Leave him."

"No."

"Keep looking."

"Elliot!"

"And if in two years you haven't found him—No. Fuck him, actually. If in two years you haven't found her, if you're not settled and well on your way to 'five-year Luce' I'll give you the kids."

Is she happy? Well on her way to where she needs to be?

Fuck, no.

She might have a fancy job and live in a different country, but if the last three days have been anything to go by, she's still the same Lucy who left four months ago.

She excuses herself from the table, and Nina instantly stands. I put my hand up and tell her without words that I've got it.

Because I have got it.

It's the one thing I've always promised her.

I walk down the hall to the bedrooms, presuming that's where I'll find her. Her room is at the farthest end of the lodge, and I walk right in without knocking.

I hear the tap running in the en suite and stride towards the door. She pulls it open just as I reach it, and she sucks in a breath when she sees me.

She tries to close the door, but I grab her waist, walking her backwards into the bathroom and putting her back to the door.

I bring my face to hers, our noses brushing as I reach into the slit in her dress.

"Elliot," she warns against my lips.

My movements are hurried as I slip my fingers into the lace of her underwear, gliding my knuckles through her slickened folds. I gather the material and pull it to the side, then hike her leg around my waist, pinning her to the wall with my hips as I work my belt buckle between us. I unbutton my trousers with one hand and pull out my cock.

I keep my head angled down, refusing to look at her when she says, "Don't do this to us."

My hand reaches around to lift her, angling her so we line up perfectly when I inch forward. I slide in deep, and my head drops to the door, my eyes drifting closed. "Where did we go so fucking wrong?"

My hips roll, and I see stars as our hearts race between us.

I hear her voice crack and squeeze my eyes tighter. "Elliot, look at me."

I roll my hips and try to block her out as she holds on to my back, her leg locking tighter.

"You'll break it completely," she mutters. "Elliot, don't do this, please. Just look at me."

She pulls on my tux jacket, my hair, anything she can to draw my head up.

"Kiss me, dammit!" Her teeth sink into my neck, and I rip my head up as a growl thunders through my chest.

My eyes sear through her as her mouth parts.

I wrap her throat in my palm, dancing my fingers over her neck as I pin her to the wall.

Her eyes roll, and her pussy clenches tight around me,

sucking me deeper as my mouth closes in on hers. I tighten my hold, and she looks up at me as I look down my nose at her, our breaths mingling as we both pant through our arousal.

"Is this all I'll ever get? All I'm good for?"

"No," she chokes out, her hand fisting over mine and clenching it tighter as she whimpers.

I hold her like she wants me to. "You like that?"

"Kiss me," she begs, a stray tear lining her face. "Please, kiss me."

Fuck. I swallow around the ache in my throat as she pulls me impossibly closer, her hands grasping my shoulders.

My jaw goes slack as my toes curl. I lean in, swiping my tongue across the corner of her mouth and up over her cheek, licking up the saltiness. "Is this not enough for you?" My cock jerks prematurely, and I groan, thrusting deep and giving her everything I have.

She holds on tight as I pull her onto me, and I choose to bury my face back into the crevice of her neck, not being able to look into her eyes as I come inside of her.

My chest heaves between us as my breath pants across her smooth skin. I let her go, releasing her throat and pulling out of her. As I take a step back, she slaps me.

And fuck if it doesn't feel all wrong.

"Are you happy?" She cries. "Does it feel any better now?"

"Luce…"

Her hands work on her dress, and then she looks back at me, swiping at the end of her nose.

My jaw locks tight as I try to find something to say.

I take a step towards her, but she holds a hand up, her

eyes filling with tears as her voice cracks. "This isn't you. You don't treat me this way!"

She leaves the bathroom in a rush, but I don't go after her, knowing she will need anyone but me.

I turn and catch my reflection in the mirror. My hair is a mess, and my tux tie is hanging half-off. I turn my neck and see the deep purple bruising forming from her teeth.

I rest against the counter and dip my head.

"What am I?"

"You're Elliot. You're different."

"Different how?"

"I don't know… I know you better than any man I've been with."

"So you'd sleep with me without being in a relationship with me?"

"No."

"No?"

"It's about the connection in that moment. The feelings. Not the relationship."

"Okay. So I have to make you feel something."

A sick feeling rises in my stomach. I push off the basin and leave the bathroom after her.

I find everyone in the living area and quickly pull Nina to one side. "Where is she?"

"Luce?"

"Yeah."

"I thought she was with you."

"She didn't come back out?"

Nina shakes her head and glares at me. "What did you do?"

"Nothing." I take off towards the bedrooms again. She has to be in one of them.

"Elliot," Vinny stops me as I round the corner. He walks

in through the bifold doors and nods his head for me to go to him. "She's gone for a walk. I was just getting Nina."

"Which way?"

"Coastal."

The sun's almost set, but there's a purple hue setting the sky alight as the winds whip up. "I'll go. Don't tell Nina."

He nods his head.

I leave the lodge and follow the coastal path I'd been on earlier.

32

Lucy

The wind whips through my hair as my feet hit the sandy path and carry me towards the horizon.

My face is wet with tears, and no matter how hard I try, I can't stop.

I'm angry at myself. I don't want to live my life holding on for dear life anymore, too afraid of what could happen when it's not reality.

Look where it's got me.

I want to prove them all wrong.

I want to prove *him* wrong.

"You plan to jump, princess? I can't see it."

Without a second thought, I run for the edge of the cliff, my heart hammering in my chest as I leap forward. I instantly look down and panic, seeing the white water and waves crashing against the rocks. I hit the water with a slap, knocking the air right out of me.

For a couple of seconds, there's quiet. Slowed, serene

silence as the water bathes me, and I almost understand the rush they all go on about. But then I swim to the surface, ready to gasp for a breath and the second I do, a wave crashes on top of me, forcing me into the cliffs with force.

I frown, squeezing my eyes tight as I reach for my forehead. "Shit."

Panic creeps up my throat, and I ease back from the rock.

As I turn, ready to swim around to the steps on the other side, someone grabs me.

"Baby."

His arm wraps around my waist as his other hand plants firmly against the cliff. "The fuck were you thinking," he pants into my wet hair.

He pulls me closer to him, holding me in his arms like I might break.

"I thought—" my voice shakes, and I swallow hard, fighting against the emotion.

He pulls me to the other side of the two rocks I've jumped between, then wraps my arms around his back and swims us towards the shore.

As soon as I can stand, I do, rushing up the beach in my soaking wet dress and feeling foolish for even jumping.

"You couldn't do it, could you," he says to my back, his voice thick with emotion.

My face screws up, and I keep walking.

"You couldn't be alone. You had to cling to something, as always. You don't even like him, do you?"

I come to a stop in the sand as tears burn in my eyes.

"You can't be alone."

I turn and look at him, his tux soaked through and his face utterly broken. "Why else, Luce? Tell me I'm wrong!"

I don't know what he wants me to say, and looking at his face makes my throat ache. All week I've demanded he listen to me, and now I can't form a single sentence.

My eyes blink and cut to the sand.

"Outta your hea—"

"No!" I ground out, shocking the both of us as I lift my head. "I won't." I step towards him. "I'm in my head, Elliot. I'm always in my head, and that's never going to go away. It's me. It's the only thing I have, and you can't control that right now or tell me to turn it off. I went to New York because of *you!* Because you told me it was the right thing to do." My face screws up as tears fall. "I fell in love with you. I fell in love with you so bad, and then you cut me off."

His nostrils flare, his taut jaw flexing as he watches me with his eyes shining. "I don't want you to change who you are."

"I know. You only wanted me to live my life. I just didn't know there were rules."

"You brought him here," he grits out.

"And I'm so, so sorry." My chin trembles. "I didn't know you were coming, Elliot."

"You let another man touch you," he says as if it pains him.

I shake my head, running my fingers through my hair at a loss. "You cut me off, Elliot! You made me feel these… things, and then you dropped me as if none of it mattered!"

"I fell in love with *you*!" he bellows, and my heart all but stops. "You think you're the only one? I fell in love with you before you left me. I fell in love with you before I even knew who you really were. From the first night I met you—from my friend to every look that followed. Every word shared. Every fear I found. I fell in love with *you*."

Elliot Montgomery fell in love with me?

"And you chose to fall into someone else."

"Ell, no."

He steps forward and grasps my face in his large palm, his other hand sliding up the back of my neck as he pulls me to him. His lips part, mere inches from my own. "You know what's worse than that, though, what keeps me awake at night?"

My tears run over my lips, and he wipes them away with his thumbs. "I *still* fucking love you."

His mouth crashes to mine, coaxing my lips apart with a kiss so full of passion, it will be seared into my memory for an eternity.

Our desperation fuels us. Weeks of nothing, and now he's kissing me. He's showing me without any more words what this is.

"Elliot."

He lifts me, holding me to him as he refuses to break our kiss. I'm weightless despite my soaked dress, completely lost to him as he carries us up the beach and to the steps.

With each step he takes we become a little more lost. A little more frantic. A little more in love.

There is no more restraint, and I feel it freely.

"Elliot." I pull on his hair, praying he drops us to the ground and gives us both what we crave.

Connection.

Him.

Us.

It's all I need.

But he doesn't let up, walking blindly until my back hits something cold and hard. I think we're back at the lodge, and I frown at how quick we got here, but when I pull away, I see that he's unlocking a different door. "Where are we?"

He looks at me, nose to nose, his eyes heavy, and his lips swollen. My feet hit the ground, but he keeps me close.

"My place."

He pulls my lips into a deep kiss before drawing away again, his eyes riveted to them.

"They clean it and keep it maintained, but the beds might not be made."

I kiss him back, not giving a crap if the beds are made.

"Hmmm," I moan.

"Baby, say it again," he hums, kissing me.

"I love you?"

Kiss.

"You say it—"

Kiss.

"Again," I pant, pulling his shirt from his slacks.

He smiles against my mouth, and my stomach bottoms out. "No."

I groan, and he pushes open the door, his mouth on my neck as he guides me backwards into the dark lodge.

"I'm going to fuck you." His tongue flattens against the hollow dip in my throat. He taunts me, dragging it up slowly then sucking at my jaw. "I'm going to fuck you properly." He smiles against me again, and I know it's my weak spot. This man shouldn't be allowed to smile, let alone when his mouth is on me.

I pull at his hair, and he lets out a growl as he lifts me at the waist.

"You fucked me against a door already tonight," I tell him, my hands working on his buttons as he grinds his cock against me. His shirt hangs open, and he leans back, placing his hand around my throat, mimicking the move from before. His thumb dusts over my erratic pulse, and I take him in.

He's so fucking hot. It's not right. Not normal.

He shakes his head. "That was me fulfilling a promise." His eyes dance with sin. "Trust me when I tell you, when I fuck you, you'll know."

"No," I paw his hand away from my throat, sliding my arms around his shoulders where I pull on the hair at the nape of his neck until his head eases back. "That was you being a prick." I force his face back to mine as I shift myself higher around his waist, using my legs to lock myself tight. Our mouths brush, and his lips part, ready for something I hold back. "Trust me when I tell *you*, when you've fulfilled that promise, *you'll* know." I lick my lips and catch his. "You'll know, Ell." I grind my hips, and he groans, looking between us at where our bodies align.

"Baby, I'm still going to fuck you against this door."

"I know. Get it over with so you can love me."

His smirk is sexy and full and makes my body heat. I expect him to take me against the door, but he must have other ideas because he turns and walks me through the lodge.

My eyes are wide compared to his heavy, lust-filled ones. He stares at me as he walks us out onto the terrace, and I don't know what it is that he sees, but it makes my throat tight.

His forehead touches mine, and he gives me a deep kiss before pulling away again. "I'm sorry. The way I treated you in that bathroom—"

I shake my head and kiss him, cutting him off.

He slides me down his body until my feet land beside a wooden hot tub. "Turn around," he mumbles against my mouth.

I turn, and he gathers up my hair, placing it over my shoulder. I feel him nearing, and I think he will kiss me again but instead, his teeth sink into the sensitive skin between my neck and shoulder, pinching, biting before he soothes it with a sucking kiss.

"I want you naked and on me," he rasps against the shell of my ear. He slides the zip down on my dress. "I need your body—skin to skin fucking, baby. I need it more than air right now."

Anticipation swims in my gut, and I roll my head back onto his chest, but he quickly rights me again. I watch as he removes the lid of the hot tub and steam billows into the air. It's not cold out, but the wind seems to whip around us, creating a chill down my arms.

Elliot faces me. His shirt is open, and my eyes are drawn to his stomach, the way his abs flex and ripple as he moves. He reaches out and slips his hand into my dress, cupping my breast as he pushes the material down my arm until it catches at my wrists. I slip my hands from the holes and let it drop.

I stand in front of him in nothing but my thong, his

hand still cupping my breast. He dusts his thumb across my nipple, then pinches it.

As he steps toward me, I take his shirt and pull it from his body so that when he brings our bodies together, our skin brushes.

"Baby, you're so beautiful. So sexy."

I slide my hands up his strong back and back down again, looking up at him as my hands drift over his ass. I slip into his boxer briefs and squeeze. He clenches tight, grinding his hips into my stomach.

My hands move around and work on his trousers, undoing the button. I push them over his thighs in a rush along with his boxers, but then he lifts me at the waist and locks my legs at his back again.

He steps into the hot tub and lowers us into the water. I cling to him as we submerge.

"Luce."

I look up and find him watching me.

"I'm sorry."

I swallow, needing more and less and the entire world he lives in. "So am I."

He takes my lips in a gentle kiss, coaxing my tongue with his own. It makes my body ache for him. A burning need that starts in my lower belly and flushes throughout my entire centre.

"You're so hard," I say, running my fingers across his scalp as his lips drop to my neck.

I roll my hips over him, and he groans.

His head lifts, and an amused smile transforms his face. "Fuck, I've waited too long for this."

I smile and laze back as he rests me against the side of

the hot tub. Elliot stands, and my legs drop to the water, but he keeps himself between my thighs.

I bite my lip as I take in his naked body.

He's phenomenal.

His penis is fucking phenomenal.

He glides his hands from my knees up to my hips, then to my waist, where he dusts his thumbs across the taut skin covering my ribs.

I know what he's going to do before he does it, and my back arches, meeting his hot mouth as it falls to my chest. His stubble scratches and tickles me, and it's completely on purpose. He knows what it's doing to me. Knows I'm desperate and needy and insatiable for him in this moment.

"Elliot, please." I look down, watching as his mouth dusts over my breast but never where I want him. "I need more."

His cock is hard and hangs heavy between us, occasionally dragging over my stomach and groin.

"So impatient. What if I want to take my time?" He skims the tip of one nipple with his chin, and I whimper.

He chuckles. "I already know it's not going to be enough. You want to know what I'm thinking about? What's making my dick weep for you right now?"

"Yes." I roll my hips against his thigh, closing my eyes when my pussy clenches, becoming slick with my need for him.

"I'm thinking about how I should take you, how long I'll have to wait to take you again if I go too hard, what you might like, what you won't like, how much you'll take from me before you reach your limit. Fuck, I hope you don't stop me before I'm done with you." He runs his hands lower and around to my ass, lifting me out of the water slightly.

I hold on to the side of the tub.

He bends, sinking to his knee, and I watch with a lust-filled stare as his shoulders move through the water. His mouth covers my pussy, and I groan. He pushes his tongue deep between my aching lips before sucking once. His mouth glistens as he pulls away all too fast, and I reach for him. "I want you to take every inch for me, sweet girl, and then I want you to take a little more." His thumb sweeps over my clit, and I moan in desperation. "Will you be a good girl and take it for me?"

I nod.

"I knew you would."

He rights himself, taking his cock in his hand and pumping three times.

With my arms lying along the top of the hot tub, Elliot takes my hips and hikes me up. He lines himself up, trailing his cock through my folds, teasing me, before he pushes in the slightest bit.

Our mouths part, and our eyes meet. We were both looking at the same thing—the way he braced against me. The way I coated him right before he—

"Take it all for me, princess."

He rolls his hips, sinking into me as he collapses forward. His arm brushes my head as his hand plants itself on the side of the tub, bracing himself.

"Fuck." He bands his arm around my lower back, taking me completely in his hold. He bends his knees and rocks slowly into me.

It's the perfect position.

Gentle.

Deep.

Close.

My arms wrap around his neck, knowing he's got me. "Elliot?" I whisper, needily pulling him tighter to me.

His eyes open, his nose brushing mine. "What is it, baby?"

I slant my thumb over his lips, and he kisses the pad. "Please, look at me."

He groans, closing the distance and licking through my mouth. I catch his tongue with my own before drawing his lips into a wet kiss. It's hungry and sends us into a frenzy.

His hips work as he guides my own, sucking at my throat then jumping back to my mouth for a messy kiss while he pulls me harder onto him with his arm that's wrapped around my back.

The water sloshes over the sides, and it's euphoric—all of it. The sky above us and the wind that whips through my hair. The water we fuck in. The way Elliot's jaw hangs slack, his eyes almost closed, but *never* fully.

This is ecstasy in its purest form.

"I'm sorry," I say in a whisper, frowning the moment the words are out.

We're in the master bedroom of the Montgomerys' family lodge, and I watch transfixed as the sun rises up over the cliff's edge. We haven't slept. I'm not sure we would've even if we wanted to.

The need we shared to consume ourselves with one

another was too overwhelming. Elliot couldn't stop, yet I still begged him for more. Every time he'd pull away from me, I'd be on him, holding him, wrapping myself in him and making him hold me for longer.

I know I'll never find a better lover than the beautiful man currently sprawled out across my stomach, and that realisation makes the guilt burning in my stomach seem all the more bitter.

"What are you sorry for, princess?" he murmurs, his voice gruff and sounding sleepy.

"I don't know, exactly." I shrug as my fingers run through his hair. "There's lot of things, and I wish I could explain them all to you. And maybe that's the problem. I don't know. I'm never truly sure."

Elliot doesn't say anything, and I can't seem to stop.

"You probably deserve someone better than that. Someone who can stand up and make clear exactly what they want."

He lifts his head and studies me, a frown pulling his brows together. "I've not always seen you. Not really. Not the man you really are. You never deserved my doubt, and maybe that's what I'm sorry for." I look back out through the bifold doors, eyeing the horizon so I can escape his intense gaze. "But I do love you, Ell. It's not enough, but it's the only thing I'm sure of."

"Stop." He kisses my stomach, his lips lingering on my soft skin as he speaks. "I'm not like you. I didn't fall for a dream or a *what-if.* I fell for you day one, and I'll fall for you through every moment of finding who you want to be. I told you," the words muffle as he leans down to kiss my side. "I don't want you to change who you are. You can doubt me all you want because I'm not going anywhere."

I grin down at him, my throat tight. "That was entirely too sweet for your filthy mouth, Elliot Montgomery."

Something sparks in his eyes. "Fuck," he says, smirking.

He rises on his knees, grasps my hips and pulls me down the bed. He pinches my nipple, and I can't help but chuckle as I attempt to roll away. "How about we dirty it up a bit?"

My laugh fills the room, and I hastily shoot forward, grabbing his neck and kissing him in a rush. He pulls me up to my knees, matching his position on the bed. Our smiles seem to slip away a second after our lips touch, and then his hands drift over my body in our silence, one wraps around my waist, and the other moves up my spine to hold me at the nape, moulding me to him.

Our kiss is gentle, slow, and unlike anything we've shared before. I swear he can sense it too. The way his arms are fixed so fiercely on my body, and the way his heart thumps, so in rhythm with my own.

He pulls back an inch, our lips barely part. "Outta your head, baby. You're mine now." His mouth drifts over mine, then higher, where he places a lingering kiss on my forehead. "It's not even up to us. It's never been up to us."

33

Lucy

We take our time walking back to the lodge. The idea we had to leave at all seemed unfair, but as we do make our way back across the cliff tops, I feel reality lurking in my every shadow. I have things to put right, and I know I can't put it off any longer.

Elliot called Mason late last night to let him know we were staying at the house, and I can't help but wonder what they will all be thinking.

I came to this island with another man, and yet I've spent more time with Elliot—been intimate with him, which will be obvious to them all. It doesn't feel wrong, and I don't carry the regret I probably should, but it *is* wrong.

"I'm going home early. When we get back, I'm going to book a flight. I need to go to New York and put everything right."

"No, you're not."

"I have to, Elliot."

He pulls on my arm, our linked hands twisting and moving to my back. We come to a stop, and he looks down his nose at me, challenging me. "You're not going anywhere. I've just got you back. Enjoy the next couple of days with me, and we'll fix everything else when we get home."

"I can't do what I need to do with Max over the phone. He lives in Ralph's house. I need to explain everything. Then *we* can move forward."

"Come on, Luce, I watched him shove his tongue down someone else's throat—you watched him. He can go fuck himself if he thinks he deserves an explanation. You're not leaving me." He walks off down the coastal path, his tux jacket thrown over his shoulder.

I carry on forward, not rushing to catch up. "It doesn't make it any less wrong," I call out.

He shakes his head, slowing his steps.

"It's not just about Maxwell," I tell him as I fall into step beside him. "He does deserve the truth, but this is about you, too. And me. I won't have us trapped in this situation any longer. It's not fair to anyone, and I don't want anything between us."

I squint up at him when a minute passes, and he doesn't say anything. I find him grinning down at me with that panty-melting smile.

"What?" I ask, wondering how his mood can flip so easily.

"Nothing."

"I'm going home," I tell him, resolute.

"So that you can be my girlfriend?"

I roll my lips in an attempt to control my face. Still, my stomach flips and my face burns.

"What if I don't ask you, princess?" he teases. "What if I don't want a girlfriend who lives thousands of miles away?"

"What if you moved to New York?" I swallow and look up at him.

His face drops, and he steps back. I catch the faintest smile that traces the corner of his mouth like he can't control his gut reaction to my question.

"For the rest of your internship?" he asks, frowning still.

I nod.

His teeth scrape across his bottom lip as he considers it. "We'd live together—"

"We could have separate rooms or even our own floors. You've seen the house."

"I'd be inside of you every night."

"Oh."

"I'd need to sit down with Lowell. Fuck, Luce. Nina's pregnant." He rubs his fingers across his forehead. "I want to. Uninterrupted Luce time for eight whole months." He pulls me to him, bunching up my still damp dress and lifting me in his arms. "Where do I sign up?"

I grin down at him as he spins me. "I didn't think. It's really bad timing, isn't it?"

"You couldn't get worse timing," he agrees. His forehead meets mine as the sun breaks the horizon fully. "I need him to experience every bit of this pregnancy, Luce."

I nod, falling impossibly further. "I know."

"But you're going to do this, baby. It's only eight months, and this time, you belong to me."

I smile, knowing I can do it this time. Knowing I'll have Elliot right there.

And my girls.

"Come on," he murmurs, kissing my jaw as he lets me slip down to the ground. "Ellis will be wondering where we are, and I don't need a week of questioning from him."

We start back on the path, and Elliot entwines our fingers again. "He'll miss you, you know. If you leave early, I won't hear the end of it."

I groan, resting my head on his shoulder. "Don't guilt me. I have to go back."

I'M NERVOUS.

My plane touched down in New York at ten o'clock this evening, and I take all the time in the world as I walk down the street towards my house.

Maxwell can react without thinking sometimes, can say things he doesn't mean, and I know he will be upset over what I've done behind his back.

That doesn't mean I'm not going to do what I need to. But it also doesn't fill me with any hope that the situation will be pretty.

The lights are off when I approach the house, and I peek around the steps to see if Alec is home.

I wonder if Polly is back yet.

My key turns in the lock, and I push forward through the door, instantly knowing the house is empty. A relieved breath expels from my chest, and I make my way to the kitchen, switching on every light in the house as I go.

I pour myself a glass of wine from the fridge and gulp down the contents before filling it again.

I take my full glass and bypass my suitcase, walking up to my room so I can change into something comfy.

Maxwell should be home soon. Or maybe he won't? Quite often, he and Alec will be away for days at a time on a job.

The coward in me hopes that tonight is one of those nights.

I shower and dress in an oversized T-shirt and shorts. Then I crawl into bed and wait.

I CAN HEAR MAXWELL. He's outside my door speaking to someone. Or at least he sounds like he's close by.

He's yelling.

Who is he yelling at?

My eyes peel open, and I'm met with darkness as my eyes adjust. For a second, my brain short-circuits and I have to remind myself I'm in my bed in New York. I'm not on the island, curled up to Elliot's side while he draws circles on my back.

"Alec, fuck! Hurry up!"

Frowning, I pull back my covers and hurry to the door. I pull it open without thinking and gasp in shock when I am met with a wide-eyed-looking Polly standing just feet away from me.

I grab my chest, feeling thankful she's here, when a loud bang rings out from the top floor. "Lucy, get back inside," she whispers. "You don't leave this room, do you understand me? You do not leave this room."

I frown at her tone. At her urgency. "Pol, what's going on?"

"Can you lock the door?"

"What?"

Lock the door?

She forcefully pushes me back and into the room while looking over her shoulder. When she checks over my door and turns back to me again, she does it with a gun held out in her grasp. "You take this. You do not fire it unless you need to protect yourself. Do you understand me? Tell me you understand."

"No. Polly, what—"

She throws the gun onto my bed and rushes for the door. "Stay here."

"Polly!" I whisper-shout.

She pins me with a stare, and I swallow my words. The second Polly leaves my room and my door clicks shut, I rush around to the other side of my bed, and I grab my phone from the nightstand. I look down at my shaking hands and then the gun sitting on top of my sheets.

I blow out a breath before fleeting on unsteady legs to my wardrobe—no gun. I shut and lock the door, keeping the lights off and knowing it will take time for anyone to break through it.

Then, I call the police.

Detective Murley Wright

I ALWAYS KNEW this day would come.

My feet swipe at the tarmac with precision, propelling me closer and closer to the house. It's one I know.

One I've lived in.

I jog up the stoop, skipping every other step before softening my footing and slipping inside.

At first, I don't hear a thing, but then an all too familiar voice hushes from a higher floor. With my hand on my gun, I lean towards the bannister and look up through the railings.

I'm almost certain I could walk up there and pretend I've been away, and they would both be stupid enough to believe me. If they weren't being tracked by the wrong people right now, I would. I'm not about to lose my badge for doing something stupid.

Two years.

It ends tonight.

I go home to my family.

They go to prison.

I place a foot on the first step, followed by my other, slowly creeping up the first floor and then around to the second set of steps.

Halfway up, I stop and listen.

Once I'm certain I'm right, I make the call. "This is Detective Murley Wright. Two white males, likely armed, potential ambush as planned. I am inside the building and will wait out with caution."

Slipping my phone back into my pocket, I mentally run over the footprint of the third floor. There are two bedrooms on this level, and I make my way towards the one at the front of the building, knowing it will give me a vantage point of being able to see up the stairs.

I take three strides forward, and just as I near the first bedroom, the door flies open.

My heart sinks when I see Lucy standing in the doorway.

Why is she back already?

She shouldn't be here.

I planned it perfectly to keep her out of it.

I snap into action as a thud sounds from upstairs. "Lucy, get back inside. You don't leave this room, do you understand me?" I lock eyes with her. "You do not leave this room."

Her brows pull in, and I know she's confused, but the panic in my chest doesn't allow me to soften.

"Pol, what's going on?"

"Can you lock the door?"

"What?"

I look around the landing, quickly ushering her back into the room. I check the door and see there isn't a lock. I close my eyes and think, my hand on my pistol. "You take this. You do not fire it unless you need to protect yourself. Do you understand me? Tell me you understand."

"No. Polly, what—"

"Stay here." Her hysterics rise, and I know I have to move.

"Polly!" she hisses, clutching at her T-shirt.

She shouldn't be here.

Why is she here?

My jaw locks tight, and I turn, pinning her with a look that tells her to shut the hell up.

I contemplate going to the bedroom as planned and

waiting for Felix, but now I know Lucy is here, I can't waste time, and I can't put her in danger.

Pulling out my phone, I text Bishop.

Murley: ETA?

Bishop: 6. We're talking about this when we get back. The fuck were you thinking Murl?

Murley: Lucy is home. Cut Felix off outside and keep it quiet. I'm not waiting.

Six minutes. I push my phone into my pocket as it flashes with a call. I know I'm breaking rules, but I also know there isn't a detective on this side of the island who would walk back down those stairs. If I wait, we run the risk of missing this moment, and I won't. Not after all the work I've put in.

All the work *they* have put in.

Alec has been working on this run for months. The fact it's gone tits up before they could make it out of the borough is laughable.

They're panicking. Which also confirms there's a rat amongst the pact because someone tipped Alec off—he knows Felix is coming for them.

But what they don't know is that *I'm* coming for them. I might not be able to take them all down tonight, but I'll take Alec.

I slowly climb the stairs, knowing the bedroom door is open. My mind works as I try to listen.

"What you're saying is one of us is fucked," Maxwell spits out. I peer over the top step, spotting his sneakers shuffling just inside the door.

"We're both fucked!" Alec huffs, sounding winded. Probably from moving his stash all the way from the basement.

"At least one of us stands a chance if we split. We leave this here and hope it's enough."

"You got me into this! You're going to get me killed!"

I hear things being pushed around—boxes, I presume, scraping across the wood floor.

When Alec doesn't respond, Maxwell stalks forward. I hear a thud, followed by another.

"You stupid—"

I make the most of the opportunity, knowing they're distracted.

I rush the room, pulling my gun from my ankle holster.

"Keep your fucking voice—"

"You're under arrest! Turn around and put your hands behind your back!"

Alec spots me the second I walk in, but Maxwell has to spin, his face turning as white as the powder they have stashed in the twenty-plus boxes at their feet.

"Pol—"

"FUCKING NOW! Move!"

Alec pulls a gun before I can get the words out fully, matching my stance from across the room.

"Don't be stupid, Polly. Put the gun down. Now." His voice is calmer than it should be, and it has the hairs on the back of my neck standing on end.

"Fuck you! You're done, and you know it, Alec."

"Am I? You don't think I'd pull the trigger on you?"

"I know you wouldn't," I sneer, watching as Maxwell side-eyes Alec.

Alec always knew I wasn't who I said I was, or he at least suspected it recently. He fell harder than he was supposed to. I did my job too well in the beginning, and I plan to reap every second of what I've sown. "I have a team waiting for you outside, front and back. They're ready to stop Felix under my orders."

I see Alec's brows flinch.

"You have a choice. You can walk down those stairs in handcuffs, or I can make a call and have them stand down, let Felix up here with his minions." I tip my chin at his gun when I see his jaw flex. He knows I have him, the little rat. I step towards him, knowing he won't shoot me. "You don't steal from the boss, baby. You got greedy. I saw it happening. Closer and closer." I walk to him, just a foot away. "You brought them to me."

"You little bitch!" Maxwell seethes, throwing his fist into my cheek. It's so unexpected, I lose my footing and fall to the floor. My gun flies from my grasp. "FUCK!" I hear Maxwell roar, losing control as he kicks his foot through a box.

I try to clear my vision.

"Alec, let's go," Maxwell urges.

I attempt to get up, but my body isn't working at the same speed as my brain. I can't move.

Shit, he got me good.

A split second, and I slipped.

I lost focus.

I see Alec coming closer, and he bends so that he's face to face with me. "You tipped Felix off?"

My lip curls, and I shake my head. "No," I say, rubbing my fingers over my cheek. "That would be against police policy."

"You're laughing at me, Pol, yet you're the one on the floor."

I blink twice, trying in vain to clear my vision fully. As I find my focus, I feel a sharp tug at the back of my head. A loud groan leaves me as I'm pulled upright, and I scramble with unsteady feet as I try to find my balance. I look over my shoulder and spot Alec backing us out of the room and then down the stairs.

My cheek throbs, and I can tell it's swelling by the way my eye seems to close in on itself.

"What's your plan? Do you even have one?" I taunt, mentally figuring out my next move.

Alec aims the gun at me as he dashes down the last few steps. I flinch internally but keep putting one foot in front of the other.

They'll be waiting for us outside.

They said six minutes.

As he reaches the bottom step, he starts to say something but quickly cuts himself off. The door to Lucy's room is slightly ajar, and it snaps shut the second Alec pauses.

Before I can stop him, he kicks his foot through the wood.

Lucy

THE SOUND of Polly's struggle has me up on my feet and at the door before I can think twice about it. The dispatcher is still on the phone, but her words seem to fade out as I flick the lock on the wardrobe door.

"Can you hear me?"

I step from the wardrobe and scan my bedroom. Everything is how it should be, and I quickly make my way to the door, twisting the handle gentle enough to not make a sound. I have no idea what or who could be on the other side of the door, and the fact Polly offered me a gun tells me it's not anything good.

I can hear shuffling outside the room, and I tentatively pull it open.

A slither of light streams in, lining my face. I blink at the intrusion, open my eyes again, then I see Maxwell.

He's jogging down the stairs from the top floor, and I instinctively take a step back.

That's my gut reaction, and it terrifies me.

Why would he run in the other direction while Polly is clearly struggling upstairs?

He passes me in a rush, and I watch as he pulls out a key for the small door that leads to the basements staircase.

He's skittish, on edge, as he glances around the landing with wide eyes.

I go to pull the door open further, ready to call him out for scaring us, but then I hear boots thumping down the stairs.

"What's your plan? Do you even have one?"

My blood turns cold. I watch in horror as Alec shoves a gun in Polly's face. My heart becomes out of control, and I grasp my chest with a hand still locked tight on the door.

What's going on?

This isn't real.

This is Ralph's home. Tears fill my eyes. Who have I let into his home?

My chest seems to get tighter and tighter, and I know I'm panicking.

A soft voice echoes through the phone. "Ma'am, is it safe for you to speak?"

The next intake of breath I gather isn't a full one.

No. No. Breathe.

I push the door shut in a rush and step back.

"I can't breathe," I panic.

"Lucy, are you safe?"

I can't breathe—

The bedroom door flies open, smashing into the chest of drawers at its back. I take three steps away as my palm rubs at my breastbone.

"Why the fuck are you here?"

My eyes dart between Alec and Polly's, her face full of remorse. Maxwell appears at the door, and his shoulders drop.

"Luce? What are you doing home?"

He takes a step towards me, and I flinch, my breathing getting worse. "No," I heave.

Realisation seems to filter over his face, and his own panic sets in. He looks over his shoulder then back at Alec. "We have to go. Now."

There's the telling sound of the front door crashing open downstairs. Glass smashes, and I know it's the frames falling from the walls.

The police.

They're here.

"Fuck." Maxwell's voice is barely above a whisper, and I watch with my heart in my mouth as the blood drains from all three of their faces.

"Move. Now," Polly orders, stepping from Alec's hold

and grabbing my arm. She moves for the door when Alec steps in front of her.

There are people shouting and hollering downstairs, and I wonder why they aren't helping me.

I want to call out and tell them I'm here, but I don't think I can form the words.

"Nobody double-crosses me."

Polly steps forward, my arm still in her grasp. "Alec, let her—"

"No," he whispers it. He whispers it so calmly, it sends a chill up my spine. "You wanted me tonight, *baby*, and I'm giving you Felix instead. You fucked up, didn't you?" He laughs. "Well, you're welcome." I watch in horror as he spits in Polly's face, then hits her around the head with his gun.

"Polly!" I cry out, trying but struggling to break her fall. "Oh my god," I mutter, my body physically shaking as I look up at Alec from the ground.

"Lucy, get up," Maxwell demands from the door.

"No." I take a deep exhale.

"Get up!" he shouts, stalking towards me.

"Get… away from… me."

"Leave her." My eyes shoot to Alec's as he backs out of the room. "Fucking leave her, Max!"

Maxwell's gaze locks with mine as footsteps thud up the first floor and across the landing.

Then, he turns on his heel and runs.

There's only one set of stairs between the police and this floor, and my breathing seems to calm as the realisation that someone is coming to help us sets in.

"Polly. Wake up!" I shake her, and she stirs. "Pol, it's me, Luce."

She sits up in a daze, looking around the room, disorientated. "Where are they?"

"I think they took… the stairs to the basement."

Footsteps get closer and closer, and she stands, losing her balance before quickly finding it again.

"Get back in the wardrobe."

"What?" I mutter, kneeling on the floor. "No."

"Lucy, please. I beg you. Listen to what I say."

Something in the tone of her voice terrifies me.

A loud crash sounds in the next room, and she points to the bed. I frown before realising she wants me to hide.

I lie on my stomach, thrashing my things out of the way as I slide under.

Seconds later, they stalk into the room.

I can see chunky black boots—lots of them. And as the air shifts I know it's not the police.

My hand lifts, and I cover my mouth, knowing if I don't, my breathing will give me away.

I watch in horror as someone walks to the wardrobe and looks inside, then the bathroom, and then they stop beside my bed.

"Police! Stay where you are!"

Polly's black trainers step into view, and I fixate on them. They don't budge as the heavy boots step up to them, toe to toe.

"The fuck did you just say, silly girl?"

"You're under arrest," she says, full of conviction. "*All* of you."

There's a laugh. It's light and dark and has my mind wondering who it could possibly belong to.

Who is this man?

"I don't want to hurt you, darling."

"You're under arrest for suppl—"

Polly hits the floor with a sickening thud.

A tear slips down my cheek as I squeeze my eyes tight, my hand plastered to my mouth.

She quickly scrambles to stand, and then a moment later, something unexpected happens.

He hits the floor.

All two hundred pounds of him.

He startles for a moment, just as shocked as I am. I see the other boots in the room move towards Polly as he stands, and then there's a click followed by silence.

Polly's trainer shifts half an inch, and I still.

Something lodges in my throat, and I try to swallow past it.

"You're going to shoot a police officer? Think about it, pretty boy."

I instantly search for a footing on the floor, knowing I can't lie here and let Polly be alone in this. There's not one talent I possess that can help her, but doing nothing isn't an option.

There's a scuffle, and I see Polly trying to keep her feet sturdy, but there are two sets of boots by her, and her grunts tell me she won't be able to take another hit.

The image of Alec cracking her over the head with his gun flashes, and my stomach turns.

Get up, Lucy.

Now!

I plant my hand down on the floor and push forward, but it slips out from under me. I peer down to find an envelope stuck to my damp palm—the edges still crinkled.

For when you need something to fixate on.

My eyes close as my mouth parts, finally expelling all the air in my lungs with ease.

The envelope is clenched tight in my hand as I pull myself forward and swipe at the legs of the man who's stood in front of me.

He stumbles but doesn't fall. And then, before I can make a move to stand, a boot connects with the side of my head.

I hear the sound of the room erupting in chaos.

I hear Polly's fight leave her as her grunts become barely audible.

I finally hear sirens.

And then, I get outta my head.

34

Lucy

When something bad happens, people always say, I never thought it would happen to me. Yet as someone with constant plaguing thoughts, chances are I have thought about it. Like what happened back at the house, I've thought about that exact moment. Not with Maxwell, or Polly, or the policeman sitting across the hospital room from me now, or even the details that make it all so very real. But there's always been this faceless fight in my mind. They bring me down, grab hold of me, and yell in my face. I run, they catch me, I find a way out. I would've been lost in my mind at the time, thinking up a scenario so far from my reality. It would've had my stomach turned up in knots.

Although it wasn't ever me I'd see.

There's this woman in my mind. She isn't me, but she looks like me. She speaks with my very voice, only it never shakes. She's brave, strong, lives for herself and makes the best choices. *That woman* has lived through this already—a constant stream of what-ifs. She analyses the situations, going over them time and time again until she wins.

She always wins.

She's the bravest person I know, and tonight was the closest I've ever come to feeling her strength.

Tonight I learnt that I have the solutions to all of my fears because I gave them to myself.

I just have to use them without being afraid of everything going wrong.

"Her name's Murley," I say with a frown, my gaze still trained on the hospital bed.

I feel his eyes on me briefly, but when I turn to face him, they're already back on her.

"I had no idea," I mutter.

"You weren't supposed to."

I watch him for a minute. I watch him watch her. The way his elbows rest on his knees, and he openly seethes. He's mad. And it seems to be directed at Murley.

"She was incredible, you know. It was terrifying—they had a gun aimed at her. She knew they were about to find me and made sure they didn't." I shake my head, thinking back to how she stepped up without a second thought. "I don't know where anyone finds the courage—"

"Years in training will do it."

I nod, swallowing the rest of my words.

Mr Angry Pants doesn't want to talk.

Noted.

The door opens a few minutes later, and an officer steps in. "Bishop, a minute, please."

He throws me a look before standing to leave the room.

Watch her.

I nod, wondering what kind of a relationship Murley has with the detective.

For a while, I sit in the quiet room, processing everything that's happened. The hospital called my family while I had tests carried out on my head, and Mum and Dad are trying to get a flight out now. I asked that they don't tell the others right away—my intentions were only to give them their last two days on holiday before they all panic and rush back, because they will.

My gut tells me my parents wouldn't have listened.

They're already on their way.

I stand and move to sit on the edge of the bed. My eyes drop to the envelope, still crumpled in my hand. I flatten it before flipping it over.

"He'd kill me if he knew I told you what's written in here," I tell a sleeping Murley.

I peel open the seal and start to read it out loud.

Luce,

If you've opened this, then I first want you to know that you are without doubt the most remarkable, ambitious, and beautiful girl on earth, and you most certainly don't need my words, secrets, or fears to get you out of whatever pitiful situation you're currently in; you are far superior to every single one of them.

I'm not sure I'll ever fully understand your mind, and for that, I'm sorry. But when you tell me you can't focus, eat, sleep, or even breathe, I might just understand that feeling.

You're probably rolling your eyes, but there have been too many times in the short time I've known you where you've left me so fucked, I've been unable to do anything but take the next breath.

Sometimes, I think you look at me and see it, and maybe you do. Like in the restaurant the other night. The way your eyes seemed to tell me more than those sweet lips did.

Shit. If anyone walks into my office right now. You're not even here, and you're fucking with me, making me inappropriately hard under my desk.

The things I do for you, Morgan.

Alright, here goes...

My secret? My secret is that I probably shouldn't want you to fall in love with me. I'm not sure what type of person that makes me. A selfish one, maybe?

But I still hope that you do.

I don't know what I'd even do with it, but sometimes I'll be sat watching you, and you'll catch me out, you'll throw me that uncertain smile I love, and I get this incredible warm feeling that spreads throughout my chest.

I wonder if it would feel a little like that?

And as for my fear? My fear is that one day you'll need me enough to read this, and then I'll have to be the man I'm not sure I am nor will ever be. Terrifies me, actually, because you deserve more than that.

More than me.

I haven't given you a ton of advice here. You're either feeling better, and you're laughing, or I've fucked it, and you can no longer read the words from distress.

Just remember, you're the motherfucking main character, princess.

You don't need anything but a catchy beat and a dress made of magic flowers.

Elliot.

Tears run freely down my face, and although I want to focus on the words, my mind is doing its thing, and all I can think about is how I've had this letter since the day I left for New York and never opened it.

"I can barely look at you right now. It hurts my face to cry." My head snaps up at Murley's voice, and I find her cheeks lined with her own tears. "You never told me about Elliot."

"I wasn't sure you even liked me some days." I chuckle, taking her hand. "Do you want me to get someone? Bishop?"

She smiles and looks away, emotion taking over her face as it screws up. "Did they get away?"

I shake my head, but she doesn't see. I scoot closer and squeeze her hand in mine. "No, no, Pol, they got them. You did it. They got all of them."

She turns back to look at me. "What?"

I nod and wipe my face. "You did it. I heard the police officers talking, bigging you up about how you pulled it off."

"Felix, too?"

I smile and nod again. "I don't know what I would've done if you hadn't shown up. Thank you, *Murley*."

She laughs, but I can sense her pain as she winces slightly before trying to move up the bed. "You weren't part of the plan, Lucy. When I met you in that bar that first night I wanted to tell you to run far and wide."

"Why didn't you?" I question unapologetically.

"You brought me closer. I never had a good reason to stay out with them in the evenings, and I definitely didn't have the same access to Maxwell that I've had since you showed up. My superiors looked at you as the perfect in. When Maxwell suggested we move into the house, I should've said no. I'm sorry for that."

"Are you?" I ask, looking between us. "It set it up perfectly, right?"

"It meant I got them quicker. But you were always to be left out of it."

"It worked out in the end and—"

"A word when you're done here, Wright."

My eyes widen, and I don't dare turn. I bite my bottom lip at the tone of his voice, smiling through it at Murley. "You never told me about Bishop." I pop a brow.

She rolls her eyes and composes herself while I block her from view. When she gives me the nod, I stand and leave.

"They want you to stay the night to keep an eye on you. Your family will arrive shortly, and I imagine they will be able to help you with the house?"

The house. I forgot about the state it was left in after everything happened.

"Uh, yeah, my family will help me," I mutter, turning on the threshold.

"I'll be over once I get out of here. I can help you."

Bishop frowns as he looks back at Murley. He faces me

again, that annoyance firmly back on his handsome face. "Thank you, Lucy." He nods, dismissing me.

As the door creeps closed, I hear, "It's wild to me that you think I'd let you out of my sight in the next decade, let alone a week from now."

I smile to myself as I disappear down the corridor.

My parents arrived in New York early this morning after catching the first available flight out of London. They've been trying their hardest to hold it together, but the moment we walked into the house and Mum saw the mess left behind, she broke.

So did I.

Dad sent me to bed to rest, but I opted for the sofa instead. Truth is, I don't want to go upstairs just yet. I know the police cleared away the surface mess and the drugs. They took pictures and checked the entire house for anything that could've been hidden away.

The idea that Maxwell is a criminal doesn't seem real to me even now. How could I live with him, spend my mornings, nights, and weekends with him, and not know?

Drugs. Fucking drugs stored in the basement of this house. The police told me it was the perfect opportunity for them living here. Quiet, out of the way, and private. It makes me wonder if Maxwell used me for that very reason.

Maxwell. Alec. Polly.

Not one of them was who I thought they were.

"This is Ralph and Elsie?"

I peer over the sofa at the frame my mum is holding. A

smile slides into place, and I stand, walking over to her and taking the picture.

"I need to get new frames."

"Will insurance cover all the damages?"

I shake my head, my temples throbbing with the movement. "I don't know. I should call him."

It's been weeks since I've checked in with Ralph. I told him I'd call after Bora Bora, and I know this is something that has to come from me.

"From what you've told me, he will understand this, Lucy."

"He will." I look up at my mum with tears in my eyes, giving her a sad smile. "It's the type of person he is."

"Go lie down. You've had a scary couple of days."

I go back to the sofa and pull out more tissues, anticipating what's coming. "Mum?"

"Yes, darling."

"Will you stay with me here, at the house, just for a little bit?"

She looks across the room at me, her own eyes shining, and I know she wants to say something, but she can't, so she nods instead.

I DON'T KNOW what time it is, but I startle awake when the front door snaps shut. I hear my dad's voice and instantly relax into the sofa again. My eyes drift quickly, and I'm almost asleep again when I hear a slight sniff and shoes being kicked off. The sofa dips, and I roll with a frown pulling at my brows.

The lamp in the corner of the room illuminates his beautiful broken face, and I instantly wish it didn't.

Never in my life have I wanted to reach for something just as badly as I want it to disappear.

"Ell…."

He shakes his head as he looks down at me, telling me to stop.

His body settles alongside mine on the sofa, and he lies on his back.

I reach up and wipe at his cheek, but he quickly stops me, grabbing my hand and twisting his neck to look at me.

He kisses my knuckles, resting them against his mouth as he speaks.

"Lucy, your face," he mutters, distraught.

"I'm okay."

"It's *not* okay." His voice cracks, and it kills me.

"Don't do this to yourself, Elliot. Please."

"We couldn't get back. We did everything we could, but I couldn't get back to you."

I pull him close.

"There was nothing you could've done if you were here. I've been resting all day."

"I'm so angry."

"Me too," I tell him. "But I'm also thankful to be okay and here—alive."

His nose brushes mine, and I lean in to kiss his lips, desperate for the contact and sensing he needs it too.

"I need you to put your arms around my body and hold me for a while, princess. Can you do that for me?"

"Yeah. I can do that."

Elliot

I'VE BEEN awake for hours, watching her sprawled out over my chest while she sleeps. It has to be one of my new favourite past times and not one I'm willing to give up —ever.

The sound of everyone upstairs should probably have me moving my ass to help, but they know as well as I do that Lucy doesn't need to relive what she did on Wednesday night, and I'm unwilling to let her out of my grasp.

Never in my life have I experienced the dread and unease that I felt when Maggie called to tell us what had happened.

Being in London would've been hard, but I would've been by her side within hours. Being in Bora Bora with a storm slowing us down and grounding our plane meant that it took us nearly two days. I've never felt so helpless, and when Charlie looked at me with utter hopelessness at the airport, I knew there was nothing any of us could do.

"I can hear you thinking."

Her words settle over me, and I smile through the ache in my chest.

"Your heart started to beat a little faster." She lifts her head and rests her chin on my chest. "I thought you were dreaming."

I run my palm over her cheek and into her hair, dusting her jaw with my thumb. "No, I was awake."

She watches me, and I watch her back. Her eyes are heavy, and she looks drained, her cheeks lacking the colour that usually gives her a glow. My gaze is constantly drawn back to her temple, where a blackish-blue bruise is spreading around her forehead and cheek.

It has to fucking hurt.

"I need some paracetamol," she tells me, matching my racing thoughts.

I nod to the small table beside the sofa. "Nina got you your prescription already. You need to eat first, though." I lean over and pick up the other tablets and water to pass them to her, keeping a hand on her back, so she doesn't try to get up. "She said you can take these whenever, but not paracetamol."

"Nina's here?"

"And Mase. The kids stayed with Charlie and Scar."

"Megan?"

"You think they wouldn't come?"

She shrugs as tears fill her eyes. "I knew they'd want to, but it's hard with the children."

I move us up the sofa, keeping her cuddled to my body. I refuse to let her go. "Take the tablets."

She sips the water and swallows them down.

When she looks up at me and smiles, I bend tentatively and kiss her bruised temple. I twist my fingers into her hair and bring her back to lie on my chest, dusting over her scalp in smooth circles. We lie for a while just listening to the noises rattling through the house, and I almost think she's drifting back to sleep.

Almost.

"You don't put bleach on these floors! Maggie, speak some sense into this man, please!"

Both Lucy and I chuckle as Nina's voice floats down the stairs.

"I read the bottle and diluted it with water, woman! I'm not wrong," Mason responds.

"Nina's rolling her eyes," Lucy observes, sliding her hand up and down my side beneath my T-shirt.

"Yeah, and Mason is just about ready to give her a good spanking. Nina was stressed trying to get us all here. I almost felt sorry for Mase."

"We should go help them," she suggests.

"Or we could go shower, have some breakfast." I look down at her, hoping while not hoping that she can feel my cock growing stiffer between us. Because that would be dickish of me.

She lifts her head and cocks a brow. "Mr Montgomery, my parents are here."

"Your parents love me." I grin, gathering up her hair and leaning in to kiss her neck. "But also." Kiss. "I'm pretty sure they are far too busy." Kiss. "To worry about you taking a shower."

"Ell..."

"Hmmm," I reply, nibbling at her jaw.

She nuzzles into me, searching for my mouth, which I happily give her. Our lips meet, and I instantly want more.

Her body slides up and over me until she's straddling my waist and my hands curve around the tops of her thighs. I pull back and gaze up at her, at her still swollen face.

I swallow the bullshit lump in my throat.

She has all the right intentions, and fuck if I want her.

I need her.

"You need a shower, then you need food, and then you need rest. This isn't happening right now."

Her jaw drops as I slip out from under her, placing her down on the sofa before I can change my mind.

"Don't look at me like that," I warn, the reprimand more for my own ears than hers. "You've just got out of the hospital. You need to rest."

I go to the hallway and get her the dressing gown her mum left out for her. When I walk back into the room, she's scowling at me. "Luce." I huff with a light laugh, pulling her up and sliding the robe over her shoulders. "You need nurturing right now."

She gives me a look that says *exactly*.

"Not that kind of nurturing." I kiss her, but she doesn't kiss me back. I frown and pull back. "Kiss me."

She shakes her head.

I kiss her again, longer and harder. "Kiss me," I groan.

"No."

My tongue traces her bottom lip before I pull it between my teeth. I lick across the spot before whispering, "Kiss me. Kiss me now, and I'll let you ride my face like you want to."

Her mouth parts. "Promise?"

I grin and take her hand in mine, pulling her behind me and up the stairs.

Maggie is coming from Lucy's bedroom as we round the top step and her face lights up with surprise. "Oh, Lucy darling, you have some colour back in your cheeks."

I bite back a laugh and squeeze Lucy's hand in mine. "She does, doesn't she?"

She elbows me in the ribs, and it's the least subtle move

she could've made. Maggie eyes us both before her own cheeks colour. "Well, then. I have plenty to get to."

"I'm going to shower before breakfast. Elliot said he's more than happy to help you, Mum."

"Oh, yes. I have a job for you, actually. It's the wardrobe on the top floor. I saw—"

I eye Lucy as she snakes past her mum and leaves me. She knows I wanted that promise just as much as she did.

Maybe more.

I look down at Maggie, who's still talking about the boxes on top of the wardrobe. "Of course, Maggie. I'd be happy to help."

"Wonderful. I just need to get everyone a cuppa, and I'll be back."

I watch as she flits off down the stairs, then my eyes move to the spare bedroom Luce just slipped into. I don't want to leave her alone, but I also don't want to push her boundaries.

Before I can think about it for too long, I knock on her door and wait. She opens it seconds later.

"I'm sorry. I am in full nurturing mode. You may come back in three to five business days."

I shake my head at her sass and laugh, not realising how badly I needed to hear it.

My head dips, and I sober the air surrounding us without even meaning to. When I lift my gaze again, she's studying me with a tilt to her head.

I clear my throat and lean against the wall, my voice only loud enough for her ears. "You'd tell me if you needed me, right?"

She stares transfixed at me, and her eyes tell me everything her words don't.

Not being able to help myself, I lean in and kiss her once more before turning and walking down the landing.

When I arrived last night, I had one and one place only that I wanted to be. I haven't been up here yet, but I know from what John told me on the phone that it's a mess.

I push against the bedroom door, a slight trepidation as to what I might see behind it. But then I find my best friend of thirty-five years with a mop in his hands and a bucket at his feet, cleaning up everything that went to shit.

35

Elliot

We spend the next couple of days cleaning the top two floors of the house, making sure they're as Lucy found them when she arrived. She tried to help us, but no one would let her. It was unanimous. We wanted her to rest, and we didn't want her mind stuck on what happened.

Nina and Megan took her out for the day yesterday, and I know she secretly hated it by the deep sigh that left her when she crawled into bed late last night. She loves her friends, but I know she isn't getting the rest she needs. I wrapped her in my arms and told her she didn't have to do anything she didn't want to and to stop trying to please everyone else.

She gave me a soft smile and was asleep in seconds.

I'm on the hunt for her in this maze of a house when I find her in her en suite. She disappeared after lunch, and I know something's up.

She's riffling through a cosmetic bag, and I lean against the door, watching her.

"Mase said we could go out this evening, get some food," she mutters, not looking at me and placing her products haphazardly on the counter.

I tighten my eyes on her, not answering as I walk to where she's got herself in a fluster at the sinks. I stand behind her, looking in the mirror.

She stops what she's doing and follows my gaze to her temple. Her jaw clenches when she sees what I do.

"Turn around."

She does. And then I leave the anger that's clawing at my insides at the door, choosing to worship the woman at my feet instead.

I lift her, placing her on the counter and stepping between her legs. I take the cleanser from her grasp and pump it into my hand.

"Do you want to go out tonight?" I ask, lathering the cream in my hands to warm it. Her hair is pulled back from her face with a band, and I do my best to apply the cleanser across her cheeks without getting it in the loose strands.

"What are you doing?" she asks with a smile.

I look down as I sweep gently over her temple. "Leave me be, Morgan. Do you want to go out tonight?"

She sighs, sitting quietly for a minute. "Not really. I feel like everyone just stares at me. Like even though it's impossible for them to know what happened, it feels like they do."

I pause my task and lift her chin. "They stare because they have small minds. It's what makes *you* so damn beautiful." I brush her temple again. "This mind. It might just be my favourite thing about you."

"My mind is fucked up, and we both know it." She laughs.

There's a washcloth beside her on the sink, and I rinse it with warm water, removing the cleanser like she would.

I pick up the toner next.

"Your mind isn't fucked up." I swipe the pads over her nose and across her cheeks. "If everyone put as much thought into their day as you do, I can promise you the world would be a better place."

"But you love me." I drop my eyes as she rolls her lips, a sexy smile playing on her mouth.

"I do." I lean into her further. "Maybe I'm biased."

"You most definitely are." Her hands sneak up the front of my T-shirt as her legs pull me in closer.

I open the lid on the exfoliator and start to apply it. "Does that hurt?" I ask, massaging in small circles.

"No," she says softly, closing her eyes and tilting her head back. Her nails scratch gently over my ribs, and I refrain from doing all the things I want to do.

"I'm staying in New York." She works on a swallow, her eyes still closed.

I try to control my flinch when she adds, "Alone."

A frown creases my brow, and I push a loose strand of hair behind her ear as I focus on removing the product from her face.

"Why?" I ask simply after a beat.

She peels her eyes open, regarding me with an amused smile as her hand slips out the neck of my T-shirt and glides lovingly over my face. "Because I'm the motherfucking main character."

My brows shoot high, and I drop my hands between us. "You opened it?"

I wonder if she can feel the way my heart is pounding against her forearm.

"I did. I was in the hospital, and I was fine at the time, but I found it when I was here, under the bed." She frowns as she says it, and I lean in to kiss the space between her distorted brows. "I was so afraid, and I could've stayed there and watched everything unfold, but something told me to move. I couldn't just lie there."

"You were brave," I admire.

"I've never been in a situation like that ever. My mind was absolute."

I frown, not really understanding where she's going with this.

"I don't know that I want to stay here, which is frankly infuriating. But I also know that I dreamed about it once. It's not what I thought it would be, and I know it's probably not going to get miraculously better, but I also know I owe it to the girl under the bed to finish the internship. I want to do it for me."

I ease back slightly, a small smile fighting its way through. "You wanna stay alone?"

"I do."

I nod, pulling her close again. "Then you stay alone."

Lucy

It's been six days since everyone left New York and three since I noticed the guy in the BMW following my every move. You'd think someone would warn me, considering I recently went through an insanely traumatic experience.

A quick picture, which I snapped from my bedroom window, and some top FBI work from the girls, and we worked out that the man sitting outside my house is Vinny's right-hand man—Scott.

"Good morning, Scott." I hand him a freshly made coffee and give him a wide smile.

"Good morning." He nods at me, taken aback, his eyes unsure. "And thank you… for the coffee."

"Nearly done with the night shift?" I ask.

He places a hand on the steering wheel, shaking his head. "I don't know what you're talking about."

"Oh, I spoke to Elliot." I smile, waving him off. "He knows I know and said that you absolutely may not sleep inside the house, as I suggested." I sigh heavily for effect. "Men…. Are you warm enough out here?"

"Wait, what? Elliot told you I work for him?"

My mouth pops open, a shocked chuckle working its way out. "Oh my god, you're terrible!" I step forward. "How much do they pay you?"

Scott's face pales, and a teeny tiny fraction of guilt seeps in. "Lucy—"

"Hey, it's okay. We won't mention this to anyone."

I'm definitely telling the girls.

It feels good to mess around with someone. This is probably the most confident I've felt in weeks, and it's solely down to the girls hyping me up over the phone this morning.

"Will you be following me into work today?"

He tightens his gaze on me before giving in and nodding. "Yes."

I can tell he's annoyed with himself, and it makes me feel even worse.

"Can I get a lift with you? I normally walk, but I picked out these heels, and they're stupidly—"

The sound of a phone dialling echoes throughout the inside of the car, and then, before I can speak, Elliot answers.

I look at Scott's stoic face through the open window, then shake my head *no*.

"Montgomery, I have Lucy with me. She'd like a lift to work this morning."

There's a pause, and then, "You spoke to her?"

"Something like that." Scott leans back in the leather seat then glances at me standing like a lemon on the pavement. "She's entirely too smart for you, my friend."

"She's beautiful, isn't she?" I can hear the smile as it takes over his voice, and it makes me miss him even more than I already do. "Is she there now? Fuck, I'm jealous you're looking at her."

"I'm here," I call out.

"Good morning, princess."

My cheeks burn, and I momentarily wish I never came over here. "Good morning."

"You don't feel like walking in today?" Elliot asks me.

I eye Scott, and he looks away as if it gives us some kind of privacy. "I had this plan with the girls, and it unfolded quicker than I anticipated."

God, I feel like a child.

"A plan?"

"To make Scott crack." I shrug to no one. "We knew he worked for you."

Scott shakes his head as he turns to look at me again. He's secretly loving this.

"I'm sorry," Elliot says in earnest. "I should've told you."

"I'm not mad. I actually think it's why I slept so well last night."

Elliot makes this noise in his throat, and it instantly makes me hot. I want to reach into the car and smash the speakers before it translates, but—

"Nah, baby, I think that had more to do with—"

"Elliot," I warn, cutting him off.

"Scotty?" he calls, and I can sense his smirk through the phone.

I turn and compose myself.

"Yep?" Scott calls back with a chuckle.

"You're travelling with precious cargo now. You'll drive her as if there's a bomb on her lap, got it?"

Scott cocks his head to tell me to get in, clearly not feeling a need to respond.

I quickly jump into the car and strap myself in.

"Luce," Elliot addresses me.

I close my eyes, dreading not knowing what will come out of his mouth next. "Yes?"

"I'm proud of you today. Have a good day at work, yeah?"

My confidence goes out the window, and I shamelessly ignore the world as I reach into my bag and pull out my phone.

Luce: 227 days feels like too many sometimes

Elliot: You'd rather it was easy, sweet girl?

Elliot: Epic isn't easy

I think about that and what he means. This isn't easy, but for superficial reasons, and that makes me lucky. People have far worse things happen to them. Horrific things that they live through and carry with them for years.

I'm just in love.

Elliot: Outta your head. You're sexy when you think and I can't see you. What's going on in that mind?

I smile as I type the words.

Luce: Not a thing x

Three Weeks Later

The buzz around the office is exciting.

Or at least it should be.

We landed a huge campaign last week, and today Monica came in to tell us who will be moving upstairs with her and the top floor designers to work on it.

She looked at me with pity in her eyes when I didn't get a spot, but everyone, even me, knew I was never going to get it after being away for weeks.

Still, I should be excited. This is huge for Almendo and sets me up to work in roles that are now available in other parts of the company.

It's going to create a shuffle, and that might mean no more bullshit from the bitch squad.

I've been doing my best to ignore them, and my mind has been occupied by Christmas, which is only weeks away. And then Ralph. I've not been able to stop thinking about him either. It's been nearly a month since I spoke to him last. He was never good at calling, but he normally got back to me by the end of the week.

I need to tell him about what happened at the house, and the longer I don't, the more uneasy I feel about it all.

"Lucy, did you need anything on the order? Chelsea is sending it out in the next five."

I turn to find Tanner standing at my back. "Yeah, I put the Post-it on her desk yesterday."

"You did?"

I frown, thinking back. "Yep."

"Huh." He goes back to their office but reappears at my door after a couple of minutes, his face screwed up in the signature bitch squad way. "They won't have these fabrics." He holds up the Post-it. "Chelsea doesn't appreciate you wasting our time when you know what's available to us already. You're not new anymore." He sticks the note to the door and stalks out of my office.

I close my eyes and count to ten in my head, not wanting to snap.

I've always kept my cool in these situations—the need to be professional far more important than stooping to their level.

I know it's what they want.

Rolling back my chair, I stand and untack the Post-it from the glass. Then, I walk across the hall and into their office.

"Knock knock."

The three of them give me a bored look.

When I realise I won't be greeted with anything more, I walk forward and place the order in front of Chelsea. "I phoned ahead and had the fabrics preapproved. I've been watching the supplier for a while to secure them. They're actually for the Pernel designs."

She looks up at me when she realises the fabrics will end up back in her hands.

Her project.

"I'd love to see the campaign work out for you, Chelsea. I thought these would really give it an edge." I tap the top of the note and then walk from the office.

Internally, I'm giving them all a massive middle finger.

I SLIDE into Scott's car at the end of the day, feeling defeated. My feet ache, I miss home, and I'm so hungry I feel sick.

"Rough day?"

I think about my problems.

"Just a long one," I reply, keeping my positive head firm.

Every day I cross out another number that sees me one step closer to being home. I need to get the next 206 days done, and then I can start my life in London again.

"Have you eaten?"

"If you offer me food right now, Scott, I might cry. I think I'm a little hormonal."

"Montgomery told me you have a love-love relationship with food," he remarks, tapping a finger on the steering wheel.

"He knows me too well." I smile. "Years of coming home from nights out and making him cook for me, I guess."

"Do you want me to stop somewhere?"

He looks over at me, and I nod appreciatively.

206 days.

Three weeks later

Snow started to fall in New York City this morning, making me smile my first real smile in days. I'm walking back from lunch, my hands bundled in my coat pockets and my face half-submerged in my scarf, when I spot Scott's BMW parked and empty across the road.

I pull my scarf from my neck and dig in my bag, looking for my phone to text him.

"Lucy."

I lift my head, finding him walking out the doors from Almendo.

"Hey! Is everything okay?" I ask, wrapping my arms tight across my chest to keep warm.

He nods, but it's not in answer, and his eyes are full of something I can't place.

"Luce—"

I hate that feeling. When you know the person in front of you is about to tell you something that will tear a little piece of you away forever.

I swallow and glance around the street as my heart starts to strike my chest. "What's wrong? What is it?"

He drops his head, and I stare transfixed, waiting. "I ended up going out to Ralph Mendes home when you said you couldn't get a hold of him."

I shake my head as my face screws up.

"Lucy, I'm so sorry."

"Oh." Sadness floors me, and I fight hard to stay on my feet.

"This was found at his home." He hands me an envelope. "I jumped through hoops to get this in your hands."

"It's open." I frown, trying to control my emotions.

"I don't think it was ever sealed."

I blow out a shaky breath, and as I look up, I see a client walking toward the office doors.

"Shit, I need to clean myself up. I'm going to go speak to Monica, see if I can leave early."

"Of course. I'll be right out here."

"Thank you," I tell him, walking backwards quickly into the reception and towards the bathrooms.

I slip inside and pluck three tissues from the counter.

The door to one of the cubicles opens, and Chelsea steps out. The second she sees my tear-stained face, she tuts.

I blink twice as she pumps the hand wash, her eyes flicking up at me.

I'm still in shock.

"Seriously, we've tried speaking to Monica about it, but clearly no one is going to say anything, and I'm just about done with the waterworks. You can't walk around with your tail between your legs every day, expecting people to feel sorry for you, Lucy. And honestly, after your absence last month, I don't understand why you're here."

She shakes her hands off and goes to open the door to leave.

Everything inside of me seems to rattle, and I know the next words out of my mouth will be pure, unfiltered emotion.

"Chelsea," I snap.

Her eyes glare over her shoulder as she waits.

I swipe at my eyes and bin my tissue. "Thank you."

"What for?" she sneers, rolling her eyes.

I step up to her, lifting my chin as I look down my nose at her. "For being a first-class cunt and making this easy for me."

Her jaw just about hits the floor, and I push past her into the reception. I don't go to my desk, and I don't tell Monica I'm leaving.

Instead, I push out through the doors and take the thirty-minute walk to St Paul's Chapel.

To a dear friend,

Well, Lucy, I woke this morning feeling quite awful, and instead of calling you like I normally would, I felt the need to pick up a pen and paper. It's been many years since I've written a letter and something tells me you'll enjoy receiving something a little different from me.

How are you, Lucy? I hope your trip has been full of joyous, sunny memories with your family? I've been sitting in my chair out in the sunroom thinking about the vacations I went on with my Elsie.

There wasn't many and nowhere near enough in her eyes.

Another grave regret of mine, unfortunately.

If I could go back, if I had that second chance, I'd drop everything to take one more trip—we'd go to Italy!

The days seem to feel slower here compared to

back home. Time hasn't felt the same for many years, but it's as if I'm counting down the days as I pull myself from the bed each morning. The silly thing is, I have nowhere to be at the end of it.

No one is waiting on me.

Elsie and I wanted to retire here, and I know I should stay and live out the dream.

She'd be looking down on me right now smiling, I'm sure of it.

She couldn't devote a full lifetime to me or her dreams, but I plan to give her everything that's left of mine.

Crazy thing is love.

The letter ends abruptly, and I struggle to comprehend what that means.

I look up at the sky from the bench I'm sitting on. The first time I met Ralph was on this very bench, and I revel in the moment as snowflakes settle like pricking needles on my cheeks, reminding me that I am very much alive.

It's as if I'm counting down the days as I pull myself from the bed each morning.

175 days.

Elsie and I wanted to retire here, and I know I should stay and live out the dream.

"And I know I should stay and live out the dream." I smile, shaking my head as tears leak from the corners of my eyes and run down my temples.

Although I feel an insane amount of sadness, I also feel so much fulfilment. I can't imagine living a life without the one person you love, and to think Ralph is at peace with Elsie now, makes it all feel a little less shit.

I read over Ralph's letter many times before I stand and leave the chapel. The BMW is waiting for me by the pavement, and I slide in, the letter still held in my hand.

"Scott, will you take me home?"

"Of course."

I shake my head, but he doesn't see, already pulling out into the traffic. "No. I mean—"

"*Home*," he emphasises the word, slowing his movements as he catches on immediately.

He turns to face me.

I sit with that feeling of absoluteness like a drug in my veins, and I nod. "I want to go home."

EPILOGUE

CHAPTER ONE - THE REUNION

Lucy

I SHOULD'VE GONE HOME AND GOT CHANGED.

That's all I can think about as I ride the elevator to Elliot's floor. When we touched down in Heathrow, there was a car waiting for Scott and me. He was easier to convince than I expected and agreed to not tell Elliot that we were coming home.

When Scott asked where I'd be going from the airport, I hesitated for all of a second before I told him to take me to The Montwell—which is the explanation behind my leggings, sweatshirt, and trainers.

It's comfy, and I'm totally rocking it, but it definitely garnered some questioning looks from the ladies at the front desk.

George is at the reception desk when the elevator doors slide open, and I have to lift my hand to tell him to shut up the second he sees me.

"No frigging way!!" he exclaims. "What are you doing here? I thought Elliot was coming out for Christmas?"

I shake my head, smiling. "I'm coming home."

"Oh," he mutters, his eyes sparkling. "Oh, Lucy, this is the most wonderful thing I've heard all year!"

"Thank you, George. I hope your boss thinks so too."

"You already know how that man is going to take this."

I chuckle as he smooths out the wispy pieces of hair that have fallen from my bun.

"I wish I could be there to see his face."

"Is he in?"

George nods, walking a few steps with a hand on my back. "He's working, but you're going to be a welcomed interruption."

"Thank you, George." I give him a warm grin and walk down the corridor.

When I reach Elliot's office, I pause. I spent the entire plane journey thinking about what I want and need to say, yet I know the minute I step through these doors, I'm going to come out with something completely different.

I'm not even afraid of his reaction.

I'm afraid my words won't be what I need them to be.

I knock and push open the door, knowing he would scold me if I wait. My eyes lock on the back of his chair as I walk in, his head resting on the back as he slowly spins to see who's walked in.

His head tilts in question before he frowns. "Luce?"

"Hi."

His face transforms into a megawatt smile, and he mutters a barely audible, "Fuck."

He places the phone in the cradle, not even saying goodbye to the person on the other end as he rounds his desk and pulls me into his arms. "What are you doing here?"

I push up onto my toes and kiss him, annoyed that he didn't do it the second we were close enough. "I needed a favour," I murmur against his lips.

"A favour? I was supposed to fly out in ten days—"

"I quit," I cut him off. "I quit, and I'm not going back."

He pulls back an inch, smoothing his hands down my back. "What?"

I blow out a breath, feeling lighter than I have in maybe ever. "When I was a little girl, I wanted to be just like the women in all my favourite movies. Driven. Independent. Strong. I was inspired by them and their ability to turn their lives around. It gave me this dream, and for so long I chased it, thinking it would be the catalyst to the person I wanted to be. If I could make it in New York, become a designer at a top brand, and then find the happily ever after to tie the knot in the perfect bow… I'd be her."

"Luce, you're—"

"I don't believe a dream is truly what we think it is. It's so much more. I was never going to become that girl I aspired to be, but setting the goal post and pushing myself to chase her, it created a journey that's shown me exactly who I am. I've learnt a shit ton about myself by following that dream, Ell, and I'm nowhere near done yet. The goalposts are always going to get further away, and the triumphs will always be bittersweet because life won't always go the way I planned it. I'm blessed. I'm surrounded by people who love me, people who I rely on heavily. And that's okay. Because although I might need a little holding up some days, I know there's more for me, and I know that with every step I take towards my goal posts, my dreams… *our pact.* I know that I'll be finding a truer form of *me.* I'll get a little stronger. A little more independent." I shake my head as a tear slides down my cheek, my voice cracking and cutting me off. "I'm certain of it."

"You have no idea how incredible you are. How the fuck did I get you?"

I smile and try to wipe at the corner of my eyes, but he takes over.

"Sorry," I say. "I've been overthinking everything the whole way home."

"Don't ever apologise for being you." He bends at the knees so he can look at me better. "You're home for good?"

I nod my head yes and smile. "Uh-huh."

He flashes me his teeth, straightening again. "And that favour?" he asks, making me believe he will agree to almost anything.

"Take me out tonight." I bite my lip, excitement for this new journey with him to begin too much to maintain. "Take me out tonight, Elliot Montgomery, and I'll tell you what it is."

I reach up on the tips of my toes and brush my lips over his.

"I love you so much, it makes me fucking crazy," he mutters, his eyes heavy and glued to me as I back away.

"I know."

CHAPTER TWO

THE PACT

Lucy

Everything is perfect—courtesy of my girls. When I left The Montwell, I texted the group chat and told them I was home.

They freaked out. Cancelled all their evening plans. And turned up, as always, standing by my side whilst I got ready for my date.

"You look stunning," Megan tells me from the back seat.

"Stunning," Scarlet reiterates, poking her head forward between Nina and me.

"Thank you, girls." I slip my phone into my clutch bag and unlatch my seat belt.

My dress is blue. A silky, open-backed masterpiece that I've been saving for the perfect occasion.

This is it.

"He's going to love you," Nina tells me, placing her hand on my arm. "And on the days he doesn't, when he's playing you up, we'll be here."

"Do you reckon men do this?" Megan asks with a hint of amusement in her voice. "Imagine Mase being like… 'hey, Elliot. If Luce is being a little bitch slut, you come right on over. I'll kick my wife out of bed for you any day.'"

"He wouldn't fucking dare," Nina deadpans.

"Don't kill my fantasy." Megan tuts.

Our chuckles fill the car, and I look to my hands, my fingers fiddling with the zipper on my bag.

"I'm so nervous," I say, looking out the window and into the restaurant. "Do you think he's here yet?"

"He's here," Nina confirms.

"Do you think I'm crazy?"

"I think he'd be crazy to say no."

I love you so much, it makes me fucking crazy.

"Crap. I'm just going to go for it." I pull open the door and slide from the car. I turn to look at the girls and find them all smiling at me.

Nina lowers the window. "I feel like we should part with some advice. Wisdom."

"Oh, oh!" Megan calls, shooting forward in the seat.

"No!" Nina cuts her off, holding her back with her arm. "Not any of your wisdom." She chuckles, lifting her eyes to mine, and I think she's going to say something, but she doesn't.

"You deserve this, Lucy. You both do."

Nina's face softens as she twists in the seat to look at her sister-in-law.

"Thank you, Scar," I say.

Nina nods in agreement, beeping her horn as I step back. "Go get him, *little bitch slut*!"

Elliot

IMAGINE FINDING SOMEONE LIKE LUCE.

She steps through the door at Groulx, and my heart sets off like a racehorse. I stand as she approaches me, not being able to stop the smile from pulling at the corners of my mouth.

"You know, I'd have much preferred driving you here myself."

She steps in close, kissing my cheek as if that's enough. "Where's the fun in that?"

I lean in before she can sit down, lowering my voice to a whisper. "Baby, there would have been plenty of fun in that." I pull back, keeping our faces close. "You look perfect." I kiss her. "You're perfect." I kiss her.

"It feels so good to be home," she murmurs, resting her forehead against mine.

"Hmm, we should sit down," I groan, my hand dusting up the exposed skin at her back. "As much as I want to take you home and show you just how much I've missed you these past six weeks. I should try impressing you a little first."

"You don't need to impress me." She chuckles, stepping away.

I pull out her chair and wait for her to sit down before I take mine. When I first arrived and found the place settings on opposite sides of the table, I asked the waiter if we could change it.

Luce slides her hand over my thigh, angling her body towards me as she asks, "Good day?"

And this is why. I won't have a distance between us.

Jesus, we had thousands of miles separating us for too long. Screw anyone who tries to keep me from her again.

Even a fucking table.

"The best." I run my eyes around her face, appreciating her immaculate makeup. "You?"

She dips her head, and I frown.

"Luce."

"I had an incredible day, but yesterday I had some sad news."

I tighten my eyes on her, waiting.

"Ralph passed away," she tells me. "Around a month ago. It's why I never heard from him."

I watch as pain swims in the pits of her eyes. "I'm so sorry, Luce."

"He wrote me a letter." She smiles, blinking and clearing away the tears. "I feel so lucky to have that."

I nod, covering her hand on my thigh.

"I think it made me realise how important not wasting a second is. And I know you don't like to make plans, and I'd never force you to make plans with me, but—"

"I want to make plans with you."

"You do?" she asks, shocked.

I lace our fingers under the table, keeping her close. "Luce, ever since this started, all I've been able to do is make plans. It's been endless thoughts that keep me up late into the night and wild fucking feelings I chase into the morning. You were thousands of miles away, and all I wanted was you beside me, telling me exactly what we're going to do next. Forever. No track changes. No detours. Me and you, Luce."

She blows out a breath, her eyes blinking wide. "Why did we take so long to get here?"

"I don't know," I admit. "But if you don't want to waste another second… then we won't."

Her chest rises and falls, and she rolls her lips, her eyes not leaving mine.

"If there's something you want, princess, you'll ask me for it."

She swallows, and I wait. "You promised me something no man should promise on a whim—"

"It wasn't a whim."

"I was with another man, and you offered me your children."

"And I'd do it again."

"You would?"

"Are you asking me if our pact still stands?" I ask.

"No."

I frown, disappointment stirring in my gut.

"I want to make a new pact. One that's not just for me."

She has no idea.

"One that's for us—"

"I want kids. Lots of them."

I cut her off and she breaks out into a wide grin, laughing as she tips her head to the side.

"What else do you want?"

"Movies—your kind."

"I knew it."

"Dinner—every Sunday with our parents."

Her eyes glaze. "Okay."

I lean in, dusting her lips. "Sex. All the fucking time."

"Keep going," she utters.

"You'll be my wife."

She smiles. "I'll be your wife," she repeats with confidence.

My mouth slides over hers, a slow deep kiss that has my cock twitching. I pull away. "How long do we have this time? How long is our pact?"

She grasps my neck, pulling me back desperately. "I don't know."

"A year? Six months? Maybe nine if we're smashing out kids."

"Elliot?" She bites down on my bottom lip.

"Hmm," I groan, knowing it's time to shut the fuck up.

"I'm not hungry. I want it now. Number four." Her nails drift over my forearm that's lying in my lap and then over my thigh.

"Luce."

She squeezes my erection, panting against my mouth. "Take me home, Elliot."

CHAPTER THREE

THE HOUSE

Lucy

Four Months Later

"EVERYTHING'S OFF UPSTAIRS." I ROUND THE BOTTOM OF the staircase and smile over at Jean, who's behind the desk.

"I'd call that perfect timing," she tells me, flicking her eyes to the front of the shop.

I spot Elliot's dark-grey Aston Martin parked outside on double yellow lines.

"What's he doing here?"

Jean chuckles under her breath, and I give her a look that tells her I don't need her to answer the question.

"You'll think about my proposal, yes? No rush, of course. Take Monday off if you like. Spend time with your family and really think it over."

"I don't need Monday off, Jean."

"That's up to you. I'm giving you a day off if you want it."

"Thank you. And I appreciate it. You're too good to me."

Her lips twist as she looks out at Elliot. "You'll get the boy a ticket."

I sigh, pulling my bag onto my shoulder. "He'll get himself a ticket. I'll see you on Monday."

She shakes her head as I walk out of the shop, and I smile, knowing she wants me to take the day off.

Elliot rolls down the window as I approach the car. "What's that smile? Tell me immediately."

I pull open the door and slide in, reaching to place my bag and coat on the back seat. "I have some news."

"Yeah?" He gives me the most wholesome smile, and it makes my chest warm. He doesn't even know what I'm going to tell him.

"Jean wants to make me a partner."

He doesn't flinch, his face knowing and sure as he leans in and kisses my forehead. "Of course, she does. You're a powerhouse," he mutters, brushing our lips.

"I'm going to accept," I tell him. "I knew the moment she asked me, but I thought I'd look a little too eager and desperate if I jumped too quick. I need Charlie to look over the paperwork too."

"Of course. You're sure you don't want to wait; go at it on your own one day?"

I shake my head before I can fully think about it, my gut answering for me. "We're established. And it's very much a *we're* thing already. People call the shop and ask for me. They know me, know the brand we've built."

"I think it's perfect. Especially if you're happy...."

"I am. I could carry on as it is now, and I'd be happy. It

will be more work, but we plan to grow the team once we renovate next door. The potential is huge."

"Sounds like you have it all worked out, princess."

"I do." I smile, watching him through heavy lids as he sits close. "What are you doing here anyway? I thought I was staying at home tonight."

He tilts his head, giving me a bored look.

"What?"

"You haven't been *home* since you got back from New York."

"Exactly, and every time I try to have a night off, you talk me around. You've got me locked up in your house and won't let me leave."

"Well, I actually changed the locks today."

"You did?" I ask, frowning as he pulls out into the traffic.

"Hmm. The security system wasn't what I wanted it to be. And I agree, by the way…" He glances across at me. "You should go home tonight."

Okay, I definitely didn't want to go home. But he wants me to?

Did I piss him off?

I think back on the conversation.

I don't think I said anything—

"Outta your head." His hand slips under mine, and he lifts it, kissing the tips of my fingers. "I've got you."

Elliot

I'M MOMENTARILY WOUNDED that she could think for even a second that I wouldn't want her in my bed tonight.

We pull up to my house, and I open the gates.

"I knew you wouldn't take me home," she admits, giving me a coy smile.

"I presumed you'd need your charger and things.... Run in and get them."

Her face drops, and I have to bite the side of my cheek to keep myself from cracking.

"Uh... okay. Just a sec." She opens her door and rushes to my front door, her face hard.

I slowly climb from the car and walk up behind her, catching her between my arms when she realises she doesn't have a key.

"Here." I dig into my pocket and pull out the new set.

She unlocks the door and quickly makes her way up the stairs.

"You not going to wait for me?" I call out, smiling at her back as I take the steps behind her.

She's at the top by the time I reach the fourth step. And I can tell she's a little salty by the way she looks down at me.

I can't help but smile.

"You okay?" I ask, meeting her on the landing.

"I'm fine."

"You seem a little mad."

"I'm mad at myself."

I frown. "Yourself?"

"I said I wanted to go home, and now I want to sulk because you're sending me home, but I don't actually want to go. It was a polite thing. Like... tell him I'm going home so he says *stay*, and then it's his idea, and I won't look beggy."

I whistle, stepping closer. "Manipulation, Luce."

She shrugs, her lip curling as I wrap her in my arms. "The apartment doesn't feel like home anymore."

"Do you have somewhere that does feel like home?"

Her eyes cut through me, and I know she already has the answer. "You."

"Me?" I slide my hands down her arms, and I link our fingers. "I feel like home, or this house does?"

"Just you," she answers honestly.

"Do you not like it here?"

She looks over the bannister at the entrance lit up by the evening sun streaming in through the windows. "Of course, I like it here."

"That's good," I say, leaning in and kissing her. She pulls me closer as my hands drop to her hips, around to her ass. "Can I fuck you before I take you home? I've been thinking about you on your knees in that shower all day."

"I'm sulking," she mutters against my mouth.

"Sulk with my cock in your mouth." I pull on her bottom lip. "It might cheer you up."

"It probably will."

I chuckle, pulling away. "Go get your things."

Her shoulders drop, and she frowns up at me, searching my face. "Are you okay?"

"Why would I not be?"

"You need space. I just wanted to make sure you—"

"I'm perfect. Now go and get your fucking things!"

She watches me as she takes steps back, her feet moving blindly towards the bedroom.

As she slips inside, I readjust myself in my trousers, wondering if we have time for a cheeky shower before dinner arrives at the house. I'm pretty sure I could get us both off quick enough.

Lucy's head pokes around the doorframe, and I roll my eyes at her tears. "You've just set us back fifteen minutes."

"What is this?"

I cross the hall and step into the room.

"Where are all your things?" She holds up the paperwork I left in the middle of the carpet. "Is this. . . ."

"It's contracts," I confirm, walking further into the room. "I planned to move you in here. It's what I planned for us when you were in New York—before all the shit."

"You didn't say anything."

"I didn't want to show you all my cards at once."

Her lip twitches and I know she is thinking about the night of her birthday.

"Why would you sell this place?"

"I'm not."

She frowns, not following.

"Lance needs somewhere when he gets out. He won't ask for help, and I need to keep him close. Obviously."

"It's your home, though."

I go to her, pushing a strand of hair behind her ear. "You know when Lowell sold the penthouse, and none of us understood it. He loved that place. Nina loved it. Well, I think I get it now. I've lived through so much here, Luce. And yeah, it's full of memories, and it's always going to feel like home for me in a way, but it's my memories. Nothing about it is ours. I want to tell my kids stories—stories about the house they sleep in that I'm actually proud to tell." *Not how I fucked three women in the pool house when I was twenty-two.* "I want to tell them how I searched for months for the perfect home for their mum, how I spent weeks off work getting it ready for her. How I thought about their bedrooms long before they were even conceived."

"Elliot."

"Sign that contract, so we can carry on the story. Sign it so we can go make our kids proud of something."

"When you talk about kids." She leans into me, rubbing her body against mine. "God, when you talk about *our* kids.... Why are men with children so fucking hot?"

"Man with kids," I correct, shifting her hips and rocking into her.

"You're never going on the school run. They'll eat you alive," she purrs.

"I'm doing the school run every day." I take her lips in a light kiss.

"Mase used to think so too."

"Baby," I whisper, needing her to shut up.

She opens her eyes, her hand drifting down my neck to lie on my chest. "Hmm."

"Let me take you home. We won't tell the kids what I did to you when we got there the first day."

CHAPTER FOUR

THE TUESDAY CLUB INITIATION

Lucy

Six Months Later

"You're idiots. Fucking idiots."

"Listen. I didn't get this lucky, so stop being so ungrateful. We all know you like a toy or two, Luce. Don't be shy."

I hold up one of the butt plugs and shake it in front of Nina's face. "Shy? You think this"—I scoop up the emptied basket of toys they've surprised me with—"is me being shy?"

"Just looking out for you, princess." Megan stands on the bed behind me, and I look up as she gently places a set of anal beads around the top of my head. "Tonight, we crown a new champion."

I watch Nina struggling to contain her bladder as she doubles over. I pull them off. "You girls…." I laugh along with them, dropping the toys to the bed.

"You'll thank us, trust me," Nina assures me.

"What if I don't like it?" I ask, holding up the underwear I purchased hours before. "I know he wants it—he's snuck in a finger pretty much every time I've been on all fours lately."

"Did you like the finger?" Scar asks, her brows popping.

"A finger was fine. But we're talking about a different level of girth here. And it's *girthy*."

"Beep beep," Nina mutters, poking me in the ribs with the butt plug. "Lube me up and slide me in. This is where you go next."

"Hmm, still doesn't feel like a finger." Megan shrugs, looking at me deadpan. "You just gotta suck it up."

"Every inch," Nina snorts.

For fuck's sake.

"Get out of my house!"

"Go wash your asshole!" Megan yells straight back.

"Girls," I warn.

"We're going." Scarlet gives me a sympathetic look, pulling on the girl's arms. "Wish Ell a happy birthday from us."

They walk towards the door, their steps only slightly sloppy from the cocktails we consumed at lunch. "Hey," I call out.

They all turn.

"Thank you." I smile.

"Coffee at The Elm in the a.m.! We'll get the sofas." Nina throws me a wink, and they leave the room.

I walk to the bed and look down at everything they bought me. Or bought *us*, I should say. My eyes land on the pack of cards I picked up, and I reach for them.

He's going to fucking love this.

Elliot

I FIND Lucy in the shower when I get home. She doesn't spot me right away, and I stand and watch her from my spot at the sinks for as long as I can before giving in. I'm unbuttoning my shirt when she turns, her eyes growing as hungry as I feel.

"You're early," she mutters, her arms dropping to her sides. "I had plans for us."

"Does it involve me fucking you against that shower wall?"

"No, but—"

"Then your plans are changing."

"Are you sure that's what you want? I have *big* plans."

I smile, popping a brow. "Why don't you tell them to me whilst I fuck you? We can multitask."

I see her think about it, and my lip tips up. I pull off my socks and lose my boxers, then I stand naked, letting her see me.

"Or… how about you tell me exactly what you want."

She drops to her fucking knees.

I step into the walk-in shower, my dick saluting her as I near. My hand reaches out, and I curl my pointer finger under her chin, lifting her face until her eyes are back on me.

"Hey, princess." I smile down at her, biting my lip as precum beads on the head of my dick.

"Hi."

"You won't be able to tell me your plans with this in your

mouth." I work myself in my other hand, purposely brushing her bottom lip and watching as she darts her tongue out.

"Maybe you're wrong."

"You think you can tell me with my cock in your mouth?" I smirk, loving how she looks on her knees. "I can't dismiss your enthusiasm."

"You underestimate me." She lifts my shaft and licks from my balls, up my underside, and over the tip. "Dangerous, Mr Montgomery."

I lift it for her. "Do that again, baby."

"This?" The warmth of her mouth covers my balls, licking and sucking before her tongue flutters as it dances up my cock.

"Fuck yes."

She palms my heavy sac, her fingers inching a little way past my scrotum.

"Luce," I warn.

She leans in, taking me in her mouth until I hit the back of her throat. Her head works from side to side, and I give it to her. I push deeper. Her grip on my balls tighten, making the heels of my feet leave the tile.

She pulls back, and I groan as she hollows her cheeks. My hips roll forwards, my patience slipping with every inch she takes.

"I don't feel like being gentle with you, Luce. Fuck, that feels good."

One of her fingers eases over the skin between my balls and asshole, and I squeeze my eyes tight before they snap down at her.

Her brows jump in knowing, her mouth fucking full of me.

This.

I tighten my gaze on her, my head tilting to the side as I try to decipher what that look is.

And then the tip of her finger is poised right there.

My nostrils flare, and I jerk my hips as I grow harder.

The tatters of my control are completely in her hands as she draws back, her lips sucking over the smooth head of my cock.

This.

She takes me deep and swallows around me, then pulls back as she sucks me in again. It's slow. It's torturous. It's fucking insanity.

And then she's pushing into a place no fucker has ever been before, and I momentarily lose my fucking mind. My hands fist in her hair as my jaw goes slack, my hips pumping unforgivably, and I can't even see her.

Stars. I see fucking stars.

I reach blindly for the tiled wall at her back, knowing it puts her in an awkward position, but she's taking one for the team here.

I need this.

I hear her make a sound as she struggles, my cock sliding deeper than I've ever been.

"Gonna—"

She slides into her knuckle, and I go off.

I GO OFF.

I'm not sure what happens in the time between Lucy's finger fully penetrating my asshole and me ending up on my knees straddling her face, but as the stars clear and I find focus on my girl—she's fucking smiling at me.

Lucy

"I CAN'T BELIEVE I became a member of the Tuesday club before you."

I crawl onto the sofa, curling in his lap and snuggling into his chest. He wraps me in his arms, and I close my eyes.

"Things went south fast." I chuckle softly. "I had it all planned out."

"What were your plans? Tell me about your day?" His hands thread through my hair, smoothing over the strands he had twisted in his fists only hours ago.

"I went shopping with the girls." I grin. "We had a bottomless brunch and ended up in a sex shop."

"Of course, you did." He sniggers. "What did you buy?"

"Me? I bought you another birthday present."

I look up to find a sinful smile on his mouth.

"Do you want to see what I got you?" I sit up, straddling his waist.

"I've not been gentle with you tonight, baby. Will your present make me hard?"

"You can't break me, Elliot."

"That's a yes."

"Well, I hope so…" I climb from his lap and back out of the room. "Wait here."

I run up the stairs and into our room. The toys lay scattered on the bed, and I quickly throw them into the basket.

I pull off Elliot's shirt and slide on my new bra and panty set.

I rush back down the stairs and peep around the door to the lounge and find him in the same spot, one arm thrown behind his head as he lies with his eyes closed.

I sneak in, dropping the toys to the floor as I climb back onto him.

His eyes open.

"The first gift is a bit of fun for me."

He bites his lip, sitting up and running his hands up my waist. "Baby, no. This is all for me."

"It's princess," I correct. "And you're wrong."

I reach down and pull out the first gift, feeling silly. Still, I place the gold crown on his head.

It fits perfectly.

"Don't say anything," I tell him, suppressing a giggle.

"Luce."

"Open this." I hold up the neatly wrapped piece of card.

"What is it?"

I tilt my head and give him a droll stare.

He leans in and bites my nipple through my lace. "Tease."

He unwraps the paper and frowns before realisation sets in. His face transforms. And then he flinches, and I know he's thinking about what happened in the shower.

"Ace. For my Prince Charming. Judge me on this kink, and I'll tell everyone you like my finger up your arse."

"You're giving me your ace." He smiles, finally understanding. "I didn't catch on in the shower."

"You were having too much fun." I roll my lips and pop my brows, taking the card from him and slipping it into my panties. "You think you can go for round three tonight, big man?"

"With a fucking crown on my head."

I nod, knowing he'll do anything for me. "Happy birthday, my noble prince."

"Nah." He stands, hoisting me up in his arms as he walks through the house and up the stairs. "Happy fucking Tuesday, princess."

CHAPTER FIVE

THE KIDS

Elliot

One Year Later

I'VE NEVER WANTED THE WHITE PICKET FENCE. THE HOUSE didn't even come with one—it had a stone and wrought iron boundary wall instead.

Close enough.

But as I pull into the driveway of mine and Lucy's home, her bare feet dusting the ground as she sways on the swing seat out on the porch, I realise this is all I'll ever want.

"Hard day, Mr Montgomery?" she asks as I near.

I smile down at her, her stomach swollen with my babies.

"Is that a new dress?" I remark, already knowing it is.

"I couldn't fit into the others." She stands, spinning around to show me. "Do you like it?"

My fingers catch her waist, and I pull her to me. "I love it."

"And your day? It was a good one?"

"Long one," I mutter, sliding my hands over her body.

She looks at me through heavy-lidded eyes. "Hmmm, what do you need?"

"You."

I kiss her despite her wide smile, and she reciprocates, twisting her lips with mine.

I back her into the house, spinning her, so she walks in front of me.

The house is bigger than anything she wanted or would have asked for, but I know she loves it here. When I found it, I was driving home from my parents' estate. It's strange how I must have driven past the house hundreds of times over the years, yet on this particular night, it caught my eye.

Stone Castle.

It's not officially a castle but lit up that night as I passed by, I'd have believed it was.

It has two wings, with a small tower in the centre which opens up the grand entrance.

"Can I take you out for dinner?" I ask her. "I don't feel like cooking."

"Hmm, I suppose I could show off my new dress before it doesn't fit me tomorrow."

"Let me go and get dressed." I take off up the left staircase. "I'll call and book a table. Anywhere in particular you want to go?"

I look over the bannister at her, the crystal chandelier slightly swaying just in front of me.

"Anywhere is fine," she mutters, waving me off.

"No, no, no. I'm not playing that game."

She frowns and snakes a hand over her stomach.

"You'll tell me you don't mind, but you're wild when you're hungry, baby. I'm not sure I can handle getting it wrong tonight." I smile. "You pick. Tell me what you fancy, and I'll call ahead." I disappear into our bedroom, quickly showering before changing into a black shirt and trousers.

I find Lucy in the kitchen when I get downstairs. She's on the other side of the island.

"Where are we going?" I ask, pulling out my phone as I scroll through my contacts, already searching for her favourite.

"The hospital seems like a safe bet at this point."

I shift my gaze up.

"I wrecked my pretty dress." She looks down at her feet, and it has me rushing around the kitchen.

She's standing on a towel, her dress wet and clutched in her hands. "I think our babies are coming."

Fuck.

"Now?"

"I've had twinges all day. But now…." She blows out a deep breath, her knuckles turning white against the blue on her dress. "I'd say it's getting a little more intense."

I go to her, sliding to my knees and holding her stomach. "They said to come in if your waters break. The fuck are we going to do?"

She sucks in her lips, but not in pain. "Are you laughing at me? This isn't funny, Luce!"

"I know, I'm sorry. Stop panicking." She winces, and my heart jolts. "You need to drive me to the hospital, okay? I'm okay."

"Do you need some paracetamol?"

She shakes her head no, slipping her hand through my

stubble and into my hair. "I love you. I can't wait to officially make you a *daddy*."

I blow out an unsteady breath. "Are you not scared?"

She shakes her head no. "Not even a little. Are you?"

"You're in pain." My brows crease. "I don't like it."

She looks down at me, a soft look settling across her delicate features. "You want this to be easy?" She smiles. "Epic isn't easy."

She throws my words back at me, and I stand.

"I'll get the bags. Don't move."

Lucy

I HAD A BIRTH PLAN. Every detail was set in stone. Elliot knew. My midwives knew. Everything I thought I wanted.

The pain medication.

The birth partners.

The outfit I'd come home in.

We arrived at the hospital, and within minutes of being assessed, chaos ensued. The birth plan went out the window, and I was rushed straight to surgery.

The epidural I swore I wouldn't have made me numb from the waist down, rendering me temporarily bedbound.

And my birth partner? Well, he dropped like a sack of shit when the surgeon informed the room he was making an incision.

I once said that once you get the ick, you're done—there's no coming back from the ick. But as Elliot Montgomery lay on the ground with a flannel on his head, two nurses crouched around him, I knew I'd been telling myself a lie and that I would, in fact, love him for a lifetime.

Our beautiful daughter, Elsie Montgomery, was born via C-section at 8:34 p.m., on the 12th of November 2023, showcasing an impressive set of lungs and weighing five pounds, three ounces.

Her brother came four minutes later, challenging his sister's cries as he screamed and flailed his arms until he was by her side again—Mr Ralph Montgomery, weighing a respectable six pounds, ten ounces.

"You know, princess," Elliot leans over the hospital bed, placing a kiss on my forehead before smoothing a hand over Elsie's. We're in a private room, soaking up every second of our babies' first hours on earth. "We wrote a pretty epic tale for ourselves."

I chuckle despite the pain it causes, looking down at our future. "One for the history books?"

"Damn straight it is."

My head tilts. "Do you think Elsie looks like you or me?"

"Hmm…"

Elliot shuffles around beside me, but I'm transfixed on her.

"She's seems so small compared to Ralph."

"Well, I think she has my nose but my wife's lips."

"Wife?" I lift my head, finding Elliot standing with a ring poised in his fingertips.

I'm stunned to complete silence.

"I don't have a speech planned, Luce. I bought this ring knowing you'd be my wife one day, but no moment has been special enough to give it to you. I don't know…. this feels right."

I nod through my tears as he sits on the edge of the bed, taking my hand.

"I love you so fucking much. More today than I ever thought was possible, and yet tomorrow's never felt so exciting. There's no one else I want to do this with. This is it for me. You three are it for me."

I purse my lips as salty tears coat them, choosing to not speak.

"Marry me, princess. Be my wife."

I nod. "Yes," I whisper, my hand shaking as he lifts it. "Of course, I will marry you."

CHAPTER SIX

THE HAPPILY EVER AFTER

Lucy

Three Years Later

Lowerwick Estate, London: Antlis Memorial Ball

If there's one thing the Lowells know how to do, it's to throw a party. We're at the estate, set up as a family in the east wing in one of the house's largest rooms. Of course, Elliot's parents will be taking the twins back to Rosestone later tonight.

We've had them here with us for the week while we prepare for the ball, but my husband is an insatiable man when it comes to time with his wife, and who am I to get in the way of that?

I'm sliding the back on my earring as I walk out onto the balcony, searching for my tribe, when I find the three of them looking out over the estate. Elsie and Ralph both standing on what I know are two very expensive plant pots, their best shoes collecting soil onto the soles.

Elliot stands between the two of them, his muscular back stretched wide under his white dress shirt as he leans on the wall.

"Can you tell us the story again, Daddy!" Elsie pesters, tugging on Elliot's sleeve. "The one about the princess and the pact."

Ralph grins at his sister, nodding when his dad looks to him for hype.

Elliot leans down further, making them huddle in closer. "It was seven years ago on this very night. The grounds were lit up like they are now, and the string quartet was playing so loud, you could hear them all the way at the end of Nanna and Papa's lane. People were—"

"Was Papa Anthony and Nanna Ellis deaded still?" Ralph cuts in, frowning down at the garden where Mason's parents are buried.

I lift my hand to stifle my laugh.

"Yes," Elliot tells him. "Yes, they were."

"Oh," Ralph mutters, dropping his head.

"That's a really sad story, Daddy," Elsie sighs, not impressed as she drops to one knee and climbs to the floor.

Her eyes light up again when she turns. "Mummy's dress!" She runs for me, and I scoop her up. "It has so many flowers."

"You're not terrorising Daddy, I hope?"

Elliot smiles over his shoulder, righting himself and helping Ralph down.

"You look like a princess!" Ralph tells me, coming closer and fiddling with the sheer overskirt on my dress.

My children are beautiful, but I can't help my eyes fixating on Elliot as he walks toward me, a look on his face I'll never tire of.

"She does," he agrees, coming to a stop and gazing down at me. "Hello, wife."

"Hi." I smile.

"Daddy! Elsie!" Ralph gasps, his expression one of pure excitement as if he's just figured something out. "A catchy beat and a dress made of magical flowers," he tells them, holding up my dress.

"See, Elsie?" Elliot smirks, tapping her shoulder and bending down to one knee. "Sometimes you have to trust that the happy ending will come, even when the story seems really sad."

My heart swells, and I swallow the lump in my throat as Elliot looks up at me and winks.

I love you.

"I love you, too."

I hear our bedroom door open then clatter shut, the sound of a broken sob carrying out onto the balcony.

Both Elliot and I frown, Elliot rising to his feet before striding into the bedroom.

"Scarlet?" he questions, halting in the middle of the room.

I take the twins' hands and follow him in, my heart racing as I take in my friend. "Scar? What is it?"

She looks up at us, her mascara running as she holds a trembling fist in front of her mouth. "Lance," she says, breathless. "It's Lance. He's being released. He's—"

The doors push open in a rush. Waverly stands attentively on the threshold. "Mum?" she asks, her voice shaky. "What's wrong?"

THE END

Are you screaming at me?
I think some of you might be…
Well, I'm taking you back to the beginning. Back before Mason found his Pix. All the way back to the day Lance Sullivan met Scarlet Lowell.

You can pre-order Lance & Scarlet on Amazon
While the release date is set for April 2023, please be aware that this WILL be much sooner!!

AFTERWORD

Thank you so much for reading!
If you enjoyed The Grand Pact, please consider leaving a review on Amazon.
Reviews are so important to authors!

Want to be notified about future book releases of mine?
Sign up to my Newsletter via my website
www.jchawkeauthor.com

Come join my Facebook reader group for a first look at sneak peeks and teasers. This is a PRIVATE group and only people in the group can see posts and comments!
Hawkes Hangout - JC Hawke's Reader Group

ALSO BY JC HAWKE

Grand Lies

Grand Love

ACKNOWLEDGMENTS

Writing a book isn't easy. It's lonely, tedious, frustrating, and damn right insanity most days, which is probably why I've never encountered an author who willingly does it alone.

I have a team, and it's the best fucking team in the world.

My husband and children lose hours upon hours of time with me. They have to grab tea—sometimes something fried or frozen. They do bedtimes without me. Weekends at Nanny and Pappys or Granny and Bampys. All so that I can follow a dream. A dream they have all chosen to follow with me. Thank you for that, team. It means more to me than you'll ever know. I'll always strive to balance the scales for us.

Although my family is supportive, they don't always get it—understandably. I have a person for that. Someone to tell me I can do it when the tight deadlines come around. That I'm more than my fears on the bad days. And someone who loves my characters and me enough to tell me to go back and fix the shit parts. Jess you know how much I appreciate you. This journey wouldn't be what it is without you and I'm blessed to have found you. LY

Pulling inspiration can be hard some days, but I have incredible people around me. They don't push me or tell me to do the shit that needs doing—we barely speak some days.

They work on their own shit, and they do it so well, with so much determination, it has my butt moving. Katie and Bills, you are without doubt fucking impeccable businesswomen and humans. I aspire to be a little more like you every day.

My beta team…. Why you put up with me is wild. I throw you these words, and you drop everything to devour them. You help shape my stories to be the best they can be, and without you, they'd be a lot less whole than they are. Thank you, Rach, Jo, Lindsay, Pam, Katie, and Lauren.

My *Butt Slut Society*: I get emotional thinking about you ladies. I don't know how I found you so soon on this journey, but I am forever thankful that I did. The way your messages motivate me, lift me up, and inspire me is more than I could ever ask for in a street team. I know we have something special going on. I mean, a day of the week dedicated to our asses. It's beautiful, right? I hope you do this thing with me forever.

To the members in Hawkes Hangout and the Cygnets, thank you for supporting me. I adore you all.

Murphy and Ellie. You ladies need a special mention. Murphy, you get it right every single time! Ellie, your communication is everything my anxious little ass needs—your edits are decent too. LOL. I picked two of the best in the business and got damn lucky. Thank you for being patient with me and for making everything shine.

To my reader

You're the most special of them all (Shh, don't tell the others ^). You put trust in me and this story with no clue if it's going to be any good. So, for picking this book up, or maybe all of them, thank you. You're making my dreams come true!

Until next time,

Stay Wonderful

xo

ABOUT THE AUTHOR

JC Hawke is an author of contemporary romance. She lives in the South-West of the United Kingdom with her husband, two curly haired daughters, and beagle woofer.